GREATER LOVE

UNBROKEN BONES— BOOK 1

GREATER LOVE

ALANA C. MARKS

Dedicated to my mother, a woman of character, strength, and kindness. Your greater love shaped me in ways that only pure love can. Thank you, Mother, for everything you gave and gave up for me. It's my deepest desire to demonstrate how your unselfish sacrifices were all worthwhile.

"Remember now thy Creator in the days of thy youth…"
Ecclesiastes 12:1

Table of Contents

Preface ... ix

Prologue: Mathias: The Advent ... 1

1. Natasha: Peculiar Guide ... 6

2. Dr. Betsy: Divine Design ... 15

3. Mathias: Zariah ... 25

4. Natasha: Strained Relationship ... 33

5. John: The Competition ... 43

6. Natasha: Old Ben ... 50

7. Mathias: My Haven ... 59

8. John: Dysfunctional Home ... 66

9. Natasha: Timely Sermon ... 77

10. Natasha: Surprise Revelation ... 87

11. Mathias: Base of Operation ... 99

12. John: College Dream ... 109

13. Dr. Betsy: Miserable Memories ... 117

14. John: Trail of Suspicion ... 127

15. Mathias: My Communion ... 137

16. Natasha: Unexpected Discovery ... 146

17.	Graduation Nightmare	157
18.	Natasha: Contentious Gift	172
19.	Mathias: Rasmus I	184
20.	Natasha: Hidden Treasure	192
21.	Natasha: Fascinating Find	204
22.	John: Threatening Proposition	215
23.	Mathias: Rasmus II	222
24.	John: Enlightening Observations	229
25.	Natasha: Buried Mystery	237
26.	Natasha: Unforeseen Fright	245
27.	Mathias: Commissioned	252
28.	John: Crossing the Line	262
29.	Mistaken Identity	271
30.	Dr. Betsy: Greater Love	280
31.	Aziel: Trapped	289
32.	John: Twist of Fate	295
33.	Natasha: Together Again	303
34.	Natasha: Making Amends	309
35.	Amazing Grace	318
36.	Aziel: Flashback	331

Preface

A bedtime story. That's really how this book got started. My kids were story-holics. They wouldn't go to bed without a bedtime story, and they would beg me to tell them stories throughout the day. One night as I tucked my girls into bed, they began their usual pleading: "Mommy, are you going to tell us a bedtime story? Mommy, please, just one more, and make it a long one."

I would always make up a story on the fly, though I made sure it served a purpose. There had to be a lesson about lying or stealing or being disobedient. I developed a group of regular characters such as Teeny and Tiny the mice and Chip, Dale, and Hank the chipmunks. But that night, I veered off my usual path of characters. I made up a new one. Her name was Natasha, and she had discovered something interesting in a cave.

The next night, I did not return to my typical characters and themes. I continued with part two of the story, and every night, for weeks, the story went on and on. What was even more extraordinary was that I continued the story for an entire summer. More characters were added, and the plot thickened. Best of all, the story actually made sense and was intriguing. I started to record the story as I told it to my kids. We all felt this would make a great book one day.

I made several attempts to write this book but could never bring the story to life on paper. The years rolled on, and my young children turned into teenagers. My life kept getting busier and busier, and writing a book was the last thing on my mind. I figured, whenever my kids went to college, or maybe when I retired, I'd finally find the time to start writing this story.

In January of 2019, something changed. My plate was overloaded with responsibility. I was holding down three jobs and taking a music theory class with my girls at the community college they were attending. I was also running my girls all over town to piano, violin, cello, and guitar lessons as well as taking them to school and orchestra. I couldn't imagine being busier. The new job I had accepted involved a significant amount of driving. There, in the silence of my car with the beauty of nature around me as I drove countless miles, that story was reborn. It poured into my mind like a river overflowing its banks. All I had to do was find the time to write. I squeezed it in while waiting to pick my kids up from a class or by cheating myself of some needed sleep by waking up at 2:00 or 3:00 in the morning. Over the next twelve months, I wrote chapter after chapter and layer after layer effortlessly. A year and a half later, I had a readable copy of the story.

Ultimately, this book aims to broaden the scope of the imagination toward the world of light. However, I also tried to address particular topics that are sometimes difficult to discuss, and certain aspects of this story are likely to be controversial. I am not a minister or a biblical scholar. It is not my intent to establish the truth for anyone, but I hope those who read this book will be inspired to think about what they believe and why they believe it. Though this book is fiction, I believe there to be a line of truth and biblical principles throughout the story.

Unbroken Bones is a trilogy that begins with a family secret and some bones in a cave but ends with discovering truths we often lose sight of in our world of darkness. If you make it to the end of the trilogy, I pray you will be inspired and happy to have read a great story about the most important elements of life: love, loss, worth, value, friendship, and family.

Matthias: The Advent

Whispers of my name, like wisps of air, echoed in haunting tones throughout the canal. A vortex had pierced its way through space, making a passageway from the realm of eternal light to the universe governed by time and night. A journey of extraordinary significance awaited my first steps, yet I stood frozen at its entrance, contemplating the enormous responsibility now resting upon my shoulders. My heart was filled with trepidation. Was I prepared to confront the darkness?

This darkness was not the darkness of night. It was the darkness that came from "beings" separated from the source of light. Beings who surrendered to evil and wickedness of every type. Beings who had been banished from the realm I was about to leave behind. Cloaked under the guise of a thousand lies, these fallen ones had brought utter despair to a once majestic planet, the place of my destination.

My world was bathed in ethereal light emanating from the glorious presence of the One Who created all things. It was a world of exquisite delight. There we cherished intimate relationships with beings from home and foreign universes, bonds that grew in depth and love for endless ages. Unimaginable discoveries and opportunities for learning stretched us to grow in every capacity of our being and fueled our intense desire for knowledge unknown. Most endearing was the all-encompassing love that perpetually enveloped us in a comforting bliss of peace, confidence, and assuredness. To leave such a place to dwell within the exact opposite was a formidable and daunting reality.

Though the time had come for me to play my part in confronting the darkness and shielding the precious ones from the fallen creatures of the night, my thoughts at the moment were not of this unfortunate planet and its inhabitants. Instead, I was consumed with whether I was ready to perform the task expected of me. *Was my training adequate? Will I be able to bear the sorrow and pain that will sear into my soul? Can I vanquish beings who once stood as angels of light?*

I turned to face the magnificent immortal who was to escort me on this, my very first mission to the fallen realm. He was a being of dazzling brilliance. Four massive wings stretched out from his chiseled form, and his intense eyes flickered like flames of fire. Confidence, might, and power exuded from his soul. My father, Adriel, fluffed his wings and folded them toward me. Instinctively I folded mine to him, and as our wing tips touched, a force field of love developed about us. This heavenly embrace dissipated my apprehension, and my father's faith and trust in the Omnipotent One infused into my spirit as his voice rang out loud and clear, beseeching his Maker in prayer.

"I thank thee, my Creator, for the joy and peace in which we live. As we journey to Earth, I plead Your Spirit to enshroud my son, Matthias. Enable him to decimate the demons that attempt to destroy his mission to protect and save the precious ones."

His impassioned tone intensified. "May he find the answers to the questions that trouble him. May his eyes be opened to see through the deceptions that masquerade as truth. May he realize Your unchangeable laws are just, right, and true."

Stunned by his words, I raised my head and peered at him. An expression of sorrow pervaded his brow.

Does he really believe my questions challenge the very foundation of our joy? Then why allow me to embark on a mission such as this one? I pondered as he whispered, "It is well with my soul. Amen."

Immediately, the Spirit of our omniscient Creator descended upon us in a flame of holy fire, causing us to let out a shout like the roar of a lion, claiming victory won even before I had begun. As I stepped into the portal, colors of light coalesced into exquisite patterns that danced in unison with the melodic sounds this passageway emitted. Instantaneously, we spanned an immeasurable distance through the sinless galactic universe.

But instead of the usual radiant light that awaited us at the entrance to our heavenly realms, my vision beheld a surreptitious blackness. My eyes, designed to recognize light in all its luminous faucets, needed to be transformed to see through the inky murkiness we were heading toward.

The dazzling illuminations dimmed within the canal, the pulsating energy weakened, and the euphonious chorales ceased when we arrived at the veil. This singularity of space served as a wall separating the universes of light from the universe of night, and when we crossed it, I felt as if a malevolent presence was pulling me into an abyss of gloom. A sense of doom surged through my being. My spirit recoiled, and my confidence wavered. We were now on enemy ground and within the habitation of legions of demons. My father, sensing my apprehension, encircled me while uttering words of courage.

I intensified my vision to take in this minuscule and virtually non-existent planet. This grain of sand in the vast, endless ocean of space had moved all the heavens into action. This point of attraction, though a spectacle of sorrow, had secured the sinless universes of light for time eternal. Here, the Creator had revealed a side of Himself unseen in all eternity—a display of His immortal goodness confirming His beauty and love for all His created beings.

Drawing his leviathan sword in preparation for an imminent attack, my father sliced through the blackness like a blazing comet streaking across the night sky. The legions parted like the Red Sea, howling and shrieking like a frenzied pack of wild wolves chasing down their prey. These were the weaker ones with no strength to resist my father's might, and their screeching almost eclipsed a sound I had never before heard. It was the cry of a world gripped in misery, pain, grief, and despair.

Earth soon came into view. The tiny blue ball of life created to sustain its inhabitants for endless ages had disintegrated into a catastrophic state beyond repair by any human abilities. Ragged mountains, plastic-filled seas, and colorless reefs devoid of living things met my distraught gaze. A putrid odor encircled the atmosphere, bathing the cities and countryside with its poisoned stench. Inconceivable horrors enacted by minds given to evil produced rivers of human-filled blood. Seemingly stripped of value and worth, they walked about, entrapped in their degenerating bodies. Depression, guilt, and shame draped about them like thick, heavy chains.

Sorrow and sympathy swept over me with an intensity I had never felt before, and I began to weep. Again, my father enshrouded me with his consoling light. We were not to focus on that which was lost but on that which could be gained. He pointed to the few shimmering stars in the darkness. These were not the lights of distant galaxies. They were the lives of those who reflected the source of light and whose hearts were filled with faith, hope, and courage despite the constant onslaught of discouragements inflicted upon them by the fallen ones.

Ominous grey thunderclouds clashed together and billowed high into the atmosphere. Lightning crackled with splintering tentacles of white lights across the darkened skies. Strong winds howled while stripping leaves from branches that bounced back and forth in a disorganized frenzy. People rushed to find cover as large drops of rain began to fall.

We had arrived, and with a fury of hatred, they flung themselves at us. The ground trembled by the sheer force of energy generated from beings battling for the souls of humankind. They knew it not, for they could not see us, nor could they hear us. Most would never know we walked among them, at times as men, and at times as beings of light. Summoned from the eternal throne, we were to minister and guide the precious ones in their journey of life.

But my arrival was for a very singular purpose. A crucial truth was on the brink of revelation—a truth that could dissipate the fog surrounding the history and worth of humanity.

Bones. All that is left after they die is a pile of bones. Buried beyond sight within the earth, they are often forgotten. But all bones tell a story of the past that can impact the future, and all bones hold within them the source of life, especially the unbroken bones.

CHAPTER 1

Natasha: Peculiar Guide

A pile of dirt collected behind Natasha as she forced her shovel back into the ground. With each toss of the shovel, the extent of her exertion became more apparent. What began as labored breaths had turned into grueling grunts, and beads of sweat had coalesced into salty rivers careening down the sides of her face. Determined to find what she believed to be a treasure, she continued at a frenzied pace.

Suddenly, something hard repelled the force of her thrust. Retracting the shovel slightly, she scraped the dirt away. A yelp of victory echoed through the rocky cavern as the light from her headgear danced across the walls, in unison with her excited leaps. It was some sort of box made of wood, and a hollow thud sounded every time she tapped its surface. Searching for an edge, she continued to shovel and push away the dirt, but try as she did, it seemed as if there was no end to the larger-than-expected structure. Out of breath and running out of patience, Natasha took a break to collect her thoughts and figure out what her next move should be. Then every muscle in her body froze as fear gripped her heart. She heard it coming even before the ground began to tremble.

"Earthquake!" her mind screamed. "Not now. Not here," she cried. Pebbles bounced in every direction as dirt loosened from the corridor walls. Grabbing her pack, she tried to escape her enclosure before it caved in. Instantly, everything went black.

⊰o⊱

Grey-bellied cotton ball clouds sailed effortlessly across a deep blue sky. They appeared to be on a journey to somewhere important, perhaps as intent as she at arriving at their destination. Twigs snapped under her feet as she hustled down the narrow dirt trail that wound its way past a large pond before she headed toward a forest.

It was mid-April in San Francisco, California, and spring was in full bloom. Bright yellow daffodils gathered here and there about the pond in groups, like a community of families. Their slightly bowed heads bounced about in the evening breeze as if greeting one another. Ripples silently spread their reach across the pond, having been born by the splashes of ducks and their cute fledging ducklings swimming behind them. The air was sweet with the sound of birds tweeting their high-pitched melodies and the scent of abounding life from grass to trees.

Natasha hastened past the beauty that thrilled her heart with delight. How she wished she could spend a few moments taking in its invigorating spirit. On any other day, she would have settled down on a patch of grass with her notebook in hand and sketched the tantalizing scenery. Today, she mustn't waste any time, for the sun had already begun its slow and steady descent toward the horizon.

Kennington Park was eerily silent for a place with such breathtaking beauty. No giggling or laughter erupted from the joyful mouths of children running about. No men in lounging chairs with fishing gear at their sides and hooks swaying in the water were flanking the pond. No couples walking hand in hand or rowing across the still waters were gracing the park with their presence. Instead, a stillness pervaded the area, as if something unexpected was about to happen.

A moment of doubt made her hesitate before she passed into the waiting forest. Standing at its edge, she looked up at the enormous trees standing like sentinels at its entrance. The path ahead appeared somewhat darkened as the rays of the sun were blocked by the thick green canopy crowning the forest. Gathering her confidence, she stepped inside and was greeted by much cooler air than what was winding its way through the field she had just trodden.

Believing she had never been down the trail, she cautiously took in her surroundings, noting the variety of ferns and other vegetation encroaching the dirt path. She was on her way to a special place that only she could find. Her grandmother had left her the directions on a map, but it was not a city map with neatly outlined roads and highways. It was a map to something. A path through the forest. A redwood tree. A signpost. An X with a ray of light above it. Was this a hidden cave with hidden treasure?

Her grandmother was in no way an eccentric person, so her leaving a map to a hidden treasure was as surprising as it was intriguing. Grandma Cunningham lived an ordinary life and had an ordinary job, a botanist by profession, and nothing more. Her passion was plants. Microscopic and enormous. Unsophisticated and complex. Plain and beautiful. That was why discovering the map was an unexpected find that aroused her curiosity to the highest level.

She had discovered it in the least likely place one would expect to find such a map. Her grandma had tucked it inside her Bible. Natasha had mulled over why her grandma would leave it in such a place, but as she thought of her grandmother's peculiar ways of teaching her Bible truths, it began to make sense. Grandma Cunningham always found a unique way to express her beliefs about God, His love, and the destiny He had planned for those He had created.

"The Bible is the place where people should search for things of extraordinary value," Grandma Cunningham would often say. "It is the place that holds remarkable mysteries and the greatest stories of people who experienced the most profound lessons ever learned."

But her Bible had been callously tossed into the darkest corner of her bedroom, cast off as a useless book that held only broken promises, empty hopes, and mysteries no one could ever understand. Two years had passed before Natasha happened across it, for she had forgotten about the night that sent her into a rage of despair. Thrown to the ground, it had slid under her bed, far from reach and sight.

When she spied the book in her search for a misplaced slipper, she knew not what it was until it rested once again in her hands. Then memories rushed in like a flood. Flipping open its pages, she found what her grandmother had placed within. Surely destiny or the guiding hand of some unseen entity had devised a path to its location.

Seeing a signpost a few meters ahead, she hoped it would be the one written on the map. "Fox Meadow," it read. Her heart leaped with joy. It was just half a mile away, and destination X was somewhere close beyond that point.

She didn't know what she was searching for. Her grandma had left no other information except to bring a light, a helmet, and a shovel. Trying to guess what her grandma had hidden left her in a state of anxious expectation. Grandma Cunningham didn't place value on temporal things, so why would she leave her a physical treasure? Or perhaps it wasn't physical at all. Maybe it was just an explorative experience that would remind her to acknowledge Him.

Grandma Cunningham had often sent her on treasure hunts in meadows, gardens, and forests, but the treasure never was some tasty treat like a chocolate Easter egg or a desired gift like a necklace. It would be a plant of exquisite beauty or design or some other living thing from which she would draw words of wisdom she hoped would help to guide Natasha through life.

Natasha gasped in awe as she eyed a small grove of redwood trees clustered about the trail a short distance away, exuding power and majesty that made them feel like extraterrestrial life forms. Her heart filled with admiring wonder as she passed those colossal giants that reached skyscraper heights.

The sight of them made her ponder whether her grandma had indeed brought her here before. For she could hear Grandma Cunningham's voice ever so clearly. "Look at this, my child. It is an ancient one from an ancient world. Its grandeur is a reflection of its Maker and His intent. Can you not feel its life force beating within you? Walk among trees such as these and study them, for they contain knowledge lost in this world."

She even remembered the Scripture Grandma Cunningham had quoted and insisted she memorize. Psalm 1:3 had been etched in her mind. "And he shall be like a tree planted by the rivers of waters that bringeth forth his fruit in his season; his leaf also shall not wither, and whatsoever he doeth shall prosper."

A strong gust of wind kicked up dust and sent dried leaves spiraling into the air. Sneezing repeatedly, she fished out the ever-present ball of tissues she kept in virtually every pocket of the clothing she owned. She had already been sniffling from the allergens floating imperceptibly through the air, but that blast of wind fully awakened her response.

Looking around, she tried to figure out how such a powerful draft could have made it through the thick vegetation surrounding her. Out of the corner of her eye, she noticed something behind some trembling shrubs. Veering off the trail, she began to pick her way toward it, pushing back tree limbs and stepping over the soft earth littered with rotting leaves.

Instinctively, she knew it had to be the spot, for something peculiar had guided her to its location. Now she fully understood the circle on the map that she had thought was a tree stump or something similar. An opening in the ledge that ran alongside the trail, perfectly hidden from view by the densely packed shrubs and foliage, was before her.

"A cave?" she wondered aloud, before the realization sank in. "Of course, a cave. Why else would she need a light and helmet? Trembling like the leaves fluttering around her, she fought with herself. Her fear of the dark and tight places was in a heated battle with her desire to discover whatever it was her grandmother hoped she would find.

"She wouldn't ask me to go if it wasn't important," she reasoned. "And if I don't go, I will never know."

Summoning an inner strength she rarely called upon, she braced herself for the unknown. Her heart pounded wildly as her hands sank into the damp earth. Crouching down, she managed to slither through the small opening, dragging her pack behind her. It led to a chamber as large as her bedroom in its height and width but with rugged rocks for its walls. Across the earthen chamber was a slender corridor whose end she could not see. The darkness eventually consumed the beam of light she flashed down its path, but the light had revealed what she had hoped to see. It was only a few feet down the ominous hallway. In the middle of the path, the ground had clearly been disturbed, and she figured that the person who had disturbed it must be none other than her grandmother.

⊷o⊶

Dirt pressed upon her lips when her eyes finally opened. She was lying face down. Trying to sit up sent a shrill of pain piercing through her ankle, causing her to slump back to the ground. Her breathing was heavy and rapid as her fear intensified. Waving her arms about as if swimming through a pool of water, she searched for her flashlight.

It was nowhere within reach, leaving her with just the dim light of her helmet and the encroaching darkness.

Clenching her teeth in sheer determination, she braced herself for the pain she knew would come as she rolled her body over and pulled it into a seated position. Tears spurted from her eyes, and she cried out in agony. The sound waves of her voice rippled through the cavern and bounced back at her, accentuating her moans.

She was in a predicament, stuck within the belly of the earth, like Jonah, who had been stuck within the belly of a whale. And like him, the God from Whom she had been running away was the only One Who could hear her now.

Pulling her phone out of her pocket sent a new wave of panic and fear rolling through her anxious veins. The digital display read 8:58 p.m. How long had she lain unconscious? As she felt her forehead, a lump met her fingers. Surely she must have suffered some level of concussion. Her trembling hand increased its intensity with the thought that she was now trapped in a cave in the dead of night.

Fumbling to press the icon to ring her mom brought to light yet another appalling obstacle. No signal could penetrate her tomb-like enclosure. It was as if He had brought her to this place for her to recognize that she could not get out without Him.

Biting her lip and punching the ground, she yelled, "What do You want from me? You already took everything. Why are You doing this?"

Surrendering to the conflicting emotions within, she wept long and hard before conceding, "You win. I need You. Please help me, Lord."

"Prayer without action is the futile attempt to get what you want without effort." Those were the words Grandma Cunningham had quoted as they watched an army of ants lifting objects twice their size while marching with determined precision to their mound. That was one of those discovery treasure hunts her grandma had sent her on.

She had written questions on colored index cards and hidden them throughout her vegetable garden, which had led Natasha to the ants. The saying became a mantra Grandma often repeated, especially when she realized Natasha believed that just her prayers would help her pass a math test or play a new cello piece exquisitely well.

Alone in the dark, the words echoed in her brain, helping her realize what she must do to end this nightmare of misadventure. When the fresh night air finally filled her lungs, she laughed happily, thanking the One Who had strengthened and coached her. Despite the agonizing pain, she dragged herself inch by inch out of the cave.

Sadly, her night of misfortune had only begun. The cacophony of sounds emitting from the forest heightened her awareness of her untimely demise. The path to the trail and the twenty-minute walk back to the parking lot were an impossibility on her own. She would have to beg for help from the very last person she wanted to know about her quandary: her mother. It was her mother who had dropped her at the park that evening, but Natasha had not divulged the truth as to why she was supposed to be there. Valerie had no knowledge of the map and believed Natasha was going to work with a group of interns. She assumed the group would travel back to the nature center, and from there, Natasha would catch the city bus home.

Lying wasn't something she liked to do, but she was in the habit of occasionally stretching the truth. And that day, Natasha chose to stretch it like a rubber band, for she suspected her mother would not be the least bit happy about what had truly inspired her trip to the park. Valerie would be angry that she had to leave work to pick Natasha up.

She tried her best not to be a bother to her mom, who always seemed to be on the brink of a nervous breakdown. She had been that way for as long as Natasha could remember. Sadness hung about her like a permanent cloud over her head. It had etched itself into her face, making her appear older than her forty-five years. It had seeped into her bones, causing her to shuffle like an old woman, and it had sunk into her mind, leaving her no choice but to constantly utter negative, discouraging words.

Shivering from shock, fear, and the cool air that now circulated through the brush, Natasha pulled herself up to a sitting position. Taking a deep breath, she dialed her mother. Barely had she begun to explain to Valerie the situation and location when the phone went dead. Anxiety threatened to overwhelm her as she realized her only lifeline had been abruptly cut off.

Her breathing accelerated, and beads of sweat erupted across her forehead. The thought of being out all night with creepy crawlers and night prowlers wandering about was more than she could bear. She fought to regain control as she slid back to the ground.

Trying her best to slow her breathing, she rolled onto her back and placed her hands across her chest. Her tears moistened the ground while she lay helplessly looking up. A break in the canopy revealed the heavens above. Her eyes caught the light of a myriad of twinkling stars. The vastness of the heavens and the depths of the dark forest made her feel vulnerable and tiny, yet at the same time she knew He could see her, and He alone could send her the help she desperately needed.

Then a Scripture came to mind—Psalm 56:3. "What time I am afraid, I will trust in thee."

Her spirit calmed as she silently mouthed the words over and over, recognizing that He had managed to bring her to a point where she could trust only in Him. Suddenly, a warmth seemed to encompass her, and for reasons she could not explain, she knew she'd be okay.

CHAPTER 2

Dr. Betsy: Divine Design

Dr Betsy's hands were trembling, as hands often do when fear grips the soul. Snatching the keys off the peg on the wall of her foyer, she barely had time to put on her jacket as she rushed toward her Jeep Wrangler. Shoving the key into the ignition, she pulled the stick shift into gear, clicked on the headlights, and pressed on the gas. The Jeep revved loudly as it swung onto the road in the dead of night.

Shifting effortlessly from one gear to the next, her feet and hands worked in perfect synchrony. She loved stick shifts; they represented the old way of life, a life that was more difficult yet more rewarding at the same time. She liked knowing that despite her age, she still had the ability to drive something most people couldn't.

As the Jeep picked up speed, her thoughts were a frenzy of unanswered questions and suspicions. Then, right when she felt she was well on her way and would soon reach her destination, she heard a familiar dinging. Looking at the gas gauge, she felt her heart sink. Her tank was almost empty.

"What the heck?" Dr. Betsy cried in distress. She'd forgotten she needed to get gas in the Jeep. "There's no way I'll make it to Kennington Park and back with this little amount of gas."

Finding the closest gas station, she pulled in behind two other cars and waited impatiently. After filling up, she traveled less than ten minutes when she came upon flashing lights signaling a train was about to barrel down the railroad tracks. "What is this?" she yelled, throwing her hands in the air. "Do You not want me to get there?"

It seemed like an eternity before the last car of the train rattled down the tracks. So intent was she on making up time that she didn't notice she had passed a highway patrol car sitting like a predator in the dark.

Blue and red lights began to whirl behind her. "Oh no. Not now," she moaned loudly. "I don't have time for this. I'll never make it there on time if he's pulling me over."

—◁◦▷—

Dr. Betsy had been enjoying a quiet evening at home sipping a cup of chamomile tea in her rocker while reading one of her favorite books, *Les Misérables*. It was an old copy, with frayed edges, she had purchased at a book sale years ago. She had seen the title many times before but had never been inspired to make that book her own. Why would she read a book about misery when that was the essence of her own life? She had passed it time and again until something pushed her to pick it up. As she fanned through the pages, the few sketches intrigued her, as did a single word written in the prologue: "Redemption."

The spirit within her seemed to be drawn to that word, and once she began to read the book, she devoured it all at once, like some hungry beggar finding a loaf of bread. Having read it several times, she never wearied of the story of Valjean and Fantine. It spoke to her soul like no other book of its kind. As she flipped through the pages that quiet evening, a piece of folded paper revealed itself. Surprised to find anything in the book, she quickly unfolded the paper.

Three paragraphs of neat handwriting appeared among the creases. "Good Lord," she declared to herself. Had it been two years since she'd picked up this book? Had that much time gone by? She stared at the paper for a long moment as she tried to recall why she might have left it there so many years ago. She had a special place where she stored her most valuable possessions, and she considered this letter one of them. *Why did I not place it in my secret hideaway?* she pondered.

But instead of waiting for her foggy memory cells to figure it out, she began to read the letter.

Dear Phrosene,

I know you're so confused about what is going on with me right now. I admit I've been vague and distant, but it's not because of you or anything that you have done. I treasure the friendship we have, and I'm so sorry you think I'm avoiding or being rude to you. I profoundly respect you, both professionally and personally. Believe me when I say that my recent reservedness has nothing to do with you.

I've stumbled on what seems to be an incomprehensible treasure. I've spent the last few weeks and months trying to determine whether it's just one gigantic hoax, but from what I've seen, heard, and read so far, it is a truth that cannot be denied. One thing I've learned about truth is that it will not stay hidden forever. My skin crawls with disgust as I realize the extent to which men have gone to destroy the evidence of its existence.

I want so badly to share with you what I found, but I doubt you would believe me, and I fear you would think I had somehow lost my mind. Deep down inside, I know you are not ready for something like this. Not now. But perhaps at some point in the near future, you will see the need to research more about what I've found.

If you don't, perhaps my granddaughter Natasha will. She is a bright one, so eager to learn and absorb the world around her. I believe this would be something she'd be excited about researching. Please don't hinder her, and I venture to say, help her if you can, even if you don't believe in it yourself.

Obviously, the fact that I'm even writing these words suggests I have a feeling that the future is not mine. While I've been honored to make the initial discovery, I am not the one to bring it to full light. I need you to trust me, and when the time is right, you will know what to do.

Your friend,

Vanessa

Reading it again left her feeling the same emotion as the first time she read it: puzzled. Removing her glasses, she rubbed her eyes and sighed before taking another sip of her tea. She fixed her eyes on the wall across the room and beheld a painting of a sunset on the beach. Her mind failed to process its beauty; it was too busy walking down memory lane. Time and effort had failed to bring any further comprehension of what Dr. Cunningham was talking about. As she began to refold the letter, the phone rang. She cocked her head, her brow furrowed with wrinkles. No one ever called her at this time of night.

"Hello!" she said, expecting to hear the familiar dialogue of a telemarketer or the quick apology of a stranger who realized they called the wrong number.

"Where are you guys?" a woman's voice demanded.

Instantly recognizing the voice, Dr. Betsy felt her heart rate shoot up. "Who is this?" she asked spontaneously, as if her brain needed more confirmation.

"It's Valerie. Natasha's mom. Natasha just called me, but we got disconnected, and I can't reach her anymore. She told me you'd take her back to the Paleontology Insitute of Research and Development (PIRD) and that she'd catch the bus home from there."

Dr. Betsy's mind flashed back to that fateful night when that voice hurled horrible accusations at her, like cannonballs. And like cannonballs, they had done irreparable damage to her heart.

"I'm sorry. What are you talking about?"

"Sure you are," the voice retorted sarcastically.

Waiting in silence, Dr. Betsy refused to add more fuel to the fire. She had learned that this woman was as unpredictable as she was unreasonable.

"I dropped Natasha off at Kennington Park earlier today," Valerie finally responded, descending slightly from her accusatory tone. "She said you guys were doing some research there and that you'd bring her back after you were done."

Befuddled, Dr. Betsy gripped the phone tighter yet kept her tone calm and quiet. "We weren't at any park today. There was no field study scheduled."

The furrows on her brow deepened as she tried to figure out why Natasha would lie to her mother about going to a park. Natasha never came across as a liar. She was as sweet and kind as her grandmother, and smart as a whip. Dr. Betsy could hardly keep from constantly praising Natasha's venerable work and admired her razor focus on details others often passed by.

But then something clicked in her mind. Valerie had said Kennington Park, and that wasn't just any park. It was "the park."

"Oh my gosh!" Valerie's voice turned to panic. "Why would she go out there alone? She was asking me about Mom this week. Was she asking you anything about her?" she demanded in a tearful voice.

"No, Valerie. Nothing at all. And you told me not to speak to her about her grandmother." Now her heart began racing like a thoroughbred on its final lap to victory.

"I'm sorry I called you then," Valerie said before abruptly hanging up.

Dr. Betsy stood frozen, staring at her phone. "What's going on?" she asked aloud. "I just read that letter by complete accident. What are the chances of Natasha going to Kennington Park tonight?"

She pressed the number to call Valerie back, but it just kept ringing. "What is wrong with that woman? Why won't she pick up?" she seethed.

She repeatedly tried to connect with Valerie over the next few minutes, but Valerie, being Valerie, had no further need of her assistance and ignored the ringing as she rushed out of the employee lounge at the hospital where she worked.

◄○►

Bright light from the officer's car pierced a path through her Jeep windows and blinded her view as a policeman cautiously approached. Rolling down her window, Dr. Betsy swallowed hard and tried her best to smile broadly.

"Your license, ma'am," he asked roughly.

"It's in my purse. Do you mind if I get it?" Too many videos of overreacting cops had been etched in her mind. She didn't trust them even though her profile did not fit the ones from which they seemed justified in using excessive and aggressive force.

Leaning down, the officer beamed his flashlight throughout her Jeep and then nodded his approval.

"Do you know how fast you were going, ma'am?" he asked after peering down at her driver's license.

"Uh! Not really, officer."

"Where are you going in such a hurry?"

"I'm late to pick someone up. I'm sorry. I know I was speeding a tiny bit. I was just trying to hurry."

"I'll be back. You just hold tight," he said, retreating to his car.

"Lord, help him to hurry, and please let it just be a warning," she prayed under her breath.

When he returned, he leaned down again and looked directly at her.

"I knew I recognized that name, and now I recognize your face. You're the lady from that accident a couple of years ago. I remember talking to you at the hospital. I sure hope you're doing better now."

Her memory of that night was very selective, and she had no recall of this particular officer. "I am doing better, officer," she gulped. "Thank you."

"Well, I'm glad to see you're doing okay, Ms. Betsy," he said, returning her license. "That was a terrible night for you. It was a terrible night for us all. You surely don't want to be in an accident like that, so you better slow yourself down." He tipped his hat and walked back to his car.

Nodding in disbelief was all she could do. It was the third strike of the night: the letter, the call, the officer. Looking behind her, she pulled back onto the lonely highway.

It was the same highway she was traveling on two years earlier when it happened. She awoke that night on a stretcher in an ambulance, feeling horribly dizzy, as if an elephant were sitting on her chest with every breath she drew in. The sirens stopped as they pulled her from the ambulance, and she watched as another one pulled up behind them. The emergency personnel from the hospital quickly converged and rushed the injured person inside. It wasn't until hours later that she learned the horrible truth.

⤙○⤚

21

The crunch of the gravel under her tire wheels announced that she had arrived at the park. Devoid of any light except her headlights, the area was dark with not a living soul in sight.

Turning to her phone, she pondered whether she should call again. How many times had she debated deleting Valerie's number? It served no purpose in her phone. By her own words, Valerie had sworn she'd never forgive her. And she would have deleted the number had Natasha's name not appeared on one of her intern applications. Surprised that Valerie had allowed her daughter to apply, Dr. Betsy had called to thank her. She had assumed Valerie had knowledge of it.

She'd forgotten about Natasha's attempt to keep her mother ignorant of her actions, and Natasha had done it again. Both times, she'd been caught in the act immediately. But this time, her actions seemed more subtle and purposeful.

She pressed the button. Valerie picked up. "I got her. Good night."

Her tension eased, and Dr. Betsy breathed easier, relieved that the drama had come to an end. Now alone in the dark, her mind was free to release all the memories she had held back. Tears trickled down her cheeks as the familiar pain of grief squeezed her heart.

"You killed her," Valerie's heart-wrenching voice had screamed before awful wailing filled the ER. "She died because of you."

The nurse had finally finished assessing her. She had a mild concussion, and her blood pressure was sky-high, but she was otherwise fine. She looked at the nurse attending her with eyes filled with worried confusion.

"I'm sorry, ma'am. She's just stricken with grief. People blame everyone in situations like this."

"I don't understand. What happened?"

Looking at the floor with a sullen face, the nurse reported what she knew. "I'm not sure what you remember, but a car coming in the opposite direction was trying to pass another car. You would have been hit had it not been for the car behind you that accelerated and swung around. It was like the driver saw the other car coming and took the hit head-on. That's what the eyewitness reported."

That punch-in-the-gut feeling gripped her now as tightly as it had the moment she heard the news for the first time. Her eyes blurred as she beat her steering wheel. "Why did it happen, Lord? Why did it happen this way?" she cried. "Why did she do what she did? I didn't deserve to live, not at her expense. She was the one who worshipped You. She was the faithful follower. She didn't deserve to die like that. She didn't deserve to die at all."

No one was around to see the silent tears she was shedding. It had been a long time since she had let herself grieve like this. She knew it was the healthy thing to do, so she sobbed until she could sob no more, and then she began to think. Someone was trying to tell her something.

"What is it, Lord?" she asked as she opened her Jeep door and stepped outside into the cool night air. The sound of a multitude of night creatures filled the chilly air, but her attention was turned above. Pulling her jacket about her tightly, she peered up into the night sky. The story of Abraham came to mind with the numberless speckles of light that covered the blackened horizon. Like her, he had been confused and was searching for answers. Alone in the night, he had looked up into the heavens, and it was then that God spoke.

Would He speak to her too, or was she too small and insignificant for Him to hear her? She had come to believe that He truly loved and cared for her, but at times, she had her doubts. "You know I've done my best to honor Valerie's request not to speak to Natasha about her grandmother, but Lord, I also made a promise to her grandmother. Now Natasha is older, and if she's asking questions, I feel it might be time for her to know the truth."

A rustling in the grass made Dr. Betsy turn and look toward the ground. It took a few moments for her eyes to adjust, but she saw no creatures lurking about. Resting back against her Jeep, she returned her gaze upward. What seemed like dissonant noise when she arrived began to resemble a bit of an orchestra to her ears. The deep, low croaking of the frogs with the high chirps of the crickets made a rhythm of sorts.

"And then there's that research Dr. Cunningham was investigating, Lord. I know that's something I need to find out about, yet every avenue I've tried has yielded nothing."

Dr. Betsy searched the sky for some type of sign before surrendering to just listening. The longer she stood out there watching the star-filled sky, the more at peace she felt. Soon, the chirping of the crickets, the croaks of the frogs, and the buzzing about of insects were silenced, and her soul began to hear the whispers of her Maker. It was He Who had orchestrated her reading the letter that night. It was He Who had urged Natasha to visit the park. And it was He Who had brought the officer and those flashing lights to remind her of the memories she had tried to bury.

Deep within, she felt as if her life was about to change again. "What in heaven is going on?" she asked.

CHAPTER 3

Matthias: Zariah

A soft wind blew through the walls of rose vines my father and mother had weaved together, causing a sweet floral scent to permeate our dwelling place. Like many other precious items within our abode, the walls were alive and a constant reminder of the symbiotic relationship we shared with all living things, great and small. A yellow bird we named Sephora flitted about among the green leaves and deep purple roses that budded from the vines. She was a regular visitor to our home, and we welcomed her joyful melodies.

I barely heard Sephora's cheerful chirps or noticed her mischievous nosiness as she cocked her head from side to side. I was intently listening to my parents engaged in conversation in the next room.

"What is it, Adriel? You have that look on your face again," Keturah said as she stood beside her husband.

She was my father's equal in every way, stately and beautiful, her height almost matching his. Enshrouded in a soft, radiant glow, her form was barely noticeable, though her face was clearly visible. Long tendrils of braided hair cascaded down her back and through her four folded wings. Her feathered tips seemed to have been dipped in a golden reddish dye. Beyond the breathtaking glory of her physical appearance, her true captivating and attracting force was the strength and gentleness of her inner character.

"What look is that?" my father asked, turning toward his wife.

Keturah cradled my father's face in her hands. "That one. The one on your face right now. Are you worried about Matthias?"

My father's brow fell, and he looked toward the ground covered with precious stones as he thought about his next words. "Ever since I told him the story of the fall of Abner, he just keeps asking the same questions, and I have done all I can to help him understand the truth." Adriel tenderly covered his wife's hands with his own. "I just don't know what to do next."

"I think you need to be more patient. We've all had questions. You know that."

"Yes, we have, but I don't remember any of us asking the type of questions Matthias is asking." Adriel rubbed his chin and shook his head. "His questions are different. They hint at something." My father hesitated. "He's struggling with something within, and I have yet to put my finger on exactly what it is. I just hope he's not . . ."

My mother lifted his chin and peered into his eyes as she continued his thought. "You hope he's not sympathetic to them."

My father nodded.

I knew my questions were a concern to my father, and I tried to get them out of my head. Despite my efforts, they kept troubling me. The first time I expressed any questions, he answered quickly, and I felt that he wanted to suppress them at any cost. Restraining himself, he had resorted to telling me why my trend of thoughts could bring harm and confusion.

While he sought to bring my questions to an end with his words, my mother responded differently. She seemed to know that words alone would never suffice. Instead, she encouraged my father to introduce me to the Hall of Records.

He was convinced that I was not yet ready for such an experience and that he could get me to see differently. He'd engage me in debates and discussions. We would go at it for hours. He liked the challenge and was intrigued by the depth of my thoughts, but he was also disappointed that I never seemed to grasp the truth he was trying to present. I didn't like seeing my father's saddened face when our discussions came to an end, so I began to avoid the encounters and kept my thoughts to myself.

"He needs more than just your words, husband," Keturah said, squeezing his hand. "You must think again and pray for wisdom."

"Wisdom says to ask you for suggestions," Adriel said, smiling lovingly at his wife.

"Well, now that you have asked . . ." My mother walked past my father and looked out toward the large mango tree near our dwelling. Delectable fruit of every color—purple, red, orange, and green—dangled from its branches. "Why don't you have him join us today?"

"You mean to the meeting? But it's the council meeting," he remonstrated.

My mother turned to face him, lifting her eyebrows as she waited for him to respond before heading toward the door.

Following her lead, they left our abode and walked toward the tree with Sephora flying close behind them.

"But we're meeting about Earth." He sounded perplexed with her proposition, and my ears perked up even more at the mention of Earth.

Earth was our sister planet. She had been created as our complement. The virgin beauty that erupted throughout our planet, the numberless species of plants and animals that lived within our realm, and the life-giving properties that sustained our immortality were her original destiny. Together, we were to form an alliance of unity and collaboration that would define our eternal purpose. But Earth had strayed from her divine intention in her infancy and was now the only banned entity from our universe of light. While I had knowledge of her existence, I did not know the details as to why she, along with an innumerable host, had been exiled from our celestial abode.

"And?" Keturah said again as she plucked one of the ripe, succulent fruits that hung within her reach.

"I haven't even allowed him to read the records yet. He knows nothing of what we will be discussing."

"I hardly doubt that," she said, offering my father a bite of the fruit. "He knows more than you think." She took a bite and moaned with delight as the flavors saturated her buds. "I will never tire of eating this fruit," she declared, trying to wipe the juices that ran down her chin with her hand. "It might be good for him, Adriel."

"All right," he finally agreed. "Let's see what becomes of this." My father wrapped his arms around my mother's waist and leaned in to give her a peck on the cheek, but she slipped out of his arms with a pleased grin.

—◦—

The meeting was to be held at the Hiddekel Hall. It had been built over one of our glorious rivers. It was fed by a nearby waterfall which careened down a mountainside a short distance away. The building served as a bridge and was made entirely of emeralds and a glass-like substance. The sun's rays flooded the hall with light, which allowed for the growth of various plants inside. I enjoyed standing outside on one of its expansive decks, viewing the valley on one end and the cascading falls on the other. Inside the halls, the walls were lined with paintings and exquisite artwork from the illustrious hands of master artists.

When all the council members had settled into their seats, my mother, with wings fully outstretched, called the meeting to order. She was the appointed chairperson for this special council, though she filled many roles throughout her existence, as did all the beings of Zariah. Both my parents were angelic beings who served the fallen race of humans. My mother was a recorder or watcher, a being who meticulously cataloged the events and life stories of many on Earth. My father, a warrior, often spent long periods of time engaged in close combat against the fallen ones. Yet these positions were not their permanent callings; they were transitory. With eternity stretching before us, we were constantly presented and challenged with new positions that would cause us to grow and flourish.

"I'd first like to welcome one of our youths to this special council," she said as she bowed her head my way.

I stood to my feet and pressed my hands together while bowing to her and the councilmen and women. "Thank you," I softly whispered.

"From the beginning of Earth's history, this council has been in session, but only now are we on the cusp of achieving our desired mission," she declared with an authoritative voice.

Rarely were beings other than the council members invited into a council meeting without a special purpose, so I felt quite honored to be amongst them. They had not told me what this council was about, nor their agenda for the meeting, so I sat and listened intently, my curiosity piqued.

"Only one of the mortals chosen for this mission has yet to be brought to the light," my mother said.

Heads bobbed up and down in agreement before my mother continued.

"Events of life that can only be orchestrated by divinity have positioned all the others right where they need to be at this point and time. Even the fallen ones have returned their focus to this mission and are evoking their most vile plans in an attempt to thwart our efforts at achieving our goal."

Keturah lowered her voice as she paced back and forth. "We must not be defeated. Too much relies on our success. And those bones have been buried long enough. They must be brought to the surface for everyone to see."

The council erupted in applause, and many turned to their neighbor and began to whisper. "It's about time," I heard some say.

"I knew we were getting close to finishing this thing," Anna, one of the most senior members, said to me. She must have assumed I knew what they were discussing.

I was completely mystified. I desperately wanted someone to explain to me what they were talking about, but everyone, absorbed in the words my mother had spoken, was completely oblivious to my confusion.

"John McKenzie," my mother declared.

The whispers died down, and silence filled the room.

"He is the last piece of this puzzle that needs to be put into place. He has been chosen by the Almighty, but he has yet to be brought to the crossroads. If he chooses the side of light, it will expedite our progress immensely."

She turned to face the group as she rubbed her hands. "We need him, and we need to fight for his soul. His salvation will lead to the salvation of countless others."

Keturah looked earnestly around the room. "It's time we assign him a protector, a guardian. Does anyone have any suggestions as to who could best fulfill this position?"

The room was eerily silent as each one began to think of possible candidates.

"How about Matthias?" an elder named Malkiel asked. "He is young and soon to have his Communion. I have worked with him as my understudy here on Zariah, and I have seen him grow and mature." Malkiel smiled as he looked my way.

My eyes widened with surprise, as did my mother's.

"No. He is not ready for such a great task," my father interjected almost immediately while standing to his feet. "He has not even been to the record hall. He knows nothing of Earth."

"But he will be educated and trained," Malkiel stated.

"Surely there must be someone else who is more highly qualified," my father said. He looked around the room, desperately hoping someone would speak up, but no one did. "Then I suggest Bayla. She is his senior and has served as a watcher for Earth."

"Bayla already has a commission," my mother responded. "She has been assigned to work with Tobias for a different mission." My mother bowed her head and folded her hands as if she had just realized the truth. She looked at my father, who was still standing. "We don't have to make a decision right now. We will take time to pray and discuss it some more. I am sure the Creator will make His will known."

Then she looked at me. "Matthias, what are your thoughts? Would you be willing to train so you could serve as a protector?"

I was stunned by the proposition. Only a select few were assigned to Earth. I had never even considered it, but now that the opportunity was placed before me, my heart thrilled with excitement. I tried my best to maintain my composure and simply bowed my head.

"And do you have any questions right now?"

Everyone continued to look my way. "If I was chosen, would I be able to meet the fallen ones? Would I be able to speak to them?"

The room fell silent, and I heard someone gasp as the leaders looked at one another with stares that spoke concern.

"Why would he want to speak with the fallen ones?" they whispered.

I didn't realize my question would be a cause of so much consternation. I looked at my father. His face appeared devoid of emotions, but in his eyes, I read sorrow. I quickly looked down at the table, waiting for him to respond, but he didn't. He merely sat down.

Finally, Malkiel spoke up. "Your question is a good one. We have never kept anyone from speaking to the fallen ones. If chosen, we would certainly want you to proceed with caution." Looking then to my father and mother, he said, "It is my recommendation that you take him to read the records." Everyone nodded their approval. "It is time for him to read and see for himself where and how the controversy began."

"Thank you," my father whispered, bowing respectfully to the council before him. I knew he was looking my way, but I couldn't bear to meet his disappointed gaze. I looked at my mother. She smiled, and in her eyes, I could see she knew this was the path for me.

CHAPTER 4

Natasha: Strained Relationship

Crispy white sheets stretched over Natasha's quivering frame as she lay in the ER bed. Her mother sat a few inches away with her arms folded tight, eyes closed, and her head leaning back against the stark white wall. They had been waiting for over an hour for the hospital personnel to take her for X-rays on her ankle. Glancing at her mom, she knew it was pointless apologizing again. Any words she spoke now would only serve to widen the crevice that had cracked open when her mom had exploded on her during the drive home.

"I can't believe you," Valerie scolded as the car roared to life and the headlights flashed on. They beamed across a field of grass seemingly devoid of life, though both she and her mother knew otherwise. As they struggled to get back to the car, they had been inflicted with countless bites from an array of insects that had made that grassy field their home and their bodies their platter.

A scolding was inevitable, and she gave her mom credit for having restrained herself until they arrived safely inside her car. The long journey back down the dark trail had only been filled with her grunts and groans and her mother's constant questioning if she was okay. But the suppressed reprimand seemed to have fueled her mother's fury.

Natasha knew her mom would be upset but only because rescuing her interfered with her life. No matter what she did growing up, right or wrong, her mother hardly ever seemed to notice or care. When her sixth-grade teacher reported she'd cheated on a test, her mom barely even chastised her. All she said on the drive home that day was "You'll reap what you sow." And when she won second place in the eighth-grade spelling bee, she barely muttered, "Good job" when Natasha had eagerly and proudly announced her placement, before reminding her to wash the dishes. That had been the pattern of her mother's devotion or lack thereof her entire life. Yet deep down inside, she was still the only person Natasha strived to please.

"You lied," Valerie spat while accelerating past the speed limit marked on a highway post. "I called Dr. Betsy when I couldn't get ahold of you," she said, momentarily taking her attention away from the highway to glare at her daughter. "Do you know how surprised I was to find out there was no research project planned? Do you know how scared I was to think that I dropped you off at some deserted park and that you were still there out in the dark?" Valerie's voice escalated with a level of concern Natasha rarely heard her mother express. "We just had that teenager murdered in the park only a few miles from there. Here I am thinking you'd been murdered or something. And what would I do without you?"

Natasha's heart skipped a beat as her mother's voice cracked. Her joy was short-lived when her mother turned from Dr. Jekyll to Mr. Hyde almost instantaneously.

"You risked your life doing something foolish. I finally made it to work on time only for me to have to leave to pick up your irresponsible behind. I can't afford to miss another night of work. I'm going to lose my job," she yelled, without giving Natasha a chance to respond. "What were you thinking, Natasha? And what were you doing out there alone? Whatever would possess you to lie to me? And look at you. You're a complete mess. You better tell me what's going on."

"Sorry, Mom," Natasha muttered sheepishly while doing her best to appear defenseless and apologetic. "I wasn't thinking. I just wanted to discover something on my own. Everyone's so competitive in the internship program, especially John, and . . ."

Interrupting her, Valerie asked, "Who the heck is John?"

"My lab partner in science class and at the PIRD. We always get paired up together because of our grades, but he's so competitive, Mom. He tries to outshine me in everything, and I figured I'd do a little research to try to get ahead."

"Oh! I should have figured this was about a boy," Valerie replied snidely, as if she had an "aha" revelation. "Were you trying to get ahead of him or trying to get on top of him? Was he out there with you? Was this some planned escapade to be with a boy?"

The car tires screeched as Valerie swung around a corner too quickly, causing Natasha to hang on to the door armrest as pain surged through her ankle. "What? What are you talking about? I was just telling you how I was trying to get ahead of him, not go out with him." But her words seemed to fall on deaf ears.

"Were you whoring yourself out there?" Valerie yelled. Her narrow accusatory eyes searched Natasha's face for some expression that would confirm her deranged thoughts.

"Why in the world would you even think that?" Natasha shot back in complete surprise. "It doesn't even make any sense. I was one mile down the trail. If I was with anyone and they left me like that, I'd be done with them." Her smart rebuttal didn't keep her eyes from filling with tears at her mother's suggestion. "I told you, I was just taking a walk by myself, remembering Grandma. I fell and blacked out. When I came to, it was dark." She knew it was only half the truth, but it was the only truth she was willing to share.

"But if that's what you think of me, then yes," she sniffled. "That's exactly what I was doing, Mom." Her voice trembled as she spoke. "I was whoring myself," she repeated with disdain.

"Well, that's what kids do," Valerie replied, her voice seared with a tinge of guilt. "They get involved in these relationships and start sneaking around, and before you know it, they have a baby."

The car came to a stop, and Valerie pushed the gear into park. She wagged her finger in Natasha's face and sneered, "You listen here, little girl. Don't you ever bring any children around here to me. Unlike your grandma, I won't be taking care of no kid for you. You make your mistakes, you had better be prepared to live with them by yourself."

Natasha felt as if her soul was being sucked out of her. *You would abandon me if I ever made a mistake?* she thought, before finding the words to respond. "I'm tired, Mom. I'm tired of trying to convince you that I'm not that evil person you've created in your head. I'm not a bad kid," she said. "I don't take drugs. I've never tasted alcohol. I don't smoke. And I've never had sex with anyone. I take care of you and me. I go to school and do my work well. Why would you think such a thing? Why are you always thinking the worst of me despite everything I do?" she bellowed.

"I knew I couldn't expect more than this from you. You're nothing but disrespectful and rude. It was just a matter of time until you revealed your true self," Valerie replied with a tone so condescending that it made something inside Natasha break free.

Natasha threw her hands in the air and screamed. "Didn't you hear a word I said, Mom? You don't ever hear me. Only Grandma ever did. And only she ever cared. The last thing you'd ever have to worry about is me bringing a kid to you. You're the worst mother I've ever known. Don't worry about me, Mom. What you need to worry about is when someone," she said, using air quotes, "takes me away from this pathetic life with you, and you're left all alone. And if you hadn't noticed, you're not getting any younger, and you've run every person away who ever cared for you. So, if you think you can do a better job than me or find someone else to deal with you, good luck."

She had imagined telling off her mom time and again but never had the courage or the heart to do so. Now the words she thought would demonstrate her boldness and confidence brought her little satisfaction, and she felt disappointed in herself for having said them.

"That's real nice, Natasha. "You'd leave me alone? I guess I should have left you alone out there, right? Ignored that brief phone call with absolutely no directions on where you were exactly." Valerie's eyes met Natasha's regretful gaze. "Thank goodness I remembered the time Grandma took us for a walk at that park and down that trail, and thank the good Lord you had me to call or else you'd be still lying out there alone."

—◄○►—

A warm, luminescent glow saturated the forest trail while Natasha seemed to be hovering like some angelic being watching from above. Two young boys playfully pushed and tugged at each other before pausing to watch a black squirrel scamper up a tree. Completely enamored, they pointed excitedly at the animal before returning to their fun. A little girl, fingers intertwined with the man and woman at her side, swung like a swing between them. Her delighted screeches filled the air as an older grey-haired woman strolled and hummed softly behind. They all seemed so contented, smiles on each face as they stopped to look at some natural wonder along the trail or listen to the enticing sounds of the forest.

The first movement of Beethoven's *Fifth Symphony* began to sound and gradually louden. It was her 7:45 a.m. alarm. Turning it off, she rolled over and sighed loudly. That dream was always the same—a family on some trail to nowhere but blissfully happy in that moment. Repeated dreams were warnings of some future event or suppressed past events. That was what her grandma had told her, and she wondered if this dream, which seemed to be increasing in frequency, was somehow showing her the future or her past.

Pushing her aching body into a sitting position, she sat on the edge of her bed with her arms folded and winced slightly from the pounding inside her head. Her dream faded from her thoughts as the events of the night before flooded her memory. What she had thought would be an evening of adventure had turned into a night of trauma and disappointment.

Every muscle in Natasha's face tightened before a cold splash of water bathed it. She patted her face gently with the grey towel that hung from the small circular silver ring next to the bathroom sink.

Opening her eyes, she stared at the image reflecting back at her. Her brown face, round and chubby, made her frown with displeasure. How badly she wanted to lose some weight. If only her ability to physically push herself matched her mental agility. Her mind was quick and witty. It absorbed information like a sponge, allowing her to spit out facts and figures like a computer. She was the epitome of being in mental shape, but her body was something entirely different. It had a mind of its own, and no matter how she schemed to get those extra pounds off, they stuck to her like white on rice.

Her disheveled hair brought even more self-loathing. Perming to straighten her hair had weakened it, causing breakage along her side edges. Never finding the best products to care for it left it dry, brittle, and difficult to style. She quickly brushed it and tied it back with a scrunchie.

Tightly clutching the stairway railing, she attempted to descend with her bookbag slung across her back. She had left the crutches she'd been given by the hospital at the bottom of the stairwell. They were useless in helping her up or down the stairs, and she figured she could balance on one leg while using the wall for support to get around upstairs. But she was unsuccessful in keeping her entire weight off her ankle, and the pain had intensified to levels that caused her to grimace with each step.

Grabbing the crutches and tucking them under her arms, she swung herself into the kitchen to get something to eat. Her mom had returned to work after dropping her home and was due back at any moment. She normally took the school bus, but having missed it this morning due to the extended time it took to get ready, she needed a ride and prayed her mother would oblige.

Valerie barely ever budged from her back-from-work routine. She'd arrive home, get something to eat, watch the news for about thirty minutes, and retreat to bed, leaving Natasha, on non-school days, to figure out how to get to where she needed to go. That was where the city bus came in. She learned its many routes from a young age and had come to depend on it for her primary mode of transportation apart from the school bus. But today, she hoped her mother would be sympathetic to her injury and texted her at 7:00 a.m. to plead for a ride, the exact time her mother was supposed to leave work.

The ring of the microwave summoned her to recover the bowl of oatmeal she had placed inside. Scooping a huge spoonful of smooth peanut butter from its jar, she swirled around the steaming cereal until it dissolved into a creamy mixture of sweet nutty goodness. It was her morning favorite, and she ate it at least four days of the week while she mindlessly watched TikTok clips. TikTok was a regrettable and addictive choice from her usual devotional routine, but her grief and its resulting apathy after her grandma perished caused her to abandon many of the healthy, life-sustaining practices she had previously enjoyed.

"I called Dr. Betsy." Her mother's words crawled back into her mind. It had troubled her momentarily before the scathing words that followed distracted her from figuring out how it was that her mother had Dr. Betsy's phone number. Her eyes narrowed as she scooped a hot spoonful of the thick porridge into her mouth. *Was Mom talking about the number to the PIRD?* she thought pensively. If so, that would have been easy enough for her to get. A simple search on the internet would have yielded the number. Or was she talking about Dr. Betsy's personal phone number? For some reason, the way Valerie mentioned it made her think it was the latter. If that was the case, she wondered why that would be.

As she rinsed her mouth with a swig of soy milk, her mind grappled with the idea of how her mother somehow knew Dr. Betsy. Their worlds were as far apart as the Earth and the Andromeda Galaxy. Her mother was a nurse and Dr. Betsy a scientist. It was virtually impossible for them to cross paths, much less have friends within the same circle. Then she remembered her mother's strange remonstrance when she mentioned she was applying for an internship at the PIRD. Eventually, she backed down, but Natasha never forgot her mother's response.

The rumble of the garage door opening made her hasten to wash up her dishes and wipe down the table. Reaching for her crutches, she readied herself to move toward the door.

"Good morning, Mom," Natasha greeted cheerily the minute the door swung open.

"Why are you still home?" Valerie grumbled, passing her by and tossing her keys on the table.

"Mom," Natasha replied, clearly irritated. "I sent you a text message. Twice. I asked if you could take me to school. You know I'm hurt. What the heck?"

"Don't 'what the heck' me!" her mother warned, turning around to face her. "Why didn't you call me?"

"Really?" Natasha puffed in disbelief. "I didn't call you because you were likely driving, so I texted you. And you never ever answer your phone anyway," she said, emphasizing each word forcefully. "So why would I bother calling you?"

"Well, I'm sorry," Valerie replied nonchalantly, walking to the fridge. "You should have called. Thanks to you, I had a very disruptive and disturbing night, and I'm way too tired to drive anywhere now."

"Seriously, Mom. How am I supposed to get to school?" Natasha asked, shifting her weight on her crutches. "The school bus is gone."

"I thought you'd stay home today. You did get hurt, and they gave you a doctor's note. The kitchen sink is full of dishes, and clothes need to be washed."

A gush of angry blood surged through Natasha's body and warmed her face. She bit her lower lip and tried to keep the words that hung on the precipice of her tongue from spilling out.

"I need to get to school, Mom, and you're the only one who can take me right now. It will only take you twenty to thirty minutes."

Valerie tossed a bag of bread on the counter with a package of cheese. "Actually, you have options, darling," she replied flippantly. "The city bus is still running."

Her words seemed to shove the breath right out of Natasha's lungs. "You'd make me take the city bus today when I'm on crutches?" she stuttered.

"That's on you, little girl. You decided to wander about that deserted park last night. You should be glad I took the time to take you to the ER," Valerie said with a roll of her neck.

"Okay then! Fine, Mother," Natasha spat through clenched teeth with as much anger in her tone as she could muster. "I'll take the city bus today, and I'll let you figure out how to wash your own clothes." She turned to leave but stopped right before closing the door. "Oh! By the way, where in the world did you get Dr. Betsy's phone number?"

Valerie shrugged. "I've had it for years."

"Years?" Natasha exclaimed in surprise. "Years? But how? And why?"

"Look, Natasha," Valerie said firmly. "It's none of your business, and I'm tired. So have a nice day at school."

CHAPTER 5

John: The Competition

Natasha was never late, so John couldn't help but assume she'd been excused to help in another lab. It was a privilege he would have loved to be given, but once again he'd been overlooked. He'd convinced himself they chose her over him just because of her race and because she needed the extra help to get ahead. Yet deep inside, he knew otherwise, and the seed of jealousy he desperately tried to suppress began to rear its ugly head.

Sighing deeply, John told himself to just concentrate on his work. He'd soon be out of this small pond anyway. Graduation was only a few weeks away, and then he'd be off to college and out of her shadow.

When she walked in the door with a bandage on her forehead and limping on crutches, he couldn't help but snicker silently before addressing her.

"What the heck happened to you?" John whispered.

"I'll tell you later," Natasha whispered back.

Kenisha, one of Natasha's besties, was sitting two rows ahead of them. Her eyes bugged out at the sight of Natasha, and they begged to be told what happened. But Natasha mouthed the word "later" to Kenisha, and she begrudgingly turned back around.

"Who can explain to me how the environment can shape the evolutionary path of a species?" Mr. Kennedy's baritone voice boomed through the science laboratory, filled with mostly indifferent teenagers. Silence engulfed the room as he strolled through the aisles.

Mr. Kennedy was a tall, robust man. His full beard and mustache, the well-weathered leather jacket, and the Harley Davidson that sat in the parking lot made John wonder what forces had shaped his path into a career in science and education versus a wild cross-country biker.

Regardless, he was an amazing teacher and one of the few John really enjoyed. Despite Mr. Kennedy's love of Natasha, he never failed to recognize John's outstanding academic achievements. It was Mr. Kennedy who had recommended him for the internship at the Paleontology Institute of Research and Development. It was a prestigious opportunity offered to the students with the highest GPA in the sciences. Only two students from a high school were chosen, and both he and Natasha had been recommended.

"Come on, guys," Mr. Kennedy coached before repeating the question. "Who can explain to me how the environment can shape the evolutionary path of a species?" he asked, looking around the room while eyeing each student as if sniffing out the weakest one. Then he stopped and peered down. "Kenisha, how about you?"

His sense of smell is impeccable, John mused to himself. Kenisha was very likely one of the students in the class with the lowest GPA.

"Uhh. Well. I think that . . . umm."

Giggling erupted throughout the classroom, and John couldn't help but join in.

Natasha, on the other hand, bowed her head and closed her eyes as if she couldn't bear to see her friend embarrassed and humiliated. Then, in a flash, she raised her arm, and before Mr. Kennedy could even acknowledge her, she spat out the answer.

"Perfect. Couldn't have said it better myself," Mr. Kennedy said glowingly as he smiled at Natasha. "I'm glad to see you, despite your injury. The office told me you might not be in today. Now get to your labs," he continued, clasping his hands. "Read the instructions carefully, and you should be fine." He then retreated to the back of the lab and sat down at his desk with pen in hand, turning his attention to grading the quizzes the students had completed a few minutes before.

Rolling his eyes with a sigh, John folded his arms and glared at Natasha. "Well, superwoman, once again you've swooped down and rescued your friend. And did you ever happen to think that your supposed rescue might be why she's still so stupid? I mean, if I knew someone was always going to answer for me, I wouldn't bother to read or study either."

"Shut up, John!" Natasha replied with a scowl. "I would never expect you to understand the need to help anyone since you've only ever helped yourself. And there you go again, making accusations that are just not true. I mean, where would you be without me and the work I do for all the assignments we happen to have together?

"Calling Kenisha stupid just because she doesn't have a 4.0 GPA like you is ignorant and dumb. People are more than just their GPA, John, and I'm tired of you calling my friend names. Anyway," Natasha continued, her face contorted with frustration, "this conversation is going nowhere, so let's just get on with it. Do you want to get the beakers or should I?"

"Fine. I'll get them, but tell me what this is all about," he said, waving his hand at Natasha's leg and head.

"Nothing, really," Natasha replied, shrugging her shoulders. "I just fell."

"Okay. Where? Down a flight of stairs?" He knew his tone was dripping with sarcasm, but he couldn't help it.

"It wasn't a flight of stairs," she shot back with a slight neck roll. "I just tripped and fell while taking a walk."

"Really? Sounds suspicious," he added before walking away to retrieve the beakers from the cabinet.

"Girl, what happened?" Kenisha had managed to slip away from her lab station under the guise of seeking help from Natasha.

"I was just careless and fell." Natasha shrugged as she turned her full attention to her friend.

"Off what? A horse?" Kenisha asked, rolling her neck.

John chuckled loudly as he placed the beakers on the table. "Those were my exact thoughts. I mean, it was either a horse or off the side of a cliff."

"No one was talking to you," Natasha retorted, rolling her eyes.

"Good gracious!" Kenisha said, eyeing Natasha from head to toe. "You're all beat up. Thank goodness you're okay." Her expression of concern quickly changed to a broad smile. "Can I borrow your crutches?" she asked, grabbing them and slipping them under her arms. "I've always wanted to try them out." Kenisha feigned an injured ankle as she shuffled around their lab station.

"Excuse me, but what are you doing?" Mr. Kennedy asked, looking up from his work.

"Uh! Sorry. I was just asking Natasha for some help," Kenisha replied, placing the crutches aside and returning to her station.

"I hope your broken leg won't slow us down or interfere with the project we have to complete for our intern assignment," John said, turning to Natasha. "Bethany and Ivan have been working their butts off and have theirs almost completed."

"Well, my leg isn't broken. No cast here," she said, waving her leg. "It's just a sprain. And since it's my leg that is sprained and not my brain, I think we should be fine."

Pursing his lips together, John restrained himself from responding. Natasha always had a smart quip to counter his. Why he kept getting stuck with her was an annoyance he couldn't get over. Sure, they were both the smartest in their class, but that didn't mean they needed to be stuck at the hip for virtually every assignment. He'd even made special requests to work with others, yet somehow, he'd still end up with Natasha at his side.

He'd thought things would be different at the PIRD. He'd expected them to work on their own or to partner with students from a different high school, but again he was met with disappointment. Not only were they required to work on-site together, but they were also required to attend other events as a team. He spent so much time in her presence that his buddies jokingly referred to her as his girlfriend. It was clearly a joke he didn't find funny, but the angrier he became at their taunting, the more they pestered him.

Arriving at the PIRD later that afternoon, John fully intended to finish his portion of the classification assignment they'd been working on. Muttering under his breath, he fussed with himself as to why instructors insisted on making students' grades dependent on each other. If he had it his way, he'd never work with anyone else. While he couldn't deny that Natasha's work was always superb, it prevented him from getting one hundred percent of the credit.

"I might as well slap her name on my high school diploma and college application," he fumed as he carefully placed his plant samples on the slides he was preparing. *College.* That word alone sent thrills up and down his spine. It meant so much to him: freedom, success, opportunity, individuality, and respect. Those were all the things his mother lacked because she had never finished her college education. That was the reason she had gotten stuck in a loveless, abusive marriage.

How many times had she told him it was one of her biggest regrets in life? If only she could have mustered the determination to complete her education, she could have seen herself through on her own.

And now he was stuck too unless he completed what his mother failed to do. College was his ticket to a whole new life—a life of affluence and ease with a wife who would cater to his every need. And kids too. He wanted children, but he'd make sure to treat them well. He wanted to give them the happy childhood that he and his sister, Riley, had been robbed of.

"See, you're wrong again, Natasha," he breathed under his breath. "You don't know about Riley and how I have to help her," he told himself. But as the words of justification crossed his mind, they were rapidly overtaken by guilt. He did help his sister, but barely, and not with the things that mattered most. He'd take her to school and back, but he was not the emotional support or the loving brother he should have been.

Glancing at the time made him shake his head. How Natasha managed to never be late for school but was always late for this intern rotation was beyond him. It was stuff like this that made him downgrade her excellence. Everyone else had their lab partners and were all working diligently. The assignment was due by the end of the day, and he knew she had yet to finish her portion. Working as swiftly as he could, he completed his slides and began working on hers with a sly grin plastered on his face. It was a surefire way to get the full credit for completing the assignment and a perfect way to make her look inefficient.

"Did everyone check in their packs?" research assistant Melinda asked as she entered the room. "We have a field trip tomorrow, and last time, we had two teams with missing equipment. Let me remind you that the field pack equipment belongs to the PIRD, and you are not at liberty to take it home for personal use. I know it's hard to keep track of some of the smaller items and that some might get lost on our trips, but you must make sure to inform me so I can record the lost or missing items and replace them."

Melinda then proceeded to call Team Two and Team Six to the front so she could give them the replacement items they needed to complete their packs.

John grimaced as he realized he had neglected to check appropriately in his haste to begin working on the assignment. Yet he wasn't worried. He and Natasha were the only team who had not lost or misplaced any of their tools. They meticulously tracked every item they used while on their field trips and consistently checked their packs before and after use.

"John," Melinda called a few minutes later. "You guys are usually impeccable, but your team never signed off on your pack check from the last field trip. Remember, signatures are required to ensure you have everything you need."

"Okay. I thought Natasha said she was going to do that," he replied with a concerned frown. "But I'll check and sign it off now." He retreated to the storage locker. Instead of the casual verification he was expecting, his hands rabidly searched through the pack as he tried to understand how several items could be missing.

CHAPTER 6

Natasha: Old Ben

Sitting at the edge of her seat, Natasha anxiously waited for the city bus to come to a full stop. She had raced to the bus stop immediately after her last class but to no avail. The bus was full of people and stopped to unload and reload at every stop along the way. Its progress was so slow that she felt she could have beaten it with a fast walk had she not been on crutches.

She was the unfortunate one among the interns. Not only did she not have a car and could not drive but she was also the only one to whom no one ever offered a ride. How often had she seen other students catching a ride with someone else? Even though she often worked side by side with John, he had never been polite or kind enough to offer her a ride. A glance toward the intern room indicated that the ambitious group was already busy working on their projects. *Figures,* she fumed as she stumbled through the eight-foot double doors of the PIRD. *The last one, once again,* she thought.

It was her intention to get there before any of the interns arrived, especially John, since he would be the only one to notice their field pack had missing items. And without hesitation, he would be anxious to report them as stolen. But the helmet, flashlight, and shovel that sat in her bookbag were on their way to being returned. And if returned, Natasha reasoned, they had only been borrowed.

As luck would have it, the bus ride had delayed her arrival to the point that John should have already taken inventory, something they were required to do at the beginning and end of each session. If he had, she might be walking right into trouble. Palms moist from sweat caused by both the heat and her anxiety made the wooden door handle feel sticky. A cold whisk of air cooled her down as she stepped inside.

"What happened to you?" Suzie asked as Natasha tried to wave hello while swinging herself on her crutches. Suzie, the receptionist, was one of the nicest people Natasha had met at the PIRD. She always made her feel welcome and never shied away from an opportunity to brag about her.

"I tripped and sprained my ankle pretty badly," Natasha said, scrunching her face to display her displeasure at her misfortune. "But I'm okay otherwise," she grinned.

"You poor dear. You better be more careful," Suzie cautioned as Natasha turned to head toward the intern room.

"I know. Sometimes I think I have two left feet," she joked.

Suzie smiled and waved her on through. "You let me know if you need me to do anything for you while you're here, even if it's just to get a snack out of the vending machine."

"Don't worry, I'm pretty good with these," she yelled back, slightly lifting one of her crutches from the ground.

"Oh! Wait, wait!" Suzie shouted. "I almost forgot." She quickly rose from her seat, rushed to Natasha's side, and lowered her voice. "Dr. Betsy wants to see you before you start today. She wants you to wait for her here in the lobby," she said, pointing to some empty seats.

Natasha's body stiffened. "Really?" she whispered back as her smile shrank and a knot developed in her stomach. "Why?" she asked, trying to hide her concern.

Suzie shrugged and smiled. "I'm confident it's nothing serious," she said reassuringly. "Probably just wants to commend you for the outstanding job you did on the otter display. I get wonderful compliments about it all the time. People just love it." She looked toward the clock. "She won't get out of her meeting for another ten minutes, so make yourself comfortable."

"In that case, do you mind getting me some M&Ms from the vending machine?" Natasha asked, grinning broadly.

She didn't taste the M&Ms she started popping in her mouth in quick succession. She was too absorbed trying to figure out how she could return the field pack items before her meeting with Dr. Betsy. *Ten minutes*, she thought as she looked around. She could sneak off to the bathroom and then hurry down the hall to the equipment room. Picking up her crutches, she prepared to stand, just as a familiar voice made her turn and her belly flip-flop.

John was at the receptionist's desk. "Crap," she whispered to herself while hoping he didn't ask for her whereabouts. After a few moments chatting with Suzie, he sauntered over to the vending machine and retrieved a Snickers bar.

What's he doing out here? she thought, despite knowing the answer to her question. He had to be looking for her. There was a snack machine in the hall right outside the interns' room. *He didn't have to come out here for his calorie booster.* Slinking lower in her chair, she pulled her head to her chest and hoped he wouldn't notice her.

With John hanging out in the lobby and Dr. Betsy on her way, she was sure she'd be caught red- handed. Unable to get rid of the evidence in her pack, she started sweating profusely and desperately prayed for deliverance. When John retreated down the hall toward the interns' office, she breathed a sigh of relief.

"Hello, Natasha."

Startled, she turned to see Dr. Betsy standing behind her. Grabbing her crutches, she pulled herself to standing. "I didn't even see you walk in."

"I noticed that," she replied. "You were deep in thought."

"Uhh, yes! I was just . . . kind of . . ."

Dr. Betsy faced Natasha with a warm smile. "Worried about why I want to speak with you?"

Natasha's head nodded vigorously.

"Do you mind if we take a walk outside? I know you're on crutches, but I've been cooped up in this building all day and would love some fresh air while we chat."

The smell of salty ocean air greeted her nose buds as a stiff wind whipped at Natasha's sweatpants and shirt. The quarter acre of grass that sat between the PIRD and the Pacific Ocean had been recently mowed, triggering Natasha's ever-present allergies. Sneezing repeatedly, she quickly fished out a tissue from her bag and tried to shield her nostrils from the onslaught of minuscule allergens saturating the air.

"Old Ben," Dr. Betsy said, pointing its way.

A trail of worn grass led toward a lonely but gargantuan oak tree. Even from a distance, Natasha could see its gnarled trunk which appeared short in comparison to its long-branched arms that stretched out wide and far. Laden with newly erupted leaves, it wore them like a crown upon its head. Swaying gently in the breeze, it seemed to be calling them to its side.

"Old Ben," Dr. Betsy repeated as she eagerly approached this magnificent creation. She could tell it was a mighty force to be reckoned with, for it had withstood all the storms and tribulations the fierce ocean wind could lash at it.

"I call him Old Ben," she continued with a grin. "Look at him. Old and knobby, much like me, though I don't expect I will be living as old as he," she said with a chuckle.

Seabirds, wings outstretched like a plane in flight, rose on the invisible thermals of warm air through the endless blue skies that had been painted with trails of white swirls of cirrus clouds. The beauty of the scenery invigorated her spirit with each breath she drew. Why she never wandered to this side of the PIRD was beyond her, but Dr. Betsy knew it would now become her special retreat.

"There's a bench out there, you know." Dr. Betsy raised her slender arm and pointed at the tree. "You can't see it from here, but it's facing the mighty beast of the sea."

The bench shoulders appeared first before she could see its seat. It appeared as old as the tree. The metal framework was rusted, and the salty air had eaten away at some of the fibers of wood, but it, like the tree, stood strong and sure.

Gladdened by the outdoor beauty and gentle breeze, Dr. Betsy seated herself, inviting Natasha to do the same by patting the lumber next to her.

"I'm sure you're wondering why I wanted to speak with you, or perhaps you've already guessed." Natasha shook her head no as she watched the strands of Dr. Betsy's short silver hair dance in the wind.

She had time on the walk there to consider whether she should confess or explain her "borrowing" to her preceptor. She'd been taught that it was better to confess than to be found out. But if she mentioned the tools, the next question would be *why*, and she didn't want to add lying to her list of indiscretions.

"I heard you made a visit to Kennington Park last night," Dr. Betsy said, looking out toward the ocean.

Natasha slowly nodded but kept her lips sealed. She could think of nothing to say that would steer Dr. Betsy's questions away from her actions.

"I knew your grandmother," she finally said, turning to look at Natasha before returning her gaze to the sea. "We were very good friends. I met her at a conference, much like the one you're scheduled to attend this weekend with John. She was a presenter the day of that long-ago conference and articulated her research so well and spoke with such passion that we couldn't help but give her a standing ovation. I was beyond impressed with her knowledge of the local flora and felt she would be a huge asset to my team."

"Grandma was an avid environmentalist," Natasha said, grinning proudly. "She knew everything about everything around here. She spent so much time outdoors studying nature, and she often took me with her. I think that's how I gained a love for the natural world."

"Indeed, she was obsessed with protecting the Earth and its natural resources," Dr. Betsy said, shaking her head. "But she was as smart as she was kind. And more than anything, I was drawn to her selfless spirit."

Natasha's eyes welled with tears. No one had spoken so highly of her dear grandmother before, and the thought that Dr. Betsy, with all her accolades, would express such lovely compliments touched every chord in Natasha's heart.

"I didn't mean to make you cry," Dr. Betsy comforted her as she gently touched Natasha's hand. "Here," she said, pulling out a small pouch of Kleenex from her pants pocket. "I always keep these with me," she confessed.

"Thank you," Natasha squeaked while trying to hold back her emotions. Her own mother refused to speak of precious Grandma, no matter how much Natasha prodded. Valerie's persistent suppression of her mother's memories only served to hurt Natasha and caused her to bury her grief as deeply as she could push it. It was her grandma's grace and love that had saved her and raised her. As her mind opened the doors to her memories, her heart refused to hold its sorrow any longer, and she wept.

Dr. Betsy tried to comfort her with more words of admiration for her beloved friend, but that made the tears roll even harder, so Dr. Betsy surrendered to wrapping her arms around Natasha and letting her mourn.

Finally, after moments of grieving, Natasha lifted her head and noticed the once calm ocean water was now tainted with white-capped waves across its great expanse. There were clouds in the distance, and the wind briskly tousled the leaves of the tree.

She wiped her eyes and blew her nose. "Sorry about that," she apologized. "I didn't expect . . ."

"No, don't be sorry. Your grandmother deserves every tear." Dr. Betsy squeezed her shoulders and then scooted away. She pulled her sweater about her more tightly before folding her arms. "It looks like a storm might be brewing."

Natasha nodded in agreement. "Those clouds don't look happy, and they seemed to have come out of nowhere."

"Our weather is quite unstable these days. Sunny one minute and pouring the next." Dr. Betsy smiled, and then the corners of her mouth turned down. "We need to talk, Natasha."

Natasha shook her head in agreement. "I know," she whispered.

"Why you were at Kennington Park so late at night, and why did you lie to your mother?"

"Mom wouldn't understand," she said softly, looking at the ground. Old Ben's roots bulged out of the earth like veins popping through a bodybuilder's taut skin. She could see them bubbling through the earth all the way to the edge of the embankment. "She doesn't talk about Grandma, and I went there because of her. She would never have taken me there had I mentioned her name, so I didn't. I told her we were doing some field study and experiments with water quality." Natasha kept her eyes fixed on the ground.

"But why did you go?" Dr. Betsy prodded. "And how in the world did you get hurt?"

"I tripped and fell and twisted my ankle. I had no choice but to call Mom, but then my phone died."

Dr. Betsy sighed and nodded. "I see," she said kindly. "And there's nothing else you'd like to share?"

Natasha didn't answer her right away. She thought for a long minute before shaking her head. By now the wind had picked up significantly and an occasional gust would bend Old Ben's branches in one direction.

"I know you don't know me well, but please don't speak of going to that park to anyone," Dr. Betsy said. Then, closing her eyes and taking a deep breath, she asked if Natasha would pray.

Natasha cocked her head. "Pray?" she asked, her voice riddled with confusion. She had assumed Dr. Betsy, like some of her other science teachers, didn't believe that God existed.

"You pray, don't you?" Dr. Betsy's eyebrows lifted in surprise. "I know your grandma did."

Natasha bounced her head up and down. "But for what?"

"For God's guidance and for us, that we can learn to trust one another."

Something tugged at Natasha's heart. She felt the need to be truthful with her mentor. "There is one thing I need to tell you," she said before Dr. Betsy had a chance to rise. "I borrowed or took some items from our field pack. I was going to return them but didn't get a chance to yet. I'm sorry. I know it's kind of like stealing, and that's wrong. I should have asked to take them, so I'll put them back once I return. I know you could kick me out of the program for this, and I'd understand. But just so you know, this program has been a big blessing for me. I mean, it has really helped me to have something to look forward to. And now that I know you worked with my grandma, it makes it even more special for me."

Dr. Betsy smiled and squeezed Natasha's hand. "Thank you, dear. I'm so glad you let me know. Don't worry about getting kicked out of the program. You're one of my brightest students, not just in knowledge and skills but in character. I appreciate the confession. I think it's time we get back inside," she said as the sky began to darken. "I'm going to stay here for a few more minutes. You run along."

"Thank you, Dr. Betsy. I won't forget your kindness."

"No, honey, it's your grandma's kindness I'll never forget." Dr. Betsy watched Natasha walk away before looking out to the ocean and the stormy sky. "She's hiding something, Lord. I can feel it."

CHAPTER 7

Matthias: My Haven

The day after the meeting, my father was pensive and quiet. I knew he was struggling with the recommendations of the council and his own belief that I was not yet prepared for such an undertaking. Hoping to alleviate his concern, I joined him one evening as he approached our home from a nearby trail.

"I'm sorry, Father. I didn't expect them to ask me anything, and I would never speak with the fallen ones on my own. I figured you or another warrior would be with me and . . ." I hesitated. "Don't you ever talk to them?"

My father slowly shook his head. "That time is past. There was and is no talking to them, not anymore." Adriel found a nearby tree and sat under it before summoning me to join him.

"When they were first cast out, we did try," he said solemnly. "But all they would do is taunt us relentlessly, telling us how we were the ones who were deceived and weak. They did not want to listen to our pleas, and we did not want to hear their words, which became more and more vile with the passing of time. It became clear that no communication was the only way to keep focused on our mission to protect and save the lost."

"So, you just gave up? I asked, my voice tinged with sorrow.

"Son, I thought you resolved these questions when you became silent in asking them. I had hoped and prayed that you resolved them. You must understand. All that could have been done to save them had and has been done. They chose to follow this path of darkness."

"Will you take me, Father? Perhaps when I read the records I can better understand."

Instead of giving his consent, Adriel said he needed to have more time. He then unfolded his wings and took to the skies and was soon out of view.

With a heavy heart, I called for my stallion, Naseem. He was black with a silver tail and mane. We met when I was just a child and he was a foal. We had chosen each other, and now he was one of my most faithful and devoted friends. I mounted him. He knew my heart and headed full speed for my secret place.

As Naseem galloped out of the forest, through the valley, and over hills, I berated myself. "Why do these questions plague me? Why can't I accept the explanation my father gave me?"

Naseem splashed through a stream before making his final trek up the side of a mountain from which fell a solitary slender waterfall. He slowed his pace to a trot as he banked behind the falls and followed a stream that flowed through a passageway under the mountain from which the waterfalls fell. The passage led to an opening that was the place I called my haven. I had found this intimate hideaway just a short time before, and its clandestine beauty captivated me.

The cove was surrounded by falls that fell into a pond at its center. Each waterfall poured a different color. Ruby red flowed from one side, sky blue on another side, and finally, emerald green. Yet the water of the pond was crystal clear. It was an incredible sight to see. Jewels of various colors and shapes lay at the pond's bottom and sparkled through the clear water. Plant and marine life that proliferated here were found nowhere else on Zariah.

Greenery and flowers sprang out from the cove walls and hung down its sides, which perfectly complemented the waterfalls. I would take out my flute and play praises to the Creator each time I entered as I observed His masterful handiwork. It was the perfect place to be alone with my thoughts, and now more than ever, I needed time to think and to pray.

Looking up to the heavens, I besought the One Who created me for wisdom, understanding, and guidance. I told Him how honored I would be if chosen for this great mission to Earth. Though I knew I was not yet ready, I surrendered myself to the process, telling Him I'd do whatever it would take to prepare for such an undertaking. I implored Him to help me see the truth of the fall from grace of both humans and angels so that I could fully acknowledge His mercy and love. Feeling the warmth of His presence, I knew He heard my cry and would answer me.

I then took out my flute and began to play my favorite melodies. I watched with peace and joy as the birds seemed to dance, and the flowers nodded their heads to the tones of music that filled the cavern.

—◁◦▷—

When I returned home, I let Naseem find his way to the places he loved to roam with his comrades. I joined my mother and sister, who were talking and resting on a swing that hung from one of the thick branches of the mango tree.

"When will you be leaving for Earth?" Hadassah asked as I approached them.

"Has the decision already been made?" I said, looking at my mother.

"Not formally, but I know in my heart it will be so."

I had no words. I simply watched as she gracefully rocked back and forth. My mother wore a flowing garment of light that emanated a soft, warm glow of blue lilacs that changed their hue ever so slightly from time to time. Her wool-textured hair had been twisted and tied up into a bun that was a magnificent work of art. She was crowned with a wreath of blue hydrangeas that my sister had made for her. It was studded with emerald stones gathered from a nearby stream. Long strands of twisted hair had deliberately been left out and swayed in the gentle breeze. She was stunningly beautiful, as were all the women of Zariah. Her thick eyebrows highlighted her copper-green eyes and her naturally rose-colored lips.

Keturah joined Hadassah, who was sitting on the ground among the flowers that grew around our home. She tilted her head, beckoning me to come sit with them. Hadassah's covering blended so well with her surroundings that she seemed to disappear at times. Her light garment reflected flowers of every color and shape and continuously transformed from one flower to the next.

"That's why you love to sit here," I said teasingly. "And that's why we can't find you half the time."

"I'm perfectly hidden here, right before your eyes," she said, giggling as she lay back into the bed of flowers.

"Now, back to your question," Keturah said. "We don't know the exact time, darling. We just know it will be soon."

"But why does he have to go?" Hadassah implored with an edge of disappointment in her voice. "I'm going to miss you," she said softly, hanging her head.

"We're all going to miss him," my mother said, holding her hand out to me. "But it won't be for long. When he returns, it will be a jubilant time," she smiled as Hadassah cuddled up under her other arm. "And he won't be leaving before his Communion. That comes first."

I was nearing the time of my first Communion. It was the duty of parents to prepare their children for this first intimate meeting with their Creator. It would be a life-changing event on every level, and I looked forward to it with great anticipation and excitement. I focused intently on the lessons my parents were attempting to teach so that I would be ready for this divine encounter.

"I might be here for a while," I said with a sigh.

"Tell me more about Communion," Hadassah asked eagerly as she ran her hands through the flowers around her, bending over from time to time to smell their fragrant scent.

"The Communion is a special time a person has with our Creator when they reach a certain level of maturity," Keturah explained, folding her hands and resting her chin on the perch she had created. Her eyes glowed as she peered out into the distance. "It's an opportunity to be alone with our Maker, face to face. You can ask Him anything you'd like."

"I want to ask Him how He made such beautiful flowers," Hadassah said, her voice filled with glee.

"That's wonderful," Keturah replied. "I know how much you love flowers. The beautiful thing about Communion is that you can ask Him about anything and everything. I promise you will learn amazing things, and He will show you wonders you have never before seen."

Keturah paused, and I could tell she was remembering her time of Communion. I had heard the story many times before. It was an experience she loved to speak of and one we all loved to hear. Her smile broadened as delight swept across her face, just like the breeze that was caressing ours.

I watched as she opened her mouth and thought she was about to speak, but instead, she began to sing. She sang her song, the song her Maker had sung to her during her Communion. It was her favorite, and the melody and harmony of what seemed like more than one voice filled the air. Hadassah and I couldn't help but join her as she stood and moved her body with such elegance and fluency to the song that poured out of her soul.

When her song came to an end, Hadassah continued to pepper her with questions. "Tell me again, Mother, about—"

"I know exactly what you're going to ask now," I interrupted as I headed for the large mango tree in our yard. The tree towered fifty feet into the air. Its branches reached out in every direction and provided a wide berth of shade. The leaves sprouting from the branches were of varied colors, and the tree bore more than just one variety of fruit. The fruit, though ripe on the tree, never fell to the ground. They remained ripe until picked and consumed by some form of living creature. I plucked a fruit from its branch.

"Tell us about wings," I said, before taking a bite of the delectable fruit.

Keturah fluffed out her once-folded wings. Their gentle flapping created a calm breeze of their own making.

"But how do we get them?" Hadassah asked, as if she had not been told a thousand times over.

My mother smiled. She never minded repeating her words. "Well, they are kind of like your teeth or hair. They have their roots hidden inside you, and at the right time, they are stimulated to grow."

"Will that happen at my Communion?" I asked.

"For many of us, it does, but that is up to our Creator and the plan He has for our lives.

Once they bud, it takes only a few days for them to reach their maximum size and functionality."

"I hope mine look exactly like yours, Mother," Hadassah responded.

"They will," Keturah answered, as she folded and tucked her wings neatly behind her and reached up to grab a fruit from the tree.

"I can hardly wait for my Communion time with our Creator," Hadassah said as she too reached up toward the tree.

"It will be your time before you know it," Keturah replied, looking at Hadassah. "Just keep discovering and learning everything you can about Him and the beautiful home He has given us."

"And Matthias," she said, turning to me, "I will speak with Adriel. I'm confident it's time for a visit to Uriela and the Hall of Records."

CHAPTER 8

John: Dysfunctional Home

"Stop it, Kevin. Please stop!" she pleaded as her body struck the kitchen table, causing the morning breakfast dishes to crash onto the floor. Falling to the ground, she lay motionless as Kevin ranted from above, slinging untrue accusations about cheating and lying, and hurling degrading names at his helpless wife at his feet. Rigid with fear, John had done nothing but watch from the kitchen door and hope that his father would quickly retreat.

Rushing to her side after Kevin finally stumbled out the door, John helped his mother get up. The bruises on her face and body were noticeable, but she still tried to smile with swollen cheeks and a trembling jaw.

"I'm okay," she insisted as she brushed off her dress and tried to straighten her hair. "He's just drunk, and you know he's not himself when he's drinking. He'll calm down soon. Help me clean up this mess, John. It will only enrage him again if he returns to see it."

Obedient to her request, he began to pick up dish after dish, but inside of him, a cauldron of rage and hate was bubbling and brewing like magma within a serene mountaintop. He swore to himself that he'd never again stand as a silent witness to the brutality.

Blinking several times, John brought his mind back from the disenchanting memory and turned the key in the ignition of his Toyota Camry. The striped black and grey tabby cat running across the lawn was responsible for this flashback. Years earlier, their cat, terrified by the sound of the dishes hitting the floor that morning, had bolted across his fallen mother.

At this time of day, he was usually still in bed, tossing and turning restlessly as his body awakened, but this Saturday morning he was dressed in khaki-colored slacks and a blue polo shirt and was heading toward the convention hall. It was a science convention, and attendance was required for the interns working at the PIRD.

The sun's rays sparkled through the tall glass windows, filling the registration hall with natural light. Enthusiastic banter from an eager crowd of scientists, students, and manufacturers echoed through the halls of Moscone Convention Center. This was an annual science conference where scientists presented their latest research and discussed advances in their field of study. Lining the halls and an auditorium were booths of tables laden with research posters, pamphlets, and study tools from companies hoping to sell their products or obtain new staff.

As the lines at the registration table lengthened, the mood the cat had initiated that morning began to proliferate. He would have been visiting the booths already had he not been waiting for her. They were a team, and as a team, they were expected to attend all these functions together. He slid his finger across his phone for the umpteenth time as his blood began to simmer. He told her to meet him at 9:00 a.m. so they could decide who would go to which presentation. Now it was 9:15, and his numerous texts to her remained unanswered.

"She has to be ignoring me," he concluded while tapping his foot methodically against the dark grey cement floor. Fixing his eyes on the doors, he whispered a promise through clenched teeth: "Five more minutes; then I'm going in."

But five minutes later, Natasha was nowhere in sight, and with his extension of grace rebuffed, he retreated to the registration table while turning off his phone. Now any texts or appeals from her would go ignored. His anxiety eased, and the scowl etched on his face softened. It gave him a small sense of satisfaction to return the frustration she had dished out to him.

"And you are?" The attending woman at the registration table smiled broadly, apparently pleased with the sight before her. Her curly black hair fell past her shoulders and bounced with every turn of her head. He knew what that look meant, but he wasn't interested.

"John. John McKenzie," he spoke as if reporting to a TSA officer at the airport. He hoped it would discourage any further innuendos.

"Well, it's nice to meet you, John McKenzie," she replied with a Southern twang in her voice and a slight wink. She then proceeded to scribble on a card before attaching it to his folder with a paper clip.

"And this is for you, Mr. McKenzie," she said. "The exhibit hall will be open for another ten minutes. I hope you enjoy the conference."

"Uhhh . . . thanks, Danielle," he replied with a short grin before reading the message on the back of the card. "Meet me for lunch," it read. He didn't turn back around to let her know he'd read it even though he could feel her eyes boring through him.

"Hey, young man," a voice called. Though unrecognized, it seemed to be directed at him, and he swung around to see who it might be. A tall, slender older gentleman with greying hair pulled back into a ponytail and a neatly trimmed mustache and beard called him to his table.

"I'm George," he said, stretching out his hand. "You look a bit lost and confused, son."

Shaking his head, John replied, "No, sir. I was just looking for someone." Grasping George's hand, John turned his full attention to the man and his booth. "My name is John."

A table draped in black cloth had several bones lying across it. "What do you have here?" he asked, moving closer.

"Actually, it's what I have here." George lifted an eyebrow and pointed to the large monitor sitting at the corner of the table. He typed into a keyboard, and soon a digital image of a bone began rotating across the screen in 3D.

"Wow! That's impressive," John said, bending lower to gaze at the screen.

"I work for the Museum of Natural History. I'm a part of a forensic anthropology team. Some of our research has been published in the most prestigious journals." George pointed to a bulletin board filled with colored tables and graphs.

"This is crazy interesting," John said while scanning the research report on the bulletin boards.

Reaching toward a stack of business cards lying on the table, George passed one to John. "So, who do you work for?"

"Me?" John's eyes widened as he pointed to himself. "I haven't even graduated from high school."

George looked surprised. "Sorry, I thought you were a bit older. What brings you here?"

"My internship program. I'm an intern at the PIRD," John said proudly.

"Is that so?" George replied, slowly nodding his head in apparent approval. "That's great. You must be a pretty good student. I know the PIRD program accepts only the best students in our area. You know, we're looking for interns too. If you're not already too busy, we could use some help. It would give you more experience in this field, and boy would it look good on your college applications."

"You're kidding me, right?" John said, eyeing George suspiciously.

George raised his hand and pointed to a group of students who had gathered around the monitor.

"Looks like I gotta go, but I'm serious about my offer," he added with a resolute nod. "Think about it and give me a ring. I'm sure you'd make a great addition to our team." He stuck his hand out again, and John shook it vigorously this time.

"George Peterson" was the name on the card. John gripped it tightly, wondering how a brief stop at a booth had led to an offer for an internship. He couldn't hold back the grin creeping across his face as he realized how fortunate it was that Natasha hadn't joined him. Had she been there, the offer might have gone out to both of them, or worse, just her. He removed the paper clip, let the other card slip to the ground, and replaced it with George's card. *Forensic Anthropology?* he thought. He might even consider it as a career choice.

◄○►

John's joy was short-lived as he returned home late that afternoon. He couldn't help but roll his eyes at the sight of the car sitting in their driveway. It belonged to his dad's girlfriend, Stacey. At least twenty years his junior, she looked more like John's older sister, and the idea that she might actually become his stepmother always drudged up feelings of anger within him.

It wasn't that she didn't seem to be a nice person. She was friendly enough but also stupidly naïve and blind. She had yet to pick up that his father's controlling mannerisms or choleric outbursts were just a harbinger of the future. Her vision was hidden by the jewelry he gifted her, the cars he drove, and the money he flashed anytime he took her out.

But the person he felt the sorriest for was his sister, Riley. She would be the one left to suffer from their neglect, twisted relationship, and possible abandonment if they chose to ship her off to some distant boarding school. At eleven years of age, she still had a long time before she could escape their deranged jurisdiction.

He, on the other hand, knew his liberation day was near since his high school graduation was only a few weeks away. While he hoped Kevin would agree to fund his college years, John was anticipating the move onto a campus as far away from the house as possible.

The fly in the ointment was Riley. He needed to stay around to protect her and to make sure Kevin never did to her what he did to their mother. He had stood up to his father after a beating so severe that it sent his mother to the hospital. John had warned him against touching her again. Kevin responded by kicking him out of the house, though he was only fifteen years old. He was forced to live with his aunt for a whole year while his sick and suffering mother tried to meet Kevin's selfish desires and needs. Kevin agreed to let John return to take care of Riley and himself only after his mom had passed away.

Opening the door as quietly as possible, John figured he'd make a beeline for his room. Kevin and Stacey would probably be lying entangled on the living room couch. Kevin seemed to enjoy watching John's discomfort and frustration when Stacey was around. The door slowly creaked open, but to his dismay, they were standing and kissing passionately in the foyer.

"Hi John," Stacey stammered. Her face flushed red as she pulled away from his dad. "We didn't hear you pull up. Sorry. I was just leaving." Her keys jingled as she tightened her grip on her purse.

She knew how John and Riley felt about her relationship with their dad, and it made her uncomfortable too.

"You don't have to apologize," Kevin blustered, pulling her back to himself. "It's not like he hasn't seen people in love before."

John rolled his eyes as he passed them, his nostrils picking up the familiar scent of alcohol.

"Where's your manners, boy? You need to tell Stacey goodbye."

John stopped and closed his eyes. The tempest of anger that lay quietly within him was rising to unhealthy levels. *Calm down. You'll only punish yourself. You know he's just itching for you to do something so he can kick you out again.* As much as he detested living with Kevin, he wasn't ready to be kicked out again. At least not yet.

So, he took a deep breath and turned around. "See you later," he muttered.

Stacey responded with exuberance. "Thank you so much. You're so sweet." The last time she had visited, Kevin had berated him so badly in front of her that even she had inconspicuously tried to quiet him. Her overly positive response was a clear indication she had no intention of watching a "round two" of that scene. A moment of silence followed before his ears picked up the sound of smooches.

"I'll see you later too," she finally whispered to Kevin before slipping out the door.

John breathed a sigh of relief when he heard the door close, and his anger abated as he retreated toward his room.

Kevin returned to the living room and turned up the volume on the television. The sound of machine guns and screaming soldiers reverberated throughout the house.

Tossing his bag on the floor, John heard his stomach growl loudly, and he realized he hadn't eaten lunch. He'd purposefully avoided it in an attempt not to see the girl from the registration table. Instead, he had returned to the auditorium and visited as many booths as he could while seething at the fact that Natasha had yet to make an appearance. Her absence would guarantee they would not get full points for the assignment.

As he stared into their practically empty fridge, he berated himself for not stopping to pick up a bite to eat. The fridge was empty more often than not. It was rare for Kevin to shop for anything except his favorite brand of beer. A half-gallon jug of whole milk lay beside several bottles of beer. There was some butter and a box of pizza from two nights ago. John closed the door and rubbed his belly.

Half a loaf of white bread lay on the speckled grey granite counter. He eyed it begrudgingly. He wasn't in the mood for another sandwich. *Is there even any lunch meat?* He opened the refrigerator again and then closed it in disappointment. He looked in the pantry. It was pretty sparse too, but there was a jar of peanut butter.

It wasn't the lack of money that kept the pantry and fridge bare. Kevin was a financial manager for a Fortune 500 company and made excellent money. They lived in the suburbs within a complex of million-dollar homes sitting on perfectly manicured two-to-three-acre yards. Swimming pools and four-car garages that housed boats and vintage cars were accessorizing details. Kevin himself owned three cars: the one he drove to work, a Porsche, and his black beauty, a Shelby Cobra. He also owned a motorcycle and a boat.

John smeared a large glob of peanut butter over a slice of bread before placing another slice of bread on top. "The only person who truly benefits from Kevin's wealth is Kevin. And now Stacey," he quietly muttered as he smashed the sandwich into his mouth. The necklace and ring she now wore hadn't gone unnoticed.

"Where the heck were you?" Kevin barked from the living room.

John cleared his mouth before screaming back, "I was at a conference for school."

"I thought I told you to watch your sister. Where is she?"

The volume of the television decreased. John shrugged his shoulders as he took another bite of his sandwich. "I don't know," he mumbled through a mouth filled with food. "Did you check her room?"

"No, she's not there. Where is she?" Kevin demanded again. "And where is my supper?"

Placing his half-eaten sandwich on the counter, John started muttering to himself. "With all the money he has, why doesn't he just order whatever he wants from wherever he wants? Why must he insist that someone cook for him? If you want a maid, pay for one."

Kevin's voice slowed as he spoke, "Why haven't you cooked already?"

John sighed heavily, pushing his hands through his curly brown hair. *Is he blind or has the alcohol finally scrambled his brain? I just walked in the door. What am I supposed to do? Wave a magic wand?* John waved his hand through the air. "And voila! Supper à la king," he mouthed.

He waved his hand again. "Poof," he said. "Riley's home." As he twisted the bag of bread closed, he yelled back, "What do you want, pizza or Chinese?"

"I don't want that crap again tonight," Kevin said, appearing in the doorway of the kitchen. "Where the heck is your sister? I warned you to keep up with her. I don't want another call from her school, John. I let you keep your mother's car so that you could take care of her."

Compared to what Kevin drove, his mother's car was a piece of junk. It was an old Toyota Camry that Kevin had purchased used. Kevin never got his mom anything new despite the fact that she slaved over him every day. When his mom passed away, Kevin declared that her car was his gift to John.

John hadn't been paying much attention to his sister at all over the past few months. The last he recalled, she was staying at her friend's house. She stayed there a lot, not that he blamed her. It was her way of escaping their dad, their dysfunctional home, and the painful memories of their mom. She was only nine years old when Marissa passed away—old enough to remember but too young to cope.

"Did you hear me?" Kevin's belligerent voice bellowed.

"Yes, Dad, I'm texting her now, and I'll figure out what to cook even though there's no food in this house."

"That ain't my fault," Kevin retorted. "I told you to go shopping. That's your responsibility."

"If I had some money to go shopping, I would."

"That ain't my fault either. Nor my problem. No one's stopping you from getting a better job."

It was pointless to argue about things they had repeatedly argued before. The measly amount of money John made from working at the gas station twelve hours a week was just enough to pay for gas for his car, a few bare necessities, and a couple of takeout meals. Getting a better job would mean not going to school, an option he'd never consider.

"Hurry up. I'm starving. At least your mother had my meals on time."

Kevin's mention of John's mother made him cringe, and the hairs on his arm stood up. John wanted to scream at him never to mention the woman he had tortured and practically abused to death, but he knew better than to aggravate his father any further. Kevin was drunk and ready to pick a fight.

Spaghetti, John thought. That was the easiest meal he knew how to cook.

"I'm making dinner," he replied flatly. "It will be ready in a few minutes." He pulled a pot out from one of the cherry wood cabinets.

"You better get your act together," Kevin threatened as he walked toward him. "You get your sister to where she needs to go, and you get her back here. If you can't at least do that, you don't belong here. You can't expect me to do everything."

I long ago stopped expecting you to do anything, John thought to himself. He kept his face emotionless as he stared back at Kevin. Then he walked to the sink and began filling the pot with water.

Kevin followed close behind, making John's heart begin to race. *Back off man. Back off,* was all he could think. He dared not turn to face him for fear of what that might trigger.

"Got it," he declared loudly before carrying the pot to the stove. Kevin stood watching with a demonic scowl on his face. John could tell he was trying to figure out how to get him to act out.

Reaching for his phone, John declared, "I'm texting Riley again right now. She'll be home for supper."

"She better be," Kevin snorted before retreating to the living room.

CHAPTER 9

Natasha: Timely Sermon

"Mom, do you remember when we posed for this picture?" Natasha held up her Bible for her mom to see as they walked through a half-empty parking lot. The slightly tattered blue cloth Bible cover she had been gifted had a plastic envelope at its front that allowed her to display a picture. Grandma Cunningham, Valerie, and Natasha, all wearing beautiful dresses and hats, had locked arms and donned broad smiles.

Taking a quick peek, Valerie nodded. "A day to remember. That day, Mom got us all to wear hats. I must admit, we look quite dashing in them," she said, placing her clutch under her arm.

Natasha had asked her mom to join her for the Sabbath service though she knew about the science convention. Saturday was her day of rest for religious purposes, even if she didn't attend church every week, and she had even provided Dr. Betsy with a letter from her pastor so she could be excused. When she attempted to tell John about her convictions, his critical and judgmental attitude made her think otherwise. Plus, today was her birthday, and following the example of her grandmother, she'd made it a habit to at least go to church to give a special offering of thanks to God for keeping her another year.

Sadly, birthdays were events Valerie rarely acknowledged. "It's just another day we get closer to dying," she'd often say. Then she would remind Natasha not to do anything special for her. "I don't want or need anything," she'd insist.

So, it took Natasha by surprise when her mom agreed to come with her to church. With her grandmother gone, they had abandoned going together on a regular basis. Only on major holidays like Christmas or Thanksgiving would they venture through the church doors.

Valerie straightened her back and stood taller than she normally did as they neared the entrance, making Natasha wonder if her mother was concerned with her image or just steeling herself for the expected awkward reception they were bound to receive.

"Happy Sabbath!" greeted a woman with a beautiful blend of silver and black hair styled in a pixie cut.

Then, gasping in surprise, she sandwiched Valerie's hand between hers. "Is that you, Valerie, and is this your daughter? My, my, my, has it been a long time since I've seen you two," she said, leaning backward so she could get a better view of their entire profile. "And look at you." The woman grinned from ear to ear as she sized up Natasha. "I see your grandma in you, and boy have you grown.

Natasha wasn't sure if she should take the lady's words as a compliment. The mention of her size left her feeling embarrassed, though she still felt compelled to respond kindly. "Umm! Happy Sabbath! It's good to see you too," she said, clenching the bulletin she was handed.

"But what happened to your leg, young lady?"

Shifting on her crutches, Natasha looked down and wagged her head. "Just a sprain. I kind of tripped and badly twisted my ankle, but it's getting better quickly. I probably won't need the crutches in a few days."

"Well, that's good, and I'll be praying for your healing too," she said kindly before turning back to Valerie. "Good gracious, Valerie, it's so good to see you two again."

Natasha poked her mom as they walked toward the main chapel. "Who was that?" she whispered.

"It's Ms. Bell," Valerie whispered back. "She's always been so nice, despite everything."

The familiar church scent made Natasha's nose twitch. Every church she had ever been in had that smell. It wasn't a bad or good smell. It was just a church smell that never failed to greet her. As they approached the closed oak double doors that led into the sanctuary, they could hear an elder speaking.

"Malachi 3:10 says, 'Bring ye all the tithes into the storehouse, that there may be meat in my house, and I will open the doors, that there may not be room enough to receive it.'"

Amens echoed throughout the congregation as the elder challenged them to give freely in thanks for all the blessings the Lord had showered upon them. Looking behind her, Natasha saw two men in black suits and white shirts with offering plates in hand waiting for their cue to collect the offering. Stepping aside, she let them pass. Then, slipping inside behind the men, she and Valerie tried to look as inconspicuous as possible. Finding seats near the rear gave them a good view of the congregation.

Hats of every color and style were on display on the heads of the most elderly mothers of the church. It was they who made up more than half of the people in attendance. As Natasha looked around, she could tell nothing had changed. It was as if no time had passed since she had last stepped inside the church doors. Knowing the ritual of service well, she expected that special music would be next on the agenda. The powerful voice of the dark-skinned woman in a red suit with red heels singing "Great Is Thy Faithfulness" made even Natasha acknowledge God's goodness to her.

A commanding voice from the podium drew her attention from the bulletin she was perusing while the Scripture reading was taking place. It was Pastor Anderson, and the sight of him made her tingle with excitement. His towering height, wide girth, booming bass voice, and enchanting characteristics ensured he was the center of attention wherever he went. But it was his preaching that made him the man of the hour in her eyes. His sermons were theatrical events, though deeply infused with spiritual insight and meaning. They left her mind grappling with the thoughts presented, long after the service was done.

"Would you lodge in the house of a harlot?" Pastor Anderson began, looking dumbfounded by his own question.

A lady with a large, floppy black hat waved her hand in the air with a loud "Amen, Pastor. Now you go on and preach."

Natasha exchanged a glance with her mom, who nodded her head with an approving grin. They both knew they were in for a treat and settled into the cushioned navy blue seats.

"Who among us would find ourselves in a different city and decide to lodge, of all places, in the house of a known prostitute?" Pastor Anderson paused a long moment as if to let his words sink deep into the minds of the people before him.

"My sermon today is titled 'The Kindness of a Sinner.'" He said this in a lowered voice while wiping the beads of sweat already drizzling down the sides of his dark chocolate face.

"You know how we sometimes believe that the people we judge as bad have absolutely no good in them?" He paused to let the congregation respond.

"Oh yes, Pastor. Amen," many congregants declared out loud.

"Before I go there, let's go here. Turn with me to Joshua 2:1.

"Did you hear me, folks? I said Joshua two and verse one. Now I know some of you have forgotten where Joshua is," he said, chuckling as he continued to turn the pages in his Bible. "And if you have, go to Genesis and start flipping forward.

"Now read with me, folks. 'And Joshua the son of Nun sent out of Shittim two men to spy secretly, saying, Go view the land, even Jericho. And they went, and came into an harlot's house, named Rahab, and lodged there.'

"If you know this story, you know that she welcomed those two Israelites into her home and hid them. Then she helped them escape from her own people. As they left her abode, she reminded them of her kindness. Let's read verse twelve."

Natasha's finger traced across each line in her Bible as he read.

"'Now, therefore,'" he said with a loud voice before beginning to emphasize each word, "'I pray you, swear unto me by the Lord, since I have shewed you kindness.'"

Pastor Anderson looked up from the Bible and stared into the congregation. "What did she say she showed them?"

The church replied in unison: "Kindness."

"That's right, kindness."

Then he started to read again. "'That ye will also show kindness unto my father's house and give me a true token.'

"Now, what do you think of this?" Pastor Anderson asked. "She's a harlot, and she's requesting that these young Israelite men be kind to her because she was kind to them. And how do you think they responded?" He slowly turned his head to look at each section of the church. "How would you respond to a harlot?

"Let's read verse fourteen to see how these Israelite men reacted. Yes, I said verse fourteen. 'And the men answered her. Our life for yours, if ye utter not this our business. And it shall be when the Lord hath given us the land that we will deal kindly and truly with thee.'

"Interpretation, folks?" Pastor Anderson bellowed before answering his own question. "You put your neck out on the line for us, and we'll put it out for you. They promised to deal kindly with her. They did not tell her their kindness was contingent on whether she sinned no more or if and when she stopped working as a harlot.

"As a matter of fact, they never mentioned her status or her 'profession,' even though I'm sure it was obvious. They dealt with her like they would have dealt with any other person.

"It didn't matter that she was a woman." Pastor Anderson slapped the podium.

"And it didn't matter that she was a harlot." He slapped the podium again.

"It didn't matter if she was black or white, rich or poor." He stared at the congregation as if each were guilty of the acts he'd mentioned.

"They saw her character of kindness behind her harlot's dress. Despite her profession, she had a heart for God." Pastor Anderson pulled out his handkerchief and wiped his brow. "There are folks out there who have a heart for good and a heart for God. And they don't look the way we expect them to look. They're not sitting in the pews of churches. They might be at the bar, or they might be in the whore house, but they have a heart for Him," he sang while pointing to the ceiling.

"Are we willing to look past our prejudices and ideologies and who we think measures up to be a Christian? Are we willing to open our eyes to see them and recognize who they are and that they have value and worth? Are we willing to open our hearts to love them without judging them? Are we willing to break our bones to heal their broken ones?"

The church sat silently as they awaited his next words.

"We must go deeper, folks. This is not an on-the-surface book. It needs to be studied in depth. Only as we dig deeper will we find the real meaning and the genuine treasures God meant for us to understand. These stories are not just bedtime stories that we read to our children or grandchildren. No, sir! They are much more than that. They are treasures that will help us navigate through our broken world today.

"Now let's read some more. Read with me verses sixteen through twenty-one.

"'So, they made an agreement with this woman. If she ties a scarlet cord in her window, when they return, she and everyone within her household will be spared.'

"Where is the 'If you are willing to be baptized ma'am,' or the 'You must accept Jesus as your personal Savior before I save ya'?

"Where is the 'If you repent' or 'You need to abandon your ways'? Why isn't this dialogue part of the story? Is not this what we do? Is not this what we think?

"'You can come if you change, first.' What about that one?

"Let me say it louder and slower. I know we might say differently, but we act like and insist to people we meet that they must change before they can be saved. NO, folks! NO!" Pastor Anderson reprimanded. "We got it in reverse. Acceptance comes first, and that's what Christ taught. Be loving. Be sincere. Leave the rest to Him, because it's none of your business anywayssss," he hissed.

"You do your job. Love one another, and let Him do His. You can't change no one's heart."

The preacher sucked his teeth and pushed back from the podium, flailing his arms.

"You can't change no one's mind. Don't fool yourselves, folks. It is only because of the Savior that people genuinely come to serve Him. We may lead the horse to the water, but we can't make it drink. And you must be satisfied with leaving it at that, knowing you may never see the fruit of your labor. God did not intend for us to baptize and claim the victory as our own and then flaunt the numbers to others.

"When David counted Israel, he sinned. And we sin every time we count what we believe to be our trophies," he said, calming his voice. "Instead of being concerned with them, we need to be looking at ourselves. We need to make sure we're not the ones sittin' in church and stinking up the place. You know what I'm talking about." The pastor pointed his finger across the congregation. "You be sitting in your seat and start smellin' a stink. You know it was you, but you start looking around confused."

The congregation laughed loudly.

"So, you start to look around you. And sometimes our eyes fall upon what we believe to be a 'lesser one'—someone who doesn't look like us. They might be in jeans and a T-shirt instead of a suit and tie. Their dress might be a little higher than ours that drags the floor."

Then, calming his voice again, he continued. "But folks, we cannot see. We cannot tell just by looking at the outside what is going on inside.

"Turn with me to James 2:25. Now, why does the Bible keep addressing this woman as a harlot? Isn't that rude? But we do it all the time." Pastor Anderson straightened himself as if meeting someone. "This is Dr. So-and-So," he said, reaching out his hand, "and this is Nancy. She teaches at the college.

"We identify people with their professions. This woman's profession was a harlot, and the Bible does not try to hide it. Instead, it reveals something we would have missed otherwise, something we sometimes refuse to see. A harlot was used by God to do His will and accomplish His purpose, and she remained a harlot. The story begins and ends with her being a harlot," he shouted.

Pastor Anderson searched the faces of his congregation. "Why?" he asked. "Now, we do not know the end of her story, for we know not of the rest of her life, nor her death. But the part of the story the Bible shared is making a point. We can deal with the harlots. And we can deal with those who do not meet our moral standards. We don't have to make them feel marginalized or less because they do not smell like us or look like us. Some of them are doing a work, a good work that God alone knows.

"So, she hung that scarlet cord in the window, and there ends the story."

He picked up his Bible and shook it gently in the air. "Not quite. The Bible is not finished with her yet. Turn with me, folks, to Hebrews 11:31. Y'all know Hebrews? Come on now. It's toward the end of the Bible."

The pastor flipped quickly through his Bible. "Find Revelation and flip a few books back, and you'll find Hebrews." He licked his finger and worked to separate the pages. Then, landing on it, he looked up.

"Come on, let's read verse thirty-one. 'By faith the harlot Rahab.'" Pastor Anderson slapped his hand on the podium.

"Folks, what does that say? It says her surname is harlot. The Bible is making no bones about who this woman is. But it doesn't stop there. Now let's continue.

"'By faith the harlot Rahab perished with them that believed not.' Sorry, but I got to stop you again. She perished NOT with them that believed not.

"Oh!" he said, bouncing in place. "I know the next few words is going to tell us how she converted to Israelism. And I know that's not a word, folks. I did go to college. I know some of you out there are already saying, 'I told you he was uneducated.'

"Have mercy! Well, let me tell you," the pastor whispered, "no one needs a degree to preach the love of Jesus.

"Come on now, we're going to read this thing again, and we're going to read it to the end.

"'By faith the harlot Rahab perished not with them that believed not, when she had received the spies with peace.'

"Now wait one pea-picking minute. The Bible just acknowledged she was blessed because she was kind." He scratched his head. "But I thought it took more than just kindness to be of worth, right? You got to dress the part and look the part and have a decent job.

"No? Come on, I don't hear any amens." Pastor Anderson tilted his head and waited before answering.

"How many times do we puff out our chest and turn our heads because people don't look like me or identify the same as me?" he said, pounding his chest. "And therefore, we can ignore them and pass them by as if they did not exist, like the priest and the Levite who passed by on the other side of a man wounded on the road. They did not want to acknowledge him because he was not like them.

"Does different in any capacity make their humanity irrelevant?" he demanded. "Are their lives less worthy than ours?

"No, folks," he said, wiping the sweat rolling down his face. "The Bible makes it clear that no matter who you are, you matter. No matter what you look like, you are loved by Him and should be loved by us all."

CHAPTER 10

Natasha: Surprise Revelation

The sage-colored Jeep Compass beeped as they silently walked toward it. They were both deep in thought.

"That was an amazing sermon, wasn't it, Mom?"

Valerie nodded and reached for the door handle of the car. "It's a whole lot different preaching than what we heard in our day."

Natasha pulled her seatbelt across her body. "What do you mean by that?"

"Nothing. Just thinking about what the pastor said."

"I know. He hit the nail on the head when it comes to dealing with people who we think are very different from ourselves. The Bible sure is clear on how it viewed Rahab. You know, I didn't realize she was even mentioned in Hebrews, and with such honor."

Natasha looked at her mom, hoping she'd respond, but Valerie was deep in thought.

Flipping open her Bible, she stared at the map before looking out the car window. She hadn't noticed the wall-to-wall cloud cover that had sneaked in during the church service. Only as it started to rain did she realize how dreary it looked outside. People scurried into buildings and under umbrellas as the rain fell harder. She couldn't help but wonder about the dichotomy of it all. Few people ever declared their love of a rainy day, yet without the clouds and rain, the beautiful greenery that clothed the land could never be.

Looking at her mom, she wondered if the perpetually cloudy disposition Valerie wore would ever break into a sunny day. Valerie seemed oblivious to her stare as she drove down the highway. Her mind always seemed to be lost in some dark place that had her mesmerized. It was what kept them from having a real mother-daughter relationship. It kept Valerie from talking about or even caring for things outside her world of pain. Natasha had tried countless times before to engage her mom, but her consistent failure had taught her to leave well enough alone.

Today seemed different. Though Valerie's facial expression was the same, her spirit appeared to be somewhat lighter.

"You know, Mom, I found something in my Bible the other day." She paused for a moment to gauge her mom's response, but Valerie didn't flinch. "It was from Grandma."

Valerie glanced at Natasha. "Well, what was it? Did she leave you a letter or some money?"

"No, not really. At least I don't think so. I mean, I'm not sure what it is because technically I have not found it yet."

The car halted at a four-way stop sign, allowing Valerie a few seconds to give Natasha a suspicious eye.

"That's where I thought you might be able to help." Natasha unfolded the map for her mother to see.

Immediately Valerie's expression changed as she sighed loudly. "Not this again," she groaned, shaking her head. "I told Mom to throw all that stuff out."

Natasha couldn't hide her annoyance at Valerie's response. "Why would you tell her that, and what is this map about?"

"To be honest, I don't know what the map is about. I just know your grandmother was obsessed with trees or bones, or both of those. I really can't remember. It was like she'd lost her mind in whatever it was that she was researching." Valerie turned to look at Natasha. "Has Dr. Betsy been talking to you about her? Has she been asking questions about her?"

Natasha puckered her lips and faced her window.

"Natasha Constance Cunningham, look at me!" Valerie demanded.

Natasha's head slowly bobbed up and down.

"That's it! I'm pulling you out of the program. You're not allowed to talk with that lady."

"What?" Natasha's screeched, her voice raising a few decibels higher than she intended. "Why, Mom? That makes no sense. You can't do that. I need this internship. It will help me get into college."

Tears welled up in her eyes as her voice cracked. "What is this about? You knew I was working at the PIRD from the start. I don't get it."

"Dr. Betsy is not the person you think she is," Valerie said coldly, clutching the steering wheel tighter.

"You never seemed to have a problem with her before, and she seems like a great person to me," Natasha replied.

"You don't know her," Valerie said through clenched teeth. "I let you do that internship because she said you'd be working with one of her staff and not with her. She promised me she wouldn't talk to you about Grandma."

Natasha's mouth dropped open. "Wait, wait, wait, Mom. Are you telling me that you actually had a conversation about this with her? That you told her not to tell me about my own grandma and the work she was doing? Are you kidding me right now?" she asked, giving her mom an angry stare.

Valerie pulled into their driveway before replying. "I told you. You don't know her like I do."

"Really? Or maybe you don't know Dr. Betsy like I do," Natasha replied, flaying her finger at her mother. "We interns love her. Her staff loves her, and I'm sure Grandma loved working with her too, especially since she's a Christian, and they had so much in common."

"A Christian?" Valerie cackled. "Now that's a joke. She is the farthest thing from a Christian." She leaned back in her seat and looked at Natasha. "Obviously, you two have been speaking. But all you've heard is her side of the story, and I can only imagine what nonsense she's filled your head with about her relationship with my mother."

"At least she was willing to talk with me, Mom," Natasha shot back as she folded her arms with a scowl. "I try to talk to you. I've asked you to tell me more about Grandma. But you always refuse or . . ." Natasha started to stutter as her lips trembled. "You never tell me anything," she shouted.

Natasha was surprised her mother didn't immediately reprimand her for her outburst. Instead, she sighed and closed her eyes, leaving Natasha to wonder what her next move would be.

Good gosh, she upsets me so much. I literally lost it, but now I've ruined it, Natasha thought to herself. *I'm supposed to get her to talk, not get her to clam up. I should have kept my calm and backed off,* she scolded herself. *Go ahead, Mom. Open the car door and leave like you always do when I confront you.*

"Okay, fine. I'll tell you what I know," her mom said with a stiff nod. "You think you know everything.

"Dr. Betsy liked your grandma.

"No," she corrected, hesitating momentarily. "She loved your grandmother." Valerie turned to Natasha with a "Do you get what I'm saying?" look.

"And what's wrong with that? I loved her too." Natasha signaled her mom to turn the key in the ignition so she could roll down her window. It had stopped raining, and the car windows were beginning to fog.

"No, you don't love her the way Dr. Betsy loved her," Valerie said, turning the key in the ignition. "She loved her like a man would love a woman."

The cool breeze rushing into the car allowed Natasha to take a deep breath as she processed her mother's words. She tried to hide her surprise, yet she couldn't help but look at her mom with a doubtful expression.

Valerie smirked. "Told you, you didn't know her like I did. If that woman had the audacity to tell people the truth, especially about the work your grandmother did, things would be very different now," she said scornfully.

"What the heck happened, Mom?" Natasha implored.

Valerie shook her head and closed her eyes. "It's such a long and painful story. I hate even bringing it up, especially after hearing the sermon today."

Natasha nodded her agreement. Pastor Anderson's sermon was a timely one. *Who would have thought we'd land on this topic today?* she thought. *And how am I going to get Mom to tell me more?*

"Are you hungry, Mom?" she asked, trying to alleviate the tension of the moment.

"Actually, I am," Valerie replied. She seemed relieved Natasha had backed off.

Natasha changed her tone. "Let's go inside and eat then. I made some rice and beans—Grandma's Bajan recipe," she said with a smile.

"And some fried chicken too. But you know," she said, rolling her neck, "That's not Grandma's recipe."

They both started to laugh. Grandma Cunningham was a strict vegan and had always told them they should give up their meat-eating.

"I'm sure she'd be ecstatic we went to church together and not so much mind the meat-eating," Valerie admitted as she opened her door.

Once inside, Natasha and her mom tossed off their high-heeled shoes and peeled down their stockings before retreating to their rooms to change into something more comfortable. Natasha was pulling out lettuce, tomatoes, and cucumbers from their fridge when her mom walked into the kitchen. Valerie had on a pretty floral sundress that fell to her knees and zipped up at the front.

"I'm making a salad, Mom. You just relax. Everything will be ready in about fifteen minutes. We're even having cake today," she announced proudly, her eyes glistening mischievously.

"What? You baked a lemon sponge cake?" Valerie asked with glee. "You know that's my favorite."

Bingo! Gotcha back online. Natasha's heart leaped with gladness. *Thank you, lemon sponge cake. Thank you, God. Of course, she should have been baking me a cake since it is my birthday. But whatever . . .*

Valerie sat down at the rectangular table covered with a white tablecloth with flowers around the edges. "I see you took out the nice tablecloth," she said as she smoothed it out with her hands. "Everything today reminds me of Mom."

"Please tell me more about Grandma and Dr. Betsy," Natasha begged as she sliced the cucumbers and placed them in the salad bowl her grandmother loved to use.

"Look, little girl. The only reason I'm telling you this is that you need to understand why I didn't want that woman talking to you," Valerie said sternly.

"Mom. Really? What could Dr. Betsy have done that's so terrible?" Natasha stopped opening the can of olives while she looked at her mom.

"When your grandmother first met Dr. Betsy, she didn't like her much. She was arrogant, narrow-minded, and difficult to work with." Valerie paused and stood up. "I'll set the table and make us some tea," she said, walking over to one of the cabinets.

"I remember Mom coming home so many evenings complaining about the difficulties she would encounter in trying to work with Dr. Betsy. As time went on, things started to change. I believe it was your grandmother's good influence," Valerie said as she took out two plates from their oak cabinet.

"She had that effect on people. Your grandmother always seemed to know the right questions to ask and the right points to bring out. Mom told me she and Dr. Betsy had several deep conversations about life and religion." Valerie set the table with the plates and all the accessories as Natasha continued to prepare the salad.

"Mom always came home to tell me about some new issue they were debating, and as time went on, I realized they seemed to be enjoying those discussions more and more and were developing respect for each other. So, you were right about that." She eyed Natasha as she shook her head.

"They did come to respect each other, and despite their differences of opinion, they became close friends. They flew to conferences and presented together. They both loved classical music, and they frequently took each other to concerts and went out to eat afterward."

"Wow! That sounds nice. That's exactly how I imagined their relationship from what Dr. Betsy told me. I mean, she didn't mention about them going to dinner or stuff like that, but I could tell they must have been close friends," Natasha quipped.

Valerie walked over to the kitchen sink and looked out the window. Then she turned on the faucet and started to fill a tea kettle with water. "I was a little jealous. Mom was supposed to be keeping me company and helping me out, but she seemed to be spending most of her time with Dr. Betsy."

Natasha started to plate the rice and beans, chicken, and greens as she listened intently.

"One week, something happened, and instead of talking my head off about her work like she usually did, she was strangely quiet. I kept questioning and needling her as the week wore on, but she remained silent about her work and Dr. Betsy. Finally, after about two weeks of avoiding my questions, she told me what was bothering her."

Valerie paused as she placed the kettle on the stove. "She found out that Dr. Betsy was a lesbian," she said in a subdued voice.

Natasha bit in her lower lip. "And what did Grandma do then?" she asked as she placed the plate in the microwave.

"It definitely changed things. Mom didn't feel as comfortable with her anymore. She'd never had a personal relationship with someone who was gay. She wasn't sure what she should do, and she began to doubt Dr. Betsy's intentions." Valerie peeled off a few sheets of paper towel from the holder and placed them under her silverware and Natasha's.

"But how did she find out about Dr. Betsy in the first place?"

Valerie leaned back in her chair and scratched her chin. "It was someone at work. I don't know whom, but they asked Mom if she and Dr. Betsy were going out. Of course, Mom was stunned at the question and asked why they would ask such a thing, and that's when they told her. Mom was conflicted and upset. You know how she was a hugger, and they had been hugging, I guess now and then, when they left each other's presence. It wasn't at work, but after they went out for dinner."

Valerie sighed loudly. "Mom knew she needed to confront her."

The tea kettle started to whistle, and Valerie got up to retrieve it. "When Mom told me what she found out, I was very upset. I felt like Dr. Betsy should have told her something like that before. Here they were gallivanting all over town like they were a couple." She began to pour the hot water into two mugs and then placed two peppermint tea bags into each of them.

"But they were just friends," Natasha said defensively as she pulled out a chair on the opposite side of the table and sat down. "There was nothing wrong with what they were doing. That's how I am with my friends."

"I know that, but your friends aren't gay," Valerie said, peering at Natasha. "People who knew this about Dr. Betsy thought she and Mom were involved. It just wasn't right. The Bible tells us to avoid even the appearance of evil."

"Okay, Mom," Natasha replied, holding up her hands. "I think you're forgetting Pastor Anderson's sermon. You shouldn't call things or people evil just because you disagree with them, and there was nothing evil about what they were doing."

Valerie stared into Natasha's eyes and pointed her finger. "I didn't say they were doing evil. I said she needed to avoid the appearance of evil, and that is the truth. Someone already thought they were in a relationship. It wouldn't be long before everyone started thinking the same thing."

Shaking her head in dismay, Natasha looked up at Valerie. "So, what did Grandma do?"

Valerie finished stirring the lemon and sugar in the mugs, placed them on the table, and sat down.

"Nothing. She did absolutely nothing despite my telling her she needed to address it. She told me she prayed about it and felt it was Dr. Betsy's responsibility to tell her more about herself when she was comfortable enough. I knew it was all going to come around and bite her in the butt. Not long after, a rumor began to circulate at their offices that she and Dr. Betsy were romantically involved."

Natasha sat silent, rubbing her lips, carefully listening to her mother's rendition. She didn't feel hungry anymore, at least not for physical food.

"Like most workplace rules, they had a policy about personal relationships between employees."

"But Grandma wasn't an employee there," Natasha interrupted. "They just worked on projects together, right?"

"That's true, but someone at their workplace was disturbed by their supposed relationship. They complained to management, and management felt obligated to act."

"They were two grown women and single at that. Why would the management feel they needed to do anything?" Natasha asked.

"You never know what type of things people say. Who knows? Your grandma was doing great work and being recognized for it. I'm sure there must have been some who were jealous of her, including Dr. Betsy. Anyway, that's another story.

"But now Mom realized she had to confront Dr. Betsy, and that conversation didn't go well at all. It went terribly," Valerie said emphatically. "I know Mom tried to be sensitive, but Dr. Betsy took offense and ended up making it about religion. Mom felt the need to defend her faith. They both said things they regretted, and they both agreed to end their friendship. Mom was devastated." Valerie stared at the food in front of her, then reached for her mug.

"I don't get it," Natasha shrugged. "Then how is it that Dr. Betsy holds Grandma in such high regard now?"

Valerie took a sip of her tea then continued. "Mom and Dr. Betsy were working on building the PIRD. That was their baby project, and they had already come so far. They had identified the site they wanted to acquire, selected contractors, and were in negotiation with multiple parks and museums to see about the contributions that could be made. With all the drama and tension that developed between them, Mom felt the need to back away until the dust settled, so to speak. She started spending more time on another opportunity that had fallen into her lap.

"Dr. Betsy took her stepping back as stepping away even though Mom insisted she had no intentions of pulling out. She just needed some time to think and sort things out for herself. Dr. Betsy was furious. She didn't want the project to slow down. She was ready to push forward and felt that Mom was, in her subtle way, trying to undermine her and the work she was doing."

Valerie stopped talking and looked at the food before her. "You know what, honey? I'm pretty hungry now. Let's say grace."

Natasha nodded, bowed her head, and folded her hands. "Thank you Lord for this food that has been prepared, and thank you for Grandma and Mom too. Amen."

Natasha looked at her mom, who had already taken a bite of her meal. "I have to admit, Mom, you were right. I didn't know anything about all of this. I didn't realize my grandma had something to do with the PIRD being established."

"Well, you wouldn't know, because Dr. Betsy gave her absolutely no credit despite Mom having contributed so much. At that point, Mom was already involved in her other project and didn't seem to care much about what was happening with everything else."

"Is the map about this other project?" Natasha asked, taking a small bite of her greens.

Valerie set down the chicken leg she'd bit into and nodded. "Yes, and what's funny is that Dr. Betsy tried to take that away from her too, albeit after she died."

"What do you mean, Mom?" Natasha's forehead wrinkled, and she put down her fork.

Valerie took a deep breath. "After Mom died, Dr. Betsy started asking me about what Grandma had been working on. She said that Mom had contacted her and wanted her to start working on it too. Of course, I knew she was lying. It was just one more thing she could claim for herself and her PIRD. I made sure she never got her hands on it. I took everything from Grandma's work office and put it away," she said, pointing up.

Natasha's eyes widened momentarily. *So that's where everything is,* she thought. *I'll have to investigate for sure.*

"Why would you let me even intern at the PIRD if Dr. Betsy did everything you said she did to Grandma? I don't even want to be there now."

Valerie cowardly looked down at her half-eaten plate. "Despite it all, Mom wanted to repair her relationship with Dr. Betsy." She looked up at Natasha. "And that was the only internship you could get into in this area. But that's why I don't want her poisoning your mind about anything," she said, folding her arms. "I'm sorry, Natasha, but I really think you need to be careful around her."

"Well, I'm confused and torn now that I know the real story," Natasha pouted. "Dr. Betsy has been kind to me, Mom, and she swears Grandma showed her kindness too. Now more than ever, I know God wanted us to hear that sermon today. And speaking of today, do you realize what day it is?"

CHAPTER 11

Matthias:
Base of Operation

"But he's my son," I heard my father say to my mother one evening as they crafted yet another wall from the red trumpet vines growing nearby.

"And he's my son too, Adriel. But there is no other and no better candidate for this position," my mother said as she stopped her weaving to look at my father.

I shifted my position on the swing under our mango tree and watched my father get up and walk over to where my mother was seated. "Surely you must agree with me that he is not ready for such an assignment. You heard the questions he asked at the council meeting."

My mother stood to face him. "He is searching, Adriel. He must have an experience of his own. We must let him find the truth for himself. There is nothing for us to fear."

"But to speak with the fallen ones?" My father shook his head and looked at the ground. "They are still powerful enough to hold some of us in check."

"Adriel," my mother implored as she took his hand. "The entire council was unanimous about their impression that Matthias is the one. And I agree with them. Take him to the record hall and let him start training."

My father was silent for a long moment. I waited anxiously for his response. "We must have invited him to the council meeting for a reason," he said softly, reasoning to himself. "Only the Creator could have orchestrated this, for we hardly ever allow others to join us, especially the young ones," he continued before sighing loudly.

"Let us take him to Uriela. There we will meet with Malak, and we will discuss his education and training," he consented. "If Matthias is to become this young man's protector, he will need to be strong. I have read and watched John. His misguided upbringing allowed depression, pride, and anger to be strongly rooted within him. It will be no easy task to uproot the seeds that have been planted. We are not guaranteed to win this one. This could be Matthias's first and most difficult mission if he loses him."

"Or it could be his most precious victory. We know not, husband." My mother cradled my father's face in her hands, and then they wrapped their arms and their wings around each other.

For the next hours, my mother and father were engrossed in lively conversation. They often enshrouded themselves, though I knew they were discussing the best path for my progress and preparation to become a protector.

At last, I was summoned to join them. I sat wide-eyed as they told me we'd be traveling to Uriela the very next day. There, we'd meet with Malak, who they thought would best serve as my sage, as he was currently serving on Earth. He and my parents would guide me through several stages of training to become a protector and guardian.

Uriela was the heavenly realm that served as the base of operations for Earth. On it were found the garden of Eden, the Hall of Records (containing the history of the human race), the Museum of the Saved, and the viewing rooms from which the watchers worked. It also served as a place for education and rejuvenation for any being who worked on Earth.

As we stepped out of the portal onto Uriela's soil, my heart melted within me. I had never seen such glory and splendor. Beings from all the angelic orders, as well as other celestial beings who ministered to humanity, were represented here. I stood in awe as they scurried or flew about, taking care of the invaluable business they had been commissioned to complete.

My first assignment was to read the records of men. My father accompanied me to the Hall of Records. There were seven massive ruby pillars on each side, creating a perfect square. Intricate drawings chronicling the history of man had been etched into the pillars from the crown to the ground. Within the pillars was a garden, breathtaking in its beauty. It was a flower garden, and birds and insects of every kind had made this their home. A winding golden staircase in the middle of the garden led up to the transparent building made of diamonds that contained the records. The radiant rays of the sun pierced through the perfectly cut diamonds, allowing life to flourish in the garden below. Vines with crimson red and white ivory roses had made their way up the sides of the staircase. There were several levels to which we could ascend. Each level contained the records of a specific period.

An angelic attendant met us at the bottom of the stairwell and escorted us to the first level. It was there that my father left me. He intended for me to read the records alone. I was taken to a table, and the record of the fall was placed before me. The words were etched in fire, and as I read them, it was as if I were transported into the story as a watcher. For the first time, I read of man's demise and was horrified. While the records fully enlightened me to the cause and effect of man's fall from grace, they did not give me the answers to my questions. Man was in a different position than the angels who had been banished from their heavenly home.

Next, I was to join my mother for a conference being held by the translated ones. Here I would receive even more education about the race I might be assigned to protect. I would get a firsthand perspective from those who were once sinful mortals. I could hardly contain my enthusiasm as I took my seat next to my mother in the great amphitheater.

As the three men strode out onto the platform, an enormous round of applause thundered from the angelic host and heavenly beings. We all stood to our feet, clapping our hands or fluttering our wings.

The men reverently knelt before us, lifted their hands to the skies, and began to sing in perfect harmony. "To God be the glory; great things He has done. So loved He the world that He gave us His Son, Who yielded His life an atonement for sin and opened the life gate that all may go in."

The heavenly host who had already served on Earth joined in the chorus, for they all knew this lovely song.

"Praise the Lord, praise the Lord, let the earth hear His voice.

Praise the Lord, praise the Lord, let the people rejoice.

Come to the Father through Jesus the Son.

Give Him the glory; great things He has done."

When the last notes rippled out of the theatre, we all sat down, and Moses, Elisha, and Enoch rose to their feet. Moses was the first to speak. "If they only knew of the thousands of thousands that minister to them daily." His voice rang out in all its strength.

Then Elisha stepped forward. "If they only knew that there were guardians and warriors at their sides, fighting day and night to protect and keep them."

Enoch looked at the host that had gathered before him, and in a voice filled with intensity and enthusiasm, he said, "If they only knew they had a personal guide, a constant friend, and a helper."

Moses continued, "Every session we have with you, our beloved guardians, it is our first duty to thank our Creator for His incomprehensible love. But we also thank you, this heavenly host, who, unbeknown to most of our race, have sacrificed so much to save us from our folly and our sin."

Then, pointing to a gargantuan guardian, Moses asked, "How many times did you save me, my friend? How many times did you warn me that the path of my feet would only bring sorrow? How many times did you fight with all your might to keep me safe from harm?"

The guardian named Tobias bowed his head and said, "It was worth it, for you now stand with us for eternity."

I clapped my hands as loudly as I could at those words, as did my mother and the rest of the celestial host.

When we all quieted down, each of the men came forward again to speak of their experience on Earth. Then they opened the session for questions. We were there for hours, though it seemed like minutes. At the end of the session, Elisha stepped forward to offer a prayer for those returning to service and those going to Earth for the first time. I had been infused with energy and zeal for the lost race and desired more than ever before to play my part in man's redemption.

Multitudes of angels and sinless beings walked or flew from the amphitheater out in every direction. I followed my mother to the edible gardens, where food had been spread out on large banana leaves across a grassy field. The leaves were filled with a variety of fruits, nuts, and other dainties.

My mother and I were just about to sit down when a voice called out to me. It was Malak, and beside him stood the mighty angel who was once Moses's guardian. Keturah eagerly introduced me to these mighty immortals. We in turn greeted each other with an angelic embrace.

"We were not expecting to see you until later this evening," Mother said as she settled on the ground. "I know there are many here you wanted to meet. And have you seen Adriel, Malak?"

Malak shook his head. "He is now conversing with Elisha and told me to summon you. He wants to speak with us."

"And Matthias?" she said, looking at me and then back at Malak.

"Well, he's in the best of company." Malak nodded toward Tobias.

"Indeed he is," my mother agreed as she joined Malak. "We'll be back soon," she promised as she unfolded her wings and took to the skies.

Tobias settled on his elbows as he dropped a few grapes into his mouth. "Do you want to hear a story?" he asked as I gazed adoringly at him. "I have a good one for you," he said, looking directly at me.

My curiosity was aroused. I knew the only story he could tell would be a good one. "What's the story about?" I questioned as I joined him in eating the grapes.

"Abner," Tobias whispered in a haunting voice.

"Abner?" I questioned. "I'd love to hear a story about Abner," I declared, edging closer toward Tobias.

"As you already know," he began, "Abner was the firstborn of creation, the brightest and most talented and intelligent of us all.

"He was kind, friendly, funny, ambitious, and cunning," Tobias chuckled. "He was strong, musical, and delightful. He was holy and righteous and good. He was so much to us all. His place, dwelling in the presence of the Eternal One, was the most honored and revered position, the one to which we all aspired. The glory of the Eternal One enriched and deepened every aspect of his being, so his advancement and growth exceeded us all. We were constantly amazed at his progress in strength, intellect, and character each time we met."

I had heard all this before, but not in the same way. Every being who knew Abner personally had their own story of him, each with a different perspective.

"Our order had gathered for a time of fellowship with the Creator," he explained as he placed his hands on his chin and his wings fluttered in the warm, gentle breeze. "The Creator spent several days with us. It was divine. We ate and laughed together. We danced and created new music together. It was nothing short of a glorious time. But on the last day of His visit, we decided to encourage each other through races. As you know, our races are meant to inspire each other to reach for our full potential, stretch us to our greatest capacity, and grow closer to being like our Creator. We had such a blast. But it was the last race of the day that we remember most."

I tucked my wings in and sat up as I moved even closer to Tobias.

"I think this race changed everything."

"What do you mean by that?" I questioned.

Tobias gently raised his hand, summoning me to be patient. "This race belonged to the strongest seven.

Up to this point, Abner had only watched and cheered us on, but as the angels lined up for this final race, guess who strode up to join them?"

"Are you kidding? Did he race you guys?"

"Wait a minute," Tobias chimed. "Who do you suppose to be the 'you' guys? None of us were in that race. We had long since been eliminated."

"Who were the seven?" I asked.

"You know of only one," Tobias said. "He was Malak.

"Anyway, there they were, now eight of them in a ready position, and then the unthinkable happened."

"I know, Abner backed out. I knew he wouldn't race them. Come on. I knew you were kidding."

"Can you let me tell the story?" Tobias asked, motioning for me to be quiet. "So where was I? Oh yes, Abner had just come to the starting line. The angelic host went wild with excitement. This was the first time we had seen this. Abner always stood next to the Creator and cheered us on. We never expected or thought that he would even consider joining us."

"Why do you think he joined the race?"

"Maybe to inspire and stretch those seven," Tobias explained as he let a snake with silver wings slither around his ankles.

"As I was saying, we were so enthralled. We were all hollering and flipping in the air. And then we were shocked again," Tobias whispered.

"The Creator walked up and joined them."

I jumped to my feet. "No way," I squealed. "The Creator? Why? Well, we know for sure who won then."

"I'm not done with the story," Tobias scolded. "So, sit back down."

I settled back onto the soft grass. I could see the race so vividly in my mind and realized my heart was racing as well.

"The race began. Everyone was cheering and laughing, leaping into the air, and fluttering their wings. Naturally, the Creator was ahead of everyone, and we expected there to be this enormous and impossible gap between Him and everyone else. But as the race continued, Abner started to gain on the Creator."

I couldn't believe what I was hearing. I couldn't believe what was being suggested. Why hadn't anybody told me this story before? "That's impossible. No one can beat the Creator. That's a given." My heart wouldn't stop racing although I was confident of the expected end.

"The more he gained on the Creator, the more silent it became as everyone started to wonder if he would equal Him. You could tell Abner was putting forth his mightiest effort, and no one was sure whether or not the Creator was holding Himself back. As they neared the finish line, Abner closed the gap and was only a small distance away from the Creator. Now everyone fell utterly silent. Even the animals that were grazing and romping around stopped what they were doing, and birds settled in the trees to pay attention to this race between the mightiest of us all." Tobias squinted his eyes, looked directly at me, and then jumped up to his feet and fluttered his wings.

At that moment, Malak and my mother returned. "You know, I think I'll pick this up again a little later," he declared with a sly grin on his face and a wink at Malak.

"No way are you going to stop this story now!" I threatened, pointing my finger directly at him.

"Nothing like a little anticipation," he teased. "I'll let Malak finish this story." And in a flash, he was gone.

I looked longingly at Malak, who had started to chuckle.

"Please," I begged. "Tell me what happened."

Malak and my mother were still laughing heartedly at Tobias's hasty retreat and the state of intrigue in which he left me. When they had quieted down, he replied, "You will soon hear the end of the story. I promise."

"Malak will be coming to spend time with us at Zariah, and then he will take you to Nanea," my mother added. "There you will meet an ancient one—one who was close to the fallen ones."

Thus far, every phase of my training brought me closer and closer to addressing the questions burning within my heart. I was eager to meet such a one.

"We will be returning home this evening, my son, but come," she beckoned as she held out her hand to me. "Let us visit the Museum of the Saved before our departure."

John: College Dream

John stared at the door assigned number six. The eagerness that gripped him upon his arrival had faded into apprehension.

Should I even go in? he asked himself. *Something doesn't feel right.* Yet he found himself turning the knob and pushing the door open. It looked like a lab and smelled like one too. The astringent scent of formaldehyde permeated the air and made him cough several times.

Sauntering slowly to the back of the room, he eyed every detail with suspicion. The three large rectangular tables with black countertops, the metal stools, and the whiteboard all looked fairly typical to him. He breathed a sigh of relief, content with the apparent normalcy.

Arriving at the office door, he knocked gently while adjusting his bookbag on his shoulder and then straightened himself up. Seconds went by. He shifted nervously. His ears strained to pick up the sound of papers shuffling or the whispering of a phone conversation. But no sound waves riveted past the door as the inky silence deepened. He knocked again, a bit louder this time.

George had confirmed the time of their meeting just a few hours earlier. He couldn't possibly have forgotten. John swiped his phone and checked the calendar again. He was correct and was precisely on time. Folding his arms, he tapped his foot as the seconds ticked into minutes and a bit of anger began seeping slowly into his veins.

"What the heck?" he finally moaned. "Why does everyone stand me up?" He pounded the door angrily before turning to leave.

Suddenly the door flung open.

"John," George greeted enthusiastically. "So good to see you," he said, reaching out his hand.

John could feel his face flush with embarrassment. "So sorry. I thought you weren't in your office. I knocked several times," he stammered. "I was just about to leave."

George waved his hand as if to wipe away any wrongdoing. "You know this was slated to be a summer position," he declared, pointing to a chair that sat across from his desk. "But I don't mind you starting now. I mean, graduation is not far away, is it?"

"Four weeks, to be exact," John corrected. "Though I wish it was two weeks." The mention of his upcoming graduation made him forget his anger and confusion about George ignoring his knocks.

"You must be excited," George grinned as he sat down.

John nodded and returned the smile. George's desk was a disheveled mess with stacks of unorganized papers, folders, and magazines scattered across it. Coffee or some type of brown substance had spilled on some of the papers and the paper towels he must have used to clean it up remained scrunched on his desk. Yet, no pictures or plaques hung from the walls. His bookcase held no books, instead it had become the receptor for empty coffee cups and finished bags of fast food.

Picking up a jacket and papers that were resting in the chair, John looked at George who pointed to the bookcase. "Looks like you're pretty overwhelmed with paperwork." John said, peering at his desk.

George laughed. "You see why I need some help. He said leaning forward. The research is great but getting all the information into the computer can be a real bear. So, let's talk about your position."

Two minutes later, George was done with the job description, leaving John rather puzzled and somewhat speechless. From what George described, he'd be completing menial tasks that were more secretarial than research-related. George had made it sound like he'd be his intern or understudy and that they'd work side by side completing field studies, working in the lab, and writing research papers. How else would he gain the experience he needed?

"Umm, it doesn't seem like I'd be getting much actual experience. I thought this position would be like an internship and a hands-on opportunity."

"Oh! It is," George countered. "But you can't expect to start at the top of the ladder. You've got to prove yourself and work your way up."

John's eyes widened in surprise. "Work my way up?" he questioned. "I didn't think this was a real job, just an internship."

"Oh, no, no!" George looked intently at John. "This is a real job, and it's precisely the way I got this position. It might not be exactly what you want to do right now, but look, you can already say you work in the Natural History Museum. Give it a shot before you say no, John. I promise it will get you to where you want to go in life."

John sat silent, not knowing what to say as he tried to wrap his mind around what George was offering him.

"I know you want to go to college, and you want a career in anthropology or paleontology, right? Your grades are excellent, John." George tapped the papers lying before him. "But it takes more than just good grades to get into college these days. It's competitive out there, and a position such as this one will make you stand out."

He raised his hands as if to silence John's expected rebuttal. "Don't get me wrong. Interning at the PIRD is great, but look at all the students who are already there. They're all putting that on their applications too. And I assume you're still applying to colleges since you haven't told me where you're heading in the fall." George leaned forward as if to evoke an answer from John.

He's quite perceptive, John thought, narrowing his eyes. *He's already realized the predicament I'm in, based on our conversations and apparently from my résumé.*

John had applied to several universities and hoped he'd get into Ivy League ones like Harvard and Stanford. But he'd been ignorant of the process of how the schools decided on financial aid. Having already submitted his FASFA with his father's income, he realized too late that Kevin would have to foot the majority of the cost of John's college schooling.

Kevin was more than capable of funding college tuition, but deep down, John knew it was pointless to ask. Yet desperation and hope insisted he at least try. Riley had mentioned Kevin insinuated he would pay for her college, and she maintained he meant John as well. But Kevin had always treated them differently. Though not the attentive father he should have been to Riley, he was much more tolerant of her and was occasionally willing to concede to her wishes.

"Heck no. I'm not helping pay for college," Kevin had replied before laughing hysterically. "Why in the world would I do that?"

John immediately regretted making his desire known to Kevin. It set Kevin off into a horrible tirade that lasted for hours.

"My father did nothing for me," he said, pounding his chest. "I had to figure out my own way through college and life, and I did. Your mother spoiled you kids into believing I owe you something, but

I've given you all you're going to get from me: a roof over your head and some food to eat. Everything else is up to you to make happen."

Despite having stellar grades, John hadn't been offered any full-ride scholarships. The academic scholarships he did qualify for still left a hefty gap that he was unable to bridge with his current meager income. Needless to say, the reality that he might not be going to college sent him into a period of hopelessness and despair.

"John, you're a smart kid. You'll do great in college," his mother had encouraged him. "So don't get distracted or give up."

He didn't need much convincing. Practically no one on his mother's side of the family had completed college, and they were all a financial mess, struggling from one check to the other to put food on their family's table. But even without her family's less-than-stellar example, he always had a deep drive to learn. From as young as he could remember, he loved books and learning about the world around him. As a kid, he spent countless hours roaming through the woods in their backyard. Every time he found a plant or a bug, or some other living thing, he'd google it.

Books were also his way of escaping the constant fighting and bickering taking place between his parents. Earbuds were practically a part of his anatomy as they served to block out the noise he didn't want to hear. Instead of just listening to music, podcasts and science-based audiobooks brought even more knowledge into his brain. Getting good grades in school was as easy for him as eating apple pie, and he remained at the top of his class from kindergarten through high school. The only person who challenged his academic prowess was Natasha.

But all of his hard work would be for naught if he couldn't get into college. Determined to find a way, he scoured the internet for hours at a time, hoping to find some type of financial opportunity that would allow him to fulfill his dreams, but "no" was the prevailing answer, over and over again. Scholarships were virtually out of the question. He didn't meet the financial limitation for most of them with Kevin as his dad. The other scholarships were too specific. He had to live in Indiana or be a Native American or attend a certain high school. There'd always be at least one criterion that didn't apply and would make him ineligible. Sometimes he felt that something in the universe didn't want him to succeed.

A last resort was getting a loan. The thought of accumulating massive amounts of debt made him shudder with consternation. Debt was something he loathed. He saw the heavy burden it could become and how it could bring a person to ruin. His mom's debt from her school loans and careless financial management in her youthful years was her constant bemoaning. She had an awful credit rating, making it virtually impossible for her to make it on her own. Debt was like an iron chain that kept its victims within the strong grasp of poverty. But perhaps it could be different for him. If he worked hard, maybe he'd be one of the few who could climb their way out of its seemingly bottomless pit.

"Did I mention there is a scholarship involved?" George continued.

John's brain shifted back to the conversation at hand. "No," he stuttered slightly. "You never mentioned anything about a scholarship."

"It's a Science Foundation scholarship, and it's open to anyone in a degree program at the Natural History Museum. Mary, the receptionist, can tell you more about it if you're interested."

George stood to his feet. "Look, John, you don't have to give me your answer right now, but I have some other students who would love to fill this position. How about I give you until Monday? This way you'll have the weekend to mull things over." He headed for the door as John grabbed his bookbag and slung it over his shoulder.

"The way I see it, this is a win-win for you," Steven said as he walked with John down their high school hall Friday morning. Steven was one of John's long-time buddies. They had met at the community art center when he was nine years old. Both their moms had brought their sons for guitar lessons, and the four had become immediate friends. But Steven's family was vastly different from John's. Steven had three younger siblings, and his mom and dad seemed to genuinely love each other. John couldn't help but feel a little jealous whenever he saw Steven's dad rub his wife's back or tenderly massage her shoulders.

"You said that if your dad didn't pay for your college, you'd declare yourself independent. If you take the job, plus get the scholarship to help you with your tuition, I think you could make it."

"I know what I said," John replied in frustration. "But after doing more research about declaring my independence, I realize it's not that easy. I'd have to be working full-time hours to meet all my expenses, and that's impossible if I'm in school full-time too." He sighed, digging his hands into his pants pocket. "My dad is at least providing a roof over my head and some food to eat. Putting myself in a position of potential homelessness is not where I want to be. And I still don't know what that scholarship would cover. That receptionist has issues. She gives me the creepy vibes and has refused to give me any information about the scholarship."

"But you live in fear of your dad kicking you out at any time." Steven stopped walking as they reached the biology door and quieted his voice. "Honestly, I don't know what I'd do if I were in your situation, but if he's going to kick you out eventually, you might as well do it under your own auspices, right?" He slung his arm around John. "And you can always bum with us for a while. I'm sure Mom and Dad won't mind."

John fist-bumped Steven and smiled, though his stomach was in knots with the prospect of having to follow through with his friend's suggestion. He hadn't mentioned the biggest issue with his leaving their home. Riley was only eleven and completely unable to defend herself if Kevin went berserk on her. He knew if he left her, Kevin might feel at liberty to escalate his mental abuse to physical. Yet he'd never be in a position to help her if he couldn't get on his own feet. "I'll figure this out," he told himself when he reached his car.

But before he could start his engine, his cell phone started to buzz. He arched back in surprise when he saw who was calling him. He stroked his forehead and sighed as he listened to George. "Okay, so what you're telling me is that you want an answer right now." He wasn't yet prepared to give George an answer and couldn't help but feel pressured by the sudden request to do so.

George continued to talk as John rolled his eyes and tightened his lips. "Fine then! I guess I'll have to say yes. I'll take it," he croaked in defeat. "Sure. We'll talk later, and Monday will be fine."

"That little swindler," John grumbled after disconnecting the call. "I bet he didn't even have another student in his office at the time."

Again, an uneasiness settled over him. "Where am I going to find the time to go to school, go to work, and get Riley to where she needs to be?" He pounded his fist on the steering wheel. "What have I gotten myself into?"

CHAPTER 13

Dr. Betsy: Miserable Memories

An album buried under a pile of papers sat in Dr. Betsy's lower desk drawer. She had placed it there over two years ago and had not retrieved it since. A pang of guilt mingled with grief caused her stomach to roil and tighten as her eyes fell upon a picture of her alongside Dr. Cunningham. They were both smiling broadly as they stood under the shade of Old Ben. But the joy she displayed was not the joy that was in her heart. She had been riddled with guilt and regret that day at the sight of her, for she had not expected her to be there.

"Congratulations, Dr. Betsy," Dr. Cunningham had declared. "You deserve to be recognized for the amazing work you've accomplished here."

Dr. Cunningham's compliment was genuine and kind, but it pierced her heart like a knife.

Dr. Betsy turned the album cover down as she stared out the window. A red-winged blackbird flew effortlessly from branch to branch in the California Buckeye that grew in the front yard of her cottage home. Watching intently, she hoped its mate would also make an appearance. They were the guests that always brought a smile to her face as they flitted and flirted about with each other. But today, only one revealed itself, making her wonder if harm had come to the other. Her heart sank with the awful thought of another of her precious friends falling into an untimely demise.

Her eyes drifted slowly back to the album that lay on her desk. It was a lifeless book, yet she seemed to hear it calling, telling her it was time to face the past she could no longer ignore. It was coming for her, as she knew it eventually would. And life had given her time to prepare.

"Come on, old lady; you've got to face it," she coaxed as she placed her hand back on the cover. Flipping the page, she stared at the pictures as a wave of sadness washed over her. She felt as if no time had elapsed since her dear friend had passed away. A tear made its way across her soft, wrinkled skin, and she quickly reached for a tissue to catch it from dribbling onto the pages that brought back her heart-wrenching sorrow.

"You loved me like no one ever did," she gasped through broken sobs. "Why God felt the need to take you away right when I finally realized how precious you were is still a mystery to me. But you're gone now, and my heart will ache forever." Every page she turned brought back treasured memories, and the contours of her face changed every few seconds as her emotions swung like a pendulum from joy to sadness and gratitude to grief. Then, leaning back in her high-back leather swivel chair, she drew in a deep breath, relaxed, and opened the doors that held so many painful memories of her past.

―◇―

Snowflakes drifted silently through the air, covering the homes and ground of her childhood neighborhood in a blanket of white.

Crystals of ice hung like ornaments on evergreen trees among the elaborate Christmas decorations displayed in each yard. A kaleidoscope of Christmas lights flashed about the two-story seven-thousand-square-foot mansion she refused to call home. Despite the scene of affluence from several ornately decorated Christmas trees laden with beautifully wrapped presents around their feet and fireplaces with bulging stockings, their home was strangely quiet. An air of solitude seemed to stalk about the empty halls and rooms like ghosts. Their wealth masqueraded as love, but only to those who knew them not.

She was an only child, and it should have been easy to envelop her with the time and attention she deserved, but her parents preferred to gratify the yearning of their own selfish hearts, leaving her feeling abandoned and unwanted. She was just the pretty thing they flaunted whenever they felt it would make them look better in front of others. They had never taken her to a park, driven her to school, or celebrated one holiday together. But that year was different. Dr. Bradley and his wife had flown home to attend to her this time.

Dr. Betsy batted her eyes. She could feel them filling with tears as the pain of that Christmas rose within her. All her life, she fought to forget. Forget the lights. Forget the faces. Forget the hurtful words. Forget the physical and emotional pain. "You never let me forget," she spat out as tears streamed down the valleys of wrinkles created by time and worry. "Why, Lord?" she begged, clutching the album to her chest. "Why didn't You just wipe the memory of it away like You wash away our sins? Was it not my sin? Was it not my shame?" she choked, looking up before surrendering to the flood of sorrow that caused her whole body to tremble in grief. "You let them take everything from me. You let them break me. Why, Lord? Why?"

―◦―

Water rushed out the faucet of a bathroom sink. Cupping her hands together, Dr. Betsy watched as they filled to the brim before splashing the frigid water on her face. The cold shock made her eyes widen, and the tear ducts that had been voraciously reproducing momentarily arrested their development. Then, as if steeling herself for battle, she returned to the living room.

"This relationship is over," her partner snapped as she approached her. "I can't take you and your obsession over finding her anymore. You need to get over this and live your life. Live our life."

"I want to so badly," she cried. "And I'm trying. Can't you just give me another chance? You see all that I'm doing for us. It's not easy being in graduate school and working full-time. I know I don't have much time for us. Just give me another chance," she begged.

"Listen, Frosty, I love you. You know I do, but you need help. Your depression is real. You don't speak to me for days when you're down. Then, the next thing I know, you're upset over some trivial thing. I'm either spending time alone or arguing with you, and I don't like the dysfunctionality of our relationship. You're a beautiful woman, but you're also a broken one."

Three black suitcases sat near the door of their condominium as Suzie collected the pictures, books, and other belongings they had proudly displayed in their living room.

She met Suzie in her first year of graduate school after a traumatizing breakup with her boyfriend. Shawn was obsessive, demeaning, and jealous, and he had made their time together miserable with his incessant demands for exclusivity and threats. Their toxic relationship added to her childhood trauma, causing her to become more and more unstable. That was when she seemed to have awoken to her true identity and feelings. But now as she watched Suzie grabbing everything with calculated anger, the person she had become began to haunt her.

She was broken with a hurt that bore its roots into every bone of her body. A fury like an eternal burning in the cauldron of her soul rose to the surface now and then when she lost the power to control it. Any extreme emotional situation seemed to summon it from its resting place. There was the stress and financial burden of graduate school, the fear of letting love take hold of her, and the loss of her favorite aunt, the only family who genuinely cared for her. It was all too much for her to bear. There was no fight left in her, so she sat in a daze, silent and stoic, and watched another person walk away.

Her sobbing had subsided as the thoughts of her past relationships rolled through her memory. They conjured up those old feelings of abandonment that had pulled her into a very dark and solitary space. She had shut down her emotions and her desire and willingness to love and trust anyone.

No emotions meant no pain and no existence.

"Come on, old lady," she coached as she squeezed her eyes shut as if to block the pervading emptiness pressing upon her. "Lord, help me," she cried. "I can't go there again. I need You, my precious Savior. Take this from me and fill me with Your love and remind me of my worth and value in Your sight."

Immediately, the words of her favorite Scripture, Isaiah 43:1, flashed into her mind as if being whispered into her ear by an unseen being beside her. "But now thus saith the LORD that created thee, O Jacob, and he that formed thee, O Israel, Fear not: for I have redeemed thee, I have called thee by thy name; thou art mine."

Her breathing slowed, and a peace washed over her as her thoughts returned to Dr. Cunningham.

"What a stunning person you were!" she crooned before flipping open the album again. Dr. Cunningham had been captured wearing a stylish dress with heels that accentuated her physique. But the sparkle in her eyes and endearing smile revealed a much deeper beauty. She possessed an inner confidence and purity of soul few women possessed. And the sincere courtesy and respect she had displayed toward Dr. Betsy was intoxicating to her.

"Good morning," Dr. Cunningham happily greeted one day. "Would you like me to get you something to drink, or perhaps you'd enjoy a sweet treat? I made some banana bread last night and brought some to share with everyone."

Dr. Betsy laughed inwardly. "That banana bread was the best-tasting version I'd ever had—so light and fluffy and bursting with flavor. You always made the tastiest things. And I'll never forget your thoughtfulness in sharing."

Her smile then returned to a sullen gaze.

By that point and time in her life, a professional distance characterized all her communication and interactions. For many months, she refused to let Dr. Cunningham's kindness break through the walls she had erected to protect herself, but the constant barrage of love eventually began to wear her down.

They had agreed to work on a project together to complete some field studies of the local parks. They were keen on discovering new plant species. That required working in close proximity for weeks at a time. She was used to this type of working relationship as she'd partnered with countless scientists and students on a variety of scientific studies. Yet the typical scientific banter that occurred with her previous contacts was not like the conversations she had with Dr. Cunningham. Somehow their conversations would segue into real-life issues, and it was soon clear to her that Dr. Cunningham was a devout Christian.

God had never been a part of her own life. Her father was an atheist, and her mom was completely devoted to herself. She had been taken to church a few times with her nanny's family, but God wasn't something or Someone she gave much thought to. Science was her religion, her peace, and her livelihood, and she couldn't imagine anyone or anything changing the irrefutable facts that formed the basis of her beliefs about the world and its existence. Despite their drastic differences of opinions and beliefs, she and Dr. Cunningham found themselves discussing topics they never should have been able to broach.

"How can you believe in Creation despite all the evidence we have otherwise?" she had inadvertently blurted out one morning as they traveled to a site, silencing Dr. Cunningham's humming of a hymn. She figured the expected rebuttal would be filled with useless Scripture and unproven statements, but Dr. Cunningham's response was quite alarming, clever even. She kept it personal to her and no one else.

She'd replied, "I can't deny the Hand that has guided me all the days of my life. The path I have traveled could only have been designed by One Who sees outside of my realm."

Dr. Betsy shook her head incredulously. *Now how was I supposed to answer that?* She had sat speechless for the rest of the trip. Dr. Cunningham had craftily directed her response at the real question, and those words invited no argument or defense.

Dr. Cunningham intrigued her. Christianity and science were polar opposites. Like oil and water, they could not be mixed. Yet this woman seemed to have created an emulsion of sorts with her beliefs and life that belied contradiction. As time went on, Dr. Betsy began to feel more at ease with asking this gentle lady questions that had always troubled her.

"How can you believe in a God that allows humanity to suffer the way we do?"

"It was not His design nor intent for humanity to suffer. To believe His Word is to acknowledge the opposite. He created a perfect place of joy, peace, and love devoid of all evil in which He intended for us to live."

"But He could stop the suffering. He could prevent the murders and the rapes and the atrocities. Why doesn't He?"

"Yes, He could, He is, and He will, but not in the way we think it should happen. His goals are much broader and higher than our imagination, for He seeks eternal security and not just the suppression of will that may terminate oppression for a season. Do you not prefer freedom of will?"

"Well, of course, yes, but then again . . . well, hold on. What exactly are you saying?" she countered, slightly confused.

Dr. Betsy marveled that her questions never seemed to disturb Dr. Cunningham's ever-calm and peaceful spirit, and she always responded in a non-threatening manner. Friendship was easy with this woman who embraced her despite their differences. And their relationship deepened as they gradually shared more and more of themselves.

But it all came to a screeching halt.

"She wouldn't even let me pay my respects to you, dear friend," she cried with trembling lips. "I only wanted to honor you. To let them know how much you changed my life." Dr. Betsy reached for another tissue. Blowing her nose and wiping her eyes, she peered down at the funeral bulletin she had inserted in the album.

"I met someone," Dr. Cunningham announced one morning while Dr. Betsy sat sipping her coffee in the employee lounge. "Some guy joined me as I was walking in the park. We chitchatted for a long while, and I began to realize he's just like me."

Dr. Betsy placed her mug on the table and looked up. "What do you mean, just like you?" she had questioned, her eyes squinting slightly.

"You know," Dr. Cunningham replied excitedly. "He's a scientist who is also a Christian.

Dr. Betsy picked up her cup of coffee and sipped. "Humph," she puffed softly.

It wasn't long after that declaration that she noticed Dr. Cunningham had become much quieter around her and their fellow scientists. She would go out alone on field explorations and seemed secretive about her experience.

Dr. Betsy hadn't paid too much attention until a few weeks later when she asked Dr. Cunningham about the gentleman she had met and if she was still talking with him. She replied that she was, so Dr. Betsy asked what his name was.

She simply said, "He likes to be called Josh." She then walked away to ensure no further questions would be asked.

A few weeks after that encounter, Dr. Cunningham started asking her some very odd questions. She asked about forensic anthropologists in the area and if she knew of any museums from the past that may have closed. She even asked if she was familiar with any research related to determining the precise age at death by skeletal remains. When questioned about the reason for such inquiries, Dr. Cunningham just shrugged her shoulders and said she was doing some additional personal research. It wasn't until after she died that Dr. Betsy concluded Dr. Cunningham was researching something out of the ordinary, something mysterious.

Dr Betsy closed the album and took a deep breath. She walked over to her bay window. The sun was setting, and the sky was turning shades of pink and grey. In the distance, lightning flashed from blackened clouds. She remembered the weather forecast predicted a stormy night ahead.

"I sure hope this won't be too ugly of a storm," she said, clicking the window latch closed. A brisk wind swept through the trees, causing clusters of leaves to flutter to the ground. "I better check the windows downstairs," she told herself. "Wouldn't want to leave anything open."

When she reached the stairwell, her hands gripped the railing tightly, and she slowly made her way down. Her legs were stiff from having sat so long, and she couldn't help but groan a bit as they stretched with each step she took.

After checking the windows, she made her way to her bedroom. It was tucked to the left side of the small cottage opposite the kitchen. It was only big enough for a queen-size bed with nightstands on each end and a dresser. Above the bed was a painting of a flower-filled garden whose soft pastel colors matched her comforter.

"What about supper?" she asked herself. "You said you'd do better and not skip so much. Can't be starving this old body unless you want to feel even weaker." Yet she didn't feel like she had the energy to cook that evening. All that crying had left her feeling drained, as if a vacuum had sapped away her energy.

Dr. Betsy walked to her fridge and opened the freezer. A neat selection of frozen entrées sat inside. She tugged to get one out. "Chicken alfredo it is," she declared, making her way to the microwave.

Thirty minutes later, she flipped the kitchen light off and headed back to her bedroom. She picked up the Bible lying on the nightstand. Her name was inscribed on the outer cover. Inside was a handwritten note that read, "The likelihood you read this is slim, but I've been impressed to give it to you anyway. It will show you your worth and your value like nothing else can. With love, Vanessa."

Climbing into bed, she snuggled into her soft silken sheets. She drifted off to sleep but awoke with a start soon after. Heart-pounding and drenched in sweat, she flicked on the lamp on her nightstand and peered, wide-eyed and straight ahead. *What the heck!* she wondered. *Why would I dream about him?* She had done her best to forget about that man. *What could that dream mean?* she questioned with a wrinkled brow as she slowly lowered herself back down.

CHAPTER 14

John: Trail of Suspicion

John quickly tiptoed toward George's office door. He wasn't going to miss the opportunity to find out what George and the men sitting in his office were talking about. They seemed to be heatedly arguing, with George's voice often superseding the others. George was clearly trying to convince them of something, but the men's angry responses indicated their unwillingness to concede. Try as he may, John couldn't make out most of the conversation. Despite their frustrated exchange, they all seemed to be keeping their tone down as if to ensure no one would hear them.

He'd seen these men at least twice since he started working there, and he knew they weren't staff. Everyone at the museum dressed rather casually in slacks or jeans and shirts, and everyone at the museum seemed to be pretty lighthearted and friendly, except the receptionist.

These men were different. Dressed in suits with shoes that could be heard as they walked through the cement floor corridor, they presented as businessmen, and that was exactly who John thought they were, though he wondered what kind of business they were in. At first, he figured they might be representatives from other museums, but they didn't come across as the museum type. They didn't come across as any type. That left him guessing who they could be and what business they had with George. Tight-lipped and stoic with sunglasses-clad faces, they remind him of black-suited FBI agents.

Gently pressing his ear against the door, John heard George mention Dr. Betsy's name. Then the conversation abruptly stopped. Intuition told him he had better retreat, so he silently and swiftly made his way back to the entrance door to the lab. Without a second to spare, just as he pretended to enter the room for the first time, George swung the door open.

"Oh, hi, George." He tried to sound lively and normal. The door clicked as it closed. "Sorry I'm a little late. You know I got stuck in traffic coming over here."

George looked skeptical. "You just got here?" he asked, somewhat relieved. "Give me a minute. I was wrapping up this meeting." He pointed toward his office door. "I need to speak with you right after these guys leave, and you know what? We'll be heading out to the field this afternoon, so don't unpack your bag," he said as he returned to his office and closed the door.

The men exited the room thirty seconds later, and neither looked John's way as they passed by. His stomach tightened as they walked out. Something was not right about them. He could feel it in his gut. And something was not right about George either.

"You ready?" George asked with keys in hand. "I hope you got some good shoes on. We're going for a little hike," he announced as he folded a piece of paper and pushed it into his pocket.

George drove an old Toyota 4x4 pickup truck. Its bright red color was a dead giveaway that it was made sometime in the 1990s, and it wasn't in the best condition. Rust had eaten its way around the tire rims and into various parts of its body. It looked like a leper of sorts. John wasn't the judging type, but the old rusty exterior was lovely compared to the filth he found inside. He quietly gagged upon opening the door as an eclectic mix of gassy, smoky mustiness attacked his nostrils and throat. Smashed empty coffee cups and crumpled fast food bags, among other things, had been carelessly discarded on the floor. He literally had to push them aside to find a place for his feet. The remnants of smoked cigarette butts overflowing the ashtray were a clear contributor to the strong smoke smell permeating the truck's interior.

"Where are we heading?" John asked as George shoved the key into the ignition.

"Kennington Park," he replied without further explanation.

"Oh, great! I love that park. It's so beautiful and tranquil," he said as the truck rumbled to life. "What's going on there?" he asked while trying to clear the mucus that had built up in his throat.

George didn't answer. Either he was preoccupied with his thoughts or he hadn't heard John's question due to the loud rumbling of the engine.

"George," he called out. "Why are we going there?"

"Need to check some stuff out. We shouldn't be long," George yelled back.

Sighing to himself, John turned to look out his window for the remainder of the bumpy ride, wondering why George had invited him along on a trip he didn't want to explain the purpose of. Pacifying his intense feelings of strangeness, he convinced himself that his concerns were unfounded and that George was just one of those people who did things differently.

He had only been to Kennington Park once before, but upon arriving, the view of the surrounding area was just as he remembered. The park was gorgeous with its shimmering lake and surrounding flora.

About half a mile beyond the lake was a forest riddled with walking trails that led to ponds, bogs, scenic viewpoints, and picnic areas.

"It's stunning out here," he spoke as he took in the deepest of breaths as if to clear his body of the contaminated air he was forced to breathe in during the ride.

George did not respond. He stood staring at his phone for several minutes before typing a text to someone or writing notes. John wasn't sure which, and he wasn't inclined to ask any more questions. He patiently waited with his hands deep in his pockets and enjoyed the view.

"We're going to be heading down one of those trails." George scratched his head as he looked up past the pond and then back at the park map pamphlet. "Sure hope we find what we're looking for."

"And that would be what?" He surprised himself with his unintended response, and to his delight, George answered.

"Not sure," he said with a shrug of his shoulders. "Just figured we'd take a walk and see if we notice anything unusual." Buckling his waist pouch, he headed for the forest. "Dr. Betsy brought y'all out here already?" George questioned.

It was the second time he'd heard George mention Dr. Betsy and couldn't help but wonder why. "Umm, yes, she did, but we only stayed near the lake gathering samples. Do you know her personally?"

George nodded. "I guess you can say that."

"Really?" John questioned with a raised brow. "I didn't know."

"Figured she'd never mention it," he said, turning to look at John. "But a couple of years back, I was working with Dr. Betsy on a project around here."

"Around here? On what?" John watched a chipmunk scamper across the path ahead.

"I was working on a research project for the university, and she was working on building the PIRD. We often ended up doing fieldwork and research in the same locations and sharing information. We seemed to be getting pretty close at one point. I'm sure you'd agree that Dr. Betsy is very attractive."

John shook his head, hoping the conversation wasn't turning weird.

"In her youth, Dr. Betsy was drop-dead gorgeous," he continued. "Anyway, I would invite her for coffee or lunch, and she frequently obliged. I thought we were getting along great, but one day, my boss took me aside and told me he wanted me to start working on a 'special' project."

"My boss had obtained information about a scientist named Dr. Cunningham who was working with Dr. Betsy. Dr. Cunningham had made some type of discovery significant enough for the museum director to be interested. You know how museums are always looking for the next best thing to display? Of course I wanted details, but he refused to give them and said the information was classified."

John was bewildered. *Why is George telling me this?* He just kept walking and listening.

George pulled out a bottle of water from his pack and took a few sips. "I feel pretty dry," he admitted, taking a few more sips before returning the bottle to his pack.

"He wanted me to start what he called 'observing' Dr. Cunningham. I told them I had only met her once or twice, and it would be evident if I started trailing her now. I also mentioned how Dr. Betsy and Dr. Cunningham seemed pretty tight. My boss immediately homed in on the fact that they were friends. He figured if I couldn't get through to Dr. Cunningham, I could try to get the information they were hoping to obtain from Dr. Betsy."

George cleared his throat as he swatted at a fly buzzing around him. "But there was, you could say, a fly in the ointment."

"A fly?" John asked, swatting at the same fly. "What would that be?"

"I was beginning to fall in love with Dr. Betsy." A swarm of gnats could be seen hovering in a circular mass ahead, and George shifted closer to John to avoid them.

Yikes! John thought. He had no clue things were this deep between George and Dr. Betsy. Sweat began to trickle down his forehead despite the slower pace they were keeping. The temperature had risen abnormally high for a day in May. Slapping his arm, he missed the miserable fly that kept buzzing around his head.

"Falling in love with her? I would have never guessed that. You guys don't seem to be in the same . . ." John stopped as he scanned his brain for the right word.

"It's different now. We're different now, but we weren't always enemies."

"Enemies?" John choked, his face cringing in amazement at George's words.

"I didn't tell Dr. Betsy about my feelings for her. I tried to continue as usual, but my attraction kept getting stronger."

John and George had slowed to a turtle's pace as they approached a sign that read "One mile to Fox Meadow."

"Are we walking all the way to Fox Meadow?" John asked as they stopped at the sign. He watched as George peered at the map, and then, twisting off the cap of his water bottle, he guzzled some water.

"I guess so," George said, looking around. "You see anything different out here?"

"No, not really. Trees. Foliage. Small animals. All looks pretty normal to me. But then again, you never told me what you're looking for."

"Hmm." George rubbed his chin as he thought. "I know something has got to be out here," he said, seemingly to himself. He walked off the path into the forest, shaking his head in frustration. "I don't know. Look for something like disturbed ground," he announced, turning to John.

"Disturbed ground?" John gulped at the thought of the suggestion.

George laughed and returned to the trail. "It's nothing like that. We're not looking for a dead body, or at least I don't think we are," he said with an air of mystery. He pulled out a rag to wipe his brow and then continued his storytelling.

"After working with Dr. Betsy for a couple of months, I felt it was time to tell her how I felt. I figured if we started a relationship, I would kill two birds with one stone. She'd feel comfortable telling me what was going on with Dr. Cunningham's research project. And to be honest, even though I wasn't interested in Dr. Cunningham's work, my interest increased as she seemed resistant to sharing her findings."

"Umm! I'm not sure why you're telling me this. You don't have to. I see it's pretty personal."

"This is nothing," George replied with a wave of his hand. "I don't mind talking to you. Actually, it's quite easy talking to you. Getting back to my story, on the personal side, I had it all planned out, and in my mind, I saw Dr. Betsy as my potential partner. I had never married and was hoping to find a companion. I was gravely disappointed when she flat-out rejected me. I didn't see that coming at all. I thought she had been falling in love with me too."

So, he goes from telling me nothing to telling me everything. How strange. What in the heck is going on? John narrowed his eyes and looked at George. "Whatever gave you that idea?" he asked before kicking a stone and watching it tumble down the pathway.

"I don't know why, now that I look back on it," George shrugged. "I think my feelings for her just blinded me. I took simple acts she did to mean she had romantic feelings for me. In my defense, though, I acted maturely and accepted her rejection. However, as time went on, I realized who she had true romantic feelings for."

John thought he saw something in the distance. It looked dark; maybe it was an opening. He pointed in the direction, but as they walked closer, they noticed it was just a huge hole in a rotting tree trunk.

"She had feelings for Dr. Cunningham," George declared loudly.

John stopped in his tracks. "What? You mean that woman, that scientist you were talking about?"

"You hit the nail on the head. And it was more than my machismo self could bear at the time, especially since I hadn't exactly been discreet with my feelings for her. I felt humiliated and manipulated. She had led me on. She could have told me from the beginning she had no interest. She played me," he said as if he was still accusing her. "In my anger, I determined to sabotage their relationship."

His words made John shudder. *Sabotage a relationship?* John thought. *None of this makes sense, and why would I need to know this anyway?*

John pulled up his shirt to wipe the sweat off his face while thinking how he could change the uncomfortable topic they were on. "I was wondering about the office work you had for me. Is it a lot of data entry?" he asked.

George laughed. "I guess you're tired of listening to me. I was about done sharing anyway since Dr. Cunningham ended up dying. A car accident," he said rather coolly without looking back at John. "I happened to be behind Dr. Cunningham's car one evening. We were driving down a two-lane highway. A car coming in the opposite direction swerved into her lane. She tried to avoid it, but it was a head-on collision."

A chill of horror raced up John's spine. "That's terrible," he gulped. "What did you do?"

"What could I do? I was in shock. I called for help. I ran to the car, but I could tell it was too late."

John went silent for several seconds. George was creeping him out. He didn't seem shaken up about having seen such a violent death. He seemed heartless and cold and reminded him of his father. He too brushed aside the death of others as if it were of no significance.

George stopped walking and peered at John. "You know what? I think we better head back now."

John drove like a bat out of hell all the way home and went straight to his computer. He was going to investigate George's story, though he had no clue where to begin a search with the few bits of information he had. He typed in Dr. Cunningham's name and "car accident." His back arched up when the results popped across the screen.

"Car Accident Kills Local Scientist," read the heading. His mouth dropped open while his eyes greedily gobbled up the article. He hadn't read every word in his haste, but a few moments later, he knew her full name was Dr. Vanessa Cunningham. The weirdest part was that this woman was Natasha's grandmother. By some odd coincidence, Dr. Cunningham had died the same year Natasha won the youth STEAM competition. The reporter, who evidently did his homework, mentioned that Dr. Cunningham was the grandmother of the recently recognized high school student.

He and Natasha had been going to the same schools since grade school. He was well aware of her because of her stellar academics and the fact that she had beaten even him for that esteemed STEAM award. But did he ever remember seeing her sad?

He'd never paid that much attention to her, and no memories from those years stood out to him, probably because he too was absorbed in his own grief. They both had lost loved ones, probably around the same time. It made him feel connected to her in some peculiar way.

"If the accident was real, was everything else George said true?" he wondered before typing in Dr. Betsy's and Dr. Cunningham's names together. Again, he lurched back in surprise after reading the heading that appeared. "Local Scientists Study Redwoods at Kennington Park."

Pumping his fist in the air, he hollered with excitement. "That's the connecting link," he shouted. "It's the park." That was why George had taken him there. Whatever he was looking for had to be at the park.

But his gut told him it was not plants or trees that he was looking for; it had to be something different.

CHAPTER 15

Matthias: My Communion

Entertaining guests was a regular occurrence on Zariah. Heavenly beings from distant realms, worlds, and universes were frequent visitors. Some came for just a day, while others lingered for lengthy periods. How thrilled I was that Malak would be coming to our home. He was a prodigious being whose powerful presence matched his physical girth. Malak was older than my father by more than ten thousand years, and his wingtips depicted that age difference. The older a heavenly being was, the deeper and more elaborate were the hues at the tips of their wings. Beyond the tips of their wings, there was no physical difference that would distinguish their age.

He was a dear friend of my parents, especially my father, Adriel. They met when my father was a youth and quickly bonded like brothers. My father was once his understudy, but now they shared knowledge between themselves as equals. They too were thankful for this special visit and time of reprieve since their duties did not allow them to be in each other's presence frequently.

A few weeks after my visit to Uriela, I found my father and Malak standing under our mango tree enraptured in conversation. He had finally arrived. Extending my auditory range since they had not encircled themselves in a forcefield of light that would prevent anyone from hearing their words, I picked up their conversation from where Hadassah and I were working to prepare the meal.

"Is your son ready for his first galactic travel experience without you or Keturah?" Malak asked before looking up and noticing a particularly large purple-skinned mango hanging close by. He reached up and plucked it. "I love these," he said, closing his eyes as he bit into the flesh.

"Don't ruin your appetite," Adriel warned. "I'm sure Hadassah and Matthias have a meal that will tantalize every taste bud in your mouth. But yes, he is more than ready to travel to Nanea with you. Now that he's seen Uriela and read the records, I feel it has given him a necessary level of experience and knowledge."

Malak nodded his agreement and took another bite of the luscious fruit.

"I wanted to wait," my father admitted. "But now that he is recommended to be a protector . . ."

Malak stopped eating the fruit and looked at my father. "We had discussed this on Uriela, but you never mentioned whom you thought he'd be a good candidate to protect."

"It is for a youth identified by the Council of Bones as critical to the progress of our mission. His name is John McKenzie."

Malak threw his head up and chuckled heartedly as a young doe walked up to him and nibbled on the fruit he held at his side.

"What is it, my friend?" Adriel questioned, not knowing why Malak found the information so amusing.

"I am the guardian for Natasha, the young lady who is the driving force behind that same mission. This is good news, Adriel. But why don't you seem pleased, my friend?" Malak leaned in as he studied my father's face.

"He hasn't even had his first Communion, and he . . ."

I strained my ears as my father's voice was suddenly silenced. Looking out toward the tree, I noticed they were now enshrouded in a circle of light. I would have to wait for them to reveal what they discussed if they chose to tell me. I couldn't help but wonder what had compelled them to ensure no one heard their words.

Once we finished the repast Hadassah and I had prepared, we all settled down on a patch of soft, thick grass embedded with small colorful flowers. Hadassah sat next to me. I had told her the story of the great race, and we both were anxious for Malak to finish the story.

◂◦▸

"Malak, please tell us how that great race ended?" I folded my hands pleadingly as I looked at him with anticipation.

Malak let out a hearty laugh. "Oh yes, Tobias did leave you hanging, didn't he?"

"Yes, he did, and I can hardly wait to hear the end of the story, and neither can Hadassah."

Malak stretched his legs out and leaned back on his elbows. "So where did he leave off?

"At the best part," I replied as I pulled my knees to my chest. "Abner was catching up to the Creator."

"Oh yes, and by the way, I had been dusted by them. As those two pulled ahead, we all stopped racing and just watched, frozen with wonder. The Creator passed the finish line first, but Abner was not far behind Him."

"I knew it," I shouted, shaking my fist in the air. "No one can beat or equal the Creator. He probably wasn't even really trying."

"Hold on a second. Let me explain something to you. The Creator can transform into any life form He desires. He can subdue His divinity and experience life as any of the created creatures. That day He raced just like an angel. But from that day forward, Abner started to change. Somehow, he got it in his head that it was possible for him to equal or maybe even surpass the Creator."

"That's crazy," I mused. "I mean, the Creator is God, and He created Abner. How could the creation be greater than the Creator?"

"Good point. But Abner didn't see it that way at all."

"How did he see it?"

"He believed the Creator was keeping us from reaching some higher realm. He thought he should be higher even though he was already in the highest position of any created being. He told us we weren't truly free."

Malak looked at me and then looked past me. "And some of us believed him," he said as his countenance fell.

"Do you now understand the records, my son?" my father asked as he rubbed his chin. "Surely they told you of all this. You should be well versed in the fall, why it happened, and the wisdom and justice of the Creator in preserving the peace and harmony of the unfallen realms."

"Oh yes, Father," I said softly while glancing at my mother before looking at the ground.

"What are your plans for tomorrow, Malak?" Keturah asked as she fluttered and then folded her wings.

"I was hoping Matthias would accompany me on my visits to the other Zariah families. I know you and Adriel are quite busy now."

Malak looked my way. "It would be my honor," I declared. "A whole day with you would be remarkable."

"Can I come too?" Hadassah asked.

"Not this time, Little Sis. I think we'll be moving quickly."

"I can keep up." Hadassah moved her arms and legs to show us her swiftness.

My father scooped her up and started to tickle her. "You will be my companion," he said as she giggled with all her might. "I'll take you to the Children's Discovery Garden," he assured her.

And then the unexpected occurred. Sudden and subtle, I knew not at first what was happening, but someone was calling me. Something was drawing me.

"Can I please be excused?" I asked.

"Yes, of course you can," both my parents said in unison.

Seeing the puzzled look on my face as I turned to leave, my mother asked if I was all right.

"I think so," I replied as I left our communing circle. Walking past the line of trees that encircled our home, I headed for the open fields beyond.

"Where is he going, Daddy?" I heard Hadassah question.

"I don't know," my father replied.

"I do," Malak announced. "Look up. His time has come."

—◦—

A dazzling light encircled by rainbows carried by creatures I had never before seen was approaching. The brightness banished the evening tides that had been encroaching upon the horizon. A voice continued to beckon me ever so softly. As I walked toward the light, I was instantaneously taken in and enveloped with a circle of light and fire.

I fell to my knees. I was in the presence of my Creator. The light surrounding Him was brighter than our sun, and yet I could clearly see Him Who was the Ruler of the universe. He stretched forth His scarred hands, and I reached up and grasped them. As our hands clasped together, we were transported to another realm by the traveling throne that had brought Him.

As the light faded, I realized we were in a garden. Its stunning beauty left me speechless. The Creator beckoned me forward, and I began to walk through this masterpiece of loveliness with Him. We passed an immortal bloom—a tree of life laden with twelve different sumptuous fruits hanging from its branches. I knew that at every new moon, the tree produced a different selection of twelve fruits. Every planet within our realm contained its own immortal bloom. While we savored the new fruit, we also prized the leaves, for they contained healing properties unequaled by any other plant.

We didn't stop to sample the fruit of this enchanting tree. Instead, He led me to another tree. This one was laden with only one fruit. Bright and deep was the color of its outer skin. It was a tree of knowledge, and He beckoned me to take one. It was succulent and sweet, and my tastebuds rejoiced with each bite. Here under its massive canopy, we sat down on the carpet of vibrant, luscious green grass and conversed.

In a vision, the Creator took me to worlds whose existences were unknown to me and were alive with creatures and beings I could never have imagined. He spoke of the wonders of the universes of light and revealed mysteries that had plagued my mind. I poured out my questions like a waterfall, and He answered them all.

My consciousness was heightened, and clarity filled my mind. When my eyes met His gaze, He knew I hadn't asked all the questions in my heart. Yet He didn't try to pursue a path I was not ready to take. Instead, He gave me my song. His voice was mesmerizing. The melody evoked the strongest emotions I had ever felt. His love and acceptance were beyond my comprehension, and the joy that filled my heart was so great that I closed my eyes to allow it to saturate my being.

When I opened my eyes again, I was back on Zariah.

I watched as the circular living throne lifted and swept through the air, leaving me burning with light and love and joy like I'd never known before. I looked to our dwelling place, where I knew my family and Malak eagerly awaited my return, but I couldn't go there now. I needed time alone to process all that I had seen, heard, and felt. Deep within, I chastised myself. *Why didn't I ask all my questions? Why did I withhold myself?*

I clicked my teeth to call Naseem, who came galloping through the valley. As always, he knew my heart, and I soon found myself surrounded by the beauty of my haven.

I spent the early morning hours the following day telling my parents about my experience. They were overjoyed. My father looked at me and said, "I trust your doubts have come to rest." Before I could say anything, he turned to my mother, hugged her, and wished me a good day with Malak as he took to the skies.

"How was your Communion?" Malak asked as I met up with him on a trail that led to our neighbor's home.

"It was more than I expected. So much more. I felt such joy, peace, and acceptance in His presence. My emotions reached their ultimate pinnacle, and I felt so alive. It's a feeling that I never want to fade. I have etched it in my memory and my heart."

"And your questions?" Malak asked, turning ever so slightly to face me.

"He answered them all," I said enthusiastically.

Malak stopped walking and looked straight into my eyes. "Did you ask them all?"

I listened to the birds chirping cheerily around us as I searched my mind for an acceptable response. "I was afraid to ask them all," I slowly admitted. "And now I'm ashamed of it. I know He knows my thoughts. Why didn't He just answer them?" I questioned, returning Malak's gaze.

"The Creator will only respond to what you are willing to reveal to Him. He wants you to speak freely, but He can help and guide you only if you let Him."

Malak laid his hand on my shoulder. "You have a long journey ahead of you. You need to reveal all that is in your heart. You know the Creator's love has no boundary," he reassured me. "All that has been done since the beginning has been done in love. Never doubt that, Matthias," he instructed. "We may not understand all His ways, but we can understand that He is and ever will be the truest definition of love."

We soon left behind the forest trail we were traversing and continued our journey until we reached the top of a hill that overlooked the valley. In the distance was the dwelling place of our closest neighbor. Malak fluffed out his wings and let the wind ripple through them as we enjoyed the scene. The sky was clear and blue, and the sun shone down brightly upon us.

Malak smiled as he seemed to look behind me. "Even without fully disclosing your heart to Him, He gave you His blessings," he said.

"What do you mean?" I asked inquisitively. Then, correcting myself, I said, "Of course I am blessed."

But Malak shook his head and flapped his wings.

I hung my head. "I knew He wouldn't allow me to have them if I didn't fully—" I began, but Malak pressed his finger against his lips to tell me to stop speaking.

"You have much to learn about our Creator, His love, and His wisdom. Stretch out your wings," he commanded. "You are no longer a child."

Malak stepped back, and as natural as it was for me to think of moving my arm, the thought of unfolding my wings caused a rustling sound behind me. In the shadows of the morning sun, I saw them for the first time: two pairs, like a red-tailed hawk, just like my father's wings. I bowed my head, humbled and in awe of my Creator's love, and then I folded my fledgling wings toward Malak in my first celestial embrace.

CHAPTER 16

Natasha: Unexpected Discovery

Anxious fingers scurried through bits of paper ripped from notebooks full of scribbled phone numbers and other nuanced information. Coins from pennies to half-dollars, bobby pins, and paperclips of varied sizes and colors resident in her mother's nightstand were getting pushed aside in Natasha's frenzy to find the key.

"Well, it's not in here," she mumbled as she peered at her mother's bed. The crumpled sheets strewn with dirty clothes were an annoyance hard to ignore. She was in the habit of cleaning up after her mother. Making her bed, folding her clothes, and cleaning her bathroom were weekly rituals. These weren't her assigned chores, but something in her had a compulsion for tidiness.

Tonight, however, was not the night to pacify her need; it would reveal that she had been in her mother's room, and that was what she didn't want her mom to know. Arriving at the second nightstand, she began her frenzied search again. This time a smile broke out on her face as she picked it up and examined it. It had to be the one.

The digital clock sitting on her mother's nightstand read 9:13 p.m. as she wrapped her hand tightly around the key and headed past her bedroom door. She had been warned against rummaging through her grandmother's office. Her mother had said it was because there were important papers about taxes and loans and other business things she needed to sort through.

Hey! Natasha laughed. *Business papers wouldn't be a reason to lock up a room and hide the key.* And by her own mother's words, that was not the entire truth. She hoped her mother had not noticed her surprised yet pleased look by her unwitting confession.

Several weeks had flown by since Natasha's forgotten birthday. Schoolwork had taken precedence over any detective desires, but now her opportunity had arrived. Her mom was at work, and she had all the time she needed to snoop around. She tiptoed down the hall as if someone who could catch her in her sneaky expedition were near. Beads of sweat suddenly sprang from her forehead as she eagerly pushed in the key, felt the click of release, and eased open the door.

Stale air filled with particles of dust caused an eruption of sneezes. She was prepared for this and quickly shoved her hands into her sweatpants to retrieve a folded mound of Kleenex. It had been two years since anyone had cleaned this room. As she clicked on the light, her shoulders sank with disappointment. How many times had Valerie promised she would sort through Grandma's stuff and clean up the office? Natasha shook her head at the thought. She had even offered to help in the hopes that her mom would let her use the room as a study, a music room, or a library. She could think of so many ways to use this space. BUT NO. Her mom had been adamant. She was not allowed to touch or change anything.

Boxes. Brown boxes of every size covered the floors and the furniture and even lined the walls, crawling up them like vines. Some had been dug into, with flaps peeled back or hanging at their sides, but most were stacked on top of each other and had been untouched since they had been placed there.

This room hardly resembled the place her mind remembered when her grandma was alive. Grandma kept it neat as a pin. Everything had its place and purpose. Her L-shaped executive-style desk was the center of attraction. Two stately artificial Ficus trees sat in the corners, bringing warmth and greenery into the room. There was a small couch that could pull out to a bed. That was where Natasha had loved to hang out and listen to her grandma's stories or just read books from her bookcase library.

Natasha pulled out the desk chair and plopped down. The disturbed dust caused her body to spew out another series of sneezes. From this seat, her grandma's special chair, she used to be able to admire the view of the room while feeling quite important. But tonight, the only view she had was of boxes. The desk was covered with them.

"Let's get to it, girl," she said as she stood.

Rummaging through the first box, she found it was filled with bills. "Good gracious," she declared as she held one up to her face. "These aren't yours, Grandma. These are Mom's." That realization sent a new wave of frustration cruising through her body. "Dang it!" she muttered, clenching her fist. "Mom used this office as a dumping area." That meant she'd probably have to sift through a bunch more boxes until she found her grandma's notes.

"Overwhelmed is an understatement," she moaned. "I have a test tomorrow, but with all this, I'm likely to be here all night.

"Well, complaining will get you nowhere," Natasha told herself. *That's exactly what Grandma would say,* she thought.

Fifteen boxes later, the only word she could muster was "Ridiculous!" She said it repeatedly, like a soliloquy, sometimes with clenched teeth in anger, and other times softly in despair. *Mom, you are the worst pack rat ever. These bills are from a decade ago and should have long since been shredded. I have yet to find one box filled with Grandma's stuff, and now my back is aching.*

"Figures," she mumbled aloud. "My sprained ankle has finally mended only for my back to start hurting. If it's not one thing, it's another."

Natasha pulled herself erect with hands on her hips and grimaced in pain as she stretched back. She had done this several times already, with each stretch coming sooner than the one before it.

She was ten years old when she watched her very first Olympic Games. It was exhilarating seeing the gymnasts swing through the air, tumble across the floor, and do backflips on a beam. When her grandma noticed her fascination with the sport, she asked Natasha if she'd like to sign up for some gymnastics classes. Natasha was delighted. She told her best friend, Kenisha, about the plan, and Kenisha convinced her parents to let her sign up too.

Grandma had an ulterior motive, though. She described Natasha as "thick" and "big-boned." Now Natasha understood that those were words for "fat" or "obese." "We have a lot of fat people in our family," Grandma would say, warning Natasha of her likely demise. "Your genes are against you, so you have to work hard, honey."

The gymnastics teachers were poorly trained. Some were mere high schoolers who had no formal teaching experience. When Natasha tumbled or did handstands and other gymnastic postures, the teachers didn't realize she was straining her back, and neither did she. Ten-year-old kids shouldn't need physical therapy, so after Natasha's second therapy session, her grandma pulled her out of gymnastics, albeit a little too late. From then on, her weight slowly and stealthily increased, that is, until Grandma died. Then it ballooned out of control.

Looking around to assess her progress made her groan loud and long. "There must be, like, one hundred boxes stuffed in here," she said pouting. She needed to strategize. Instead of searching every box, she needed to single out the ones most likely to have been placed there right after Grandma passed away.

"The walls," she yelled out after thinking and assessing the room more closely. "Why didn't I think of this before?"

Now the real work had to be done. The boxes against the walls were stacked five tall and two in. That meant she'd need to do even more lifting and turning. Her sweatpants and t-shirt were already moist from her exertion. "This is a workout," she declared with a measure of gladness. "You might actually lose a couple of pounds tonight."

The first box had you-know-what in it—BILLS. But she had succeeded in finding her grandma's things. "If there are more bills in here, I'm going to scream," she told herself as she reached for the third box in a stack.

Instead of a scream, she let out a victorious *woohoo*. "Bingo!" Natasha slid across the floor doing a happy dance. "They're beautiful," she sang at the sight of plant science, biology, and chemistry textbooks. Her waning energy now had a resurgence, and she excitedly delved into pulling and searching box after box. Dates were written on the cover of each of her grandma's research journals. *September 1989. January 1995. August 2003.* "At least I'm getting warmer," she said, laying a box behind her before digging into another.

But nothing in those boxes yielded anything of exceptional interest, and all the material was dated years before her grandma had passed away. Leaning against the wall, she gently pounded her head against it before sliding to the floor. She needed to find the box with the research from right before her grandma had passed.

Natasha pulled her phone from her pocket and swiped the screen. *12:30 a.m.* She gasped. *I've been searching these frickin' boxes for three and a half hours and nothing?* Yawning, she looked wearily around the room and stared at the last bunch of boxes sitting in the right-hand corner.

Warm rays from a dreamy sun filtered through the trees. Elation thrilled her soul as he tossed her small frame into the air and then caught her in his strong arms. She giggled with glee, begging him to do it again and again.

Natasha's neck dropped like a falling boulder, and she snapped awake. She had fallen asleep for a few seconds. With eyes half open, she realized it was the reoccurring dream. Were these subconscious memories or intense desires for how she wished her childhood had been? Or perhaps they were visions of the future? Her child in the arms of her husband?

She arched back. Everything ached, from her shoulders to her legs. Rolling onto her knees, she decided crawling was easier than standing up. Upon reaching the boxes, she crinkled her nose at the pungent smell of mothballs. Pulling back the box flaps brought a moment of confusion. "Bathing towels?" she questioned.

She reached in, but something hard was wrapped inside. Unfolding the towel, she found an album. "Huh! Why would Mom or Grandma wrap an album in towels?" She reached for the next towel, and again there was something hard within it. The box was filled with albums.

There were five in all. One looked like a wedding album. The others were just plain old albums. *Someone mustn't have wanted anyone to see these,* she figured. *Why else try to disguise them?* She wasn't sure who might have hidden them or why, but she was going to see what was inside.

As long as she could remember, they had no other family. It was always just the three of them: her, her mom, and Grandma. No aunts, uncles, or cousins ever stopped by. No other grandparents visited. No holidays or picnics with extended family. She hadn't noticed the oddity until she turned about six years old and was visiting her friends' families. She'd ask Mom or Grandma where her family had gone, and they'd tell her that her family was right there. It was Grandma and Mom. "No, I mean my other grandmas and grandpas," she'd pester. "And don't I have any cousins or uncles and aunts?"

Her imploring was always met with some type of vague response or a distracting comment or question. "Why don't we go shopping? You need some new school clothes, don't you?" Or "If we had other family, don't you think they'd be here?" Or "Be thankful for who you have, Natasha. Some people have absolutely nobody."

She closed her eyes. *Who or what will I see when I open these albums?* She drew in a deep breath and remembered. Her grandma always told her she had lived many lives. She wasn't referring to reincarnation but to the chapters of her one life. "There was my childhood with my mom and dad and brothers and sisters." Grandma had four other siblings. "That was my first life, Natasha," she'd say with a far-off look in her eyes.

"Then there was my life of marriage and raising my children." She always smiled broadly when she mentioned her husband, Cecil, before tears would brim in her eyes. "He was my prince, my best friend in this life." That was when her eyes would turn back to Natasha. "A diamond in the rough, but a diamond no less." Her finger would point at Natasha as if she were scolding her. "I can only hope and pray you find someone with his soul, heart, and character. His kind is a rare breed, my darling," she'd say, dabbing her face to catch the tears streaming down. "We had a beautiful life together, he and I and our children."

"But when he died, I entered my third life. That's the life I'm living now. It's my life with you." Grandma Cunningham would then open her arms and give Natasha a warm hug.

As she turned the hardcover over, Natasha's eyes scanned the black and white pictures filled with the faces of strangers. Coconut and palm trees were scattered about. As she turned the pages, she intuitively knew that it was her grandma's first life. The pictures weren't taken in America; she could tell from the background that they were in some tropical place. "The Caribbean," she whispered. "These are pictures of Grandma as a child living on the Caricom islands."

She picked up the next album. It was the wedding one. The cover was white as snow. "Grandma," she whispered as the first picture met her gaze. "And Grandpa." They were a handsome couple, and their youth made them look like dazzling superstars. The wedding was simple, but the smiles were enormous. Grandma often said her wedding day was one of the happiest days in her life. Natasha rejoiced as she took in the beautiful pictures that told the story of love sealed in marriage for time and eternity.

That means the next book, she thought, *must be about their life with their kids.* She wasn't mistaken. She recognized her mom immediately, even though she was just a child. Her grandma had three children: two daughters and one son. Grandma's son, her uncle, had passed when he was just fifteen years old. That was her grandma's first life—sorrow. Natasha breezed through the album, for she knew it was the next one that could reveal what she had been looking for her whole life. Had her grandmother kept pictures from the time she was born? If so, might it have pictures of her deceased father?

Though not often, her grandmother told her bits and pieces of her childhood. She said her dad was a wonderful man, and she regretted that Natasha did not get to experience life with him. Her mom, on the other hand, never mentioned her father. "He's dead," was all she'd say. The mention of him seemed to pierce her heart like a knife and trigger depressive episodes that would last days on end, so Natasha learned to not ask or talk about him. "That's why we don't keep pictures of your dad around," her grandma would explain. "It's just too hard on your mom."

Her hands were shaking, as if they knew the next album would hold what she had been yearning to see for so long. Leaning forward, she braced herself, turned the cover open, and stared. Nothing had prepared her for what sat on the page. Mouth agape and eyes wide, her heart raced wildly as her mind tried to decipher the image.

Grandma she recognized. Her mom was an image of youth and beauty she could hardly believe. The man in the picture had to be her father. But who in the world were the two boys sitting snugly and happily on his lap? Several moments passed before the obvious connection sank in. It hit her like a tsunami wave crashing unexpectedly onto shore: her brothers? Two of them? She had been told about one, the one who perished with her father. But there were clearly two boys in the picture, and they were twins.

In an instant, her eyes flooded with tears, for in that moment, she finally felt complete. She had found her family. So overcome with emotion was she, and so fiercely were the tears bursting from her eyes, that her vision was completely obscured. She had seen them, and they were now embedded in her mind's eye. Sobbing uncontrollably, she cuddled the album to her breast. They were hers, even if they were no longer here. And she wanted to know more.

The photo was a professional one, perhaps from JCPenney or the Picture People. Grandma stood in the middle. Her mom and dad were seated. The boys were in her dad's lap, and she was in her mom's. Three children, not one or two, but three of them. Her brothers looked to be three or four years old. She was just a toddler and couldn't have been more than a year old. They looked radiantly happy, especially her mom. Young and smiling proudly, she appeared to be a completely different person than the tired, greying, washed-out woman she was now.

"Why didn't they tell me I had two brothers?" she sobbed loudly. "What was so terrible about knowing they both existed, even if they are dead now?"

Despite the fact that they were gone, she felt whole. For the first time in her life, she felt connected and complete. She was a part of a loving family. "How could knowing your past make such a difference in the present?" she wept. She peered down at her father's image. It was the way he held the boys that made her long for him, his strong arms about them as a protector and a friend. "Just like my dreams," she wept. "Just like my dreams."

More and more beautiful pictures greeted her with each turn of the page. There were pictures from parks and playgrounds, holidays, and birthdays. Silly pictures, and some serious ones too. They lived in a gorgeous house. It had a pool and swings in the backyard. *Where did this life go?* she wondered. *My life with Mom and Grandma was nothing like this. It's as if . . .*

Natasha sighed, remembering her grandma's words. It was as if it was a completely new life, but a different one, a worse one.

She turned the page and arched back. The last few pages of the album were empty.

Picking up the final album, she hoped the images would continue. To her dismay, it too was empty. It appeared that someone had removed the final pictures from that phase of their life. Placing the album on the top of the stack, she sat with legs crossed quietly sobbing and thinking. *Why?* she kept asking herself. *Why? Why tell me about Dad's death and one brother but not the other? What difference would it make?*

Someone had wanted to forget, to erase the past, as if it never was. Her tears ebbed, and a new feeling started to arise. She felt robbed. They had lied to and deceived her. By burying the truth of her past, they had left her broken and incomplete. By hiding their memories, her mom and grandma had somehow washed away her own significance.

Natasha pushed her lips together as her jaw clenched. She returned to the album and removed several pictures. No one was going to take them from her again.

CHAPTER 17

Graduation Nightmare

The intense June sun seared down on the bleachers filled with family and friends as the sound of "Pomp and Circumstance" echoed loudly throughout the high school stadium. Happy shrieks and hollers pierced the air from time to time as the ecstatic crowd proudly watched the graduating seniors, draped in caps and gowns, march toward white chairs lying in straight rows like a fleet of navy cadets.

John barely heard the congratulatory recitations and speeches that followed. Nor did his heart swell with the long-sought-after joy that seemed to permeate those around him. As he strode to the stage to receive his diploma, the impact of her loss threatened to overwhelm him. Startled by the depth of emotions that were steadily rising, he fought valiantly to restrain his feelings.

"Grief. It's like a wave, John," the counselor had explained. "It can roll in and out when you least expect it. But those waves will surely grow out of control if you try to suppress the pain."

Pain? He didn't feel pain. He was numb with shock and disbelief. She couldn't be gone. It was inconceivable that his precious and beautiful mother could just disappear.

He had looked up at the counselor, staring into her eyes. He wanted to release the enormous pressure of anger and hate building about him, especially since he knew he was just another client to her. Looking past her expectant gaze, he returned his eyes to the floor and stubbornly waited for her to concede to his wishes.

Focusing back on the present, he felt the tight grin etched on his face twitch as the principal gave his hand a vigorous shake.

"Well done, John," he whispered, with a pat on his back. "Your parents must be so proud."

Those words sent a fresh pang of sorrow searing through his soul. His mom would have been there, cheering for him and letting him know how delighted she was of this major accomplishment in his life. But his dad? He knew better than to expect anything from Kevin though he still hoped that he would be there; it was the least he could do as his father. He hadn't made it to even one important event throughout John's high school years.

Graduation is different, he thought. Even a dead-beat dad should show up for his kid's high school graduation. He had made sure to give Kevin an entrance ticket and let him know the date and time. Kevin seemed interested and even kind of congratulated him.

"It's about time, son," he said while accepting the graduation ticket John handed to him. "I know your mom would be proud."

That was Kevin's way of saying he was pleased. Saying anything good directly to him seemed an impossibility, so Kevin had made a practice of doing it through their mother.

"Hey, man, are you joining us tonight?"

Derrick playfully wrapped his arm around John's neck, and John returned the friendly gesture. He and Derrick had been on the track team and often went running together, but running was the only thing they had in common. Derrick's favorite pastimes were girls and partying, and John was into neither even though he attracted girls like a swarm of bees to nectar. He had gone to a few parties and gotten smashed before, but he loathed what he became after consuming alcohol. The last person on Earth he wanted to be like was his father.

"Dude, you worked your butt off these past four years. You deserve a little fun."

"Yeah, he definitely worked much harder than you, man," Steven chimed in jokingly. "And he's got the cords to prove it." Steven pointed at John's neck and then back to his own. "Magna cum laude," he said, pumping his fist.

"Shut up, man." Derrick gently punched Steven's arm. "At least I'm here, and C's get degrees," he retorted loudly, causing a few heads to turn his way.

"And so do D's," John muttered under his breath through a series of fake coughs.

"You know, I'm going to take you down," Derrick teased, throwing his fist up. John unzipped his robe, revealing an attire of jeans and a form-fitting white T-shirt, and threw his fist up. The two playfully tussled a few moments before Derrick returned to his request.

"It's time to celebrate and party," he screeched, waving his hands in the air.

"Hey, you!" a woman's voice interrupted. "I see congratulations are in order."

John turned to find his Aunt Kristen, her husband Joseph, and his Aunt Marsha standing behind him. Kristen opened her arms wide. "I'm so proud of you," she said, hugging him tight.

Her tone was good-natured, but her words were a bit of a scolding. "You could have at least told me which college you got into. I had to hear the good news from your sister." John's aunt looked at Riley.

"Congratulations, John," Riley echoed sweetly while edging toward him.

She looked lovely in her lavender skater dress with sun-kissed hair bouncing past her shoulders. Why hadn't he noticed how much she'd grown? He smiled at her.

"You look gorgeous," he complimented. "You look just like Mom." She edged even closer. He rarely hugged her anymore, even when he knew she needed one, like when he'd hear her crying in her room at night as he tiptoed past her door. He couldn't afford to get pulled into her grief. It hurt too badly. Plus, the less attached they were to each other, the easier it would be for both of them when the inevitable day came for him to say goodbye.

But tonight, she dared to step into his bubble. Opening her arms, she was determined not to take no for an answer. He obliged and pulled her close.

"Where's Dad?" he whispered, pulling away. He had promised himself he wouldn't ask, but the words tumbled out, irrespective of his desire.

The look in her eyes told him everything he needed to know. *It doesn't matter,* he told himself. *I don't want him there anyway,* he reasoned, clenching his teeth in disappointment.

"You're coming over to our house tonight," Kristen declared authoritatively, with Joseph nodding in agreement. John looked at Derrick and Steven, who had patiently waited to get his attention back. He shrugged his shoulders and raised his hands with a wide grin.

Kristen turned to the young men. "Sorry, guys. You can get him later, but right now, he's coming home with us." Then, turning back to John, she let him know that she and Joseph were going to head back home to finish their preparations.

"I will take Riley back," Marsha volunteered, "but I figured I'd hang out a little longer and get some nice pictures of you." She held up her camera while John wrapped his arm around Riley and smiled.

Suddenly, the large, firm hand of a man gripped John's shoulder. *It can't be,* he thought as elation swelled within him. He swung around, expecting to see his father.

"Glad I found you. I was about to give up. Congrats, John." George's radiant smile quickly faded. "You okay?" he asked.

"No, no. I'm good. It's just that, I thought . . . well, never mind. I wasn't expecting you here, but thanks."

"This is a big deal, John. Over one million students drop out of high school every year, and only about sixty percent of males enroll in college." He spewed out the facts like a reporter. "You, my friend, have not only graduated from high school, but you have also graduated magna cum laude and have been accepted into college. That is an awesome feat, and I'm happy for you." George stretched out his hand.

John's Aunt Marsha seemed impressed by his words. "My goodness, John, and who is this?"

The way she asked the question and extended her hand caused John to blush with embarrassment. "Sssssorry," he stuttered. "Aunt Marsha, this is George. He's my supervisor at the Natural History Museum."

Marsha's eyes widened. "You're working at the Natural History Museum? When did this happen?" she laughed before grasping George's hand with a rather warm smile. John instantly noticed Riley's eyeroll out of the corner of his own.

"Well, you know, I'll tell you and Aunt Kristen about it later at the house," he retorted nonchalantly, hoping both George and his aunt had picked up on his suggestive comment. "Thank you so much for your support, man. It means a lot. We'd better get going now, Auntie."

George and Marsha were both still smiling at each other, making the moment quite awkward.

"Where are your manners, John?" Marsha piped in with a nod of her head toward George.

Aunt Marsha's look made the hairs on his arm stand up. She wanted him to invite George over, but the thought of it filled him with dread. He didn't trust George, and the last thing he wanted was for him to be around his flirtatious aunt.

Looking up in desperation, he quickly eyed a possible distraction and way to escape giving an invite to George.

"Natasha," he yelled in a voice that portrayed excitement. But the noise of the crowd around them drowned his call. "Natasha," he yelled again, moving forward.

She still had her cap nestled snugly on her head and her robe zipped up. But she looked different. Taller maybe, or was it her hair that had changed?

Natasha turned. He waved and smiled. To his delight, she seemed pleased to see him.

Quickly ending her conversation with the couple standing before her, she summoned someone at her side before making her way toward him.

John turned wide-eyed to look at George as ice filled his veins. He hadn't expected to see Dr. Betsy here. And accompanying Natasha?

His clever distraction had failed, and now his heart sank as he realized his desire to extricate himself from one dilemma had led to another.

"Congratulations, John," Natasha complimented. "It's been a tough year, but we made it."

"And congratulations from me as well, John," Dr. Betsy added.

George cleared his throat loudly, making his presence known. Dr. Betsy turned bright red at the sight of him. Almost instantaneously, the blood drained from her face, leaving her looking as pale as a ghost.

"George," she gasped. "What in the world are you doing here?"

"I guess I could ask the same question." He moved toward her with his hand raised.

She stared at it momentarily, then stepped back.

"Okay, I take that as you are not happy to see me, which is quite a shame," George said.

John's and Natasha's eyes met, and for once, they both seemed to share the same feelings, neither knowing what to expect.

"It's been such a long time, Phrosene. I imagine a good Christian woman like you would have forgiven me by now."

"Still digging where your nose doesn't belong?" Dr. Betsy shook her head, her eyes filled with anger. "Some people never change."

John's stomach flipped at her words, and his throat went dry as he glanced at George.

Folding his arms, George stared at Dr. Betsy with a scowl before changing his expression. "Well, to answer your question, I came to congratulate John, my current assistant," he grinned. "He's going to make a wonderful addition to our team at the Natural History Museum, won't you, John?" he asked, looking directly at Dr. Betsy.

John's eyes widened. He hadn't yet told Dr. Betsy he had taken up another intern position at the Natural History Museum and wasn't planning to follow through on helping her with the summer programs.

Natasha nudged Dr. Betsy with her elbow. "We best be going," she declared before Dr. Betsy could respond. "Congrats again, John." She waved as they turned away.

"And we should be going too," Marsha announced. "Why don't you come with us, George? Now that you two are working together, you should have a lot to talk about. Right, John?"

John managed a weak smile and then pulled out his phone. "Hey, Derrick," he typed. "Changed my mind. Where's the party?"

"What was that about?" Natasha asked as they weaved their way through the crowds.

"I can't believe he's out. I should have known. The Lord literally warned me. I knew something strange was going on when John never signed up to be an intern this summer. I can't believe that man," she scoffed. "Putting out his hand as if I'm supposed to pretend he's an old friend."

Natasha stopped walking. "What's going on? Who is that guy? And I've never seen you so upset. The Lord warned you about what?" They had almost reached the parking lot, which was fast emptying as cars loaded with family and friends took off to continue their celebrations.

"Good gracious," Dr. Betsy replied in a tired voice. "I thought I'd never see him again. And to think he now has John working with him. He'll twist that boy into pretzels."

"What in the heck are you talking about?" Natasha asked, almost yelling.

"I'm sorry, Natasha," Dr. Betsy said. "Why don't we talk on our way to the restaurant? They said the reservations were for 6:00 p.m., right?"

Natasha nodded even though Dr. Betsy was not looking. Her Jeep beeped and flashed. Kenisha and her family had invited Natasha to dine with them that night after Natasha told her about her mom's refusal to come.

They buckled up in silence before Dr. Betsy spoke. "His name is George, as you heard. He was an old colleague of mine. I worked with him for a while before he ruined it by letting me know he liked me."

"So, what's wrong with liking you?" Natasha asked tentatively. "You're very beautiful. I can only imagine how many guys and, umm—" Natasha nervously cleared her throat—"I mean, how many people must have fallen in love with you."

"He was extraordinarily persistent, and I dealt with his kind in the past. I was in no way interested, but some people just can't take no for an answer." She shook her head despondently.

"I should have known," she berated herself before clicking on her turning signal.

Natasha was still confused. "Should have known what?"

"He was in jail. I thought they put him away for at least five years, but I guess he's out early."

"Oh my gosh, Dr. Betsy! A guy like him? I would have never known. In jail for what?"

"He just wouldn't stop bothering me," she said, stealing a glance at Natasha and then quickly returning her attention to the road. "He bothered your grandma too. After she perished, I decided to press charges for stalking."

"Grandma? But why? What did she have to do with anything? He liked her too?"

Dr. Betsy sighed. "No, it was her research. I told you about that special project, right?"

Natasha shook her head while staring at Dr. Betsy. "What special project?" she asked as Dr. Betsy turned into the parking lot of the restaurant. *This must be the project Mom was talking about,* she thought. "No, you never mentioned anything about my grandma working on a special project."

"I thought I had already mentioned this to you," Dr. Betsy said while pulling into a parking space and sighing. "Your grandma was working on some type of project before the accident. Apparently, George was interested in what she was investigating. I didn't expect to see him tonight. I didn't expect to see him for a long, long time, but like I said, the Lord warned me. I had this dream about him the other night out of nowhere, and voila," she declared, waving her hand. "He showed up tonight."

Dr. Betsy turned off the ignition and slumped back in the car seat. "Please forgive me, Natasha. I just don't feel well. Seeing George really shook me up. I can't imagine what he might be up to now.

"And—" She paused. "He has John under his wings. I can hardly think of a worse-case scenario." Turning to Natasha with a frown and sad eyes, Dr. Betsy asked, "Do you mind enjoying dinner with just Kenisha and her family tonight? I don't think I'll be very good company right now."

Natasha could tell Dr. Betsy was very disturbed. "Don't worry about me, Dr. Betsy. I'm fine, and I'm sure I'm going to have a lot of fun with Kenisha. It's our awesome graduation night, and I know I'll have a good time. Go home, relax, and forget about all this. I'm sure it won't be as bad as you think."

⊷◊⊶

Hiding her emotions, Natasha waved goodbye to Dr. Betsy with the forced smile she had managed to muster. After Dr. Betsy was out of sight, her shoulders drooped. Her mother had been too upset with her come, and now Dr. Betsy, who was fast becoming like a surrogate grandma to her, had left.

She desperately tried to remain upbeat while dining with Kenisha's family. Afterward, Kenisha convinced her to go to one of her friend's graduation parties. Partying wasn't her vibe, but she didn't want to go home either. The thought of facing her mom made the blood in her veins boil, while the searing pain of being neglected gripped her heart.

She watched with quiet abandon until the revelry reached heights she could no longer tolerate.

"I'm going home," she yelled to Kenisha at the top of her voice. Kenisha was clearly enjoying herself but managed to pout her displeasure before being pulled back into the frenzy by a group of guys and gals intent on partying the night away.

166

As the cool outdoor breeze caressed her face, Natasha realized she had waited too long. The last bus of the night was at midnight, and it was already 11:51 p.m. She picked up her pace, trying to half run and walk to the bus station. The high heels she was not accustomed to wearing squeezed her toes so tightly they pulsated with pain. Then she watched in horror as the rear bus lights from the final bus of the night disappeared down the road just as she arrived at the station.

Tears quickly blurred her vision as she began to sob. "What the heck am I going to do now?" she cried. "There's no way I'm calling Mom," she swore. "I'd rather walk ten miles than see her wretched face apologize for not being there for me. I'll figure it out. I'll make it home on my own," she told herself as she winced in pain with every step she took.

To make matters worse, the temperature had cooled. Clouds covered the sky, and soon a misty drizzle began to fall. Natasha pulled on her graduation robe and zipped it up as she limped along. A car with three men inside honked as they drove past her. She wasn't in the safest part of town and hoped no one would notice her. But a few minutes later, she recognized the same car passing her again. This time they slowed down and began waving at her as they approached. Looking around, she realized she was alone on this abandoned street with dimmed streetlights. The stores were closed, and there was literally nowhere safe she could run.

Ignoring the guys, she picked up her pace and started to pray. "Dear Lord, help me," she wept. She pretended she was calling someone, and the car moved on. Looking behind her, she saw them turn the corner. Her heart rate slowed, and she prayed they would not return. But a few minutes later, bright lights flashing from behind told her they had returned. Instinctively she knew she was in dire trouble if she couldn't escape. They honked repeatedly, hollering and asking if she needed a ride.

Ahead, she noticed a gas station. Strangely, she hadn't seen it before. She figured if she made it there, she might be able to get some help.

"Hey, baby, congratulations on graduating. But looks like you need a ride. Why don't you come party with us? We'll take you to wherever you want to go," someone said from inside the car.

Nasty slurs and laughter could be heard coming from inside, and the smell of alcohol oozed from the car windows.

"I don't need a ride, but thank you," she yelled back before slipping off her shoes. She'd have to make a run for it and knew the heels would have to go. Her adrenaline was surging at full force when she took off running.

To her surprise, the car suddenly shot past her, but she didn't stop running. The gas station was her desperate hope.

Only after she arrived at the gas station, huffing, puffing, and completely out of breath, did she turn around, and the sight before her made her cry harder.

Dr. Betsy dashed out of the Jeep parked in the middle of the station and ran toward Natasha.

"Oh my gosh! I can't believe it's you. Thank You, Lord. Are you okay?" she asked as she wrapped her arms around Natasha. She let Natasha weep for a few seconds before helping her inside the Jeep. She turned up the heat and gave Natasha a jacket she had lying in the back seat.

"How in the heck did you find me?" Natasha asked after calming down.

"I wasn't looking for you, honey, but God knew where you were. I went home and went to bed after I left you. But I didn't sleep long. I guess I had too much on my mind. When I looked at the time it was about 11:10," she said, pulling out of the gas station. "I sat up and started to read. As I read, I got this strong urge to get some double chocolate mint ice cream. I had none in the house, so I went to the store." Dr. Betsy pointed to the back seat, where a bag sat.

"For some reason, instead of driving back home, I started to drive around to think about what happened this evening with George. I hadn't noticed where I was going, but all of a sudden, I noticed this car with flashing lights. I thought something was wrong, so I sped up and started flashing mine to let them know I was willing to help. They took off, and that's when I realized someone was running."

Natasha could hardly believe how fortunate she was. "I thought I was a goner for sure, Dr. Betsy. I know God had to have heard my cry for help. It's a miracle you arrived when you did." Natasha managed to peel off her graduation robe and replace it with Dr. Betsy's jacket.

After several moments of solemn silence, Natasha whispered, "But I don't get it. He helps me with some things and then seems not to hear me at all for other things. Do you know how hard I prayed that my mom would come to my graduation and that our relationship would get better? Why does she ignore me when I'm the only child she has left?" Natasha sniffled as a fresh batch of warm tears rolled down her chilled cheeks. "It was my night. The most important night of my life. I've worked so hard to please her. To make her happy and proud of me."

Heartbroken and sympathetic to Natasha's pain, Dr. Betsy quietly listened. She knew Natasha needed to vent, so instead of driving home, she drove to the PIRD. "The stars are back out tonight," she said softly, "and the fresh air might help. Let's take a little walk; then I'll take you home."

The cool night breeze, the salty ocean air, and the sound of waves crashing onto the shore helped to calm Natasha. Dr. Betsy wrapped her arm around her shoulder and pulled her close as they sat under Old Ben and looked up across the starry expanse.

"I'm sorry, honey," she finally spoke. "I don't have the answers your heart craves to hear," she comforted Natasha. "My own parents were just as bad or maybe worse than your mom," she admitted. "But that's a story for another day. I know it hurts, but you have to be strong."

A gentle wind fluttered the tassels still draped around Natasha's neck. "I don't know how to be strong anymore, Dr. Betsy," Natasha wept. "How can I be strong when everything she does just tears me down? She says she loves me; then she does crap like this. I'll never forgive her for not showing up to my graduation. I won't do it, Dr. Betsy," she swore with quivering lips.

"No one is asking you to forgive her, Natasha. Not now. Not tonight," she sighed. "But perhaps in the future, you'll come to understand the pain that drives people to act against their very own wishes and desires."

Dr. Betsy grasped Natasha's hands. "I think whatever is bothering your mom and making her act this way has a lot to do with her and not you. Just try to hold on. I'm sure things will change soon," she said before slipping back into silence next to Natasha.

At 2:30 a.m., Dr. Betsy's car arrived at Natasha's home, and at 2:37 that same morning, John managed to make it back to his house.

"Where the hell have you been?" Kevin's voice seemed far away as John swung open their front door. He stumbled in with his finger pointing at Kevin.

"Nope. Nope. Nope," he slurred. "Where have you been, Dad? It was my graduation today, and you couldn't even show up." Silent moments ticked away as he floundered to the railing.

"Are you drunk?" Kevin asked accusingly.

"Well! Wouldn't you celi . . . celibate if you graduated magna cum laude."

"How the heck did you make it home that drunk?" Kevin stood stoically with arms folded, staring down at John as he crawled up the staircase.

"The same way you do," John retorted when he finally reached the top.

"Get out of my face and go to bed. Count your lucky stars you didn't get pulled over or kill someone."

John wanted to scream at him, *Why don't you love me? What have I done that was so terrible it uprooted all affection for me? Can't you see how much pain I'm in? Why can't you at least say, "Congratulations, son"?* But no words came out of John's mouth.

"Did you hear me?" Kevin yelled at the top of his voice. A light mist of spittle landed on John's face. Kevin's foul breath made him cringe and pull back. Kevin had been drinking too. "I said get to bed."

John turned around, biting his lower lip; the taste of blood saturated his buds. His whole body trembled as a tear slid down his cheek.

CHAPTER 18

Natasha: Contentious Gift

Not telling her mother about the pictures she found was now a secret kindling anger within Natasha. She knew if she told her mom about her find, it would likely only make things worse between them. Valerie had somehow found out about her snooping through her grandma's office. First she accused Natasha of breaking into and entering her grandma's room. Then she kept pestering her about how she sneaked around like a thief and that she could no longer trust her.

Natasha was convinced her mother would deny her the truth anyway. It was what she'd done her entire life. Expecting something different now was pointless. "Madness is repeating the same actions and expecting different outcomes," she told herself. She had read that quote somewhere and immediately homed in to the truth of it. How many times had she asked her mom about her family and her father? Valerie was as consistent as the sun rising and setting with her response. She'd pretend she didn't hear the question, and then she'd give some vague, ambiguous reply before leaving the scene. If

Natasha pushed some more, she'd resort to manipulating her with sadness and go into a depressive state for the next few days. Natasha had been trained like Pavlov's dogs not to ask, because her mom was not going to tell.

The evidence within her hands, though, was eating her alive. She was frustrated that she could not find out more about the handsome man who spoke of his love for her through his eyes. She used to begin her morning by swiping open her phone to look at the time and then the weather. Reading the news or being distracted by video clips on her phone was a bad habit she had fallen into. Now the first thing she did upon opening her eyes was to pull out the photographs she kept in her nightstand. She'd stare at them longingly, trying to imagine what it would be like to know and live with her deceased family.

Brothers. The idea of it made her smile. Older brothers to protect and tease her and to compete with her for the bathroom and the best grades. But they were now phantoms of the past, people she could never meet. How she'd love to know more about them. What were their names? How old were they when they died? Was she like either of them in character or personality? The questions about her brothers, father, and all the rest of the people she presumed to be her family were endless.

They couldn't all be dead, she had concluded. So where were they, and why had no one in the past seventeen years come to find her? Why was her mom trying to keep her from them, or was she trying to keep them from her?

It wasn't just her mom who bore the responsibility of secretive silence. It was her grandmother as well. She had been just as tight-lipped as Valerie, even though her refusal to speak came with apologies and promises that one day Natasha would know the truth. It seemed to her that day would never come, especially after her grandma perished.

The truth had been sealed within the casket of her grandmother, and she felt it would never leak out.

Adding to the simmering flame was her mother's refusal to go to her graduation. It was a slight she felt she couldn't forgive. How hard could it have been to show up for one hour to show her support for the hard work her own daughter had accomplished in completing her high school diploma, and as the valedictorian?

The hurt she felt was like no other. It was as if all her mother's wrongs were finally sinking in, and the loathing boiling up inside her could not be held in.

Being in the same room felt like torture, so she avoided her mom at all costs. And when they did end up in the same space, they acted as if the other did not exist. By the end of each day, Natasha was emotionally exhausted from all the negative energy both she and her mom were generating. On the occasion one of them mistakenly spoke, their words and attitude would ignite an argument, and they'd explode with venomous rants and raves. Staying home was becoming intolerable, so Natasha decided to look into staying on campus during college.

The only bright spot in her day was her work at the PIRD. As the main intern, she was always busy with planning and implementing programs, which helped keep her mind off of her troubled relationship with her mom. Dr. Betsy also proved to be a source of happiness and reprieve for her. They met often to discuss the intern program and the difficulties of their lives.

One day, Dr. Betsy announced that she had a special surprise for Natasha and asked to meet her at the PIRD.

"I'll be a few minutes late, but please wait for me outside," the text from Dr. Betsy read.

Stepping off the city bus and slipping on her sunglasses, Natasha waved goodbye to Mr. Kennedy, the friendly bus driver. The bus was soon out of sight, leaving her standing in the warm summer sun watching families with small children going into or coming out of the nature center. With school out, this was the PIRD's busiest season, and each summer since their opening, the number of visitors had been steadily increasing.

Glancing at her phone, she noted ten minutes had passed since Dr. Betsy texted. The searing sun was now causing her to sweat so profusely that she could feel the trickle of moisture slowly rolling down her back. *I can see when she's pulling up from inside*, she told herself before heading toward the ten-foot-tall French glass doors with long wooden handles. But the sound of a horn made her swiftly turn back around. Approaching was a cute little blue car she didn't recognize. For a moment, she figured the driver was trying to get the attention of someone else.

It rolled to a stop near the entrance, and Dr. Betsy got out, stood up, and beckoned her over.

Happy to see her mentor, she quickly approached the car, thinking Dr. Betsy was going to take her on some type of field exploration, but Dr. Betsy stopped her as she reached for the passenger door. "Wrong side," she sang, as her finger wiggled for her to come over to the driver's side.

Confused by the request, Natasha stopped and stared at Dr. Betsy, awaiting further clarification.

"I think it's time you learned to drive." Her grin literally reached from ear to ear as she pointed to the driver's side again. "It's my graduation gift to you, Natasha."

"You've got to be kidding me right now! Are you serious?" Natasha asked. "You've got to be kidding me. I so need to learn to drive," she said, tearing up. "I asked my mom a zillion times to help me learn, and she just never took the time. I was just telling myself that I better save up my money so I can take driving lessons before the end of the summer. I can't believe this!" she squealed excitedly.

"Come on now," Dr. Betsy encouraged her. "We don't have all day, so get on inside."

"I know the basics," Natasha admitted as she adjusted her seating and fixed her rear-view mirrors. "I already have my permit."

"I heard you talking to some of the interns about driving, so I knew you had your permit." Dr. Betsy buckled herself in. "As a way of introduction, this is 'Baby Blue.' She's a Mitsubishi Mirage I purchased a few years ago. I have a home about ninety minutes from here, and once the PIRD opened, I figured I'd need a car with good gas mileage for the daily drive in. I soon tired of the drive and purchased a cottage close by.

"So, Baby Blue," she said, tapping the dashboard, "ended up sitting in my garage." She pointed to the mileage indicator. "See how few miles I've driven her? She's still a baby, thus Baby Blue. You ready?"

"Oh crap! Is this a stick shift?" Natasha asked, eyes wide with trepidation as she noticed the gears. "Please tell me this is not a stick shift." She leaned to peer at the floor.

Dr. Betsy smiled. "I love them," she declared proudly. "And they're not that hard to drive. People just give them a bad rap because they never learned to drive one. So, relax and listen up."

After several moments of instruction, the car lurched forward and idled off. A mom nearby held her kids in check, though she was clearly humored at the sight. It took several more lurches before they reached a section of the parking lot that was not being used.

"You're a fast learner," Dr. Betsy declared thirty minutes later as Natasha shifted gears and sped up. "I'm quite impressed. I think you're ready to get on the road, young lady."

That was the beginning of a summer Natasha would hold fondly in her memory, for it signaled the official beginning of one of the most endearing friendships of her life. Not only did Dr. Betsy teach her to drive Baby Blue, but they also spent countless hours together. They'd usually meet during the weekend and decide on some distant park they wanted to visit to help her get in some driving practice. The time was filled with banter about every aspect of life. It was very reminiscent of the time she'd spent as a child with her grandmother.

Their relationship blossomed even more after Dr. Betsy began inviting Natasha over on Saturday afternoons to "Holiday," her distant home.

"I usually only stay here on the holidays; thus, I gave her that name," Dr. Betsy explained.

Though she rarely went to church, Natasha held to the belief that the Sabbath was a day of rest. How thrilled she was that Dr. Betsy was willing to spend the day with her in a way consistent with her beliefs. They'd enjoy sharing the dishes they had prepared for that special day, and then they'd practice music together. Dr. Betsy played the piano exceptionally well, to the point that Natasha believed she could have been a concert pianist.

"She's gotten me through some tough times," Dr. Betsy admitted after playing an emotional rendition of "Moonlight Sonata" that brought tears to Natasha's eyes. "Playing 'Ms. Patty' somehow gives me a sense of stability and comfort. I guess I play out my feelings, and I always feel so much better afterward." She'd repeatedly tell Natasha, "Never underestimate the power of music and its ability to change the soul."

Natasha's grandmother had paid for cello lessons since Natasha was seven years old. Natasha was a devoted student and advanced quickly, that is, until her grandma perished. Her mom refused to pay for lessons, so she resorted to practicing on her own for a while, but high school became so intense that she struggled to find the time for regular practice. It had been almost a year and a half since she had even touched her beloved instrument. How pleasantly surprised she was that her fingers had forgotten virtually nothing and were able to play as effortlessly as before.

They played duets together, from hymns like "I Surrender All" to more contemporary music like Michael W. Smith's "Awesome God," and jazzy gospel music by old-time artists like the Winans and Commissioned. Often the rays of the setting sun would glisten through the six-foot windows surrounding Dr. Betsy's beautiful music room, creating a heavenly atmosphere of joy and peace.

"You're such an old soul," Dr. Betsy declared one Saturday evening. "Who would have thought you'd enjoy spending time with an old woman like me."

"You're hardly an old soul to me, Dr. Betsy. You're more like a kindred spirit," was Natasha's reply. That made them both laugh heartedly, for they both loved the *Anne of Green Gables* books and movies from which they took the phrase "kindred spirit."

Saturday nights often found them snacking on popcorn and laughing or crying while watching movies like *Tales of Light, Belle* or *the Sound of Music*. Soon Natasha found herself spending the night. Sunday mornings they'd have a late brunch and talk about how to develop more children's programs at the PIRD or how to make the intern program more enticing.

During the week, Natasha busied herself with working at Walmart and helping Dr. Betsy with the summer intern program. She missed her friend Kenisha, whose family often traveled during the summer months, though they'd catch up on the phone weekly. They promised they'd spend at least one week devoted to each other before college began, as Kenisha, a dance major, had been accepted into Juilliard, a prestigious school for the arts located in New York.

The summer weeks flew by as summers usually do, and Natasha found herself a few weeks away from her anticipated start of college life. It was then that she received a gift beyond all measure. Dr. Betsy told her Baby Blue was hers for the keeping. She thought Dr. Betsy was joking upon hearing the words.

"You can't give away your car," she had told her. But Dr. Betsy insisted, stating it was no longer any use to her now that she had her cottage. She still had two other cars, one in Holiday's garage, and her Jeep.

Tear-filled hugs and words of deep appreciation poured from Natasha's soul. The thought of no longer having to depend on the city bus for travel made her heart thrill with joy. But she would need to tell her mother, and she knew Valerie would not be happy with her receiving such a gift, especially from Dr. Betsy.

The minute she pulled into the driveway, the porch light flicked on, and Natasha's heart sank. She was hoping her mother would be sleeping and that she could ease her way into letting her know about the gift. But that hope was quickly dismissed as she watched the front door open, and her mother gazed at her with a stern face.

"Please, Jesus, help her not to have a fit, and help her to let me have it." She closed her eyes, momentarily pleading for the strength and fortitude to face the coming onslaught.

"Hey, Mom," she called out cheerily as she opened the car door. "I thought you'd be sleeping."

"I was," Valerie replied, "But for some reason I awoke early." She let the front door slide closed as she stepped onto the porch. "What's this?" she asked with arms folded. She locked eyes on the car and then looked at Natasha. Her lips shrank as she tightened them.

Screeching tires made them both turn their attention to the street. "Another blasted driver driving too fast down this road," Valerie yelled. "Don't they get it? This is a residential area." She threw her arms up toward the car. The driver ignored her angry expression and hastened off once again.

"What's this?" she demanded just as Natasha stepped inside. "You rented a car?" she asked as she crossed the threshold back into their home.

Natasha took a deep breath and shook her head no.

"Natasha, where in the heck did you get this from, and whose is it? Why are you driving around someone else's car? Girl, you don't even have a license. Do you know you can get arrested if you get pulled over?"

"It's mine," Natasha said calmly, hoping her composure would somehow reverberate back to her mom.

"It's yours?" she scoffed in disbelief. "How? Where did you get the money? You've only been working a part-time job for a few months."

Natasha pulled in her lower lip. "It's a gift." Her tone remained quiet, and she tried to sound as if it were no big deal.

Her mom's silent glare told her the wheels of her mind were turning. Her next words shot through the air like a firecracker before exploding into a blaze of glory. "Give it back," she seethed through clenched teeth. "And I forbid you from working with her again. This has gone far enough."

Natasha could see her mom's nostrils flaring and knew she was beyond the point of reason.

"I should have cut it off from the beginning. That woman is intent on taking everyone around me."

"I do have my driver's license," Natasha fiercely interrupted. She retrieved it from her purse and pushed it toward her mom. Valerie appeared shocked but pushed Natasha's hand away. "I need this car, Mom. I'm in college now, and I need to be able to get around better. I'd be late for my job all the time because the gap between my last class and the time I'm supposed to start work is too short."

Natasha took a quick breath and continued. She didn't want to lose her momentum. "I need this job. I haven't asked you for money for any of my personal items, and you seem to appreciate the $150 I give you every month. I know that is nowhere near rent, but at least it's something."

"Don't you dare talk to me like that," Valerie barked. "I have given you everything you could ever need. You don't live under a freeway pass. You don't fill the fridge with food. I constantly extend my tired self to drive you places."

"I know, Mom," she admitted, "but I'm not talking about that. I'm—"

"But nothing. If I had only known letting you be an intern at the PIRD would have ingratiated you to that woman, you can bet I would have never allowed it."

She needed to squelch her mom's attack, and her next words served that purpose. "I'm not saying you haven't done anything for me, but seriously, Mom, you've done absolutely nothing to help me get around. You act as if I'm supposed to be riding the bus for the rest of my life while you have the luxury of driving a car wherever you'd like. It's not fair. You've ignored every request to help me learn to drive, as if you want me to be stuck here with you."

Then a surge of defiance rose within her, causing her physical body to release a heat that made her instantly start to sweat. She had always complacently obeyed her mom, even if it meant she suffered. She never complained when her mother refused to go shopping every week, leaving the fridge so bare that she hardly had anything to pack for lunch. She endured the times when the lights or the water would be turned off because Valerie forgot to pay the bills. She kept her tears to herself every Thanksgiving and Christmas holiday she spent alone because her mother said they had no one to be with and nowhere to go. Valerie never seemed to realize how decision after decision she made brought misery to her daughter's life.

"I won't take it back," she stated firmly as she watched her mother move toward her as if she would strike her down. She didn't flinch. She wouldn't. And how dare her mom speak of Dr. Betsy as an enemy when she had only shown her kindness and love. "Dr. Betsy," she said, wagging her finger toward her mother, "has been more of a mom to me than you've ever been."

Natasha's voice began to crack. She immediately wanted to take back the words she had spoken as they resounded through her head like an echo bouncing off the walls of a cave. They now sounded too harsh even to her.

"And by the way, Mom . . ." She softened her tone dramatically and shifted nervously. It was time to tell her the secret she had held in her heart all summer long. "I'm moving out. It's all been arranged. I'll be moving onto the university campus next week. I didn't have a car, and I knew I couldn't rely on you or the city bus to get to and from home and school with my tight schedule."

Feeling the need to justify her actions, she continued. "I would lose too much time trying to study and commute. It would be too difficult to keep up with everything. Mom, I'm not far away, and the car will ensure I can get home quickly. I promise I'll be back every weekend. If you need anything, I'll be right here as fast as ever.

"Please, Mom, let me have this car."

Valerie's lips began to quiver. Thinking she was about to go ballistic, Natasha stepped back. Her mother's eyes dropped to the floor, her chest heaving in and out. Valerie stumbled to the couch and flung herself down. Then, burying her head into her hands, she began to weep.

"I don't want you to leave. I know I've been a terrible mother, but you're my . . ." Her sobbing swallowed the words that Natasha longed to hear. Any feelings of revenge fled at the sight of her weeping mother.

"I'm your what, Mom?" she asked tenderly, hoping Valerie would finally say something positive about her.

But she didn't. She just continued to cry, and once again Natasha found herself succumbing to her mother's emotional state, taking the role of comforter while surrendering her own grief and disappointment.

CHAPTER 19

Matthias: Rasmus I

I surged ahead of Malak as I made my way toward the opening at the other end of the portal. I didn't know what to expect. I could hardly contain my eagerness to see Malak's home and the home of the Arella order, an order of Messenger Angels. It was also the home of Rasmus. He was the one we had come to visit. I could see a glowing mist as we neared the opening at the other end of the portal, and I wondered what could emit such a harmonious and calming array of colors. When we finally stepped onto Nanea soil, we were at the top of a majestic mountain. The atmosphere was bathed in lights of varying hues from the four suns that orbited the realm. Each sun shed its spectrum of colors that harmonized perfectly with the rays of the other suns. The beams of light created a mist of colors that dispersed throughout the air. I was speechless.

"This is Mount Mahasavin," announced Malak, his voice booming behind me. "It means glorious, splendid, magnificent."

I turned to see what was making a gurgling sound and noticed two silver falls gushing out from either side of the mountain. They careened down the mountain into the valley below. The mountain was covered in a lush blanket of ever-living flowers of varied colors.

"And that is the City of Cherith," Malak said, pointing down the mountainside to the luminous light in the distance that rose miles into the atmosphere. The walls appeared to be moving, flowing like a river. "This is the city of twelve falls. They pour into twelve rivers that flow out into all the realms."

There was a path leading to the city which began at the portal's opening and led down the mountainside into the valley and ended at two grandiose gates made of silver. The path was lined with ground flowers similar to the blue evening primroses that grew on my world. These flowers could endure trampling of any kind by any being or beast. Tree flowers that looked like black-eyed Susans, the size and height of the tallest trees on Zariah, flanked either side of the path. Each had petals of different colors. Some were fiery red. Others were bold orange, and others luminous yellow. There were seven different colors in all. From the petals swayed delicate thread-like vines, and from the vines swung monkeys. Their happy sounds filled the air and welcomed us into their world, their home.

"Let us worship here on the Mount, for the suns are setting, and there is no more glorious place to observe them than here," Malak said, smiling.

And just as those words were spoken by him, the entire atmosphere took on an iridescent glow, and we took a seat on the flowers that covered the ground around the portal. The suns soon dipped below the horizon, shooting their final rays up into the atmosphere. The concentrated stream of light awakened an army of bioluminescent microbes that abided in the heavens. The microbes immediately started to fall from the sky where they had been resting. It was their feeding time and the purpose for which they descended toward Nanea's ground. Their descent was no ordinary event. As they floated to the ground, they emitted a variety of colors. The combination of the setting suns, the bioluminescent creatures, and the mist created a surreal environment enriched by the sound of voices that began to sing their praises to the King of kings, their Creator.

Soon, the sound of praise could be heard from everything that had life, from flower to tree to sea. The entire realm paid homage to their Maker with sounds of music that only sinless creatures could create. The light of day dimmed, as did the music, and evening swept across Nanea. A retinue of celestial beings gathered at the front gates to welcome us. I spent the evening meeting and conversing with the beautiful beings of this realm.

The next morning, Malak and I made our way to Rasmus's abode. As we neared, a bright form came out to meet us. Rasmus stood taller than both Malak and me. His power and strength emanated from his being. He was an ancient one. His life was measured in a thousand times ten-thousands of years, as the dark colors around his light garment and wings indicated. His eight wings were like the wings of an eagle, and they were massive. Everything about Rasmus demonstrated strength, power, and beauty. Despite his physical form, his spirit and soul emitted gentleness and kindness with a depth I rarely felt.

Malak flew ahead to greet him. Their wings folded together as they descended to the ground in an angelic embrace. They remained in this intimate embrace for several minutes. I wondered what these two ancients had to say to each other. It was an emotional and joyous moment, for they had not been in each other's presence for a long time.

"And who do we have here?" Rasmus questioned as he walked up to me. His eyes were an intense silver color and seemed to gaze deep into my soul. I immediately bowed my head and opened my wings. We embraced, and his spirit of humility and love converged with mine. "I am the son of Adriel. My name is Matthias," I said, stepping away. "I'm deeply honored to meet you."

"And I am honored to meet you as well. A new creation," he exclaimed. "Blessed be our Creator, Who never ceases to bring new life into His realm. It's always so thrilling to meet another being," Rasmus continued as he reached out to give me another embrace, but this time with his arms. "We will be close, you and I," he said. "I can feel your spirit. You are a special one with a special mission."

My heart thrilled at receiving such a heart-warming greeting from someone as admired and respected as Rasmus.

"I'm looking forward to spending time with my little brother," he said, looking back at me and then to Malak as he nodded.

Malak returned the bow and looked at me. "I will be back for you soon. You are in good hands."

"How about we go for a walk," Rasmus suggested. "I want to introduce you to my friends."

I looked around but did not see anyone and wondered to whom Rasmus was referring. He lifted his hands to his mouth and whistled a beguiling tune. Out of the forest and from the fields came animals of every size. They came walking and prancing, jumping, running, and strolling toward their master and friend. Some of them were of the same family of species that lived in my world, but many of them were not. A mammoth-like creature with tusks that appeared to be silver and emerald came and bowed his mighty head as Rasmus walked up to him and stroked behind his ears.

"This is Chasin. He's the father of all the mammoths here. We've been friends for thousands of years." Rasmus smiled while Chasin stood, bellowed loudly, and bowed his mighty head again before passing on.

"This is Amrin," Rasmus introduced. A blue rhinoceros stood before me. "She's just a baby. Her mama is over there." Rasmus pointed to a gigantic blue rhinoceros in the distance, which remained grazing on the grass. Rasmus gave her hide a brisk rub as she passed by, and an elephant's trunk curled around his waist. Rasmus laughed loudly as he grasped the trunk and turned to hug the white elephant.

"Kalei," he said. "The most loveable of them all. She makes sure to find me every morning so she can hug me." Kalei knelt before Rasmus, and he quickly mounted her.

"She is beautiful," I whispered. "She looks just like the elephants back home." Her trunk moved across my body as she sniffed every inch of me.

Then out of the skies flew a dragon with a wingspan so large that it created a blanket of shade as it flew across the plain to where Rasmus and I were standing. Rasmus immediately leaped from Kalei and onto the back of the spectacular winged beast.

"And this is Seraphina," he yelled as he reached his hand out to me. I grabbed hold of it as he swung me up behind himself, and Seraphina took to the skies. The ride was exhilarating as she seemed to perform every aerobatic move she knew. Seraphina then dove toward the ground and slowed her pace as she swept across a vast portion of Nanea. Rasmus continued to introduce me to the animals to which he had become intimately connected.

From my aerial point of view, I could see a forest with trees towering into the skies, and creatures romping through the foliage. I could see rivers and lakes teeming with life, and marine animals leaping out of the waters into the air. There were plains with herds of giraffes and zebras wandering from one feeding ground to another, and gentle rolling hills. "Look about you," Rasmus encouraged me proudly as the wind tousled my wings. "Enjoy all Nanea has to offer."

We flew for several minutes across Nanea's ever-changing terrain before Seraphina began her descent toward one of the grassy hills that flanked a lake. Rasmus pointed in the distance. "That's our destination: Lake Liraz," he said, smiling. The lake was the home of the flying manta rays, and Rasmus had promised me I would witness something spectacular. As we approached, I could see that the lake's peach-colored waters matched the peach rose bushes that grew across the hills. I watched the waters intensely, hoping to see the manta rays, but the waters were still and silent when we arrived. We dismounted Seraphina and settled comfortably on the ground flowers that had sprung around the borders of the lake.

"Have you received your commission to serve on Earth, Matthias?" Rasmus asked.

"They are training me, but I have not yet received my official commission."

Rasmus peered at me, his silver eyes flashing with light. I felt as if he could read the depth of my thoughts, and I nervously awaited his next words.

"You cannot have any question in your heart about the Creator's justice, mercy, or love, Matthias," he cautioned. "Abner will sense your weakness. He will direct his forces against you, and they can interfere with your mission. All your questions must be answered if you are to serve on Earth."

I listened quietly as I contemplated Rasmus's words. I didn't know where my questions came from or why they chose me. As I thought back to the day my father told the story about how part of our family lost their way and were forever banished, my heart couldn't comprehend the loss or the reason. I accepted that they were no longer happy because they felt they were being held back. I understood that tensions had risen and that the harmony of heaven had been disrupted, but I couldn't comprehend why they had been exiled. Why hadn't love won them back and kept them close until their hearts returned to Him? Despite nearing the end of my training, I still had not resolved these questions, and now Rasmus sensed them within me.

"I had questions too." He sat up and glided his hands over the flowers that surrounded us. "Many more questions and much deeper feelings than you," he admitted. "I was there from the beginning. I was there to hear Abner's first oration and his first attempt to weaken and deceive our hearts."

"But Rasmus," I quickly interjected. "I don't question his deceptions. I don't question his intent. I see that his arguments were unjust. I only question his banishment."

I was stunned. My thoughts slipped out so easily, almost as if Rasmus had called them forth. "I don't understand how His love that knows no bounds could let them go," I whispered, "when it was the only path back home."

I watched Rasmus settle his hand ever so carefully on the tops of the flowers. "No, Matthias." Rasmus shook his head slowly. "Do you not see that to question His love is precisely what Abner intended?" He pointed to my hand. "You are not holding them correctly. Only a light touch, like this."

I followed Rasmus's lead as I did my best to place my hand gently on the petals.

"Do you feel it?" he smiled.

My eyes widened, and a smile crept on my face. "They feel wonderful." The flowers vibrated, and I could hear a humming sound as they danced under my hand.

"These are the vibrating flowers. They only grow in certain places."

I placed both my hands down and closed my eyes. How relaxing they felt! Then I remembered what Rasmus said, and my smile faded.

"You do not see the path on which you travel and where it will lead you, and neither did Aziel."

I lifted my hands off the flowers and wrapped them around my knees. "Aziel?" I questioned, "Who is he?"

And that was when I felt it: a sorrow so intense and so deep that it caused my soul to shudder.

Rasmus looked out over the lake as the memories seemed to pour into his mind, and with them, all the emotions they conjured up.

"They were all my brothers and sisters," he said as he continued to gaze across the lake. "They were all my friends. I loved each one of them, but there was one with whom my heart was knit, one with whom I had a special bond. He was among them." Rasmus turned to me. "I feel compelled to tell you our story, but it will have to wait for another day," he added as a shadow moved over us.

I looked up to the skies. Seraphina had returned. Though Rasmus had not called her, she knew her master's heart.

"But I have not seen a single manta ray," I protested, feeling as though I had been robbed of experiencing a wonder.

"We will be back here soon," he promised as he stood to his feet. "Then you will hear my story and see their beauty."

CHAPTER 20

Natasha:
Hidden Treasure

Natasha giggled as she wiggled her toes in the dampened sand before a gentle wave of water rushed around her ankles. She splashed playfully about in the clear blue sea before fully surrendering to its subtle call. Floating effortlessly, she rocked from side to side while gently swaying her arms like waving branches as the sun caressed her face in its warmth. She felt good, and the peace that saturated her soul compelled her to close her eyes to intensify the feeling of serenity.

A streak of cold water startled her, and her eyes popped open, filling immediately with dread. Angry swirling thunderclouds now raced across a tumultuous sky, and a stiff wind whipped the ocean waters into a boiling frenzy of white-capped waves. *How could the weather have changed so swiftly?* Her mind had no time to unravel the mystery. It needed to figure out how she could reach the shore.

The deafening roar of the turbulent sea instilled fear into every cell in her body. Desire for life drove her to battle the waves despite instinctively knowing it was futile. She wasn't ready to die. And then, miraculously, she found herself back on the beach.

Panting in exhausted relief, she crawled across the sands, seeking a safe place from the angry grasp of the monstrous sea beast. But moments later, her fingers scraped across the sand, leaving deep claw-like impressions. It was pulling her back into its watery domain, intent on making her its next meal.

Wrestling herself from its grasp, she struggled to retreat to higher ground. As she began to run from the horror behind, her eyes fastened upon the horror ahead. She was on a tiny islet of sand. There was nowhere to flee. Terrified and alone, she knew she would soon be devoured. Throwing herself onto the ground, she lay face down and wept with utter abandon, awaiting her fate.

It was a human touch that made her lift her head again. Filled with compassion and love, it exuded hope and deliverance. Looking up, the sweet face of her grandmother met her gaze. In an instant, she was on her feet and reached to fasten her arms about her, but Grandma Cunningham was beyond human reach.

"Grandma, we must run and find higher ground," she cried. But her grandmother stood like a lighthouse in the midst of the terrifying storm.

"You cannot run and hide from this storm, my child. Your deliverance is in facing it. You must find your help in Him," she said in haunting tones. "He alone can guide you across the waves of life to safety. He alone can lead you to the path in which you will find the truth." And then she held up her arm and pointed toward the sea.

Bolting awake, Natasha twisted on her bedside lamp. Beads of sweat rolled down her brow as her heart thumped loudly. "It was a dream," she said repeatedly as she tried to calm herself. "It was only a dream."

Eyes wide with lingering fear and curiosity, Natasha sat up. "Grandma," she whispered, "why didn't you save me? Why would you tell me to walk into the sea?" Holding her knees to her chest, she rocked back and forth, trying to decipher the possible meaning of her nightmarish dream.

Kenisha dug her fork into her bowl of salad. "MMM MMM!" she hummed through a mouth filled with food. "This is so good. I just love the sandwiches here." Her sub was brimming with meatballs bathed in marinara sauce and melted cheese.

They were at a restaurant enjoying the last meal they would share together in what they suspected might be a long time. After they'd spent the past few days shopping, enjoying the beach, and helping Natasha move into her campus dorm room, the time had arrived for the friends to bid farewell.

"Kenisha!" Natasha tapped the table. "Aren't you listening to me? Did you hear anything I was saying?"

Squinting her eyes, Kenisha finished chewing while glaring at Natasha. "I heard everything you had to say about your grandma and your dream, but it's just a dream, Natasha," she said with a slight roll of her eyes. "It probably doesn't mean a thing except that perhaps you ate too late last night."

Natasha scowled and folded her arms. She wasn't in the mood for teasing. "Fine then," she said before taking a large bite of her buffalo chicken sandwich.

"What? You're not getting upset, are you?" Kenisha replied, batting her eyes and pouting out her lip. "It's our last moments together, and I was just kidding." Kenisha pulled a small mirror from her purse and examined her teeth before smiling at some random guys passing by their table. "I mean, it really was just a dream, and no one ever knows what most of them mean. If you only knew how many crazy dreams I've had, and thankfully none of them have ever come true."

"But this one was different," Natasha insisted. "It was so real. I felt as if I was talking to my grandma and that those waves were about to devour me. Something that real must mean something. 'And the path to the truth.' Those words keep ringing and ringing in my head."

Kenisha reached across the table and laid her hand on top of Natasha's. "Seriously, I wouldn't worry about it. There's nothing you can do to change anything, even if you did know what it meant. And there's a ton of other stuff to worry about, like your wardrobe for school and whether you might meet your future husband at college."

Kenisha turned slightly and rolled her eyes toward a table with a young man with top knot dreads and a high fade. His dark brown skin glistened with the glow of youth and health. His chiseled face was buried in a book he was reading while he slowly took bites of his sub and chips.

"I'm going to say hi," she crooned. "That tasty chocolate morsel might be my future honeybun."

"Don't you dare!" Natasha warned through clenched teeth, but Kenisha was already on her feet and heading toward the oblivious man and his table.

Natasha grimaced as she watched the brief introduction and then waved shyly as they both turned to look her way.

Grinning widely upon returning to her seat, Kenisha declared with pride that his name was TJ and that he was a senior going to the same college as Natasha. Natasha sighed and wagged her head. Kenisha had always been outspoken and bold, and rightfully so. She was gorgeous. Her straightened hair flowed down her back, swinging as effortlessly as a lasso in the hands of a cowboy. Slender and trim, her figure was always on display in her form-fitting wardrobe. While guys constantly catcalled her or tried to start a conversation, they would completely ignore Natasha, making her feel as if she didn't even exist.

She didn't blame them. She already knew she was unappealing and probably would not catch any guy's eye. Her ballooning weight was only cementing that fact in her mind. Despite the attention Kenisha constantly incurred and her antics to keep it coming her way, the two girls remained besties. As they finished their meal, the sadness they had suppressed the last few days began to surface.

"I hope you don't get too busy to stay in contact with me," Natasha said, frowning as they walked out of the restaurant toward the parking lot. "With all the new guys you'll meet, and I'm sure the new boyfriend and all, you'll get swept up in that New York lifestyle and forget about your previous life and friends." Natasha tried to be as dramatic as possible as a tear slipped from one eye.

"Seriously, Natasha. I could never do that. You're my bestie for all time," Kenisha promised when they reached her car. "And I'll always be a text away if you need me. I know you'll do the same for me." The girls hugged each other, cried, and hugged again before Kenisha got into her car and waved a final goodbye. Natasha watched tearfully as Kenisha's red Honda Civic Sport pulled out from her parking space.

"I guess you'll really miss her."

Natasha turned around to see the young man from the restaurant beside her. Instantly, her heart rate increased, and her palms became sweaty.

"I'm sorry. I didn't mean to intrude. She told me it was your last lunch together, and I saw your emotional goodbye." He stopped and pointed to a grey Mustang sitting next to the space where Kenisha's car had been. "My car just happened to be next to your girlfriend's car, and I was leaving the restaurant," he said, pointing behind him.

Not knowing what to say, Natasha stood speechless while the young man waited for her to respond.

Quickly wiping her eyes with the back of her hand and noticing the book in his, she pointed to it and smiled. "*Piercing the Darkness* by Frank Peretti?" She let out a soft laugh. "Like, who reads that nowadays? I'm shocked."

He looked down at his book, nodding his head in agreement. "Well, my grandma gave it to me, and I'm finally getting around to reading it. It's pretty good."

"I know. I read that one, and the one before it, *This Present Darkness*. They're amazing. And it's funny because my grandma also bought the books for me."

Pulling his head back in surprise, he gave her a you've-got-to-be-kidding-me look before heartily laughing. "Well, I guess we both have grandmas worried about our spiritual lives."

He stuck out his hand. "My name is TJ."

Natasha quickly wiped her hands on the side of her pants before grasping his. "Natasha," she said.

"What do you like most about the books?" he asked.

An hour later, Natasha and TJ were still standing in the same spot talking about their religious upbringings like old friends. They discussed the biblical concepts that shaped their lives and their struggle to be a positive and spiritual influence amongst their worldly friends. Never had Natasha been so invigorated and delighted by a conversation with an individual her age. TJ was certainly a different breed and seemed sincerely interested in becoming her friend. Before departing, to her surprise, he asked for her cell phone number. She must have looked at him in shock because he asked her again. It was the very first time she felt as if someone of the opposite sex noticed her.

A shrill of excitement and disbelief shot through Natasha's veins as she started Baby Blue. Her newfound friend had effectively wiped away the sadness she felt with Kenisha's departure and left her feeling cautiously hopeful that perhaps they might find their way to becoming more than friends one day.

Veering onto the freeway, her thoughts returned to her grandma's dream. "The path to finding the truth" kept repeating like a song replaying itself in her head. *The only truth I've found so far was in Grandma's office,* she thought, shifting gears as she crossed into the fast lane. *Perhaps there is something I missed,* she pondered. *I never found any boxes with Grandma's most recent work even though Mom insisted she kept all her stuff. And the last thing she worked on before she died was that special project that both Mom and Dr. Betsy mentioned.*

She hadn't intended to make a visit home, but her long talk with TJ had pushed the time later. Valerie was destined to be at work, and she wanted to check her grandma's office once again. She decided that now would be as good a time as any. Thrilled with the idea of leaving her dreary life with her mom behind, she looked forward to starting her first semester at college. But her moving out wasn't without some regret and trepidation deep within. While her mother never seemed mentally well, Valerie had always been fine physically. Recently, though, her physical health was becoming suspect.

Extreme tiredness, dizzy spells, and constant thirst, along with a handful of other symptoms, seemed to be plaguing Valerie. A firm believer that mental health can affect physical health, Natasha thought her mother's poor mentality was finally catching up with her. While Valerie didn't think she needed to be taken care of, Natasha had communicated to her mom the need to visit a doctor to discuss her worsening symptoms. It didn't surprise her in the least when Valerie refused, and Natasha felt that her duty was complete.

She and her mom were barely on speaking terms. The discomfort they both felt in each other's presence made moving to campus that much easier, and Natasha had purposefully been avoiding her.

Arriving at Valerie's room, she groaned in disappointment at the messy sight. It was as if Valerie was retreating to childhood with no care or concern for her surroundings. Open drawers with clothes hanging out, clothes and shoes strewn across the floor, and containers of half-eaten food made Natasha wonder how long it would be before rodents also made the room their residence. As she fished through her mother's nightstand in search of the key, it dawned on her that Valerie must have removed it and hidden it elsewhere.

The thought of her mother's continued attempt to keep her from finding the truth made Natasha more determined to gain reentry into her grandma's office. After a few moments of silent contemplation on how to achieve her goal, she knew her only option was to break in. Resorting to her phone for a how-to video, she soon had the door unlocked. Scanning the room, she looked intently for something she might have missed before.

"You haven't searched the closet," an inaudible voice said.

"Thank you. You're right. I haven't searched the closet," she replied as if speaking to a visible being beside her. That idea had never crossed her mind, perhaps because she believed the closet contained only her grandma's numerous coats. As she pulled back the bifold doors, her eyes swept across the area. Coats and jackets her grandmother had loved hung from the racks, just as she expected. Two hat boxes sat on the upper shelf. She retrieved them. They were light as feathers, but she searched them anyway.

"Nothing. Absolutely nothing," she breathed, staring at the varied styles, sizes, and colors of her grandmother's coats. Figuring she might as well try one on and hoping to save her the cost of a new raincoat, she peeled a light teal jacket with a black zipper off its hanger.

Then her eyes caught sight of something that made her lose her grip on the jacket. The coat crumbled to the floor right below a hole in the wall. Its jagged edges suggested someone had likely punched or hammered out the glaring gap. It was just large enough for her arm to reach in. Could her grandma have hidden something there?

Cobwebs covered the hole, indicating an eight-legged creepy crawly was likely hiding nearby. Recoiling from the thought of encountering a huge spider, or worse, the remnants of a dead mouse, she considered if the risk was worth taking. But what other option did she have? *None*, she concluded. She'd have to push past the thick, tangled white mass and hope the spider was no longer lurking about. *Gloves. I need gloves,* she thought, happy her solution-driven brain had come to the rescue at the last moment. Plopping one yellow latex glove on the ground, she peeled on the other before breaking through the labyrinth of skillfully woven silk.

Pressing her body against the closet wall, she pushed her arm in as far as it could go. Her fingertips brushed against something as smooth and hard as ice lying horizontally on the floor. It wasn't the wood studs, for they were not circular, and she already felt a puncture in the glove from the tiny splinters across their surface. She worked her hand around the smooth surface and could tell it was a tube of some sort, but its shape and angle made it difficult for her to get a good grip on it to pull it out. Every time she got her fingers around it, she'd lose leverage when she tried to bring it up. Down it would slide, back to the place where it had rested for more than two years.

Her heart leaped into her throat with the sound of the garage door sliding open. Hadn't her mother left for work more than an hour ago? She wasn't due back until the morning.

"Shoot!" she muttered, haranguing her bad luck. What were the chances that Valerie would return the very time she was snooping around? And to make matters worse, Valerie would be hunting for her because Baby Blue was blocking the garage door. Judging the time it would take her mom to park behind her car and walk into the house, she figured she could make one more attempt at retrieving the tube.

Pushing it up vertically and then placing her hand under it, she managed to angle the head right at the hole. Then, as she tilted it carefully, the tube barely sat on the lip of the jagged edge. Using her other hand like a claw, she dug her nails into the encased lid and pulled with all her might.

"Natasha," her mom yelled from downstairs, "I need you to move Dr. Betsy's car."

"Coming, Mother," she yelled at the top of her lungs. "I'll be down in a second."

Her mother's keys jingled loudly as they hit the kitchen counter. "Just pull my car in when you get down here," she yelled back. "I don't feel well. I'm going to bed."

Natasha's eyes widened with fright. She didn't want to get caught in that room. "Mom," she yelled again, "my keys are on the counter. You can move my car. I don't mind." The tube was slowly slithering out of the hole as she micro-adjusted its angle to keep it moving.

"Heck no! I won't touch that woman's car."

Beads of sweat burst from Natasha's forehead as she frantically worked at a sloth's pace to retract the cylinder. Hearing the first creak of the step her mom ascended made her cry out in prayer for help.

The tube popped through. Grabbing the raincoat, she wrapped it around the tube. Then she hustled to her room and slid them both under her bed just as the door opened.

"You're praying at this time of day?" her mother asked suspiciously.

"Umm! Yes, Mom. You know any time is a good time for prayer. Remember how Grandma used to say that?" she grinned.

Valerie sighed. "Yes, I remember," she replied softly. "I don't feel well. I got to work and vomited, so they sent me home," she said drearily.

"You vomited? Did you eat or drink something wrong?" Natasha's radar of concern escalated from yellow to red. She was used to her mom complaining about her health, but it was usually just complaints with no type of visible evidence to substantiate them.

"If I feel better in a couple of hours, I might go in for the last half of my shift, okay? Hopefully, I can sleep this lousy feeling away," Valerie said before closing the door behind her.

Natasha nodded and tried to smile. Her mom's complaints had increased dramatically since she announced she'd be moving out. Not wanting to even consider returning, she once again convinced herself they were psychologically based and maybe even an attempt to get her to unwillingly return home.

No sooner had Valerie entered her room than she called out again: "What were you doing in my nightstand drawer?"

Natasha's eyes popped open. Had she forgotten to close them back in her haste?

Stomping loudly, she returned to Natasha's room. "I thought I told you to stay out of Grandma's office. And do you think I'd be so dumb as to keep the key in the same place? You have no business in there," she chided, pointing angrily at Natasha. "Anything you need to know, you ask me," she said, pointing back to herself. "Snooping around like a criminal will get you . . ."

"Kicked out, Mom?" Natasha chimed in with a disrespectful chuckle. "Well, if you haven't noticed, I've already taken care of that, and I'm never coming back. I've asked you for answers a thousand times, and you've never answered even one of my questions honestly. All I want to know is what happened to my family. Where is everybody, Mom?" Natasha screamed. "Where are my aunts and my uncles, my cousins, and my grandparents? What have you done to them that they all refuse to find me?" she asked, breaking down in tears.

Standing like a catatonic statue, Valerie's glossy, reddened eyes stared straight through her daughter for what seemed like an eternity. Then, as she slowly backed away, her voice trembled as she spoke. "You won't understand. I'm sorry, darling," she said as tears began to roll down her grief-stricken face. "I just can't."

Valerie rushed out of Natasha's room and gently closed her bedroom door before Natasha heard her mother's sniffled weeping.

Falling back to her knees, she pled with God to shed light on the darkness that enshrouded her and to help her mom to somehow be willing to tell her the truth.

CHAPTER 21

Natasha:
Fascinating Find

Natasha's eyes pranced with joy with each item she pulled out of the cylinder tube. Beyond any shadow of a doubt, she knew they had to be her grandma's mysterious research. Thinking it was only a few pages lining the container, she was shocked at the volume of material sitting on her bed five minutes later. The tube had been packed so tightly that she was able to produce five separate piles of documents.

Fingers tingling with excitement, she grabbed the pile of what appeared to be old newspaper prints. Sitting cross-legged on her bed, she began to closely scrutinize each item. Pictures, stories, advertisements, commentaries, and detailed accounts had been crammed into nine columns of 8.5-inch by 11-inch pages. Several documents from numerous sources had been photocopied from what appeared to be microfilm. So tiny was the font of the newspaper prints that Natasha, even with her best squinting, could not read most of the words. Retreating to the old wooden desk that sat near her bed, she managed to find two different magnifying glasses.

Magnifying glasses were a must-have tool for students interested in any form of botanical science. But she'd had hers since childhood. Curious by nature, she loved analyzing things. Tiny things were by far more interesting than big things, and the magnifying glasses allowed her to observe the minutest details about whatever it was that landed under her lens.

Every page in the stack was similarly organized with tiny fonts and multiple columns of information. The *Hawaiian Star*, September 11, 1895. The *Jeffersonian Republican*, December 5, 1850. The *Wichita Daily Eagle*, December 8, 1857. The dates themselves sent shrills of delight careening through her veins. What in the world was her grandmother researching from sources so old?

At first glance, the seemingly disorganized prints yielded nothing of interest. Too much information in too small a space made them difficult to read even with the magnifying glasses. Feeling like she was looking for a needle in a haystack, she decided to abandon the stack for something that might yield more immediate clarity.

The next stack was the newspapers' polar opposite. Recent articles from professional scientific journals left her profoundly confused, albeit captivated with interest. "Forensic Anthropology: What Bones Can Tell Us" was the title of an article by Dr. John K. Lundy. It spoke of different methods used to determine gender, age at death, or height of the deceased from their bones. Another article titled "Analysis of Fragments of Gigantic Bones" had been written by R. L. Rahim. *Grandma was a botanist; why was she researching articles on bones?* Natasha wondered. It all made no sense at all.

The next pile contained pages from the Bible that had been photocopied, with specific verses or chapters highlighted. Genesis 2:3, the entire chapter of Genesis 5, Exodus 13:19, Psalm 34:20, and Psalm 51:8 were just some of the highlighted sections. Two stacks out of three made it apparent that the topic of interest was bones, but she was clueless as to why.

Then there were the photographs. She had already analyzed the pile of pictures as she withdrew them from the tube. The only recognizable person among them was her grandmother, who seemed to be on some type of expedition. She had tossed the photos into a pile but now returned to them. Unable to draw any rational conclusion about why they had been included in the tube, she turned her attention to the pile of whatnots: a few handwritten notes and some letters, which left her with more questions than answers.

One specific detail she picked up from her brief investigation was her grandmother's intent to have Dr. Betsy involved. Her name had been scribbled beside several paragraphs in both Dr. Lundy's and Dr. Rahim's articles. She figured it was her grandmother's way of marking passages that Dr. Betsy could give her more insight about as a paleoanthropologist. At least, that was how she interpreted it. But if that was the case, why had her grandmother neglected to discuss them with Dr. Betsy? And if her grandmother really did intend for Dr. Betsy to then review the information, why had she hidden it away for no one to find?

Wrapping her arms around her drawn-up knees, Natasha rocked as she thought. There was no way on earth she could unravel whatever her grandmother had been investigating on her own, and even her grandmother recognized her own need for additional professional help.

Natasha needed and wanted Dr. Betsy's help. Not wanting to make a mistake and having no one else with whom she could share her concerns, she was left with one option.

—◁○▷—

As Natasha pressed the gas pedal, Baby Blue picked up speed and barreled down the road much faster than her usual pace. She'd been driving for four months, and her skill and confidence were increasing. Tense hands gripped the steering wheel as she weaved between cars. She was headed for the PIRD and felt she couldn't get there fast enough.

Not noticing Dr. Bety's somber face upon her arrival, she placed several folders on the office table. Fanning them out while blinking excitedly, she waved her hand like a magician presenting something he'd created out of thin air.

Then, when she turned to Dr. Betsy, her smile faded. "What's wrong?" Natasha asked as Dr. Betsy's quivering hand reached toward one of the folders before stopping short of taking it.

"I don't deserve to have them," Dr. Betsy confessed. "She trusted me even though I slighted her." Grabbing a tissue from the box on her desk, she sat down, took off her eyeglasses, and laid them on the table before dabbing her eyes.

"When I met your grandmother, I was a competitive, driven woman," she began. "My career was everything to me. It's really all I had in life, and I fought hard and long to obtain it." Her gaze riveted on the folders as she spoke. "My childhood was horrible. My adolescence was a nightmare, and I was a misguided and broken adult. But once I started to study and excel in science, it brought me stability and a sense of pride in my achievements." She sighed with a half-smile that didn't linger. "It became like a religion to me, and I was devoted to it like a monk. I never noticed how detached, egocentric, and hard I'd become or that I had no sense of worth despite all the accomplishments and accolades."

Dr. Betsy paused, and her eyes returned to look at Natasha. "Your grandmother seemed to look past all my fancy successes. Her comments and questions always left me flustered or scared to speak, for my answer would reveal my true self. Those eyes of hers were keen to identify a hurting spirit, so her kindness unraveled me.

"Before you let me read these," she said, patting the folders, "I think you should know the truth, at least from my perspective. And if you feel I shouldn't read your grandma's precious information, which I know she left for you, I'll understand."

Natasha offered up a silent prayer of thanks that her request, the sign she had asked of the Lord, had been fulfilled. Then, swiping the empty folders off the desk, she replaced them with the ones that held the real documents. Dr. Betsy had proved her sincerity, and she was satisfied that they were meant to work together on this mystery. First, she wanted to hear Dr. Betsy's version of their story.

Realizing she had been tested, Dr. Betsy broke into a wide grin. "Smart girl," she complimented. Then her demeanor changed from sadness to strength. Her face relaxed as she sat back in her chair. She knew the revelation of her wrongs and weaknesses wasn't going to deter Natasha from trusting her.

"Your grandmother, Dr. Cunningham, was my partner in building the PIRD. We came up with the idea together and worked on the floor plans, dioramas, and every aspect of the nature center. It was a project that was born and driven by our friendship and respect for one another. Of course, our professional backgrounds and extensive life experience enabled us to have the knowledge and skills we needed to get such a huge undertaking off the ground. Her name should have been on the front of the building and on the deed to this property. But I robbed her of that because, well, because I was self-centered, blind, and hurt. I mistook your grandmother's kindhearted attention for something it was not, and I let my feelings interfere with my personal and professional judgment. I had been rejected so much in my life and believed, like many people, that if someone does not agree with you, they've rejected you."

Dr. Betsy let herself chuckle before continuing. "Now, we disagreed on just about everything, yet we were able to form a friendship.

Somehow, I drew a line in my head on what was acceptable and unacceptable to agree on. How wrong I was, and it took your grandmother's death to show me my error.

"I'm sorry, Natasha. I'm sorry for what my fear and anger led me to do at that time. I severed the business relationship with your grandmother and figured, since I was providing most of the financial support anyway, I'd take on this project as my own. Instead of the plaque out front being a tribute to both of us, as you can see, it is a tribute only to one. After your grandma died, I tried to apologize to your mom and told her I'd redo the plaque, but she refused and said she was happy that her mom's name wasn't next to mine and that I dare not change a thing."

Dr. Betsy and her grandma had been business partners and close friends. Now she knew that her mom had told the truth, with a slightly different twist. As she looked at Dr. Betsy's face aching with remorse and contrition, her heart knew what she should do. Walking to Dr. Betsy's side, she stooped down and hugged her while telling her she was forgiven and thanking her for telling the truth.

Her confidence in sharing the contents of the tube was solid, and with gladness, she returned to her seat and handed Dr. Betsy one of the folders. It was the folder with the photographs. As Dr. Betsy quietly analyzed the pictures, Natasha briefly explained the contents of the other folders.

"These pictures were taken somewhere in India," Dr. Betsy declared, pointing to the high snow-capped mountains sitting in the background and buildings with traditional roof shingles. "And there's one person other than your grandmother that is seen in each of these photos." Her finger landed on a dark-skinned man who stood about three inches shorter than Dr. Cunningham. They appeared to be the same age, but while her grandmother gave a gracious smile, her companion remained stoic and stern-faced.

"When were these pictures taken, Natasha?" Dr. Betsy asked.

Natasha shrugged her shoulders. "I was going to ask if you knew when my grandma went on this trip."

Placing the pictures on the table, Dr. Betsy stared at the remaining folders. "These must have been from before I knew her because there was no time I recall that she traveled abroad. It appears she had to have been visiting the country for at least a week or two. Or . . .," she said as she pondered, "could she have gone after I dissolved the business?" Dr. Betsy looked at Natasha in hopes of an answer.

Natasha's eyes brightened. "A little before the accident, she did go away for about two or three weeks. I remember her telling Mom and me how much she needed a break and wanted some time alone. I thought Mom said she was visiting one of her college friends or something like that. I really can't remember. I just recall how sad she was when she left and how happy she was when she returned."

As those last few words came out of Natasha's mouth, a light went off in her mind. Sifting through the folders, she grabbed and opened one of them. Snatching its contents, she placed it before Dr. Betsy. "I couldn't figure out this letter, but now that we're talking, I think it's about these photos. That's where she went. She went away and did research and found out something—something amazing."

Unfolding the letter, Dr. Betsy began to read.

Dear Dr. Cunningham,

I write these words to you with a heavy heart. I don't know why, but a sense of foreboding has been haunting me. I hope it has nothing to do with us, though I feel it must. After such a glorious experience, we are left to walk in darkness. So, I wanted to make sure you knew how much I appreciate what you have given me.

Dr. Betsy paused and looked at Natasha. Natasha read her mind, for she had thought the same when she read it. "They're not love letters, Dr. Betsy. Go on," she encouraged her.

I have been a man of science. I studied physical things, the things that I could feel and smell and touch and see. That was all that was real to me—observing the seen and proving its existence with the things that are unseen. But my understanding started to change when I met you. You challenged the very ground upon which I had built my factual empire. The more I opened my mind to the possibilities you presented, the more clarity I seemed to gain. And peace, wonderful peace, began to flood my troubled soul. How stubborn and stupid I had been because I didn't want to give up my prestige and respect and honor of men. None of that matters anymore. There's only One I strive to please now.

Dr. Betsy stopped again. "These words are the words of my own soul," she whispered. "That man and I, we are alike. You read the rest," she told Natasha, pushing the letter toward her.

I never expected how sweet it would be when I gave my heart to Him, Despite the trials and frustrations, the accusations, and the betrayals from the ones I loved so dear, this experience has been my stabilizing force. I stand at the pinnacle of my life at the top of my Mt. Everest. There can be nothing higher. And It has ignited a passion so deep and a desire so strong, I feel not even death can stop me.

Natasha paused to let the solemn words she just read settle in.

"But these next words, Dr. Betsy, are what send shivers up my spine," she said, clearing her voice before slowing her reading pace.

That's why I tell you we must leave out breadcrumbs for the birds. We know not the time we will meet our Maker, especially now that dangerous men are on our trail. We must realize this mission is perhaps bigger than both of us, and we must blaze the trail for those who are destined to follow.

"I think everything we're finding was meant to be. They knew they might die, Dr. Betsy. Grandma knew."

"But is this Dr. Rahim person dead too?" Dr. Betsy asked.

"I don't know," Natasha replied before turning back to the letter.

Oftentimes, I am tempted to think it was a dream. But can two people dream the exact same thing? And then there's these pictures. I never thought they'd actually come out. The light was so bright that it should have flushed all things out of sight. They too are a miracle, and I wanted you to have a copy of them as a reminder that what we felt and saw was real.

Thank you, Dr. Cunningham, for telling me to search for the invisible, for the visible can only be rightly understood by the things which are not seen. I am so honored to have shared it with you. It pains me to know I'll never see you again. We were destined to meet only once in this visible realm, but in the next, we'll be friends forever.

Dr. Rahim

Natasha sank back into her chair. Those words were echoes of her grandmother's voice to her.

"Look around you, Natasha," she'd say while out on a trail in the middle of some forest. "What don't you see?" It was a question that annoyed her as a child. She was enchanted by the things she could hear, see, smell, and touch. That was life. That was discovery to her—the slug making its way over the treacherous trail path or the chipmunk scampering up the tree while chasing another. The sight and sound of a bird warbling its song, and the trees bending in the breeze. Those were the things that fueled her spirit of exploration.

But her grandma insisted otherwise. "It's what you don't see that is the most important. Look for the invisible." She'd grab a handful of soil and then let the granules gradually tumble out of her hand like a waterfall. "It's what makes the visible possible." It had never made much sense to her, and she was still stumped to their exact meaning, but she felt her time of understanding was fast approaching.

Standing up, Dr. Betsy began pacing about her office with an expression of pure joy on her face.

"I'm speechless, Natasha. That letter confirms everything for me. We're on the right track. You were destined to find this." Pointing to the table, she asked Natasha which folder they should explore next.

But Natasha could only think of showing her the one thing she had kept a secret for a very long time. Placing the map she had found in the Bible onto the table, she confessed that it was the reason she had gone to Kennington Park that evening in April and that she had indeed found something there.

Dr. Betsy's face turned ghostly white as the blood drained from it. "Your grandmother drew a map to something hidden in Kennington Park?"

After the initial shock wore off, she explained how Dr. Cunningham had told her about a gentleman she met at one of the parks. At the time, Dr. Cunningham didn't reveal which park it was but told her they had met on one of the trails.

"I clearly remember how enthusiastic she seemed about it. She was oddly exuberant and began frequenting the park more often. I hadn't taken note of her interest or the fact that she stopped sharing about her fieldwork. I was heavily involved with getting the financing for the PIRD and contacting other nature centers and museums to see if I could obtain any samples or displays, they no longer needed or wanted.

"It was your grandmother's job to find samples from our local environment, so her excitement seemed on par with the work we were doing. She mentioned this scientist guy several times. Then, all of a sudden, she stopped talking about him or anything else about the park. Again, I noticed nothing unusual until I tried to bring it up. I asked her for his name, and she seemed evasive and uncomfortable. I figured if he knew so much about whatever park she was visiting, we should bring him on board to see how much he could contribute to our knowledge and collection. Troubled by her response, I pushed her a little more and she let me know his name was Josh. A few weeks after that, she divulged that the gentleman had passed away and the park where they met was Kennington."

Hastening to a cabinet in her office, Dr. Betsy pulled out a roll of maps. "These maps are of Kennington Park," she said. "And I've studied them several times over without a single clue of what your grandma might have found. These maps contain every geological feature of that park, from ridges to ponds to where specific types of trees are growing."

Her finger deftly moved across the surface of one of the maps she had laid flat on the table. "According to your grandmother's map, that cave you entered should be right about here." Her finger pounded on the spot. "Yet this map does not indicate that there's any such geological feature at that location."

"Oh, but there is, Dr. Betsy," Natasha said, "and I've been inside it! And I think it's time, we both go back there."

CHAPTER 22

John:
Threatening Proposition

It had been a difficult summer. His father had stuck to his promise not to devote a single penny to his college expenses. That decision forced John to move out of his home and declare himself independent. Being on his own would allow him to qualify for financial aid, though it would not cover all his expenses. He loathed the idea of incurring a mountain of debt but knew it was the only path that could guarantee him a brighter future.

Riley tried to act brave when he told her he'd be leaving, and she held back her tears until moving day. "It's going to be okay," he tried comforting her as she clung to him like a baby chimp clinging to its mother.

"I don't want to stay here alone with him. Please take me with you, John," she had pleaded. "I don't want to be in this house anymore. It's not a home. It's just a box where I happen to sleep. He doesn't even love me, and if you're not here, he might start treating me like he treated Mom."

215

But what choice did he have? He couldn't afford to take care of his little sister when he could barely take care of himself. If he never finished college, he'd never be able to take care of her well. His fears had proven to be correct; he was already behind on rent after only two months living on his own. And when he arrived at his studio apartment that evening, a note had been slipped under the door. "Unit #45, your rent is fifteen days past due," it read. He'd have to wait to pay it until his next paycheck in a week, but if he did, it would mean he'd have to go without food for a week. He was in a dilemma. Ten days later, another note had been slapped onto his front door.

Peering at the tattered "Rental Office" sign, he pushed open the wooden door with paint and varnish that had long been stripped away. It was shabby inside. The floor, filthy with stains embedded into the worn-down carpet fibers from years of traffic in and out of the office, creaked with every footstep he took. The dark curtains covering the windows had probably never been washed, and the rickety old desk that sat in the room was covered with a frenzy of papers of all shapes and sizes and littered with several empty coffee cups. He pushed his finger across his nose. The room smelled like a combination of old socks and stinky armpits.

The one-bedroom apartment and studio complex was small, with only twelve to fifteen one-story units that sat at the edge of the city in a run-down neighborhood. It wasn't listed on any apartment listings. He'd found it when driving by to investigate another potential residence. The dilapidated buildings looked barely livable, but he'd been rejected time and again and had come to the end of his options.

"Hello, son," Mr. Harley greeted with a toothless grin. He was an elderly man, probably in his seventies, and he was the owner, the handyman, the janitor, and the receptionist. He was kindhearted, and his friendliness was probably the only thing keeping his tenants from reporting the subpar living conditions.

"I've got something for you," John said, handing him a check.

"Well, it's about time you turned this in, son. I was about to slip another friendly reminder under your door even tho' I could evict ya. But I hate kickin' someone out to the streets, and I like ya, son. I can tell you're a good kid, much like my boy." Tears welled up in the old man's eyes as he sniffled. "My Johnny was a good lad."

John knew the story well but didn't stop Mr. Harley from telling it again. Nor did he stop to tell him that his check wasn't for the entire amount due.

"Ya know, the day he died, he told me how much he loved me. He was a tender boy who was never afraid to say his feelin's. Just like me, ya know." Mr. Harley pulled a dingy, torn hanky from his trousers.

John shuddered at the sight, knowing it had probably never seen soap and water in its long life.

Mr. Harley wiped his face and blew hard. "But now I don't mind anyone seein' my tears. These are for my boy. God bless his soul, and cursed be the men that took him from me." He stuffed the rag back into his trousers and reached out his hand.

John winced as he thought about the volume of microbes that had likely made Mr. Harley's hanky and hands their permanent residence. *That's what soap and water are for,* he told himself as he made his way out the door.

"You're a good kid," Mr. Harley yelled as he walked away.

◄○►

A woman in high heels and a pantsuit strutted up to the instructor's desk. She placed her briefcase on the desk and rested her coffee cup beside it. Without a single word to the class, she turned on the computer screen, its blue light reflecting off her glasses. Moments later, the projector screen slowly descended as her introductory PowerPoint slide filled the screen. Then, unfrazzled by her lateness, she smugly sipped coffee, seemingly oblivious to the students anxiously waiting for her to begin. The quiet whispers had risen to loud banter before she set her empty mug back on the desk and arose. "Okay, class, let's get started."

John was used to the ritual, but it annoyed him just the same, especially since she took the liberty to continue the lecture at least five minutes past the time the class was supposed to end. He hated leaving early but swore one day he'd have the courage to walk out at exactly the time the class should end. That day had yet to arrive, and like all the other students in the room, he sheepishly waited for the instructor to finish before making a beeline toward the exit sign.

And that was when he saw her. She was hastening down the crowded hallway, weaving her way around students walking slower than her. She halted near the entrance of the elevators, folded her arms, and looked about as she waited. Looking at the floor, he hoped the students standing between them would shield him. When he looked up, she had returned to peering at the numbers lighting up above the elevator door. He watched her until she stepped inside. Then he made a mad dash for the stairwell door.

His descent was quick and almost effortless, his heart rate only slightly heightened. Six-mile runs three times a week had kept him fit as an athlete. As he exited the cool stairwell corridor, the elevator doors opened, and out rushed the students with Natasha among them. She was heading outside. Knowing his opportunity had arrived only made him halt with apprehension. Would he really succumb to doing something that defied every moral bone in his body? Moments later, a sky-blue Mirage pulled out of the parking lot with his Toyota Camry in close pursuit.

John pressed his foot harder on the gas pedal. *Natasha's skill and confidence in driving have improved,* he thought as he slowed to allow several cars to maneuver between them. He was following her, turning when she turned, and speeding up or slowing down as if trying to choreograph her every move. But his heart wasn't in it. Angry with himself, he began to reflect on that awful conversation with George that had pushed him into this unenviable position.

⊷◦⊶

"I have a proposition for you," George had said while motioning John to sit one day toward the end of his shift.

John's stomach flip-flopped at George's words. Unless this proposition was directly related to his clerical work, he felt any "proposition" George made would not be good. Those Matrix men had visited George several times over the summer, and he was convinced George was involved in something illegal. The only reason his interest was piqued was that, for some reason, George was interested in Dr. Betsy and her work at the PIRD.

"You know how I was telling you about Dr. Betsy and Dr. Cunningham a while back?" George said after John had settled in his office chair.

Nodding his head slowly, John braced himself as his hands began to stick to the armrest he was gripping.

"I need to tell you the whole truth." George pulled his chair from around the desk and sat directly in front of John.

"Look, man. I've told you a thousand times already. I don't know anything about Dr. Betsy, and I don't need to hear anything about something that has nothing to do with me."

"Oh! But it does have something to do with you," George had replied. He scooted closer and smiled. "I was thinking about you and your situation the other day, and I think I can help."

John didn't like the smooth tone George was using. It belied something insidious. He regretted telling George about his unfortunate demise with his family and school. The less George knew about him, the safer he felt, but the information had slipped out accidentally. In a moment of utter despair, he had related his desperate circumstance in the hopes that George would offer him more hours. But George had only offered sympathy and told him things were bound to get better.

"I need some additional help and think you might be the man for the job. What do you think?" George crossed his arms and looked at John as if he had offered a golden apple on a platter.

"What would I be doing?" John asked. He knew better than to accept any offer George made without prying into the details.

George crossed his legs and tapped his fingers as he thought for a few seconds. "I need you to do some detective work for me. Nothing serious," he reassured John. "Just need you to ask for your job back at the PIRD. Think you can do that?" Without waiting for a response, he continued. "Dr. Betsy is quite fond of you, and I believe she'd be extremely pleased to have you back. I heard through the grapevine," he relayed, winking, "that she's looking for another intern. You'd be perfect."

John clenched his jaw and looked straight at George. "I thought you were going to offer me some more hours here. If this is your way of firing me, it's not funny." Standing to his feet, he turned to leave.

"Whoa!" George sang. "Sit back down and hear me out," he commanded before beginning to laugh. "I'm not firing you." His eyes pranced like ponies, and he appeared to be bemused at John's anger. "Do you seriously believe I'd do it that way? I'm not that type of guy. I'd just come out with it."

Then, straightening his face, he gave John a look of compassion. "All I'm doing is looking out for you. Working here and there would increase your hours. And that means more money for you, your schooling, and that rent fiasco you're in."

Shifting nervously in his chair, John knew there was no way he was going to allow George to swindle him into doing anything for him.

"Sorry, man, I may be in a predicament, but there's no way I'm going back to intern there when I voluntarily left. No," he corrected himself. "I voluntarily declined to accept the summer position offered me even though Dr. Betsy went out of her way to try to get me to stay." Pointing at George, he continued. "You were the one who insisted it was better I work with you than her, and now, when it's convenient for you, you want me to backpedal and plead for a job?"

George stared at the wall behind John, looking rather annoyed as he spoke. "You're in a pickle, John, and so is your family." He stopped to think about his words. "You do realize that your sweet Aunt Kristen and your Uncle Joseph owe me money." He tilted his head and looked at John as if he had an ace card in his hand. "I don't want to make things difficult for you, but I could make their lives miserable at this point. And if they're miserable, I think you'll be pretty miserable too."

John's eyes widened in disbelief. He couldn't believe the words he was hearing. Was George actually threatening him?

"Look, man, I know you need some money, and I'm trying to help you out. All I'm asking is for you to do me a small favor that won't even take much effort. Getting your job back at the PIRD is the easy way, but if you insist on not going back, here's what I'd like you to do."

Matthias: Rasmus II

We watched a herd of ivory elephants meander across a hill, their golden tusks shimmering in the sunlight. They trumpeted and rumbled loudly as they approached, with trunks raised high in the air. Bending their trunks low to the ground, they greeted Rasmus and playfully flopped their ears. Then, with heads slightly bowed, they welcomed me.

"They are just like our elephants back home," I laughed as one nuzzled the back of my neck.

"Indeed they are," Rasmus stated. "For these are the parents of those who roam your world." The herd slowly made their way up another grassy hill and stepped gingerly through the peach rose bushes toward the forest in the distance.

Seraphina brought us back to Lake Liraz. It had been seven days since I last met Rasmus, and I yearned for him to continue his story. I was also anxious to see the manta rays. I kept my eyes on the lake, hoping the waters would ripple with life.

Rasmus and I settled on the vibrating peach and silver flowers that flanked the water's edge. I tucked in my wings, rolled onto my back with my hands behind my head, and peered up into the crimson skies as I listened. Rasmus left his wings outstretched to flutter in the breeze as he spoke.

"Aziel and I came into existence at the same time, from the hands of the Creator. We grew in power and strength together, though we had our differences. We were designated different duties from the beginning. We were both messengers but to different realms and were Doyens of different things. He was a Doyen of water and I of plant and animal life. We discovered the intricacies of our world together, and we traveled to universes near and far," Rasmus chuckled softly.

"We had such a glorious time. I remember the day he brought me here, boasting of a discovery beyond my imagination." Rasmus looked out over the lake, and I could tell his mind was traveling back in time to those moments. "That day is so clear in my mind," he whispered.

"I remember telling Aziel how gorgeous this lake was, but I thought it was no more spectacular than all the lakes of Nanea. They all had a unique beauty about them. But Aziel insisted this lake was more impressive than the rest. Naturally, I asked him to prove it." Rasmus rubbed his hands together. "That's when Aziel jumped into the lake. I quickly followed him as he descended to the depths, with manta rays all around us. And that's when it happened." Rasmus paused as he shook his head and laughed.

"What happened?" I questioned as I turned my gaze from the skies to look at Rasmus.

"He disappeared."

"But how? I thought you were right behind him."

"I thought I was too. But in an instant, he was gone, and so were some of the manta rays. I was clueless. I swam around in complete and utter confusion, trying to figure out the illusion. But it was no illusion. They were gone."

"But where?" I asked anxiously as I lifted myself onto my elbows.

"While I was swimming around in circles, I felt a tap on my shoulder. It was Aziel. Wow! If you could have seen the glee on his face. Priceless. He then shot up out of the water, laughing hysterically. I was the Doyen of this region. I thought I knew the area like the back of my hand. I couldn't believe he had discovered something I knew nothing of. And he was so delighted with himself and his discovery."

"What was it?" I looked intently at Rasmus as his smile broadened. I threw myself onto the ground and grabbed my head. "Don't do this to me," I begged, but Rasmus's face said it all as his silver eyes glistened. He was going to make me wait. I pouted and put on my best pleading face, but it was no use.

"It was such a wonderful day," Rasmus continued as his smile began to fade. "He was my best friend for thousands of years before we were separated." The color in Rasmus's eyes dulled. "He who was called 'Abner' arrived that evening. His visit was completely unexpected, but he who bathed in the light of the Creator's glory and walked with Him as a friend, a brother, and a ruler had come to bless us with his presence. His authority was like the authority of the Creator Himself, for he always came to express the Creator's will.

"Every time we saw him, he had changed and grown in some remarkable way. This time was no exception. When Aziel and I finally managed to find our way through the masses of heavenly beings gathered on Mount Mahavesin, we were mesmerized by his appearance. His being and his beauty were unequaled. The garment of light enshrouding him emitted such glorious brilliance that we at first had to cover ourselves with our wings until we could endure its power and magnificence. The colors that emanated from his garments were taking on the hues of colors that emanated from the throne of the Creator. Those colors were from a spectrum we could not reflect, nor were those colors seen anywhere else in the universes of light.

"After the greetings died down, Abner told us he had come with a sacred message. Unlike other times, he never said the message was from the Creator. Instead, he started to speak about how the Creator made us with power, strength, and wisdom. He told us how special we were to the unfallen worlds as messengers, ambassadors, and beings of light. Our hearts swelled with holy pride as we reflected on his words. But this was just the beginning of his uplifting us and telling us how intrinsically special and unique we were.

"He returned several times to continue his orations. We were thrilled with his constant appearances. He had never spoken to us so consistently, but his sermons seemed to be taking a strange tone. Initially, we all just passed it off as a lack of knowledge and experience on our part. We thought we were being exposed to truths that had never been presented to us before, and we spent countless enthusiastic hours discussing and debating the main points of his orations. We figured it would take time for us to understand the depth of truth he was presenting. But over time, instead of getting more clarity, his sermons seemed to become more enshrouded in mystery.

"As time went on, I became more concerned. It became apparent that our light bearer was making suggestions that were foreign to us and seemed to conflict with the principles the Creator had established. He seemed to be insinuating injustice and unfairness built into the laws the Creator had put into place. However, it was so imperceptible and mixed with the beautiful gems of truths we knew were right, good, and holy that most of us did not perceive a need to be troubled. We thought we were fine until our discussions morphed into outright disagreements."

Rasmus fluffed his wings and stood up, and I followed his lead. He began to walk around the lake. "I remember how the conversations between Aziel and me became more intense and lengthier. He would relate a point Abner made, and I would counter or challenge it. I couldn't wrap my head around what was happening. Aziel and I never saw all things the same. We had had intense discussions about our personal opinions and viewpoints before, but our disagreements never drove us apart or made us feel like we needed to defend ourselves. Instead, they inspired us to search deeper and harder to find the truth. They encouraged us to open our eyes and look outside of our current situations and experiences to see life from a different perspective. They broadened our knowledge and caused us to stretch outside of our sphere. But now both Aziel and I felt drained and frustrated after our discussions.

"We both started spending more time apart discussing the points of the controversy with those who saw things in the light we did. I noticed that Abner seemed to be singling out individual angels and taking them into special counsel. Aziel was among them, and this distanced us even more. I was torn, confused, and, for the first time in my existence, fearful and anxious. I had a sense of impending doom. It was a feeling I had never felt before. I asked to meet with the Creator. I needed clarity and guidance, and I believe that meeting made the difference for me."

Rasmus looked at me and placed his hands behind his back as he veered closer to the water's edge. The calm waters lapped around our feet as they sank into the silky, bejeweled sand.

"I left the meeting with the Creator confident that Abner was mistaken in his assertions, and I was happy the issues would be addressed by the Creator Himself. A meeting was called with the heavenly universe, and the Creator artfully and lovingly dispensed the insinuations made by His light bearer. I felt relieved and believed our lives would soon return to our normal state of unity, peace, and love.

But I was gravely mistaken. I had underestimated Abner's influence and the impact of his delusive arguments.

"He feigned allegiance to the Creator and His laws while at the same time undermining them. This allowed him to mask his real intent under a cloak of mysticism, and I knew that I needed to awaken Aziel to his schemes. I asked him to meet me here at the lake." Rasmus's voice trembled as he continued. "I spoke my mind with no reservations, but Aziel had already made his decision. He would fully align himself with Abner. I desperately pleaded with him, outlining point after point as to why he needed to reconsider his position. It just didn't make sense to me. How could they oppose and war against the One Who made them? How could they deny that we had lived an existence of joy and bliss? How could they stand behind concepts they did not wholly understand and consequences they did not know?

"We both knew that if we stood our ground, we would be on two different sides of the controversy, but I could not convince him, and he could not convince me. The separation was inevitable." Rasmus stopped walking and looked down at the ground. "It was here on these very flowers. They absorbed our tears as we embraced. I whispered in his ears my final plea: 'Meet with the Creator. Tell Him all that is on your heart.'"

Rasmus looked up at me as a single tear made its way down his cheek and fell to the ground, landing on a flower that swayed as the teardrop fell upon its petals. He paused and looked at the water. "It's almost time," he whispered. The lake had begun to erupt into a frenzy of bubbles, some of which escaped the surface and floated into the air. "They are about to begin."

His face glowed with anticipation as he looked at me. I could see their gigantic forms swimming about in the waters, and then one exploded out of the water with such force I jumped back. It shot into the sky, twirling as it went, and when it reached a height high into the heavens, it began its descent. Its body was so streamlined that it appeared to disappear from view for a moment. And then manta ray after manta ray escaped the waters. Some ascended alone, others in pairs, and still others in groups of three or four. They ascended to different heights and performed aerial dances that would have entertained me the entire day. I flapped my wings and clapped my hands at the sight of such an impeccable display of unison and choreography.

"I told you you'd be in for a pleasant surprise," Rasmus said as the manta rays began to retreat into the water, one after the other.

I turned my attention back to Rasmus. "So, go on. What happened next?"

But in the distance, the sound of trumpets and chimes could be heard. "Is it worship time already?" Rasmus said, looking at me as the chimes started to silence. Had the day gone by so quickly?

"No, we can't stop now," I pleaded. "You were just getting started."

"We must. But don't worry. I'll pick up just where I left off." Rasmus lifted his hands to his mouth and made a bellowing sound. Seraphina appeared with a flock of leviathans.

"When can we meet again?" I asked sadly.

"I have some visitors from the Norgala universe who have come to learn how to master the art of plant manipulation. I will let you know when I'm free to meet again." Rasmus untucked his wings, but instead of mounting Seraphina, he took to the skies, and we flew alongside the dragon and the leviathans back to his home.

John: Enlightening Observations

If anyone asked John to describe Natasha, he would have quickly responded with what he thought would be an intuitive and accurate assessment.

Stupid but smart. Stupid because she believed in fairytale stories of the Bible and denied the very foundation of scientific fact about the existence of humanity and the Earth. Smart because she seemed to understand enough about the things she didn't believe to poke holes in theories and ask intelligent questions that occasionally stumped even their teachers.

Lazy but studious. At her weight, she had to be at least a little lazy. Exercise wasn't an easy task, but it also wasn't the hardest task, and he managed to fit it in regardless of his schedule. She just needed to try a little harder, like most people who were overweight or fat. Yet no one as smart as she could be entirely lazy unless they were gifted with an Albert Einstein mind, and he didn't believe she was. She had to study and work hard, perhaps even harder than he to succeed. There was no doubt she was studious.

Moralist. And not in any good type or way. Anyone who believed in God was a moralist in his opinion. Always judging others according to their own standards of right and wrong. He never heard her say it directly, but her whole demeanor sometimes made him feel somewhat less than her.

Annoying. How she got under his skin, like an itch he just couldn't seem to scratch. Every teacher who smiled with admiration when they saw her. All the compliments they poured upon her. Every award she received. She was nothing short of annoying.

But the more he "observed" her, the more his distorted view began to change. He distinctly remembered a particular Wednesday when he followed her to one of the local grocery stores. When she finally reappeared, she was pushing a cart full of groceries. It was nothing out of the ordinary, and he casually watched her until she passed her own car. That was when he sat up and stared through his rearview mirror.

Natasha had stopped at a black Corolla. He was confused until he noticed an elderly lady with a cane slowly heading toward the car. Natasha placed the woman's groceries in the trunk and gave the woman an endearing hug before returning to her car. The gratitude of the senior citizen could be seen as she waved and mouthed "thank you" several times. He couldn't help but think back to when his mom had also helped someone at the grocery store by graciously carrying the elderly woman's groceries to her car. And she had reminded him to always be thoughtful and kind. "It will come back to you, John," she'd told him.

And that act of kindness at the grocery store was not an exception for Natasha; it was the rule. She volunteered at a homeless shelter, tutored other students, participated in charity events, and often returned to her mom's house, where she'd take out the garbage and mow the lawn.

Despite Kevin's angry outbursts, John had always managed to forget to take out the garbage. Every week the same pattern continued.

Wednesday mornings, Kevin would start yelling as he left the house. Riley would rush to wake him up. He'd end up dragging the garbage cans out, barefoot and shirtless and in his pajama pants, as the garbage truck rumbled toward their house.

And the dishes. He always scoffed at the thought of washing and cleaning up the kitchen too. That was Riley's job, especially since he had to drive her everywhere. On days she forgot or just refused to wash them, they'd pile up across the counters like cars waiting for a car wash.

As he watched Natasha give of herself time and again, he began to realize that she had even been kind to him. He'd taken no real note of it before, but she had given him a sympathy card after his mom died. She'd been the only kid in school who seemed to acknowledge his loss. Despite their constant competitive bickering whenever they worked together, she rushed to his side when he accidentally stumbled to the ground one day. Embarrassed, he had insisted he was fine, but she remembered to ask how he was doing the following day. She had also given him a graduation card, wishing him the best. He knew he got on her nerves, but somehow she managed to look past her annoyance to show kindness anyway.

He, on the other hand, hadn't even recognized opportunities to reciprocate her thoughtful acts. Countless times, he had seen her walking toward or standing at the bus stop, but only after Dr. Betsy had given her a car did he realize she had been taking the bus to the PIRD. Maybe that was why she hadn't come to the conference that Saturday; with no ride, she'd have to take the bus with crutches. And the graduation card she gave him he had thrown out before he even read what was inside.

He'd been even worse with family. He ignored his aunties' texts, never remembered to acknowledge anyone's birthday, and managed to push away his sister like an unwanted rag doll. Blinded by his pain, he consistently ignored Riley's needs, watching her flounder through her grief like a fish out of water. He'd bury his guilt by convincing himself that he couldn't help her and likely made things even worse. He denied her the simple acts of a comforting hug because he knew it would unleash his own unresolved emotions.

The unwanted job of following Natasha had inadvertently caused her life to become a mirror that reflected his own. Never in his wildest imagination would he have thought she could influence his perceptions. Despite the enlightenment and flashes of self-awareness, he shut down the voices urging him to take action.

And something else was bothering him, something much worse than the pull to be kind. Imperceptible though it was, he knew it was there. Those thoughts he quickly dismantled as if unarming a ticking time bomb. For it was as ridiculous as it was impossible. She wasn't his type. Wrong race, wrong body, wrong hair, wrong everything. She now seemed to have a boyfriend of her own, which brought him a sense of relief. They looked like the perfect couple, and if all went well, she'd be consumed in a romance that would ensure his worst fear would never be realized.

―◈―

His car sat under a large white alder tree standing in the farthest corner of the parking lot. It was his favorite spot to park. Not only did the tree's foliage provide a wonderful canopy of shade, shielding him from the searing sun, but it also provided an inconspicuous spot from which he could observe their coming in and going out. "Observing" was the word he used to describe George's second option. Spying was the more precise term, but he hated the thought of it. It made him sound corrupt, so he stuck with "observing."

Today, he was nervously trying to rally his confidence to finally do what George had first suggested, as the second option was a clear dead end that had yielded no substantial results. John berated himself for procrastinating asking Dr. Betsy to take him back. It had made much more sense at the beginning of the semester than it did now. But with George's constant pushing and threatening, he had to do something that would produce results. If Dr. Betsy accepted him back, it would make it much easier for him to snoop around.

Leaving his car, he reluctantly made his way into the PIRD. "Hey, stranger, it's been a long while since I've seen you. I hear you got a nice job at the Natural History Museum and then forgot all about us," Suzie said in a friendly tone.

John smiled and shook his head. "No, it's not like that. I do miss it here. I just wanted to walk around a bit to see the new displays and check out the projects the new interns have been working on. Do you mind?" he asked, pointing to the back-office door. He didn't want to tell her that he wanted to meet with Dr. Betsy because Suzie would likely make him wait in the lobby if she was in a meeting.

"Of course not. All our old interns are always welcome," she replied before turning to address another customer.

He quickly headed straight for Dr. Betsy's office. The door was closed, but he could hear Natasha and Dr. Betsy animatedly talking inside. Instead of knocking, he decided to walk around the grounds while waiting for them to finish. An hour later and still waiting, he found he was sweating and extremely frustrated. As his hands reached to turn on the car's ignition so he could leave, he saw Natasha exit the building and head toward her car. Assuming she was leaving for the day, he quickly rolled up his windows and got out to find Dr. Betsy.

John waved to Suzie, who looked surprised that he was still there. "I thought you left," she said.

"I wanted to speak with Dr. Betsy but realized she was already in a meeting, so I waited outside," John replied.

"You should have told me you wanted to see Dr. Betsy. Once she and Natasha get together, they talk for hours. I would have told you to make an appointment for another day."

John nodded and continued to the back toward Dr. Betsy's office.

"So, what brings you here, John?" Dr. Betsy asked while offering him a seat.

The conversation was awkward and short. He got straight to the point. After some complimentary words, he asked about her program and whether he could be considered for the internship assistant again.

"Are things not going well working with George at the Natural History Museum?" she asked.

"Oh, no, ma'am!" he quickly replied. "I still work with George; I just really enjoyed working here too."

Dr. Betsy raised her eyebrows and took off her glasses. "Really?" she replied, sitting back in her chair. "You want to work for both me and him at the same time? I just want to be clear."

John nodded. "I'm on my own now and could use the money."

"I see," said Dr. Betsy. "Let me think about this for a minute."

Her chair rocked back and forth as she pensively peered at her desk and rubbed her chin.

He knew only seconds had passed, though it felt like several minutes before she spoke.

Her chair stopped rocking as she nestled her chin into her folded hands. "I'm going to give you a counteroffer, John. We'll take you back if you stop working with George. Think about it and let me know what you decide," she said as she picked up her purse and walked to the door.

Leaving George was not an option, at least not yet. John was more desperate than ever for the money. Every passing week brought him closer to being evicted from both his apartment and college. To make matters worse, George was exasperated with the amount of time it was taking him to get any useful information. He had even threatened to find someone else to do his dirty work. Spying on Natasha already felt like a betrayal of trust, but the idea of someone else spying on her or Dr. Betsy was way worse.

What if that person was as wicked as George? To what extent would they go to get the information they wanted? What if Natasha or Dr. Betsy got hurt? At least he wouldn't be more intrusive than needed and would never think of hurting them. He'd give George the least amount of information he could find, and as a silver lining, he'd find out what was pulling Dr. Betsy and Natasha together.

Failed again, he told himself as he exited the office and moseyed to the bathroom. Upon exiting the PIRD front doors, he picked up his gait substantially. Dr. Betsy had changed her clothes into athletic wear and hiking boots. John watched her slip into Natasha's waiting car before it quickly drove away.

He began to follow them, and when Natasha's car turned off the highway, his heart skipped a beat. He knew where they were heading: Kennington Park.

And what'll I do when they arrive? Take pictures of them?

No, he reasoned. *That would be too invasive of their privacy.*

Follow them down the trail or wherever they're heading? Nope. Too obvious, and at some point, they'll turn around and perhaps we'll bump into each other.

His car slowed as they neared the entrance. He pulled onto the graveled embankment near the park's wooden sign and stopped the car. He watched them retreat down the wooded road into the park.

Turning around, he started to search his disheveled car. He needed a disguise in case they were still in view. Gym clothes, dirty socks, bike helmets, jackets, and discarded fast food bags had been abandoned in the back seat. Somewhere back there had to be one of his hats. He couldn't find one, so he grabbed a bike helmet, smashed it onto his head, and pulled on his sunglasses before making a U-turn into the park's entrance.

The sound of the gravel crunching under his tires on the dirt road was drowned by the loud rattle of his engine. The noise had started a few weeks ago, but with no money for even a simple repair, he ignored the car's problems. As he slowly crept toward the parking lot, he hoped he had waited long enough for them to be about their business.

His heart pounded with anticipation as Natasha's car came into view. Pulling up his sunglasses, he searched the park. A middle-aged couple was walking their dog on the farther side of the lake. An old man sat on a bench along the water's edge with a fishing hook dangling in the water. A mom watched her three children scamper about in the children's park area, but Natasha and Dr. Betsy were nowhere to be seen.

CHAPTER 25

Natasha: Buried Mystery

Only a few days passed before TJ texted Natasha asking how she was holding up with the departure of her friend. She had thought about him more than once but figured he probably forgot about her, so the text was a pleasant surprise. She had thought about him more than once but figured he probably forgot about her, so the text was a pleasant surprise. They started to text back and forth every few days and then decided to meet again.

The the last place she thought she'd meet up with someone was at church, but that was exactly where TJ asked to meet with her. They were of the same faith, so there would be no conflict as far as that was concerned, and even though church had been clearly on the back burner of her life, TJ's influence started softening her heart toward her Maker. She told him about her struggle with her faith once her grandmother had passed. She believed that if God truly cared about her, He would never have allowed such a thing. Her grandmother was more of a mother to her than her own mom, and her death left her feeling abandoned and alone.

TJ had also suffered loss in his life. Several of his relatives, including his brother, had passed away, but his attitude about God and how he dealt with his grief was very different from hers. Instead of running away from God, he decided to run to Him. Under the shadow of His eternal Father's almighty wings, he had found a healing peace and acceptance. Despite the disappointment of loss, he believed God was still with him and working miracles in his life.

They met several times at church and always found themselves standing in the parking lot after each service, engrossed in conversation next to their cars. Each talk always began with questions about the sermon but morphed into much more complicated topics. Their cars were usually the last to leave the parking lot, and her heart always buzzed with joy when they departed.

She was cautiously optimistic about their relationship. He was definitely the type of person she could see herself becoming more serious with, but she was desperately trying to keep her feelings at a friendship level with no further expectations. TJ was a tall and handsome man whose interest in her belied her perception of who he'd be interested in. The college was chock full of beautiful women from every race, and he could have his pick with any of them. Any time she saw him on campus, some pretty girl would wave at him, but he didn't seem to be interested or care about all the attention from the ladies. To her delight, he seemed to be drawn to her, and when he saw her, his face would radiate a smile that read that he was happy to see her again.

After several weeks of talking and meeting with TJ, Natasha's confidence and apparent outward glow were becoming noticeable.

"Hey, what's going on with you?" Natasha's roommate, Jessica, asked one morning as the two of them got ready for the day.

"Nothing," Natasha replied. "Why?" she asked. She walked to the closet and started to swipe hangers across the bar as shirts, pants, dresses, and skirts flew by.

"You've been humming a lot. And you're smiling all the time now. And the most telling of all, you haven't even said anything about my mess."

Natasha pulled an above-the-knee flowered dress and a jean jacket from her closet. "I'm just feeling better about my classes and all," she said casually.

"Liar," Jessica declared as she sat twisting her long, thick black hair. "And you're going to wear that today? You're a liar. You like someone."

"Get out of here. We've only been in school for a couple of weeks. I don't fall like that," Natasha said, denying the romantic accusation.

"I know love when I see it. And you are acting like you're in love." Jessica rolled her neck and pointed at Natasha.

"Don't be ridiculous, Jessica. Look at me. I'm overweight and not very attractive."

"Hey, girl, don't be shaming on yourself. Beauty is in the eye of the beholder. And you're not fat; you just have curves. I know quite a few guys who love them some curvy girls."

Jessica hopped up and down as she pulled her skinny jeans onto her slender frame. "And not attractive? You must not have looked in the mirror for a long time. Girl, you're gorgeous! You just need to work it a little."

She threw on a shirt and fixed her hair again. "Fix your hair up and put on a little makeup. A few jewels to sparkle and . . . well, I need to take you shopping for a whole new wardrobe. I can have you rocking in no time," she said, pursing her lips together.

Natasha laughed. This was the most she and Jessica had ever talked, and it was over a guy. "Okay, so I might like someone, but it's nothing, really. And I wouldn't want to go changing myself up just for him not to be interested in me anyway. I don't know what he wants yet, but I'm pretty sure it's just to be friends and nothing romantic."

"Well, I'm here for you," Jessica insisted as she grabbed her book bag and headed for the door. "Just let me know when you're ready, and I'll get you looking your best."

Natasha had to laugh at her roommate's words. She hadn't noticed how much happier she appeared, but there was no doubt when even Dr. Betsy mentioned something that evening when she met her at the PIRD.

"By the way, you look nice today," Dr. Betsy said when she opened her office door. "I love that dress on you."

"Thank you," Natasha smiled. "I don't wear dresses very often, but I found this one at the back of my closet. Grandma got it for me, but I've never worn it." Natasha curtsied and grinned before walking over to the table where Dr. Betsy had laid out Kennington Park's map. pointing to her bag. "But I'm going to change into some hiking clothes before we get on our way. I'll meet you outside in about 5 minutes.

"What is it?" Dr. Betsy asked, easing closer to Natasha as she closed the car door.

"What is what?" Natasha glanced into her rear-view mirror before backing up.

"That smile, that look. What's going on?"

"Oh my gosh! Do I wear my feelings on my face? Everybody's been asking me that lately."

"Natasha, you just seem to have a glow about you. And you've seemed distracted lately. Come on, tell me what's going on with you."

A horn from behind honked loudly. "How rude." Natasha frowned. "The light barely turned green. These people are so impatient nowadays." Then, turning back to Dr. Betsy, she grinned as widely as she could. "Well, I sort of met someone at the college," she sang gleefully.

"Really? Like a special friend type someone?" Dr. Betsy sat down and folded her hands, waiting for Natasha to say more.

"He's a Christian who believes in keeping the 7th day Sabbath like me, which is so shocking. Thought I'd never meet another student from my denomination at school. And he's so nice and good-looking too." Natasha squeezed her hands and shook them gently in front of her while smiling broadly. "We're going to church again this Sabbath," she said excitedly.

"You mean you're dating at church?" Dr. Betsy seemed amused.

"I wouldn't call it a date. We are just friends, but it's so nice to have someone to talk with who understands me and the things that I've gone through. We have so much in common, and he really has been a great spiritual support for me."

"That's terrific, Natasha. I'm so happy for you. It sounds like it's been . . ."

"Divinely orchestrated," Natasha interrupted, her eyes wide with joy.

"Yes, that is precisely what I was going to say. I knew you'd find someone. And you thought you weren't pretty enough to attract anybody."

"I don't know, Dr. Betsy. I'm nervous. I've never dated anyone before. I don't know much, if anything, about love. And I already know I don't trust people much. I keep doubting TJ's friendship, thinking he'll just disappear and stop talking to me one day after he gets bored with me, or when some other genuine beauty walks by. It's horrible because he senses my insecurity and keeps telling me to lighten up."

Dr. Betsy looked compassionately at Natasha. "I'm not your grandmother," she said, "but I'd be happy to listen to you if you need someone to talk to. And I get the not trusting anyone. I had the same problem when I was younger. Everyone seemed to like me because of my looks, but no one seemed interested in me—the person behind the pretty face. It caused me to become very insecure and untrusting.

From what you're telling me about this TJ guy, he seems different. Give it time, Natasha. You'll know if you've found someone special."

"Enough about me," Natasha insisted. "We're almost there. Are you ready?"

"Are you kidding me? I've waited weeks for this. Of course I'm ready," Dr. Betsy declared, smacking the hiking pack lying at her feet.

—◦—

Two balls of light flashed across damp, rugged walls as Dr. Betsy cautiously followed Natasha down the dark corridor of the cave.

"How much farther?" Dr. Betsy anxiously whispered. "We have no clue how safe this enclosure is, and with all the rain we've been having lately, I fear the worst could potentially happen. That entryway is tight, and if it collapsed, we'd be trapped."

"Almost there," Natasha replied. "Watch your step," she said, pointing her flashlight downward. The enormous root of a tree bulged out of the ground. It was probably the very one she had tripped over in her haste to get out of the cave on her first visit.

Holding her hand up, she motioned for Dr. Betsy to halt before pointing ahead.

"See that?" she said, twirling the flashlight around. "That's where it is. Come on," she coached. "I think I can see a piece of the box already."

"Isn't that the sound of water I hear?" Dr. Betsy asked, pointing her flashlight down the corridor.

"I think so, but I haven't gone past this point."

"Fascinating." Dr. Betsy's voice echoed. "This is absolutely incredible! There's probably a pond or lake down there that no one has even investigated. For your grandmother to have found this is amazing."

"You mean to have been shown this?" Natasha said, placing her flashlight on the ground.

As Dr. Betsy watched her brush away the dirt, her eyes widened with fright. "A coffin?" she cried out. "This is a coffin."

The words made Natasha halt and step back. "You think?" she asked in astonishment. "I thought it was a treasure box, not a coffin. If that's a coffin," she said, pointing directly at it, "we should leave it alone and get out of here."

"No, no!" Dr. Betsy insisted, grabbing her arm. "We need to find out exactly what or who this is. Help me," she said, kneeling.

They worked like little badgers to remove the rocky soil until they found the words etched into the wooden box. "My goodness! It is a casket!" Dr. Betsy declared while brushing the remaining dirt away.

"Herein lie the remains of Jeremiah Conley" were the words inscribed on the top.

"Who is Jeremiah Conley? Is that the guy's name?" Natasha practically screamed. "He's inside here?" she asked in a high-pitched voice.

Doctor Betsy shook her head. "No, his name was Josh and he had just died, there's no way it could be someone who was recently buried. This coffin looks like it has been here much longer than two years. Look at the decomposition of the wood. I would suspect this coffin has been here for a couple of decades."

The mention of decades brought the newspaper articles to Natasha's mind. "You know what? One of the folders had newspaper articles from the 1800s. I looked them over but couldn't find anything of interest, and we didn't look at them together the other day. Did you get a chance to look them over?"

Light from Dr. Betsy's helmet flashed sideways. "No," she sighed. "I didn't have time to review everything yet. I've been so busy with managing the PIRD. I need to go back and check out every detail of everything in those folders. We know she was researching something about bones, and now we find this gargantuan casket from at least, from what I can tell, about century ago."

Pulling her phone out of her pocket, Dr Betsy began taking photographs of the site. "Now help me cover this up. The last thing we need is someone else finding out about this before we know exactly what it is."

CHAPTER 26

Natasha:
Unforeseen Fright

"Mom," Natasha called as she walked through the front door. She had arrived at her mom's house later in the evening than she wanted. With a boatload of homework to complete, she debated whether she should still stop at her mother's house, but she had spoken to her mom the night before and promised she would.

"Mom, are you here?" she yelled again as she peeped into the living room. Clothes and bedding had been dumped on the living room couch, some of which had spilled to the floor. Natasha wagged her head as she headed for the kitchen. She didn't expect anything different but had hoped her mom would at least try to keep things tidier for herself.

"Mom!" She went around the corner and entered the kitchen. Her nose immediately recoiled from the stench of something rotten. She sniffed the sink, cluttered with plates and bowls with scraps of dried food stuck on them. Granted, it had been over a week since she last visited, but she had made sure to wash the dishes and tidy up before she left.

"It's like you're trying to keep things a mess," she muttered as she tried to locate the source of the smell. She peeked inside the pizza box lying on the counter. The remaining slices were curled up and hard as a rock. Closing the box, she picked it up, along with some half-eaten containers of her mom's favorite Chinese food, but the smell persisted even after she took out the garbage.

"Mom!" she yelled as her frustration began to turn to fear, remembering the condition in which she left her mom the last time she came home. Like now, her mom had not answered when she arrived. She'd found her sleeping like the dead and smelling like she needed a bath and a good washing of her mouth. Apparently, she had stayed in bed for a few days because she was feeling so weak and tired. Natasha made her get up, take a bath, and get dressed, but even then, Valerie seemed slightly confused and disoriented. After tidying up her mother's room, Natasha had made her some dinner and watched her guzzle down a couple of glasses of water with the complaint that she was constantly thirsty.

Reaching for the pantry door, Natasha sensed that the smell had become much more pungent. She was practically knocked off her feet when she opened it. Inside lay a bowl of rotting potatoes that had turned to mush. Disgusted at the sight and smell, she quickly discarded the contents into the outside garbage and cleaned the bowl before opening the kitchen window to air out the smell.

Natasha made sure to call her mom just about every day either before she left home for work or when she returned. While her mom sounded drearier than usual, Natasha continued to believe that it was just the stressful change that had taken place. Her mom admitted that her new reality was tough to deal with.

"It's just that I'm not used to being alone," she had cried. "Somehow I thought you'd always be here. I know you can't be, but it's just something I hoped would never happen. I need you, Natasha. I really do."

But her words fell short of telling Natasha she loved her, like they always did. Now that Natasha was in college and completely absorbed in her schoolwork and meeting many more people who seemed interested in her, the sting of her mother's apathy seemed less painful.

Assuming her mom was knocked out again, she headed for Valerie's bedroom, but her mom wasn't in her bed. Perplexed at the sight of the empty, unmade bed and the overall quietness of their home. Her mind raced with horrible possibilities as she rushed to her mom's bathroom, but no one was there. Now her heart was palpitating rapidly. She called for her mom again before turning to leave. That was when she noticed the feet on the floor by the far side of her bed.

Screeching in horror, she ran to her mother's side. Valerie was lying face down. Her body was limp, but her skin was still warm. Too afraid of the sight she might see if she rolled her mom over, Natasha searched for her phone. In sheer panic, she tore at her pants pocket before realizing she had left her phone downstairs next to her keys. The adrenaline rushing through her veins brought some sensibility back to her brain. Looking frantically for her mom's phone, she found it lying beside Valerie's hand. Her mom had to have grabbed it in those lost moments before she collapsed.

"Turn her to her side and see if she's still breathing," the 911 operator commanded.

"But I'm too scared," Natasha cried.

"If she's alive, it will help her to breathe better if she's on her side. I know you're scared, but listen to my instructions so we can help your mom. The ambulance is on its way."

Everything seemed surreal as the ambulance crew rushed into their home. The swirling red lights of the ambulance, its sirens wailing through the air, and her mom on that stretcher were more than her mind could bear.

"Please, dear God, save my mother," she wept over and over with her mom's hand in hers. "She's all I have, dear Jesus. Please don't take her from me now."

Arriving at the hospital, her mom was whisked away, and Natasha was led to the receptionist's cubicle to answer mundane questions about her mother's name and age, her past medical history, and her medical insurance coverage.

And then came the most awful time ever. The waiting.

"Have you heard anything about Valerie Cunningham?" Natasha asked after an hour of waiting in the lounge.

"When we hear something, we'll let you know," the receptionist replied, barely looking away from her computer screen.

"But I've been waiting an hour. I just need to know if she's alive," she managed to choke, her voice cracking as she spoke.

"Hold on. Let me see what I can find out for you, okay?" the receptionist consoled before leading her to a private waiting room.

Another wretched hour of waiting passed before a middle-aged white gentleman walked in.

Natasha stood up, and he stretched out his hand.

"I'm Dr. Edwards. Are you Natasha Cunningham?"

She nodded, and he motioned for her to take a seat and then pulled up a chair beside her.

"Your mother is not dying, at least not today," he said with a reassuring smile. "That's the good news." Then his face turned serious. "The bad news is that your mother almost did die."

Natasha's lips trembled violently. "Oh my God! From what? A heart attack? A stroke?"

She had done some research while waiting in the lobby. African Americans were at a significantly increased risk for high blood pressure, strokes, and heart attacks. Her mom had at least four of the stated risk factors. She was black, obese, over the age of fifty, stressed, and depressed.

"No, she didn't have a heart attack or a stroke. Her blood sugar was too high. Your mom has diabetes."

Natasha breathed a sigh of relief. "It's just diabetes?" she asked enthusiastically. "There's lots of medicine for that, right?"

"We do have medicine for diabetes, but it is still a very dangerous disease. It places her at risk for heart attack, stroke, kidney failure, amputations, and blindness. We're going to keep her here for the next few days while we work to improve and stabilize her blood sugar. But she'll need to follow up regularly after that for the rest of her life."

Dr. Edwards looked at Natasha somberly. "She'll need lots of support right now to help her get started on this new journey. She's been admitted to the hospital, and you can go see her in a while. She'll likely be asleep, though, because her body is exhausted. Our nurse educator will be around to explain to you more about type 2 diabetes. Our social worker will also come to visit to make sure you guys have the services and resources you need. Do you have any questions for me?"

Clasping his hand, Natasha thanked God for saving her mom's life and thanked Dr. Edwards for his care.

Her mom looked peaceful when Natasha arrived in the room, despite the tubes running into her veins. A surge of relief brought tears of gratitude and whispers of thankfulness from Natasha's lips to her Creator. But all her fears were not abated. Those long hours of waiting alone made her realize how isolated she felt.

She didn't have to be alone. They did have family out there somewhere; she had seen the pictures. Maybe that was why God had her find those precious photographs when she did. He was trying to let her know she was not alone. Maybe it was time she stepped outside of her mother's will to find the family she knew existed. Her dad, brothers, and grandma were gone, but there were loads of pictures of people who must have been her aunts, uncles, cousins, and maybe even some other grandparents who were still alive and well.

Relaxing back in the hospital room chair, she sent a quick text to Kenisha and Dr. Betsy letting them know about her mom. She'd stay the night and wait until the doctors saw her mom again in the morning before deciding what to do next.

A few hours later, her mom's eyes opened. Natasha greeted her with weeping, hugs, and kisses and then called for the nurse to help her explain everything.

Valerie listened calmly while tears slid down her face.

"I'm so sorry that you saw me like that, honey," she wept. "I know it must have been horrible. I know how scared you must have been." Natasha handed her mom a tissue.

"I should have known," Valerie repeated time and again. "Looking back, I had all the classic symptoms. I was thirsty and peeing all the time, and starving hungry. How I didn't put the pieces together, I don't know," she said, shaking her head. "A diabetic! Good gosh, I could have prevented this. God had been trying to tell me to change my ways, but I just wouldn't listen."

She blew her nose and reached out for Natasha's hand. "Darling," she said, rubbing her hand tenderly. "I haven't told you this in a long, long time and I'm sorry. I love you, honey. Thank you for saving my life." Natasha sat speechless as she wept beside her mother. It was the moment she had always dreamed of, and now that it was here, she prayed it would last forever.

But the morning light brought bad news. The doctors reported that her mother's labs indicated she had advanced chronic kidney failure and would need to start dialysis immediately. The news was a blow neither of them was expecting, and they both cried as the doctor explained what dialysis was and why she needed it.

When her phone rang later that morning, Natasha excused herself from the room and tearfully updated Dr. Betsy about her mother's terrible condition and her fear of being left all alone.

"You won't be alone, Natasha," Dr. Betsy comforted. "I'm always here for you. And don't worry about your job at the PIRD for now either. You have so much on your plate. You know, I was thinking last night how John never got back to me about my offer. Maybe I'll give him a ring later and see if he's still interested."

CHAPTER 27

Matthias: Commissioned

I had returned home to Zariah while I waited for Rasmus to complete his duties. When he was done, we returned to Lake Liraz. It was evening, and the sun was quickly setting below the horizon. The shadows of the evening were upon us, and a soft, warm, gentle breeze rustled our wings. Once again, we settled on one of the grassy hills surrounding the lake.

As Rasmus began to speak, the rolling hills covered with rose bushes, the still peach waters of Lake Liraz, the birds gliding through the skies, and the chipmunks, squirrels, and other small animals that scurried around faded from my view. My ears began to shut out the chirping, the roars and bellows, and even the soft musical tones that always bathed Nanea with enchanting sounds. All I saw was his story being played out in my mind's eye. All I heard was his voice—deep, strong, melodic, yet filled with sorrow.

Rasmus pulled his knees to his chest and let his outstretched wings flutter in the breeze as he began to speak. "My heart and soul were shattered as we bid my friend farewell. Aziel returned to Abner's side, and they departed Nanea, along with a host of other angelic beings.

I felt that I needed to speak with the Creator again and immediately put in a request. Surely He had a plan to win Aziel and all the other angels back, I surmised. Was He not the Creator? He could restore anything, and I couldn't believe Abner was powerful enough to take the souls who belonged to Him.

"The Creator was quick to respond to my request. He assured me that all the power of the Godhead was being employed to win back the hearts of those who were now aligning themselves with Abner. Both the Father and the Creator had already met with Abner and had expounded on the law and love of God and the rightful order of authority in heaven. Abner, however, kept asserting his claims and took the forbearance of the Creator as a sign of weakness. During this meeting, the Creator told me of the Godhead's plan to bring back the peace of heaven. We would need to prepare for war. I had never heard this word before. I asked Him to explain to me what the word meant. Horror filled my heart as He described to me what it entailed and what the results would be. Abner and all who pledged their allegiance to him would be banished from our heavenly home.

"When I returned to Nanea, I was still shaken to the core. I needed time alone to process all that I had been told. I came here to Lake Liraz. Aziel and I had spent much time here playing, talking, and discovering. I slipped into the clear waters and watched the manta rays swim gracefully around me. They began to descend to the bottom of the lake, and I followed them. Then like Aziel, one by one, they dove into the ground and disappeared. I grabbed the wings of a large manta ray named Kai as she prepared to dive. The next thing I knew, she was flying. My wings fluffed out as the air rippled over them. I had entered a different realm beneath the lake. Letting go of Kai, I spun widely around as I attempted to get my bearings. This was a hidden world, a secret realm. Three moons, one larger and two smaller ones, cast their ethereal glow throughout the atmosphere. Misty clouds spread across vast plains, some of them sailing low to the ground. This is what Aziel was so excited about and anxious to show me.

"The plains were covered in orange grass, and violet-blue ground flowers erupted everywhere. Streams of rivers made patterned paths through the grass. Mammoths, dinosaurs, and elephant-like creatures roamed the land, which was dotted with enormous craters. From the center of each crater grew a single tree whose crown reached just above the crater's rim. I flew across the plain to get a close-up view. Everywhere I looked was exploding with life. Each one hosted a habitat different from the next. I descended into a place filled with plants and animals of the rainforest. Immediately, creatures great and small approached me, curious to find out who I was. I smiled and reached out my hand, as I was just as interested to understand and know them.

"Then I remembered what had brought me there. My world was changing before my eyes, and I was powerless to stop it. Beings I loved for thousands of years who had been my friends and companions would be banished. Where would they go? Would they simply vanish? Couldn't we just keep talking to them? Would they eventually see the light again? They had to, for all we had ever known was light.

"The depth of my pain was like a bottomless pit. I couldn't bear to lose so many. I couldn't bear to lose even one. I accepted that we needed to fight but not to banish them. We needed to fight to draw their allegiance back to Him, the only source of light and life and happiness."

Rasmus was touching the very thoughts that had troubled me for so long. *Why hadn't they fought to keep the family together? Why had they been banished? The Creator's power knows no bounds. He could have changed everything.* I peered across Lake Liraz with my knees pulled to my chest as I listened intently.

Rasmus continued. "I don't know how long I had been there when I felt the presence of another. The Creator Himself had found me. Once again, He conversed with me and explained why there was no other option. I knew He was right, but my heart was slow to believe. But He had not come just to comfort me. He needed a commander, a leader for a new class of angels. We would be known as the warriors, and we would be the ones who would form the front lines at the time of confrontation.

"I resisted His request. I was a lover of plants and animals. I had never pursued strength and might and power. But the Creator reassured me that the quality that mattered most was a compassionate heart. Power was needed, but so was kindness. Strength was required, but not without gentleness. And most important of all, I was not to rely on my strength. I was to lean on Him Who was the embodiment of all strength and power and glory."

I could envision all that Rasmus related to me and sat entranced by his words. We were deep into the evening hours, and birds of the evening had now taken to the skies. I could see their silhouettes soaring high. "What happened next?" I asked, hoping Rasmus was not done.

"All of heaven was in upheaval as a clear line of delineation was made between those who supported Abner and those who remained loyal to the Creator. There was unrest and confusion, sorrow and sadness, as well as defiance and despair. Abner was emboldened by his success in winning the hearts of so many and was planning on extending his reach to the other worlds and universes. Aziel had been made a commander, and now we were clearly against each other. When I happened to be in his presence, I could feel the struggle of his soul and his yearning to make things right. Now no one changed their position.

"And then it happened. The call was made for all of us warriors to report to the Creator. He informed us that the time had come to secure the universe, as Abner was now in open rebellion and inciting revolt. The time had come for us to defend our home and the peace, harmony, and love that had always saturated the heavenly universe. God could not permit these seeds of discord to be planted in any other place. Unless we acted immediately, the disharmony and sorrow we now felt would fill the universes of light.

"Abner had already gathered his forces and was proudly making demands and threatening to seize to his side all the beings God had created. The Creator summoned us to fall into rank, and we marshaled our angels into order. The tension cruising through our bodies was immense. We had never fought before, though we were now well trained.

"A multitude of us stood with Abner. I looked upon those who stood against us ready to war. They were beautiful. They were light. They were still one of us. Tears streamed down the faces of every warrior in our ranks. As commander, I was at the front line, as was Aziel. Our eyes met, and we fixated on each other. I was pleading with all that was within me, but he broke my gaze, and my heart shattered. At that moment, the Creator gave the command to fight as He raised His sword high in the sky. Everyone on either side drew their weapons of war. But I could not. As they all surged forward, I abandoned my post and fled back to my haven."

I sat dumbfounded as I looked at Rasmus. He had not fought. I had no words. I was so shocked. We sat in silence for many moments, and then I saw that the waters were stirring again and had begun to bubble. The manta rays had returned.

Rasmus stood and walked to the water's edge. He said nothing as he slipped in, but he turned around and looked at me. *Will he take me under? Will he share his intimate haven with me?*

There are no words to express the awe of seeing something your eyes have never beheld before. Though Rasmus had described the place to me, it was much more marvelous to behold. Excitement thrilled through every cell in my body as we glided past crater after crater before Rasmus began his descent toward one. Waters tumbled over its edges. We were surrounded by falls. A lake had formed in the crater, and Rasmus artfully crafted a raft from the vines that hung from the gargantuan tree that arose from the depths of the crater. We settled on the craft as it drifted around the tree, and the mist from the falls fell upon us.

"It was the Creator Who found me when the battle had been won. I was ashamed. I had failed Him. I had failed to fulfill my God-given mission. I had abandoned my post. I had abandoned my comrades. I felt I deserved to be banished for my sin, like the others had been for theirs. But He told me I had not sinned. I was just afraid, and my heart was not entirely convinced we had taken the correct course. I handed Him my sword and my seal of command. I was not the warrior He meant me to be, and I certainly was not a commander. But He refused to take them and assured me my time had not yet come."

"Did you ever see Aziel again?" I asked as I watched creatures I had never seen before swimming about in the lake.

"Yes, I saw him again, but not face to face. He no longer stood taller than I. He was bent over from the weight of sin that constantly oppressed him. His strength had waned, and his beauty had left him. I looked at his face, and there was no light in his eyes. Evil had etched itself into every expression. His smile was sinister, his frown was unsettling, and his anger was horrific."

I moved toward the edge of the raft and dangled my feet in the cool waters. "When did you see him?"

Rasmus shifted toward the other end of the raft to balance it. "I refused to watch the happenings on Earth, unlike most of the angelic hosts. Instead, I chose to read the records of the history of man. That is, until the Creator's time came. Then I joined all the unfallen beings who dwelt in the universes of light. We watched Him from the time He was born as a babe. No detail escaped our vision. Every temptation, every act of hatred instigated by them, was seen."

Rasmus swept his hands through the waters and pushed the raft toward the falls.

"I watched them hoarding around Him in Gethsemane. I saw their delight as blood dripped from His brow onto the earth. I heard them join the rabble in their shouts of 'Crucify Him.' I shuddered as they defiled Him and beat Him and spat upon Him. How was he who had stood as my friend from the time of our awakening able to bring himself to commit such crimes? How had he who had been my brother become the embodiment of darkness and evil and shame?"

As we drew closer to the falls, the spray of moisture grew heavier and heavier, and large droplets of water rolled down my face. My heart broke for Rasmus. I did not personally know any of the fallen. It was virtually impossible to feel the depth of his pain. I thought of my Zariah family and all those I had met and connected with in our unfallen world. It would be excruciating to lose even one, much less an entire host, equal to one of the heavenly realms. The loss of love and friendships, companions and coworkers, and gifts and talents and knowledge all seemed too much to comprehend.

I looked back toward Rasmus. Water rolled down every part of his majestic form, but it couldn't hide his tears.

"How could they end the life of the One Who gave them life? They descended upon Him like a pack of ravenous beasts as He hung on the cross. They desired to separate Him from all light and submerge Him into their darkness. They worked themselves into a frenzy with their desire for His blood and their yearning for His death. They were no longer the fallen angelic host. They had transformed themselves into something utterly different. They were a demonic host. When the Creator moaned, 'It is finished,' my sympathies had been completely uprooted. I knew if they could do this to our Creator, they would do it to me and every being in our universe. Their hatred was not just against Him. It was against all who pledged loyalty to our King. The cross brought me unmistakable and convincing evidence of what would have happened had they remained in heaven."

Rasmus stood to his feet, and I joined him. He flew to the falls and let the waters wash over him. I followed him and let them wash away my tears. When he flew out of the falls, I rushed to his side and extended my wet wings. We embraced. He had told me his story.

—◦—

Immediately after my visit with Rasmus, my mother and father informed me that I was to return to Uriela. While I was now thoroughly educated about Earth and the fall of both men and angels, I had yet to undergo the physical training that would allow me to develop defense skills. I would be entering into enemy ground and needed to know the right strategy to resist and fight legions of demons. I would train with those who had already served on Earth and had faced and fought the demonic host.

I was told that it wasn't just about strength or might but about who was better able to wield mastery over their light or their darkness. If the fallen ones better wielded the darkness, they could overtake us and hold us for a while. This would set off a cascade of events that would dampen the efforts toward those whom we had come to save. More of heaven's resources would be taxed, and angels would be called from their service in the universes of light to aid those in the world of darkness. But if the unfallen better wielded the light, they would overtake the darkness and hinder their efforts and their impact and influence for evil.

Finally, the day came when I was told I was adequately prepared for my mission on earth. My training would continue throughout my service on Earth, but I had reached the level I needed to begin my work.

I had not, however, received my official commission. That came directly from the Creator, and I couldn't become John's protector until then.

Weeks passed by, and I received no word from the Creator. I found myself retreating to my secret place more and more as my mood sobered with the thought that the Creator must have found me insufficient for the task. One evening when I arrived at the cove, my sorrow was so intense that I was not taken up by the beauty before me, and I fell to my knees. *Why have I not received my commission? Am I still unprepared, even after all the training and education I have received? Do I have lingering doubts? Has He found another to fulfill the mission?*

My prayers intensified as I prostrated myself on the ground with my wings completely covering me. Suddenly I sensed a presence. Looking up, I saw no one. I turned around and quickly surveyed the cove. Something was coming. The birds that had been casually swooping and cooing as they flew across the expanse now retreated to a perching position on the plants that sprang from the sides of the cove. The beavers that had been playing about in the waters settled down. I felt the ground begin to tremble. Not knowing what to expect, I stood to my feet, wings fully outstretched.

The sound of a rushing wind filled the air as a light streaked across the sky. I winced and closed my eyes for a brief second as a bright light filled the cove. When I opened them, there was a mighty one before me. She was dazzling, beautiful, magnificent, and strong. She stood a few feet above me and was cloaked in a garb of colored lights that formed an armor with a shield that was the length of her body. She had three pairs of wings, like the wings of an eagle. Her eyes were the color of gold, and her stare seemed to pierce straight through me. At her side was a living sword ablaze with a fire that did not consume. It spoke in unison with her, and their voices blended in perfect harmony.

"I am Amara, of the Seraphim order, messenger, warrior, and commander of hosts. The Creator has sent me."

I was stunned, silent, and frozen in the place where I stood. Amara stepped forward, and instinctively I stretched forth my wings. She met me in an angelic embrace. "You have been chosen for a special mission," she whispered. Then she stopped and looked me in the eye. "You will be enclosed in darkness before you see the full light," she said as she handed me a scroll.

I looked down at the scroll she placed in my hands and looked back up to thank her, but she was gone. *It is official. I have been appointed as John's protector.*

John: Crossing the Line

A few weeks passed, and John's lack of providing George with any pertinent information had caused him to display his true character. Flailing his arms about like a madman and yelling at the top of his voice, George promised John that, without immediate results, the deal would be off and that he wouldn't pay him a dime of the promised money. John had tried to reason with George, but there's no reasoning with angry minds committed to darkness, and that darkness was quickly infiltrating his own soul with feelings of discouragement and defeat.

Numb and silent, John sat in his car like a statue for what seemed like an eternity. He was about to cross the imaginary line between right and wrong that separates the law-abiding from the common criminal. Glancing in the mirror, he saw his father's empty, cold, angry eyes glaring back at him. He closed his eyes, refusing to believe that the person he just saw was his father's reflection. He was different. He was being forced to do something he despised. He derived no thirsty relish or deranged satisfaction from what he was about to do. Like a trapped animal, he had no other alternative but to act in a way that would preserve his own life. The wheels of life that shape a person into one thing or the other were turning, whether he liked it or not. And he was standing at the crossroads of choices.

Fearing the consequences of making the wrong choice, John had talked himself out of doing anything of the sort, time and again. But if he didn't do it, he'd never get paid. He was already two months delinquent on his rent. Humiliated and frustrated, he'd tried his best to remain invisible. He felt like his ineptitude was splattered across his forehead for everyone to see. And if one of his neighbors saw him, they'd feel compelled to turn him in. The last nail to be driven into his looming coffin was the letter from the registrar's office reminding him to pay the last installment of his fall semester tuition.

Ghosts and gravestones littered the yards. John couldn't help but chuckle to himself. How perfectly fate had manipulated events to open the unimaginable opportunity for him to break into Natasha's home. Halloween, that time of year when demons danced, devils pranced, and people's minds were turned on by the darker side of life, coincided with his untimely demise. Opportunity could not have knocked at a better time. He was desperate—desperate for money and desperate for this whole escapade to be over.

He had arrived at his planned destination ahead of time, 4:22 a.m., and any lingering hallowed spirits appeared to be dissipating in the thick fog and drizzling rain that enveloped the neighborhood. The miserable weather made him feel better. Perhaps someone was on his side. It was the perfect cover for his covert operation.

Zipping up his jacket and flipping on his hoodie caused a surge of adrenaline to circulate through his veins, leaving him feeling flushed and hot before his trek had even begun. He slipped out of his car and quietly closed the door. He didn't bother to lock it. He was sure he'd be the only thief on the block that day. A slow jog was his anticipated pace, though his heart was racing wildly.

Parking one mile down the road on a different street was his clever strategy to ensure no attention came his way. Who would notice a jogger on this early foggy morning? A strange car would stand out much more, he had reasoned, and they'd have the make, model, and license plate number of the getaway car. Of course, that was only if he got caught, and getting caught wasn't something he was planning to do.

Keep focused on the task at hand, he kept telling himself every time his mind wandered back to rehearse the events that had brought him to such a low point in his life. His brain wasn't ready to accept defeat. It kept trying to figure out what other possible alternative he might have that would keep him from enacting the disturbing tasks he was literally running to complete.

◄○►

In a rare stroke of luck, Dr. Betsy had called him the other day. She'd explained to him Natasha's unfortunate circumstances and the likelihood that she'd need some time to get her mom settled into a more comfortable regimen. She wanted to know if he was still interested in helping out with the high school interns. He was quick to say yes and to explain how much he appreciated the opportunity. Naturally, he felt a hint of guilt, knowing his ulterior motives, but he also felt a sense of relief. It all would be over soon. George would be off his back, he'd be able to pay his rent and school fees, and things would get back to normal. No more following Natasha or Dr. Betsy. He would even quit working at the Natural History Museum and find another job far away from George.

Dr. Betsy's invitation to return to the PIRD had brightened a very dark day. It was the same day his aunt had given him some extremely bad news. The minute he saw her phone number come up on his phone, he felt chills racing through his spine. Had George followed through on his plan to contact them?

His Aunt Kristen refused to tell him anything over the phone; she'd insisted he come to her home.

The freshly cut grass had been mown with little regard. The edges remained, with thick, uneven patches of grass. Weeds in the same proportion as flowers had grown high in the beds surrounding their home. Children's riding cars, strollers, buckets, and balls were strewn across the yard. The blue-paneled house appeared to be in disrepair. Aunt Kristen and Uncle Joseph were busy tending to young children and dealing with their rebellious teens while trying to make it on a mechanic's and store clerk's salaries. Yet they were the ones who made the sacrifice to take him in when Kevin had kicked him out. And they were the ones who made sure his mom had a proper funeral.

A quick beep of the horn brought Aunt Kristen bursting from her front door. The look on her face instantly told him something was wrong. Her eyes were red, and her face was tear-stained and drawn. That was the exact look etched on her face two years ago when she sat him down to let him know his mother had passed away.

His heartbeat quickened as he followed her into their home. Motioning for him to sit at their dining table, she pushed leftover breakfast dishes aside before pulling up a chair beside him. Eyes brimming with tears before she even spoke a word made him fear the worst.

"John," she choked softly, "I texted several times over the past few days. You've got to do better with responding. You told me that texts work best, but then you fail to answer them. I know you're busy in school and all, but not even Riley could get ahold of you."

John glanced down at his feet. He had ignored the texts, not even taking the time to read them. They never seemed to contact him for anything serious, and he figured it could wait until he had more time to speak with them. "I'm sorry, I was . . . umm . . ."

Kristen held up her hand to stop him. "Never mind that for now, as long as you try to do better."

His legs fidgeted nervously, and he rubbed his sweaty palms on his pants as he waited for her to continue.

"This is about Kevin and Riley. He's selling the house, John. He got a job in Florida and is moving right away."

"What?" John gasped. "What do you mean, selling and moving? He can't do that. He can't just leave us like that."

"You know I never liked him," Kristen said, grasping his hand. "He treated Sarah so badly, and he's always neglected you two, but this?" She stopped to catch her breath and blow her nose. "This is next level.

"I can understand him leaving me, but uprooting Riley now? This is her first year of middle school, and it's the middle of the year."

Kristen wagged her head. "Riley called me in a frenzy the other night. She was hysterically crying and begged me to take her in so she wouldn't have to leave you and live alone with Kevin. It took me several minutes to calm her down and figure out what was going on. Can you believe Kevin didn't even have the audacity to let us know?" she said, rising to her feet. "I'm sorry. Do you want anything to drink, John? I have some lemonade."

John nodded. It was all he could do as he tried to think about how he could possibly help his sister.

"I figured she could stay here, and we could become her legal guardians," she said, handing John a tall glass. "I'm planning to talk to Kevin about it, but first I wanted to catch you up on what's going on."

John pulled in his lower lip to keep it from trembling as tears welled up in his eyes. "Can we keep him from taking her, Auntie?" he asked. "I'll do anything to keep her here with me, but I can't take care of her. I can barely take care of myself."

Kristen squeezed John's hand tightly. "I know you'd be willing to be her legal guardian too if you could. Don't feel bad. His timing is all wrong. We can only pray he'll listen. But that's not the only reason I wanted to speak with you." Kristen turned and retrieved an envelope from a kitchen drawer. "Your mother wanted you to have this," she said, pushing the envelope into his hand and dabbing her eye with a tissue. "She told me to wait until you were on your own, and now you're really on your own."

He had placed the envelope in the glove compartment of his car when he left Kristen's house. He didn't want to read it then. He figured his mom might have written something that would deter him from the task he'd committed himself to completing.

◄○►

As he neared Natasha's home, he picked up his pace. A sense of relief had already begun to settle in. Within the hour, he'd be done and on his way to visit George.

He glanced at his phone; the time read 4:55 a.m. It was still dark with no hint of the coming light of day. Everything was working according to his plan. With Natasha living on campus and her mom in the hospital, he had no pressure to get in and out at the speed of light. He'd already sneaked into her dorm room and searched around for any information. He had timed that event pretty well too. He waited until she went to visit her mom and her roommate went out for dinner. He pretended to be the custodian with a broom in hand, a baseball cap, and reading glasses to partially hide his identity. No one bothered to question him, and he realized how easy it was to get away with robbery. The miniature experience fueled him with confidence for this bigger and more complex heist.

But he'd done his homework too, like any good student or robber should. He'd been jogging through the neighborhood for the past few days. It was another ploy he had thought of to throw out any suspicious activity on "D" day. One of those mornings, with the same cap and glasses as a disguise, he had pulled out their garbage can. He knew garbage day was Thursday mornings, for he had seen Natasha pulling it out on a Wednesday night when she happened to return home. He'd then taken the liberty to sneak into their backyard. That was when he noticed that the kitchen window wasn't fully closed. "Bingo," he had told himself. He had found his entrance site into their home.

The house was dark, as expected. No porch light was on, unlike most of their other neighbors' porches. He jogged across the street, looked around to ensure no one was looking, breathed a *thank you* to whoever had brought the fog, and slipped into their backyard.

His sneakers sank into thick mud that circled the base of the house. The recent rains had turned solid ground into a slushy mess. Staying as close to the wall as he could, he struggled to lift his shoes out of the heavy and sticky sludge. "Crap," he whispered. He hadn't planned for this unexpected mess, and it was going to be a problem. He couldn't wear muddy shoes into the house. He'd have to leave them outside under the windowsill where someone might see them. But the fog was still pretty thick, and he was confident no one could see him, much less his shoes. Wiggling his feet free from his sneakers, he pushed the window up and then deftly hoisted himself through the opening and onto their kitchen sink.

He was inside and could now be officially categorized as an intruder. He didn't feel any different, though his mind kept telling him he'd crossed the line of no return. How he hoped he'd be able to forget his actions and move on with his life. Twisting himself around, he landed on their kitchen floor. It had been thoroughly cleaned and tidied. He lowered himself out of view and turned on his phone light.

Creeping about like an animal in the night, he searched every crevice he thought someone might leave or hide a folder. His search of the lower living area yielded nothing. He glanced at his phone and whispered epithets through clenched teeth. It was taking him longer than expected, but he needed to be thorough, for he only planned to do this once in his lifetime. Eyeing the stairwell, he quickly ascended and looked for her room. Surely that would be the most likely place for her to keep those sacred documents. But again, he came up empty-handed from his exhaustive search. Opening the door to the room next to Natasha's made him gasp in horror. It was filled with too many boxes impossible to thoroughly search if he was to get out of there anytime soon. The sight, though, didn't keep him from snooping and sniffing around like a prowler who might get lucky.

That was when his ears picked up a sound that caused the hairs across his entire body to stand on end. SIRENS! "Are they police sirens, ambulance sirens, or fire engine sirens?" he spoke to the empty house. Astounded, he realized he'd never tried to decipher the difference, and if he had unconsciously done so, the knowledge had been scared out of his head.

As he stood there like a sentinel, every auditory cell strained to determine which direction those sirens were headed. Then, just as he thought they might be coming his way, they went silent.

Breathing a sigh of relief, he realized the intensity of the moment had triggered his bowels. Rushing to the bathroom, he soon relinquished control. Frightened by the thought of leaving any genetic evidence behind, he repeatedly flushed and cleaned the toilet's surfaces and handle.

As he reached the stairwell, another noise made him freeze with terror. A dog was barking nearby, and voices could be heard. *Are they in the neighbor's yard, or is it hers?* He couldn't tell but figured he'd better exit the premises immediately. Like a ninja, he stealthily crept down the stairwell.

CHAPTER 29

Mistaken Identity

The bang of the front door.

A cool breeze hitting his face.

Pistols pointing his way.

The stern command: "Hold up your hands."

Slow motion. Blurred voices. Blue and red lights. Handcuffs. The back of the officer's car. The flash of light for the mug shot. The cold jail cell.

Catatonic stare. Bail. Ten thousand dollars.

The wheels of life had turned against him, and now he had no one to call but the man he loathed to the core of his being. He doubted Kevin would consider it, but maybe he'd do it as a farewell gift.

When Kevin walked into the holding area, the words that poured from his mouth were much more shocking than John could have ever imagined.

"Your sister was in a car accident," he blurted out. "She was hurt and is in the hospital. That's what you get for forgetting to pick her up from her Halloween party."

That was when everything started to swirl. He heard someone crying out but didn't recognize the anguished voice as his, asking if she would be okay.

And after those words cut into his heart like a knife, Kevin drove it in even deeper.

"You're not my son. I read the blasted letter your mother left me. I should have known all along that you were not mine. I'm leaving for good. You have gotten everything you will ever get from me in this life. Find your own way out of the mess you're in."

Stern as the officers were, even they stood by looking at him pitifully, like a puppy that had been left out in the cold.

Hours passed with John in a state of stupor, holding in his anguished groans and rocking himself with knees to his chest while sitting on a dirty thin mattress. He had no one else to call. He couldn't bear to burden his Aunt Kristen, who had voluntarily taken on Riley's care. He'd have to figure this out himself or rot in that jail until his time was served.

Hours later, an officer entered. "You made bail," he declared as metal clanked against metal and the doors swung open.

Dumbfounded, he sat looking at the man as if waiting for him to start laughing at his joke.

"Are you coming, or did you get comfortable in there?"

"My father?" he questioned, trying to rally his weak legs to move.

"No, dim whit. That sleaze bucket made it clear he was doing nothing for you. Your grandma bailed you out. You left your phone in the arresting officer's car. She called asking for you. We told her you were in jail."

"But I don't have a grandma. They're both dead," he said in a daze of confusion.

The officer shrugged his shoulders. "Then I guess it was your guardian angel," he replied sarcastically. "We have some paperwork to fill out, so hurry up."

"And my phone?" John asked with hand outstretched.

"Umm! Sorry, son! That man who said he's not your father said the phone was his."

—◦—

Dr. Betsy had awakened at 5:00 a.m. that Saturday. An early start would ensure she'd make it to her home ninety minutes away and then be able to return the same day to make a meeting with Natasha. But sometimes even the most organized plans are *strangely* disrupted for a higher purpose.

A sense of peace and joy pervaded her soul, and she hummed happily to herself as she sped down the freeway and began to witness the sun's glorious entry into the morning sky. Bubbly clouds covering the great expanse were slowly absorbing the rising light and had begun to display hues of pink, yellow, and orange. As she reached for the radio dial, her hand brushed against her phone. She hadn't realized she had inadvertently called someone until a voice echoed out of the receiver.

"Hello?" asked a male voice.

Assuming it was John she had dialed, she answered. "John. "I'm so sorry, I—"

"Ma'am, your grandson." It was a strange voice that interrupted. "John McKenzie got himself in some trouble."

"I'm sorry, what? You said John McKenzie, right?"

"Yes, ma'am."

"But I'm not his grandmother. You must have the wrong number."

"This is his phone, ma'am, and you're the one who called."

Dr. Betsy glanced at her phone to make sure it was John she had accidentally rung.

"I'm sorry. I'm so confused. This is John's number, but he's not my grandson. I just spoke with him the other day, sir. Somehow our lines must have been weirdly crossed. I don't know."

"I don't know either, ma'am, except that no one is related to that boy today. Okay," the officer sighed. "You have a good day."

Dr. Betsy eased her foot off the gas, turned on her blinkers, and took the next exit off the freeway. It took several moments for her to process the conversation. "Is John in trouble?" she whispered to herself. "My Lord, there must be some mistake." She looked at her phone and pressed the icon to call the person back.

◄○►

The rays of the late morning sun piercing the sky seemed like beams of blessing when John stumbled out into the street. How could this be? Who had bailed him out? Surely his auntie and uncle could never have afforded this.

But his elation was short-lived. As he began the long walk back to his car, his troubles rolled back in like a swift spring thunderstorm. Riley, his beloved sister, was in the hospital, and it was his fault she was hurt. He'd forgotten he had promised to pick her up from her Halloween party. How irresponsible and neglectful he had been. Protecting her was the promise he had made on his mom's deathbed, but in the past few years, he'd managed to do the exact opposite. He had never expected her to get hurt. Not like this. Kevin had failed to tell him how badly she was injured.

His legs moved quicker as he hastened to his car. He needed to get to the hospital to see his sister before anything worse happened, but then he stopped. What would he say to her? His apologies were empty promises neither she nor he believed anymore. How could he live with himself if she had sustained lifelong injuries, or if she passed away?

The anguish in his soul couldn't be held inside any longer, and the tears freely flowed as he began to walk again. Looking at the time brought another forgotten reality back to his remembrance. Mr. Harley had warned him that he'd give him until 5:00 p.m. that day to pay off his rent, but if he neglected to do so, the superintendent said he'd have no choice but to change the lock on his apartment until he received payment. John had apologized profusely, but the old man kept repeating that he just needed to get the rent money by the first of the month, which was also the final day his tuition payment was due. The money George promised would have covered all of it. November 1 was supposed to be his liberation day, but instead, it had become his incarceration day.

"What's going on?" he asked himself through clenched teeth. "How could so many things go wrong in such a short period of time?"

Reaching his car, he sank into his seat and wept. He had no energy or desire to face anyone at that moment. The spirit of regret, guilt, and a haunting foreboding began weighing on him so heavily that he felt as if his very breath was being sucked out of him.

Everything that meant anything to him had been stripped away in a single day. Overwhelmed with sorrow, he punched his steering wheel, wishing he'd wake up from this nightmare. With no incentive to push himself, no aspirations to grasp, no love to embrace, and no words to encourage him, he wondered if life was even worth living. He had reached a low from which he did not know if he even wanted to recover.

It wasn't the first time that depression had gripped him in its wretched hold of despair. It wasn't the first time the siren calls to end his own life had played over and over in his head. Now, at the time he was so weak, the memory of her loss returned.

"She's gone. I'm sorry, son. Your mom has passed away."

As he stood in the hall of the hospice house where his mother spent her last days, several nurses surrounded him and Riley when the minister announced the heartbreaking news they had been anticipating for so long. But when the words were finally spoken that fateful day, something broke inside him. The life force that had sustained him withdrew itself, his legs weakened, and his hands became cold as ice. Even so, he forced himself to remain standing and held back the army of tears that stood ready to fall at his command.

Those tears never received their marching orders, and they crystallized into salty droplets of rage within the caverns of his troubled soul. And the flame of life that kindles at some point within every human consciousness was drenched. Though he managed to go about the ritual of living, the passion to fight the battle for life had been dampened.

Now that passion had been depleted to the point of disappearing. No money to continue his education, knowing Riley's suffering was because of him, and a jail stint to stain his record for all time threatened to extinguish the faint flickering of life still within him. Mindlessly, he started the car and began to drive somewhere—anywhere that would end his suffering.

◄○►

Now Dr. Betsy was driving back home for the second time that day. Her mind was distraught as she came to comprehend the enormity of what had happened to John. She knew beyond any shadow of a doubt the real person behind John's injudicious actions. And if George was behind it, she and Natasha needed to beware. Her heart quaked at the extent George was willing to go to get what he wanted. It was that very delusional persistence that had landed him in jail before, by her testimony against him. How she had hoped he would remain in jail longer or at least learn his lesson and abandon this reprehensible pursuit. If he was seeking revenge upon her, what was he capable of doing if he was willing to induce others to perform his twisted desires? No longer could she take their safety for granted. They'd have to be diligent to ensure no one was stalking them, and she needed to get John on their side. She was convinced that the Lord had orchestrated events to inform her of his situation. Her choice to bail him out would be the very thing that could pull him in her direction away from George.

The attempted robbery was still unknown to Natasha. It was probably her mom and deceased grandmother that the police department had tried to contact unsuccessfully. Dr. Betsy was glad for that, as Natasha was already dealing with so much. Her mom was supposed to have been discharged from the hospital after two days, but they ended up keeping her longer upon the discovery of her poor kidney function. Valerie's extended stay would allow Dr. Betsy to gently break the news to Natasha while establishing the need not to press charges against John.

The sun had reached its peak when she finally turned into her driveway. It had been a while since she'd come home, and the spiders had taken advantage of her absence. Webs crowded every corner, and spider poo splattered the walls. "A few weeks gone, and you guys have moved back in and made a mess for me to clean, you miserable buggers. I've come back for one thing and one thing only," she muttered to herself. "I won't have time to clean things up now."

She considered herself a bit of a clean freak, always taking time to make sure that everything was in its place and that dust did not have the opportunity to settle itself on her furniture. Her home was large, with three bedrooms, each with an ensuite bathroom. There was a living room and sitting room, a parlor and music room, and a library which also served as her study. Finding the time to keep it looking pristine was a chore, but on weekends when she visited, what else would she do? It kept her quite busy bustling around like a bumblebee while mumbling to herself. But the pride she felt when she finally could sit back and relax with a cup of her favorite chamomile tea and admire the work of her hands was pure satisfaction.

When she opened the door from the garage, her nose immediately turned up. She hated the smell of an unlived space. "Too long, too long," she said, reprimanding herself. Her knees cracked and popped with each step she took up the staircase. "Good gosh! You're getting to be such an old lady now. How much longer do you think you can climb these stairs, Frosty and how much longer can you keep this home?"

It saddened her to think that sooner than she wanted to accept, it wouldn't make much sense to keep her beautiful home. The cottage was better suited for her elderly years. Back in the day, she had purchased the cottage as her second home, a place much closer to work, but it had now become her primary residence.

When she had retrieved the sought-after items from her safe, she placed them on the bed and stared at them. She remembered the day she and Dr. Cunningham shared their complicated family history. It was neither of their intent when they began talking, but somehow the conversation twisted and turned itself until they found themselves expressing the guarded secrets of their lives. How many times had she wondered what made their tongues so lucid on that gorgeous May morning?

The clear blue skies seemed to have been paint-brushed with cirrus clouds by some master hand artist. The air was sweet with the smell of new life as springtime flowers erupted from the ground and budded on trees. The sun's rays, bright and beautiful, warmed their skin as they searched for just the right plants for their herbarium.

It felt as if they were in a different place that morning. Their hearts were full of gratitude at their newfound friendship and the respect and trust that had developed between them. The cool morning breeze, the beauty of the day, and the warmth surging in their souls must have melted away their cautious reserve.

She could never have imagined the loss and pain Dr. Cunningham had experienced. She had assumed the woman had lived an enchanted life, for the peace and joy she exuded in no way belied the difficult time she had gone through. When their lips finally exhausted their hearts' hidden anguishes, they worked in silence, inherently knowing their secrets had found a safe resting place.

Months later, Dr. Cunningham handed her two envelopes. "I've been impressed to give these to you just in case anything ever happens to me," she said solemnly.

When Natasha told her about her mom's hospitalization, Dr. Betsy knew she had better delay no longer. Valerie's illness changed everything. How she had wanted to give it to Natasha earlier, but she feared Valerie's possible reaction. She had already experienced the uncontrolled rage of that woman twice in the past, and she did not want to ignite her anger against her again.

The time had come for Natasha to be told the truth, especially if Valerie's condition worsened. Dr. Betsy caressed her forehead as she shook her head.

Falling to her knees, she earnestly prayed for God's wisdom and guidance. A feeling of assurance washed over her when her prayers came to an end, and she knew exactly the right time and the right place to speak with Natasha.

CHAPTER 30

Dr. Betsy: Greater Love

Asmile spread across Dr. Betsy's face as her car pulled into the parking lot of Kennington Park. Every time she came here, its beauty encouraged her heart and stirred her soul. There was something about this place that was special beyond her ability to fully comprehend.

Today, though, her peace was mixed with apprehension despite believing her decision was the right one. She still feared the impact it might have on Natasha. It could completely sever her affection for her mother at a time when Valerie needed her the most. Or it could bring such emotional distress that she wouldn't be able to concentrate on her schooling. Dr. Betsy truly hoped it wouldn't affect their relationship in any way.

When Natasha's car rolled to a stop beside hers, Dr. Betsy quickly exited to greet her. Natasha immediately recognized the canoe resting atop the jeep.

"I was on the rowing team in college," Dr. Betsy explained. "I was hoping to make this day special and figured we'd take her out on the pond."

Natasha clasped her hands in exuberant expectation. She had never been in a canoe before. Neither she nor her grandmother could swim, so Grandma Cunningham never took her out on the water. Instead, they always watched from the sidelines as others glided effortlessly across ponds and lakes, laughing and enjoying themselves in their watercraft.

But Dr. Betsy said they'd first have a talk and led Natasha to a particular bench that sat at the edge of the pond. It was a larger pond that could almost be called a lake because of its size. As the main attraction at the park, there was always a soul or two fishing from its banks, enjoying a canoe ride, or simply staring at its calm and pristine waters.

"How's your mom?" she asked as they picked their way through the tall grass and shrubbery that sat between the dirt trail and the bench.

"Much better, Dr. Betsy," Natasha replied, smiling. "I was so worried about her. I thought she might die."

"I know, honey. I was afraid for her too."

"Diabetes is one thing, but kidney failure is a whole other thing." The concern on Natasha's face was apparent as she spoke. "She'll have to start dialysis while in the hospital, and we're looking for an outpatient dialysis clinic near our home. It's all so much to take in. I might even have to move back home so I can help her."

"How's her spirit, Natasha? How is she holding up emotionally?" Dr. Betsy was gauging the situation to determine if now was still the best time.

"Surprisingly, she seems to be doing well. This whole ordeal seems to have changed her in a completely unexpected way. I for sure thought her depression would move to a new low level, but I guess almost losing your life can also change your perspective for the better." Natasha turned to look at Dr. Betsy. "She's appreciative for having a second chance."

Dr. Betsy bowed her head and smiled. It was the sign she was waiting for: a miracle of sorts. "Yes, Natasha. I know well how facing death can change one's perspective on life. It's really what happened to me when your grandma died. That's why this park is such a special place for me, though I hadn't come here in such a long, long time."

Leaning back, Dr. Betsy turned to look across the lake. Her piercing glare indicated she was deeply engrossed in thought. "It was here that me and your grandma had one of the most important conversations of my life. It was right after we'd been accused of being in a relationship together."

Dr. Betsy shot Natasha a look that asked if this was something she had heard about. Natasha's face did not hide the truth.

"I figured as much," Dr. Betsy said. "These are difficult things to talk about because I can't say that I have all the answers. I know the words your grandma said to me that day are words that will stay with me forever: 'No matter who you are or how you identify, there is one thing that we all need to become whole. We need agape love. We need to know that we are loved exactly the way we are, and that type of love helps us to become something more.'"

"Agape love? I don't remember Grandma mentioning that word to me."

"Despite my educated background, I had never heard the word 'agape' before your grandma said it. I asked her what she meant by it. Your grandma shook her head and said I would know when I have received it.

"After all the drama that took place with us working so closely together and all the rumors that were flying around, many of which painted your grandma very opposite to who she was, she was still able to offer me what I needed the most. I was very angry at that time because what they said about me was true, and I hated the fact that

I was being targeted for who I was. I felt I was left alone, fighting the battle to preserve my identity, and there was no one to stand up or defend me. I wanted your grandma's support, but she didn't give it in the way I expected.

"She brought me here to talk with me about it. I guess she also felt the subtle spiritual power this place seems to possess. I was prepared for a fight to defend my decision not to have her return to the PIRD and to let her know I was fine with the end of our friendship. The first words your grandmother said that evening were, 'I am so sorry for what I said and what I believed. You are a special person who is worthy of love, and I do love you.'

"That, of course, took me off guard. I wasn't expecting a confession of that sort. Those were words I had always yearned to hear even at the ripe old age of sixty-one, but no one except your grandmother ever said them to me with such genuineness and sincerity, and I couldn't help but believe her.

"I was speechless," Dr. Betsy went on. "I didn't know what to say in response to that. She then began telling me how much she enjoyed our friendship and what a special person I was. I felt she was seeing me, and not just the Dr. Betsy I wanted everyone to see, or the strong, smart, pretty woman everyone thought I was. Her eyes seemed to pierce my soul. They could see the flaws, the hurts, the fears, but they could also see my desire and passion and strength.

"She asked me a question. 'Who shared the most powerful and the most intimate relationship on earth?'

"I said I wasn't sure, for I had never experienced a truly powerful intimate relationship.

"Then she asked me another question. 'If you could repair one relationship, which one would that be?' I said the relationship between my mom and me. I never felt that my mother loved me, and that left me with a gaping hole in my heart and a constant yearning for unconditional love."

Natasha stared at the ground, listening intently as Dr. Betsy spoke. A praying mantis, disguised at first by the grass in which it hid, became visible. Still as a statue in its position, it appeared to be waiting for its next meal to pass by. She knew exactly how Dr. Betsy felt.

"Your grandmother pointed out how one of the most impactful relationships on earth was a non-sexual one. It was something I hadn't thought about before, so I was intrigued by what she was saying. She explained that, while many people seem to crave romantic love, it isn't the love we need the most. We need something much more powerful, profound, and sustaining.

"I asked if she was trying to say that romantic love or sex was pointless. She told me that romantic love and sex were very important, but she had come to understand that sex was not the ultimate expression of love between two human beings. She believed that the ultimate expression of love between any two humans is the sacrifice of one's life for another. She quoted John 15:13: 'Greater love hath no man than this, that a man lay down his life for his friends.'

"I balked at those words and scoffed at that Scripture. She ignored my response and said that it is love that makes a difference in people's lives. That's why the bond between a child and a parent is so special. A parent is willing to lay down their life for their child. When a mom or dad or anyone else loves you like that, it changes your life."

Dr. Betsy turned to look at Natasha. "We talked for about two hours that day, and by the end of our conversation, one thing was clear. I knew that we would be friends for life."

Dr. Betsy's voice started to quiver as tears welled up in her eyes. "Your grandmother stretched out her hand and said, 'I offer you my *Greater Love.*' Then she handed me this envelope."

Natasha looked down at the envelope. "What is inside these is your family history and secrets closest to her heart. Her giving them to me, entrusting me with them, told me she was trusting me with a part of her that was hidden away. My anger had been completely dismantled, and I sat humbly like a child basking in the love of their parent. As I reflected over and over on her words and her actions, it changed me in a way I could never have imagined."

Dr. Betsy wiped her eyes with a tissue she had pulled from her purse. She stood and stretched and pointed to the pond before passing Natasha her letter. "You know what?" she said excitedly. "Why don't you read that letter while riding in my canoe?"

Natasha's eyes glistened. "I can't wait to get on the water," she said as she stood up. "Everyone always seems to be having so much fun when they're out there." Then she stopped and stepped close to Dr. Betsy. "Thank you so much for sharing your heart with me," she said before embracing her.

"Oh! And one more thing, Natasha," Dr. Betsy said, pointing to the back seat of the bench. "I never wanted to forget the place or the conversation that changed my life."

Looking back, Natasha noticed an iron plaque that had been inscribed with the most endearing words, in remembrance of her dear grandma.

> ***In dedication to my best friend,***
> ***Dr. Cunningham, who showed me "agape" love.***
> ***"Greater love hath no man than this, that a man***
> ***lay down his life for his friends" (John 15:13).***

Natasha and Dr. Betsy started to make their way back to the car to retrieve the canoe, but upon arriving and opening the trunk, Dr. Betsy cried out in dismay. She had forgotten to bring life jackets.

"Please," Natasha begged. "Let's still go. It will be my first time, and right now feels so special. It will be such a wonderful place for me to read this letter," she pouted.

Skillfully, Dr. Betsy rowed them out to the middle of the pond. Then, placing the paddles inside the boat, she let them drift at the water's will. Natasha's excitement at being in the canoe was equal to her eagerness to read her grandma's letter. Breathing in deeply, she took in the scene of the park from an angle she had never seen before. Then, resting her eyes upon the letter, she began to silently read.

My dearest granddaughter Natasha,

I am so sorry I agreed to keep this from you for so long. It's funny how decisions you think will last for a moment turn into years. Needless to say, it was very poor judgment on my part, and I'm truly sorry for the pain I know you'll feel when you hear the truth.

Your mother and father had been happily married for seven years when you were born. Your birth was such a blessing to our family. You were the girl they always wanted, and they were so thrilled to have you. They decided to have a big party in celebration of your first year of life. They were also going to celebrate your brothers' birthday, which was only three days after yours.

The boys, identical twins, were going to be five years old. Your parents Valerie and Brian Thomas Bailey, invited everyone, from family to friends from church and even some from their jobs who also had small children. Your parents had a beautiful home with a pool in the backyard. The pool was going to be the source of much of the fun they intended for their guests to enjoy. They had already started the boys with swimming lessons.

At some point during the party, your mother went to the backyard to bring in some chairs from the porch. Your dad instinctively reminded her to lock the doors and reset the door alarm when she returned. She must have placed the chairs inside and then became immediately distracted. She returned to the kitchen, bustling around to finish prepping the food tables. Your dad and the rest of the men were distracted watching the football game on TV. The party was in full swing when we heard a horrendous screech from one of the parents. Your brothers had made it outside, and both had fallen into the pool. Every adult ran outside, and several jumped in to save the boys, but only one came out alive.

Tears began to slowly glide down Natasha's cheeks as she read. A clasp of thunder rumbled through the air, causing both Natasha and Dr. Betsy to look up. Ominous dark clouds were rushing across the sky, a squall as its front. Dr. Betsy grabbed the oars as Natasha returned to the letter.

The loss of one of her twins was too much for your mother to bear. She blamed herself. She had forgotten to reset the alarm door in her haste to prepare for the party. No one saw or heard when the boys opened the locked door. Every time your mother looked at the twin who survived, she saw the twin she lost. Her grief and guilt consumed her. She was inconsolable.

Natasha stopped reading and looked at Dr. Betsy, who was pushing the oars through the water with all her might.

"If only one of the twins died, then when did — ?"

"Natasha," Dr. Betsy gasped between breaths. "We must get to shore. This storm came out of nowhere. You can continue reading the letter later, but they're alive."

"They're what?" Natasha shouted.

Forgetting she was in a canoe, she stood to her feet in utter shock. Everything went into silent slow motion from that moment—Dr. Betsy flailing her hands and yelling for her to sit down, the forceful rocking of the canoe as she tried to correct her mistake, the canoe flipping, tossing her and Dr. Betsy into the cold dark water of the pond.

As the water enclosed her, her heart rate pounded as if being played by some maniac drummer. Murky darkness was all she could see when her eyes opened. Thrashing about, she managed to bring herself to the surface, but only for a moment before she descended again. By the time she bounced back up to the surface, she had no time or breath to scream out. So mighty was her effort to save herself she exhausted all her strength in mere minutes. As her body began making its final descent, her soul cried out to her Maker.

"Save me, Jesus."

CHAPTER 31

Aziel: Trapped

Aziel looked around with fiendish delight. These were the events that inspired him; they curdled his blood and satisfied the deepest desires within him. Terrorists with rifles pointed to the sky crept around buildings and ducked for cover with the noise of the slightest motion. A rat scurrying too close to a soiled, empty tin bowl was enough to get them shooting blindly toward the phantom target. Their nerves were frayed, and fear pulsated through them with every beat of their hearts, yet they pressed on in blind obedience for a cause many of them could not even recite.

Some were so easy to manipulate that it was no longer fun to even try. Where was the intrigue or challenge if there was no resistance? But he couldn't resist their cries and agonizing moans, especially when he knew their lives were coming to an end. It was like a drug, watching them in utter desperation when they realized that they were mortally wounded and their life was slipping away with every drop of blood that flowed out of them.

Aziel closed his eyes as he sailed over the scene of violence before him. He just wanted to hear it, so he listened carefully. He didn't want to miss even the most inaudible sound of their miserable suffering in their final moments. The whispers of mercy from a God they never served. The prayers for deliverance from their agony. The curses of a hardened heart.

As the fighting died down and the wounded were whisked away by their comrades, he watched the corpses being covered and collected. Men and women with bodies distorted and disfigured soaked in their own blood. So many of them were sealed forever in their sins. He counted everyone carefully in his neatest writing, hand trembling with excitement, and added their names to his list. Their list. He was their master recorder. The unfallen hosts weren't the only ones who kept impeccable records. Now he had to hurry. He had somewhere he needed to be.

Aziel hovered over John's car, then slipped inside. He wanted to be right beside him. John was driving blindly with no destination in mind as the demons did their best to infuse him with their morbid desires. He needed to know exactly what John was thinking, even though he had a good sense of the human's troubled thoughts. And why wouldn't he, for he had been the cause of most of the turmoil throughout John's young life.

His mind flashed back to his crafty work during John's childhood. John had cried himself to sleep for so many nights because kids at school were telling him he was stupid and dumb. He'd made sure John didn't like speaking up in class even if he did know the answer. Every time the boy tried to speak, he'd stutter as if the words had been scared straight out of him. And of course, his classmates would break into laughter, mocking and repeating his failed attempts.

He hadn't always stuttered, sounding like a woodpecker pecking endlessly away at a rotten tree. Aziel stroked his chin as he reminisced. He had capitalized on the perfect moment when Kevin was in the worst mood. His plan had worked flawlessly. Kevin would yank John up by his shirt and pull him to his face while yelling accusations at him before asking why he was such an idiot boy. Tears would stream down John's five-year-old face as he tried to come up with an answer that would satisfy Kevin's unmerited rage. *What kid would have the right answer to those types of questions? None,* Aziel declared to himself as he chuckled. After a couple of those incidents, the stuttering had begun.

Then there was the dog John's mom bought him for his birthday. To Aziel's annoyance, it brought John much delight. But worse, it helped him cope and handle his emotions better whenever he was petting and hugging that despicable creature they had named Beethoven. Aziel hated how the unfallen ones almost always had better control than they did over the animals that roamed the earth.

Aziel scoffed as he remembered that John's stuttering ceased as he affectionately played with the puppy. He feared all the good that little creature might bring to the loathsome child. He needed to destroy it. He needed to destroy them both, so he made sure to ignite Kevin's dislike of the harmless fuzz ball getting in the way of his plans. Kevin called them "filthy creatures that were slaves to their desires and deserved to be mistreated and abused." Aziel laughed with barbaric pleasure at those words being spurted out of Kevin's mouth. He couldn't have said it better himself.

But those words cut into the hearts of everyone else in that house. John's mom would slam the bedroom door so she wouldn't hear his rants, and John's sister would run to her room crying. That left John, who would grab Beethoven, run into his closet, and close the door. He'd pray to God to protect his little friend.

Aziel waited until John had consistently prayed for the revolting creature before he tried to act. The more the humans pled to Him, the more likely they were to curse Him if things didn't go their way.

Aziel groaned with pleasure as he remembered every moment and the minutest details. John had taken his dog outside for a bathroom break. Aziel enticed Kevin to call John back into the house to collect the garbage. John told his dad, "In a minute," but Kevin came to the front door, third glass of wine in hand, and demanded John come in right now and do it. John obeyed.

Aziel danced a demonic jig. He loved the sounds that came a few minutes later—the screeching tire, the stupendous thud, John screaming the name of his dog. But the sight of it was even more enjoyable: John's young legs running out of the house, leaping over the lawn mower; the boy finding Beethoven lifeless in a pool of blood. Aziel could picture the panicked driver crying and apologizing. John's mom trying to comfort him and pulling him away from the scene. His sister looking on from her second-story window, trying to wipe the tears raining down her face. His dad, now on his fourth glass of wine, demanding that John get his butt back inside because it was "just a dumb animal anyway." It was like the unifying sound of an orchestra. Every instrument played its part in perfect timing with perfect harmony, such beautiful music to his ears.

Aziel looked at John in the present. He looked like he was in some type of trance, and he was. He was now in the perfect frame of mind for absolute possession. Aziel had been working to control him and bring him to this point for years. The power he now had over his slave was incredibly satisfying. His slithery tongue licked at the air. He could already taste the victory.

Aziel called his imps to join him for what he believed would be their final ride with John. He wanted to tell them the story of the crafty plan he had put in place to ensure John's slow descent into degradation, misery, and shame. They packed the car and hovered around it like a swarm of bees. He needed to remind them how to master this temptation from beginning to end. But first, he should start with an analogy. *Hmm*, he thought. *What analogy can I use for it? Oh yes, it is just like a pit of quicksand. We only need to lead a person into the pit. It won't devour them right away, but slowly, over time, they will continue to sink lower and lower until, well, I don't even have to say it. We all know the end of every story we love to tell. But I can't restrain myself. Until they perish*, he sang, holding the note as long as he could.

His imps gathered like a group of schoolchildren around a teacher who had taken the class outside to observe a baby bird's nest. He'd tell them how to trap the hapless victim with a habit that could undermine a soul so effectively that it could ruin his life, his relationships, and his mind. Aziel looked about him with glee and then began to tell the imps about the act that could bring their prey effectively into their iron-clad clutch.

Changing his tone to sound more like a schoolteacher than the demon he was, he began his riveting rendition. "John's childish innocence was quickly disappearing, and in its place was growing a frustrated teen. He was thirteen and had just found out his mom was very sick." Aziel cackled softly. "I couldn't have planned a better time for him to find them. They were littered all over Kevin's home office. He didn't bother to hide them, so when he asked John to retrieve his briefcase, he was sure to see at least one. Like any precocious and curious teen, John was quickly drawn to the lewd nude photographs. And just like that—" Aziel snapped his finger—"my little boy had fallen into my well-designed trap.

Aziel hissed; his imps scattered. His story was done, and John was nearing his final destination. Aziel clapped his hands in euphoric joy and started to snicker. He had worked so hard to bring it all together at just the right time. The arrest, the abandonment by Kevin, his sister Riley, and his college plans thwarted. The snicker grew into a frenzied cackling moment. He had managed to do a "Job." "Job" was the annoying man whom they had attempted to overwhelm with a prodigious amount of misery. They swiped away his wealth, his children, and his health in a single day. Their attempt to sever Job's relationship with God had failed, but it was a successful tactic for millions of weaker souls like John.

"Free yourself," Aziel whispered ever so gently, like a mother comforting a child with a wounded knee. "Free yourself," he whispered again before throwing his hand up like a conductor for the legions who followed him.

"Free yourself," they chanted, like an army of soldiers giving homage to a dictator.

"Your mother is gone, the only person who ever truly loved you. You have no father. Your life is in shambles, and you've likely destroyed your sister's life too. What's the point of going on? What's the point of living? You're worthless. You're nothing more than a collection of cells with no destiny, no hope, and no future."

Aziel stood back from whispering in John's ear. He thought he heard something. His devilish ears perked up, but only silence sounded throughout their domain of darkness. He raised both his arms up high so he could fill the void with the chants of his horde.

But before he could conduct his farewell melody for John, a flash of light came out of nowhere.

CHAPTER 32

John: Twist of Fate

Blood-curdling screams reverberated through the air. Instantly, John's body responded. As he approached the scene, adrenaline pumped into his blood like water through a firehose, empowering him with fearless confidence. People were jumping up and down on the banks of the pond, pointing to an overturned canoe though being drenched by the driving rain that had descended upon them in moments. A lone man swam toward an elderly woman.

Peeling off his shirt and pants and tugging off his shoes, he powered his muscular legs past them all and splashed water wildly about as he ran. With a powerful leap, he careened into the water. Swimming with strokes like an Olympian, he caught sight of the girl's hand slipping into the darkness.

Reaching into the murky waters, he caught hold of a limp body. He wrapped his arms tightly around her and brought her to shore, where he then fell face down on the ground, shaking from fatigue. He crawled out of the way of the paramedics rushing toward the crowds who surrounded the rescued individuals. Trembling from the chill of the water, he watched from a distance until the girl was whisked away

295

in an ambulance with sirens blaring. Then he slinked back to his car and changed into some dry dirty clothes he found in the back seat.

"You're a hero," a middle-aged man with pepper grey hair declared as he approached John's car. "I saw everything. You came out of nowhere and saved that girl's life."

A woman with silver hair holding onto the man's arm shook her head in agreement.

John shrugged and shook his head. "I did what anyone else would have done."

"We don't know how to swim," said the lady. "We didn't know what to do. I just cried out to God, and then, like some angel, you appeared and jumped right in. With all the commotion and that freak downpour, we lost sight of you, but we're so glad you're still here." The woman pointed behind her toward the lake. "Those officers were looking for you."

John had seen the police when they arrived. It was one of the reasons he had hastily left the scene. It had only been a few hours since his arrest, and he didn't want to be back on their radar for any reason.

"Umm, well, there's no need for them to speak with me. I'm sure they got all the information they needed from everyone else. I wasn't even supposed to be here."

The couple stepped back from the car. "Be safe and God bless," they said, waving.

As he pulled away, the whole ordeal started to sink in deeper. *You jumped into the lake and pulled a woman out. Where in the heck did that come from? What if you got to her before she stopped fighting? You should have grabbed a floaty or something and thrown it to her. That's the first rule of helping a drowning person. But you did it. You hurt someone, and you helped someone today. What kind of karma is that?*

It was as if someone was directing his life, purposefully moving him from one place to another. "You should have moved me past Natasha's house," he said aloud. "And helped me remember to pick up my sister," he grumbled as he pulled into the hospital parking lot.

He sat in his car, afraid of entering yet anxious to see Riley. Thinking back to Kevin's tirade in the jail, he realized he had yet to read the letter his aunt had given him. Maybe that would give him some clue about what Kevin was referring to.

Now it dawned on him the reason he had unintentionally driven to the park. He wanted to find a quiet place to read that letter. Looking around, he saw that he was surrounded by empty cars. *It's as good a time and place as any*, he thought, reaching for the glove compartment.

Green bills floated onto his lap like butterflies when he unfolded the letter. His eyes bugged out at the sight of so many Benjamin Franklins. He wept uncontrollably as he counted the money—$5,000 in all. How could this be? It was more than what George had agreed to pay him and enough to cover his rent and his school fees. He sat back and let the tears flow as he started reading.

My dearest son John,

I'm very sorry for the life you and your sister endured because of me. I believed I could shield you guys from Kevin's cruelty and rage. How wrong and naive I've been. After watching you risk your life to protect me, I was determined to leave him. I got a part-time job working as a waitress and saved every scrap of money I could. But fatigue and tiredness overwhelmed me, and my body hurt to the core of my being. I thought it was because I was working too hard with my new job, taking care of you two, and catering to the selfish whims of Kevin. I was horribly mistaken. Two weeks before your fifteenth birthday, after a series of doctor visits and tests, I was diagnosed with metastatic breast cancer.

Cancer quickly took everything away from me, John. It took my choice and ability to leave Kevin. It took my strength and fight. It took my aspirations and hope. It brought me to the lowest point of my entire life. I always thought I'd be the one to tell you this myself when the time was right, but fate has determined otherwise. So I'm writing this letter, and I hope you understand and forgive me.

I started college right out of high school even though I had no inkling of what I wanted to study or become. It was there that I met a wonderful man. He wasn't like anyone I had ever met before—strikingly handsome and brilliant. He was studying to become a civil engineer. Though a few years older than I was and a senior in college, we fell in love hard and fast. His name was Michael Walker.

Despite our frequent dating, he was very committed to his education. I see him in you, as you're so smart and serious about your schooling. He got accepted into the graduate civil engineering program at Michigan State University and was beyond thrilled.

The only problem was that I had just found out I was pregnant with you. I pressed Michael to see if he wanted to marry me, but he was not interested in marriage. He said it would be better if we waited so that he could devote his time and attention to school without having to worry about taking care of a wife. I reasoned that, if he didn't want a wife to be bothering him in school, he surely wouldn't want a baby.

My sister begged me to tell Michael so he could make a decision, knowing the truth. But I refused. I didn't want him to feel obligated to marry me just because I was having our baby. Instead, I broke up with him.

In my anger and frustration, I went out for a night of partying with friends. The next thing I knew, I was waking up in bed with Kevin. He seemed smitten with me, so I agreed to start dating him. With Michael out of the picture, I needed someone to support me, and Kevin was already working.

I had no family I could rely on. I had never met my father, and my mother's mental issues were the reason I ran off to college in the first place. I was close with my sisters, but Marsha was a wild thing and still in high school, and Kristen was already married with a child.

I lied to Kevin and told him he got me pregnant. A few weeks later, Michael apologized and asked if we could get back together. He said he loved me and was willing to see if we could make a long-distance relationship work. I was sure being pregnant would be a game changer, and I didn't want to be rejected twice. Kevin, on the other hand, had asked me to marry him the minute he found out I was pregnant with who he thought was his child. I wasn't in love with him but figured it would be the wisest choice.

I hid the truth deep in my heart and made my sister swear she'd never tell anyone. Kevin's infatuation with me was short-lived, and I think he began to realize I had only married him because I was pregnant. We were both miserable in the marriage, but things changed for the worse when he started drinking.

I swore I'd leave him one day, and ironically, I will, but not in the way I had hoped. Leaving you and your sister with him is my greatest fear. The thought of it crushed me, but that was before my newfound faith. You are in God's hands now. I have no choice but to trust your lives with Him and to believe He will find you two and bring you to the light of His love, just like He found me.

John, please take care of your sister. You're all she has. You must be her protector and her friend. Don't let Kevin define who you are. You're not his son by birth; don't be his son in character.

And listen. Open your ears to hear His voice.

I don't have much to give, son. The money in this envelope was all I was able to save. It's not much, but I hope it helps with something. Share it with your sister. I love you, son. I love both of my beautiful butterflies.

Always and forever,

Your Mom

"Trust in the Lord with all thine heart; and lean not unto thine own understanding. In all thy ways acknowledge Him, and He shall direct thy paths" (Proverbs 3:5–6).

"Michael Walker," John whispered over and over through his tears. "That's my real father. Kevin's not my dad. He's really not my dad." Now Kevin's words made perfect sense. When he was younger, John had considered the idea that he was not Kevin's child. He didn't look anything like him. His skin was naturally tan, while Kevin's was stark white. Kevin was five foot ten, and he six foot one. Kevin had dusty brown hair and blue eyes. John had curly brown hair and brown eyes. But none of these physical differences were a guarantee he wasn't Kevin's kid. Lots of kids he knew didn't look exactly like their parents.

And what about Riley? he thought before quickly concluding she had to be Kevin's. She, on the other hand, had honey-blond hair and blue eyes, and her facial features resembled his.

As his thoughts turned back to his sister, his heart sank. He hadn't done what his mother desired. He hadn't protected his sister, and now he had to face the reality of his poor choices. Gathering his courage, he placed the letter back into the glove compartment.

He wasn't prepared for the sight that met his gaze when he walked into Riley's hospital room. He assumed she couldn't be hurt too badly since Kevin had been more concerned with the fact that John wasn't his son, but he was mistaken. Her face was scratched and swollen, and blood had seeped through part of the bandage on her head. Her left leg was in a full cast and elevated in traction. But she was alive and fast asleep and looked very much like an angel in his eyes. He tenderly rubbed her cheek with the back of his hand and stroked her lifeless arm. She didn't respond, making him wonder if she'd ever return to consciousness.

"She's on some pretty heavy medications," his aunt said as she approached with open arms. Lowering her voice to a whisper, she leaned toward John. "Her leg was badly damaged, John. They're hoping it will heal well enough for her to walk again."

His chin began to tremble. "She might not walk again?" he questioned in absolute horror. "It's all my fault," he moaned. "I was supposed to pick her up, and I—"

Aunt Kristen shook her head no and hugged John again. "You're not to blame. Things happen in life that no one understands or can prevent. Don't blame yourself, John. Right now, Riley needs you to be strong." She grabbed hold of his hand and squeezed it tightly, as if to bolster him for her next words.

"Kevin is still leaving. I've been arguing with him all evening," she said disappointedly. "Not even this has kept that selfish man from reconsidering his decision. Once he heard that she was not going to die, he said he'd have his lawyer draft the papers to give me and Joseph full guardianship. It's like he doesn't want to be weighed down by her needs right now. I just can't comprehend how he could be so wickedly apathetic at a time like this."

John's body seemed to lose all strength, and he floundered to a chair near Riley's bed. His chest felt tight, and he began to sweat profusely. His heart began to beat faster and faster.

"Are you okay?" Kristen asked, rushing to his side. She quickly filled a glass with water and handed it to him. "Just relax, John. It's going to be okay."

CHAPTER 33

Natasha: Together Again

Natasha heard panicked voices before her eyes rolled open and cheers erupted around her. Her chest ached terribly every time she tried to take a shallow breath. It felt like it was filled with cement embedded with chards of glass.

"Thank you, God!" It was Dr. Betsy's voice. Natasha turned her head toward it. Her friend's tearstained face broke into a smile. "You're alive!" Dr. Betsy wept, grabbing hold of her hand while walking beside the stretcher as the paramedics carried her to the ambulance. "I'll meet you at the hospital," she promised as they closed the doors.

Moments passed while she listened to the ambulance sirens and watched the paramedics scamper to stabilize her before she recalled what had led to her horrible demise.

"They're alive," she whispered to herself.

"I'm sorry, what did you say?" a paramedic asked. Then, assuming he had heard her words, he replied with a smile, "Yes, you're alive and going to be just fine."

Natasha returned a weak smile before closing her eyes and trying to remember more of what she had read in her grandma's letter. One of her baby brothers had drowned because her mom had forgotten to lock the door. Now she understood the sorrow that had etched itself into her mother's face. *No wonder she was so depressed all the time,* she thought to herself.

And then she thought of the news that had stunned her senseless. Her father and brother were alive. But how? And where were they? *There's no way that can be true. Perhaps Dr. Betsy misspoke.*

If only she could read the letter in its entirety. She knew her grandma would explain everything. A pang of disappointment pierced her heart. That would likely be impossible because the letter was probably at the bottom of the pond.

And if they are alive, why would Mom and Grandma lie to me? And why haven't my father and brother come to see me? Tears rolled out of the corners of her eyes as she began to sob. She was utterly confused and angry that her family could keep such a secret from her.

A paramedic grasped her hand in sympathy. "Honey, you're going to survive this. I know you're scared, but I promise you, you'll be feeling like yourself in no time. And you'll probably only need to stay one night in the hospital."

"What hospital are you taking me to?" Natasha asked as she tried to sniffle back her tears.

"UCSF Helen Diller Medical Center at Parnassus Heights," replied the paramedic.

"That's where my mom is," she said, sobbing harder. "She's been there for over a week."

"Oh my goodness! I didn't know. What is she in for?"

"We found out she's in kidney failure and needs dialysis."

"I'm so sorry. I hope she'll be fine too," the paramedic said before turning her attention back to making sure Natasha was secure in the stretcher as the ambulance doors swung open.

Dr. Betsy stayed by her side through the entire admission process. Once she was settled in her room, Natasha began to question her in earnest about her family, but Dr. Betsy didn't want to say anything more.

"Natasha, I'm sorry, but it's not my place."

"How could they do this to me?" she cried. "Why would they rob me of my family? Why wouldn't they trust me to know the truth? You even knew it," she spurted out angrily.

"It's time for you to rest," Dr. Betsy said, ignoring her accusation while pulling the covers up to Natasha's chest. "You've been through hell today and this past week. You need to relax and rest."

She turned and sat down in the chair near Natasha's hospital bed. "I delayed giving you that letter for so long because I knew it would destroy you, and I wanted your mother to be the one to tell you this." She looked down at the ground. "It's hard for her too, Natasha. Facing the past and feeling guilty about the choices you've made. You just want to run away and keep it hidden. You don't want to feel that pain. And losing a child is a pain like no other in this life."

It was the way Dr. Betsy spoke that made Natasha's spirit calm down. She spoke as if she had endured such a loss, and compassion rose within her. "Dr. Betsy, I—"

But Dr. Betsy quickly interrupted. "I struggled with whether it was the right time to give it to you. How I prayed for wisdom. And then your mom became ill. It was like a sign, and I knew the time had come."

Natasha looked at Dr. Betsy. She had one last question for her.

"Your mom knows," Dr. Betsy said, as if she had read Natasha's mind. "Your mom knows I gave you the letter and that you now know that your father and brother are alive." She stood up and squeezed Natasha's hand. "I love you, Natasha, and I'm always here for you. I have to go now, but I'll be back in the morning."

She leaned in and gave Natasha a long hug. "You'll be okay," she whispered. "God will see you through. Trust Him."

When Natasha opened her eyes, her mother was at her bedside, mourning as if she'd lost her firstborn child.

All the anger that had ingrained itself into her heart and soul over the past weeks melted away at the sight of her mother's anguish. She knew instinctively that Valerie was not just weeping for her but for her lost children. She had unwittingly lost them all.

Valerie tried to compose herself and speak. "I have no words that can take away the pain I've caused. I almost lost you too because of my foolishness. God kept pressing upon me the need to tell you the truth, but I kept it hidden for so long, I feared losing you completely, and you're the only child I had left. Because of me, I lost both my boys. I lost everything."

"What do you mean, you lost everything?" Natasha cried. "I thought that my dad and one of my brothers were still alive. Dr. Betsy said . . ."

Valerie couldn't stifle her tears and for a long moment continued to cry uncontrollably. "They are alive, Natasha, but I wanted to explain first. When I lost JT in the drowning, I couldn't bear the loss, the guilt, or the shame. It destroyed me. I blamed myself because it was my fault. I had forgotten to lock the door."

Blowing her nose and wiping her face, she tried to continue without crying. "Every time I saw his twin brother, I saw him. I couldn't bear to see my own son," she said and started to cry all over again. "After months and months of just pure depression, your dad couldn't take it anymore. It was affecting Thomas Jr. horribly. He had lost his brother, and it was like he'd lost his mom too. I could barely look at him without crying.

"We tried everything: group therapy, individual therapy, and even medications. We tried different therapists and prayer sessions, anointings, and fasting, but nothing seemed to work. I was hopelessly lost in my grief. That's when Brian suggested we separate for a time. He hoped that by having you kids and himself out of the way, I might be able to heal and cope better.

"But I insisted on keeping you. You were still a baby, and I thought that taking care of you would help me through my grief. In the end, your dad took only Thomas Jr., but it became clear that I wasn't up to taking care of you either. That's when your grandma moved in to help me.

"Instead of getting better and truly healing, I just got worse."

A rapping at the door silenced Valerie, and they both turned to look at the closed hospital room door.

"It's them," Valerie whispered nervously.

"It's who?" Natasha asked with eyebrows raised.

"Come in," Valerie said as she wiggled herself to sit up better in her wheelchair.

The door slowly crept open, and in walked a good-looking black man, clean-shaven with neatly trimmed peppered gray and black hair. He stood about six feet tall and had a round belly. He was dressed in brown slacks, a yellow polo shirt, and a light brown jacket.

And behind him walked TJ.

Thinking at first that he happened to visit her at the same time as this man she now knew to be her father, Natasha smiled graciously. Her heart was overflowing with gratitude that her dear college friend had come to see her. Her spirit of gratitude turned to shock and disbelief when TJ fell onto his knees and into her mother's arms. Valerie wept without abandon, crying, "My son, my son."

Her father ran to her bedside and enveloped her with tears and apologies as she sat spellbound and briefly emotionless. As the truth sank in, her emotions exploded like an erupting geyser. Her father was not only alive, but he loved her, and TJ, her wonderful friend, was her brother.

Still kneeling, TJ turned to her and kissed her hand before they embraced with laughter and tears. No one but God could have ordained events in such a way as this.

Brian approached Valerie and hugged her respectfully. Then he reached out one hand toward Valerie and the other to Natasha. TJ completed the circle.

"We're a family again," he said through tears. "My God, thank You. You have brought my family together again."

CHAPTER 34

Natasha: Making Amends

Looking at the time, Natasha knew she'd be late. She rushed out of the classroom and ran-walked to get to her car. She'd been discharged from the hospital three days ago and had returned to school. It was the end of the semester, and despite all the commotion within her family, she needed to buckle down and be prepared for her final examinations.

She hadn't spoken to Dr. Betsy since her hospitalization and was anxious to share what had transpired with her family. They planned to meet under Old Ben. Arriving at the bench, she found Dr. Betsy quietly peering at the sea in deep meditation.

"Sorry to interrupt," she said softly before sitting down.

Dr. Betsy smiled and reached over to hug her. "I'm so glad to see you. You look great. How are you feeling?" she asked, leaning back onto the bench. The leaves of Old Ben were now flushed with fall colors. Varying orange, red, and yellow hues permeated the leaves that glided from its branches and carpeted the ground under which she stood.

"I feel great," Natasha beamed. "And my family is great. And you? How are you doing? I realized I never even questioned how you survived the canoe catastrophe."

"Oh!" Dr. Betsy blushed while giving Natasha a grateful tap on the knee. "I am fine. I must have completely panicked despite knowing how to swim. I really don't remember everything that happened. It was all so fast, and with all that rain, I couldn't even see who helped me out of the water. Plus, it was you that I was worried about the whole time. And I must apologize. I should never have taken you out there without a life vest. None of this would have happened if we'd had those on."

Natasha watched the calm waters of the ocean. "I think everything happened just the way it ought to have happened. I think God was in it all. Think about it," she said, looking back at Dr. Betsy. "The fact that I got hospitalized pushed my mom out of being the depressed person she'd become. It pushed her to finally tell the truth. She called my dad and brother to the hospital."

"Oh my gosh! You met your family?" Dr. Betsy's eyes brimmed with tears. "That is a dream come true for your grandmother. Oh, how I wish she were here to witness it!"

"It was surreal," Natasha admitted. "It was a family reunion I never dreamed possible, and now Mom seems like a completely different person. My dad says he sees life in her eyes again. It's funny how you or someone close to you may have to die, or come close to it, for you to live."

Cocking her head, Dr. Betsy grinned. "Look who's declaring words of wisdom and recognizing the omnipotent guiding hand of God. How great Thou art," she sang, raising her hands to the sky.

There was so much to tell Dr. Betsy that Natasha found it difficult to stay focused on one topic. She told her how her parents were committed to working on their relationship and figuring out how they could move forward. There was still a lot of hurt and shame from the past, but they knew they needed to try.

To her surprise, her parents informed her that they were still married. They had separated but never formally divorced. Her mother had reverted to using her maiden name when she felt her marriage was irreparable, and after several years of hoping they'd reconcile, her father had an affair. Jasmine was his twelve-year old child from that relationship. While he hadn't brought her to the hospital, he was excited for them to meet her.

"And we're going to spend Thanksgiving together," Natasha announced like an excited five-year-old. "I mean, who could have imagined that I'd be with my family this Thanksgiving, for the first time in my life?" Then her eyes brightened some more as she clasped her hands together. "And we want you to come to our Thanksgiving dinner. Please come," she begged.

"I don't know, Natasha," Dr. Betsy sighed. "You know your mom and I—"

"No, no, no!" Natasha said, waving her hands as if to dispel Dr. Betsy's thoughts. "Mom said she wants to talk to you, so expect a call from her. I tell you, she's like a whole different person."

Despite Dr. Betsy feeling unconvinced that Valerie would welcome her to their Thanksgiving meal, she promised she'd consider it if the invite was given.

"Are you still thinking about moving back home?" she asked.

Natasha shrugged her shoulders. "I'm not sure yet. Mom says she's fine now, but my dad and I don't think she should be on her own. We're not even sure if she can continue working now that she's on dialysis. She'll probably need someone to help her with meals and housework. From what the medical team told me, she might feel pretty drained after treatments." She bowed her head and smiled. "Dad even suggested maybe coming back home, you know, if everything works out with him and Mom. I mean, they're still married."

"I can't imagine how thrilled you are," Dr. Betsy said, squeezing Natasha's hand. "And TJ? How's he taking everything?"

"Oh! He's terrific!" Natasha expressed happily, wiping away her tears. "He's the best brother a girl could ask for. I had already liked him, but now I love him. He's supportive and listens to me and all my crazy ideas. He's always giving me hugs, even when we meet in school," she laughed. "I never had that. It's so wonderful. People think I have this awesome new boyfriend, and then I tell them it's my brother, my real brother."

"It sounds like everything is going well."

"For once in my life, it actually is," Natasha shouted out, pumping her hands.

Dr. Betsy winced and drew in a deep breath. "Well, I need to tell you something that might rain on your parade a bit."

"Oh, please! No bad news. What is it?" Natasha moaned, drooping her head.

"Your mom's house was broken into the day we had that episode on the pond."

Dr. Betsy quickly explained that John was the culprit but not the real criminal. He had confessed to her the deal he made with George and his true intentions to provide him with as little information as possible. He also admitted his desire to find out what was really going on.

The police department had left a message on Valerie's phone and mailed her the details of the break-in. "Please convince your mom not to press charges," Dr. Betsy begged. "I know the type of person George is, and we both know this is completely out of character for John."

Natasha didn't completely agree with Dr. Betsy. She knew John was competitive but had never felt he had any ill will toward her or that he would try to hurt her in any way. However, she couldn't get over how he had violated her home by his unlawful entry, and she didn't sympathize with the excuses he told Dr. Betsy.

"I've been desperate for money so many times, but I would never cross the line to steal from someone. It's just something I wouldn't do, and the fact that he did says something about him, Dr. Betsy. If he's able to be influenced just for money, how trustworthy can he be?"

Natasha also reasoned that, with her dad back in their lives, he probably wouldn't be so willing to excuse the infringement either. He noticed the footsteps around the back of the house and asked her and her mom about it. They had shrugged it off, telling him it was probably one of the utility guys, but her dad insisted they needed to get a security system in place.

"I know it looks bad on John, and I can't completely defend his actions, but I can tell you that I felt impressed to post his bail that morning. It was as if God designed it for me to accidentally call his number. Upon finding out more about his circumstances, I felt even more certain that divine destiny had stepped in. It's not just about the money he needed, Natasha," she said solemnly. "It's also about family."

Natasha promised she'd try to keep an open mind but found the whole thing unsettling. She assured Dr. Betsy she'd speak with her parents but said it would be totally up to them how they wanted to proceed.

The next day, she returned to the hospital to meet with a social worker who would provide them with information to make an informed decision about Valerie's health care. Before the meeting, Natasha's family did not fully understand the treatment options available to Valerie now that she had end-stage renal failure and was on dialysis.

As they waited in the hospital lobby for their appointment, Natasha watched the news playing on a TV attached to the wall across the room. She distracted herself with a magazine that lay on the end table beside her seat. Soon, a woman walked in with a beautiful golden retriever and approached the desk. Natasha smiled, figuring it was a therapy dog and that they were on their way to visit and cheer up ailing patients. She then returned her attention to the magazine.

"And now, an update about the heroic deed of an unknown young man," a reporter spoke. Video footage from Kennington Park began to roll across the TV screen. "The police are still hoping to find the young man who bystanders say appeared out of nowhere to rescue a drowning young lady Sunday evening."

Natasha nudged her mom, who was already staring at the screen. The police had visited Natasha before she was discharged from the hospital because they needed her testimony as to what caused the canoe accident. She cooperated, telling them the truth about what happened. She also asked if they knew who had rescued her, as she'd love to thank them. They informed her that they had been unable to find her heroic rescuer, but when they did, they would be sure to contact her.

"Anyone with any information about the event is asked to report to the police," the reporter continued.

Then Natasha's ear picked up the conversation between the receptionist and the woman with the dog.

"Oh my gosh!" the woman declared to the receptionist. "We met the guy who rescued the girl that day."

Natasha sat up, and her ears homed in on the conversation.

"That heroic young man had immediately left the scene. My husband and I caught him before he left the park. He refused to think anything of it, but my husband made sure to get a photo of his license plate when he drove off. We'll be sure to hand that over to the cops. I'm sure that young lady would love to thank him."

Natasha wondered if she should let the woman know that she was that young lady but decided against it. It would bring undue attention to her and serve no other purpose. The woman continued to chat about the event before the receptionist instructed her on how to get to the hospital ward she intended to visit.

Soon after, Valerie was called in for her appointment. The social worker, a talkative and friendly woman, was extremely informative. She explained the different types of dialysis and the pros and cons of each, as well as the benefits and drawbacks of getting a transplant. Natasha and Valerie were disheartened to realize that the waiting period for a kidney transplant could be years.

The social worker also gave them information about dialysis clinics near their home, telling them they needed to make a choice immediately so that Valerie would stay on schedule with her dialysis treatments. They left her office with a packet of pamphlets and booklets about dialysis and renal disease.

Walking out the hospital doors with her mom on her arm, Natasha noticed the woman with the therapy dog excitedly speaking with a man. His back was turned to them as he scooted down to pet the dog. She smiled at the adorable scene. As they were about to pass each other, the guy stood up and turned around.

"John?" she gasped as their eyes met. For a fleeting moment, she thought about walking the other way. He looked embarrassed as his face flushed the shade of Pink Lady apple. He broke the gaze, looking down as she approached him.

"Oh my gosh! I can't believe this," the woman with the dog suddenly declared. "You're the girl who almost drowned," she shouted. Then, pointing to John, she declared in the same loud voice, "He's the one who saved you." She then covered her mouth with both her hands, completely astonished.

Natasha's arms went limp as they fell to her side. Valerie looked at Natasha and then at John. "You know him?" she asked before rushing toward John and hugging him. "You saved my daughter," she cried. Then, stepping back, she reached out her hand. John grasped it, though his eyes were fixed on Natasha.

Shaking his head in disbelief, he said, "This can't be. You're the girl?"

The woman with the dog stepped in. "I got a good look at you that day. I saw that birthmark on your upper arm," she said, pointing to an oblong black mark three to four centimeters long on Natasha's arm. "I don't forget faces very easily either, especially a pretty one like yours."

Natasha stood speechless. The compliment went unnoticed due to the conflict she felt inside. Was she supposed to thank the very person who had also violated her privacy and home?

"Thank you, John," she finally said. "How were you at Kennington Park though at that time?"

How was it you? she thought to herself as her mind tried to put the pieces together.

John just kept shaking his head no. "I don't know. I just happened to be there. I had no idea it was you."

"I can't thank you enough," Valerie said, reaching her hand out to shake his again. "God bless you and keep you, son."

"Well, umm. I gotta go," John said, looking toward the hospital lobby. "I'm happy you're okay," he told Natasha before walking away.

"You guys know each other?" the woman asked with glee as they watched John enter the hospital. "That's unbelievable. And he's probably the humblest person I've ever met."

The woman walked with Natasha and Valerie back to her car, chatting about the incredible coincidence of their meeting like that and the significance of her role in making the connection happen. She invited Natasha to their dog farm, where they bred and raised dogs.

"I know that the trauma of an event like you went through is dreadful. I'd be happy to gift you one of our newborn puppies to help you in your recovery," she offered. "They are a tremendous form of therapy," she said, handing Natasha her card.

"You barely thanked that boy," Valerie scolded her when they got into their car. "He saved your life, Natasha. You should have at least shaken his hand or given him a hug or something to show your gratitude."

"It's complicated, Mom," Natasha replied as she turned the key in the ignition. "I'll catch you up on the drive home."

CHAPTER 35

Amazing Grace

The scent of pumpkin spice and bread baking wafted through Valerie's home. It felt like Christmas morning to the residents there, but it was not, though it was a holiday. This holiday was the one that truly merited their attention and reflected the emotions swelling in each heart.

"Natasha, turn up the music and come here," TJ yelled as his favorite Christmas tune, "Jingle Bell Rock," inspired dancing vibes. He grabbed Natasha's hand, and they danced like children on Christmas morning in their matching pajamas.

The family had decided to make Thanksgiving their main holiday that year. Gratitude and thankfulness for the miraculous events of the past few weeks filled each of their hearts. Natasha reached her hand out to Jasmine as she joined them in the living room. Jasmine's thick braids bounced up and down as the girls giggled and jived until the song was done.

Passing Jasmine three index cards with the words "Thank You" written on the front, Natasha carefully instructed her, "Write three things you're thankful for. Then we'll put the cards on our Thankfulness

Tree," she said, pointing to what appeared to be a Christmas tree decorated with traditional lights, ornaments, and thankfulness cards. "I'm going to pass these to Mom and Dad," she said, leaving the room.

"Natasha, can you check the pies in the oven?" Valerie asked as she stirred a pot on the stove filled with greens.

As Natasha pulled back the oven door, a stream of hot air rushed out. Inside sat an apple pie, its thick, sweet syrup bubbling at the edges and running down the sides of the pan. A sweet potato pie decorated with buttery pastry leaves sat beside it.

"Oh, my gosh, Mom," she swooned. "They smell and look so good." She kissed her fingers and waved her hand. "Incredibly delectable."

After closing the oven door, she picked up a pamphlet sitting on the counter. It was titled "Holiday Eating Tips for Dialysis Patients."

"So, how long did you soak the sweet potatoes?" she asked while scanning the instructions. "Here it says you should have soaked them for at least four hours."

"I cut the sweet potatoes into little cubes and soaked them overnight," Valerie bragged. "Aha!" she said, pointing the spoon she used to stir the greens at Natasha. "You thought I paid that booklet no attention, didn't you? But I'm trying, baby. I'm trying."

Natasha smiled warmly at Valerie, her heart satisfyingly content to see her mother caring about herself.

"I know you're having fun out there with your brother and sister, but you need to start the green bean casserole. Remember, that's one of the dishes I can have seconds, so don't oversalt it like you did the last time you cooked those veggies for me." Valerie picked up a knife and started slicing a stalk of celery. "You guys can always add salt later."

Natasha sneaked up behind her mom and hugged her. "You're paying great attention to your diet."

"Well, the dietitian at the dialysis center put the fear of God in me after she explained all the complications that could result if I didn't watch what I eat. I have a long way to go in learning and doing everything right, but I'm trying."

"You're off to a good start, and I'm proud of you," Natasha said, grabbing two bags of green beans from the freezer.

Valerie stopped what she was doing and turned to face Natasha. "I'm very proud of you too, Natasha. Way prouder of you than you could ever be of me.

"So, what time did you tell our guest to arrive? And where is your father? He promised to make his Jamaican macaroni pie, chicken pelau, and some Sorrel drink, but he hasn't started any of them. I know it's only 8:00 a.m., but time flies.

"What time did you say they'd be arriving? I hope you didn't tell them any time before 2:00 p.m.; there's no way we'll be ready before then.

"And could you please help TJ to tidy up the sunroom?"

"Mom! Whoa! Please slow down. You're asking me to do a gazillion things at once. I know how late you always are, so I told them to show up by about 4. I'm going to put on my green bean casserole, and then I'll work with TJ on cleaning up the sunroom."

Valerie breathed a sigh of relief. "I'm sorry, honey. I'm just a little uptight. It's been a while since I've had guests over, and I'm nervous about everyone coming. Everything has happened so fast, and I know I've said this a thousand times, but I truly feel as if I just woke up from some type of trance-like coma. I'm sorry, Natasha. I'm so sorry for ruining everyone's life."

"Stop it, Mom," Natasha said, looking into the fridge. "I know you're sorry, and you can't change the past. Let's just focus on our future and today. I just want to relish everyone being here," she said, hugging her mom.

Yet Natasha couldn't help thinking about the past few weeks. They had been a stir of activity and wonderful events. Her dad had brought Jasmine to their home. She was a beautiful girl with a devious smile. Her hair was a collection of neat box braids that cascaded down her back. At twelve years old, she was taller than most girls her age and already taller than Natasha. She was respectful, just like TJ, answering "Yes, ma'am" and "No, sir" in response to every inquiry.

"It's the Jamaican way," her dad would say in his Jamaican accent while waving his finger at her. "Ya be speaking Patois too 'cause da di way we speak a fiwi language," he'd promise. Patois, an eclectic mixture of English, West African, Irish, Spanish, Hindi, and other languages, was the true language of all the folks from back home. Natasha squealed with delight and admiration every time they reverted to speaking it to each other and often begged for them to speak it just so she could hear it.

Brian loved to honor her request by complimenting his daughter. "Ya smart and ya pretty, na man," he'd say, giving her a bear hug. Her dad was already thinking about moving back to their home with Jasmine. They lived about two hours away, and he drove the distance each day for his job. "And mi wife need di help." Being a diabetic himself and having watched more than one relative end up on dialysis, he understood that Valerie shouldn't be left alone. He also wanted Natasha and TJ to remain on campus and stay focused on their schooling.

Her mom was not opposed to the idea either. Brian was a wonderful cook and showed himself to be a thoughtful caregiver. He had taken the last three weeks off work just so he could become reacquainted with his family and help Valerie adjust to her new life on dialysis.

"We have a lot of catching up and healing to do," Valerie expressed to the children one Sabbath evening.

"Rebuilding our broken home will be no easy feat," Brian added. Natasha and TJ promised they understood and were committed to bringing their family back together again.

—◄○►—

Returning to school after meeting her family was difficult. Natasha could barely concentrate on her work and was constantly being interrupted by phone calls and text messages from TJ, her dad or mom, and even Dr. Betsy. But it was the text from John that stopped her in her tracks. He asked if they could meet up so they could talk. Feeling the need for privacy, they decided to meet under Old Ben.

At first glance, she thought John had chickened out of their meeting. He was never late, and she arrived ten minutes after their agreed-upon meeting time. He wasn't sitting on the bench as she and Dr. Betsy always did. Then she caught sight of an outstretched leg. He had chosen to sit on the ground between Old Ben's gnarled roots.

John hadn't noticed her approaching, so she stopped and watched him for a few seconds. He stared at the ground, slumped forward as his hand massaged his forehead. He looked different to her, but she couldn't tell why. At a loss for words on how to greet the person who had robbed and then rescued her, she decided a simple greeting would do.

"Hey, John," she called as she neared the tree. She had chosen to wear a pair of blue jeans with some ankle boots and a button-up shirt that hung past her behind. Wearing jeans and boots wasn't her typical attire, but her dad had infused her with a sense of confidence with his constant compliments, and Jasmine, as young as she was, had an eye for style. It was she who convinced Natasha to change her look that day.

Scurrying to his feet at the sound of her voice, John stood, looking at her momentarily before responding.

"Umm, thanks for coming. I wasn't sure if you'd show up."

"I said I was coming. I wouldn't leave you hanging like that."

"Well, actually," John started to say before halting himself and shoving his hands into his pants pockets. "I just wanted to let you know how sorry and embarrassed I am about what I did and how much I appreciate that your family didn't press charges."

He didn't sound like the John she had come to know earlier. That John could never have brought himself to apologize for anything. Instead, he would have found a way to make her the culprit.

"You don't have to feel obligated to be nice just because of what happened at the lake. I'm no hero, Natasha. I just happened to be at the right place at the right time."

"How did you end up at Kennington Park after being in jail that morning?" she asked before her eyes started to follow a sparrow that was flitting about in Old Ben's branches.

John shifted his position and slowly shook his head. "I really don't know, to be frank with you. After I was released from jail, I wanted to find a quiet place to be alone before I faced seeing my sister in the hospital."

"I'm so sorry about your sister, John. Dr. Betsy told me about the accident. Is she okay?"

John's jaw clenched, and he looked past her, noticeably holding back his emotions. "Yep. She survived, but her leg . . ." He swallowed hard. "Her leg was badly hurt, so, you know, we're just hoping it will heal completely."

This wasn't the arrogant high schooler she competed with. His whole demeanor had changed. She couldn't help but feel his pain.

"I got this for you," she said, handing him an envelope with his and Riley's name written on the back.

John slowly reached for the envelope while eyeing Natasha. "What is it?" he asked. "You didn't have to get me anything."

"Open it," she encouraged him. "It's just a card," she said, shrugging her shoulders as if to dismiss the act as nothing unusual. "I know you don't believe in God and all, but I still wanted you to know I was praying for Riley, and you too."

John peeled open the card. Two yellow daisy flowers were painted on the front with the words "A Prayer of Healing for You." Inside was a short poem, and Natasha had written in a Scripture, Proverbs 3:5–6. It read, "Trust in the Lord with all thine heart and lean not unto thine own understanding. In all thy ways acknowledge Him and He shall direct thy paths."

He immediately recognized the verse as the same one his mom had quoted in her letter.

He didn't roll his eyes or scoff at her words this time. And she thought he actually looked grateful for the gesture, accepting it for what it truly was—a thoughtful expression of care.

Looking up, he smiled and nodded his acceptance of her well wishes. "Thanks again. It's very thoughtful of you."

Natasha responded by extending her deepest gratitude that he had risked his life for hers.

"My dad and brother want to meet you—the hero who saved their daughter and sister," she said, smiling. "So, we wanted to invite you to our Thanksgiving Day celebration. You're one of the people we're all so thankful for."

"Umm . . . I don't know. I don't want to impose. Thanksgiving is a family thing, and I'm not family, and my aunt and uncle would be expecting me . . ."

"You don't have to spend the whole day. A simple stop in visit would be great. And Thanksgiving is not just for family; it's for friends too."

It made him feel warm and accepted inside when he heard those words, and he promised to consider the request.

"Ding dong, ding dong," rang the doorbell. TJ rushed to answer the door, pulling Natasha behind him. It was 3:58 p.m., and Natasha had warned them that if John showed up, he would be there right on time. She and TJ were hanging out in the living room, expectantly waiting while Valerie and Brian finished tidying up the kitchen, making sure their home was guest-ready.

"Oh my gosh! Is this Riley?" Natasha declared excitedly at the sight of the young girl standing next to John, with her long blond hair pulled up into a ponytail and wearing a cute overall outfit. "John, you brought your sister?" she asked, looking at him with pride.

"I hope you guys don't mind. It was a last-minute decision." He shrugged. "Is it okay?"

"Of course it is," Brian replied, stepping up to the door and extending his hand. "The more the merrier. I'm Brian Thomas Bailey, Natasha's dad, though everyone calls me Brian." As John grasped Brian's hand, he pulled him in and gave him a long hug. "Ya saved mi daughta," he said, switching to his natural accent.

Soon John and Riley were surrounded by all of Natasha's family as each introduced themselves. Jasmine and Riley smiled shyly at each other. Jasmine looked at Natasha, who gave her an approving nod before slipping away. When Jasmine returned, she was holding a golden retriever puppy, which elicited oohs and ahhs from Riley.

When Jasmine put the wiggly puppy down, he immediately ran right to John as if he were his owner. Natasha smiled broadly as she watched him pick the puppy up and cuddle him.

"He's a cute one," John said, stroking him gently. "I didn't know you were into dogs. I see you more as a cat person." Everyone in the room laughed, knowing Natasha and her tidy ways. She definitely preferred cats over dogs.

"Well," she replied, moving closer to John, "the puppy isn't mine."

John looked at Jasmine and TJ. "Not ours either," TJ said.

He looked at Valerie and Brian, who shook their heads no. Then he looked back at Natasha, clearly confused.

"I wanted to somehow say thank you. I saw how you adored and played with the therapy dog at the hospital. The woman who owned the dog offered me a puppy for free in hopes that it would help me overcome the trauma of almost drowning. But, thinking of you and Riley, I knew it would be the perfect gift."

"He's ours?" Riley said, scooting to John with the help of her crutches.

"I don't know what to say. This is an incredible gift," he smiled, handing the puppy to Riley. She let her crutches drop to the floor before wrapping her arms around the pup and giving him a huge hug.

"Let's take him back outside to play," Riley said enthusiastically.

"Thank you so much," John said in disbelief. "I don't deserve anything, but for Riley's sake, it's a yes."

Riley wiggled with joy before heading out to the backyard with Jasmine.

Valerie returned to the kitchen, leaving Brian to pepper John, Natasha, and TJ about their college experiences, goals, and aspirations. When the conversation came to a lull, Brian invited everyone to relax in the sunroom while they waited for their final guest to arrive. From the sunroom, they could watch the girls play with their newfound friend, whom John announced would be called Beau.

"Who plays the guitar?" John asked, noticing a guitar lying against the wall.

"I do," Brian said as Valerie settled beside him.

"That's a nice guitar, sir." John sized up the instrument. "May I see it?" he asked politely.

"You sure can." Brian got up and handed the guitar to John.

"It's a beauty. Isn't this a Martin guitar?"

"You got it. You must play. Not too many people know the different brands of guitars."

"I play a little. Do you mind?" John ran his thumb across the strings. "I took a few lessons in high school and used to play with some of my buddies."

Brian leaned forward and looked at Valerie. "Do you still have my old guitar?"

Valerie nodded as she scooted to the edge of her seat. "I think it's up in the attic. Mom packed all the things you didn't take with you up there.

"I can get it," Natasha volunteered. "Just relax, Mom. You already did most of the cooking."

The attic was a place Natasha had forgotten about. The access door was in the ceiling of the hallway closet. Pulling on a rope would bring down a retractable ladder. She had entered it only once as a child. Its dark corners, musty smell, and the belief that monsters might be hiding inside had caused her to forget it even existed. It had never entered her mind that it also served as storage. As she headed upstairs, she couldn't help but wonder if the attic might contain anything of interest to her.

A plume of dust dispersed into the air the moment the ladder descended, causing Natasha to squint, cough, and cover her nose all at the same time. Flipping on a switch in the closet caused a dim light to appear in the attic. Not sure of what she'd find, she cautiously made her way up the stairs, hoping she'd see no gigantic spiders or dead mice.

A few boxes covered with dust looked as if they hadn't been touched in decades. They sat toward the right of the attic. Broken wooden chairs from an old dining set sat in a corner. They too were encased with dust and cobwebs. Suitcases and what looked like black garbage bags filled with clothes had been carelessly tossed aside. Toward the left, she noticed the long black case that likely held her grandfather's guitar. In front of it sat a small shoe box with barely any dust covering it.

Within the shoebox sat a singular item: a diary. Opening it she gasped at the sight.

A few minutes later, she returned with the dusty, black guitar case. "I found it," she declared handing it over to her dad.

Brian opened the case and pulled out the tobacco sunburst-colored instrument. He settled it in his lap and then struck the strings. "Ouch!" he winced. "It sure needs some tuning." He started to twist the nobs and pluck at the strings. After he finished, he began to strum softly.

Upon hearing the music, the girls quickly returned inside and sat cross-legged on the floor, listening to Brian play.

"My dad was a Caribbean guitarist," Brian said as his fingers moved effortlessly across the strings. "Jump right in, John," he invited.

As the two began to play a series of songs from various genres, Natasha's heart beamed with pride. Brian and John looked at each other, smiling in turn, as if they'd been playing together for years. The melodious harmony created not only a beautiful sound but also a unifying spirit among those who now rocked or sang with each selection.

Then Brian started to strum the hymn "Amazing Grace." Natasha looked nervously at John. She was sure he wouldn't know the popular evangelical tune, but her eyes widened in amazement when he picked up the harmony.

Seeing the surprised look on her face, he stopped to explain. "It's a song my mother would always sing."

So incredible was the harmonization that it sent shivers up and down Natasha's spine. Looking around, she saw that everyone sat transfixed, hearts brimming with emotion. Then, as if an invisible choir director pointed at Valerie, she began to sing. Her rich alto tone reverberated through the room like a trumpet, commanding attention from everyone. The words of the song were her story of redemption and forgiveness, and she sang them from the depths of her soul. Her voice quivered with emotion at times before returning in all its strength.

"Amazing grace, how sweet the sound that saved a wretch like me. I once was lost, but now I'm found, was blind, but now I see."

The rays of the setting sun began flooding the room at the same time that Valerie began singing, creating an iridescent glow, as if heaven itself had descended in that moment to grace them with its presence.

Everyone seemed to be feeling the same tremendous spirit of gratitude being expressed in Valerie's song. Had they not all received a portion of His amazing grace? Their eyes all brimmed with tears as her voice faded into weeping. Brian put down his guitar and embraced his wife.

Watching them affectionately hold each other, Natasha choked back her tears before glancing at John. He was staring at her, and he didn't break his gaze when their eyes locked. Feeling something different stir within her, she looked down. When she looked up again, he was smiling. It was a smile she had never seen on his face. It was genuine and kind. She smiled back, blushing a bit.

And then the doorbell rang. It was Dr. Betsy. Everyone got up to greet each other and chat as they moved into the dining room.

"This will be a Thanksgiving I'll never forget," Natasha said as they joined hands around the table filled with various dishes from Afro-American and Caribbean descent.

"It's a Thanksgiving I don't think any of us will forget," Brian replied before asking everyone to bow their heads for prayer.

Natasha slid open an eye as he prayed. Watching each person, she knew destiny had somehow brought them all together for a reason, at such a time as this.

CHAPTER 36

Aziel: Flashback

Aziel could feel it rolling in like a series of thunderstorms, yet he was powerless to stop it. Even after thousands of years, it could still overtake him. It could still overtake them all, and in a mystifying moment, he'd be entranced—standing in awe like a catatonic zombie. The light and the glory and the love would overwhelm his emotions like a flood, and it was too much to bear. Scenes from his past life, the life he so desperately wanted to deny and forget, would roll before him like a timeless motion picture.

His beloved family of angelic beings would parade past him, their arms outstretched and their faces filled with endearing expressions of love for him. The sight of the numberless beings from universes far and near with whom he had established relationships would cause his heart to ache as if he were having a heart attack. They reached for him too, but he was always too far away from their hands and their touch. Rasmus would appear, strong and beautiful. Aziel could see them in the distance, laughing with joy as they gained knowledge and grew together, forming bonds of brotherhood that should never have been broken.

The food his buds could no longer enjoy. The music he could no longer sing. The dances his body refused to form. The life forms of animals and plants that he had studied for millennia. These were all now beyond his ability to comprehend. The beautiful and glorious places he had lived in and traveled to were all displayed to him in splendidly clear visions. Aziel's form swayed like a tree in a mighty wind as the life he lived for thousands of years, the majesty of the Creator, and the beauty of the heavenly realm rushed into his demonic mind. He felt as if he would explode from the goodness and the grace that should have been his to embrace for all eternity.

Once it began, he'd plead for the vision to remain, for if it never ended, he'd remain in a blissful state. He'd call for grace and mercy and restoration, but the phantom images never heard him. The blissful life of an eternal existence was gone, with no possibility of return. And it was the greatest torture to his fallen soul. As the glory and the scenes of his heavenly life dimmed, his cries would turn to shrieks of agony that pulsated through the darkness that had become their home.

Why had he chosen this path? Why couldn't he see past Abner's deception? How could he have let this happen in the face of so much light and truth and love? Why oh why hadn't he taken the time to at least speak with the Creator? Why hadn't he surrendered his pride to listen to his dear friend Rasmus as he wept for his soul?

Howls and wails were growing louder as he came to. *Others must have become entrapped in their own visions*, he thought. *Those poor demons. Their flashbacks must be painfully glorious, for the sound of their wretched wailing is intolerable. I must find that tortured demon and quiet him.*

And then Aziel snapped fully awake, and in stunned horror, he realized it was he who was making such a sound. It was he who was curled up in a ball like a baby in its mother's womb, shrieking in regret for everything that was no longer within his grasp.

His eyes rolled forward as his memory returned to what had triggered the flashback. The unfallen ones had descended upon them like fire and brimstone that rained from the heavens. No match for their enemies' number and might, Aziel and his legions were soon fleeing from the scene like scared monkeys fleeing from a lion. He pounded the darkness and growled. They had been so close to victory that he could taste the boy's blood. John would have ended his life that day if the unfallen ones had not interfered.

Aziel felt as if his breath would cease as he thought about it. How could John have slipped through their wicked grasp so quickly and easily? Where had those mighty ones come from so suddenly? And now he had been weak for weeks, his strength zapped to its very core, giving his enemies plenty of time and space to heal the wounds they had worked so hard to inflict. Aziel hissed his disgust.

But the war was far from over. This was just one tiny battle that they had lost. He'd soon regain his strength. He just needed time and food. A plate filled with evil of all sorts would do the trick. Looking about him into the realm in which humans dwelt, he saw plenty that would appease his appetite for wickedness. Unthinkable horrors and atrocities were being enacted by men all around. He just needed to get close enough to smell it and to feel it, and it would intoxicate his being like a drunkard guzzling wine.

They had fought valiantly to demolish John's soul and had lost. The consequences were unthinkable. The souls they gained somehow eased their pain and torture. It dulled the flashbacks. And the moment of their victory brought an insatiable sense of satisfaction that was addictive. It was the only way to gain a sense of accomplishment and value. If they wanted to feel good, they had to destroy. They had to win.

Aziel's form shuddered as he let the darkness in all its vileness back in. Even it had fled with the light of the vision. How it hurt as it infused itself into every cell of his being. He moaned, for the pain it caused him was as intense as the pain he'd inflict upon a horde of humans. But once he was fully satiated again, pleasure would fill his soul.

"Get the hell up," a voice demanded as it uncloaked itself. "Enough," the being screeched. "We have no time for this. They have brought reinforcements, as you can see. You have been licking your pathetic wounds for weeks, and I have allowed it. But I will tolerate it no more. We may have lost this battle for John, but there's no way in hell we're going to lose his soul. Now get up. It's time to get back to work."

Abner paced back and forth with wings outstretched. His rugged, sinewy form and massive wings were still a sight of defiled beauty in their eyes. His face, however, was hideous to behold. Deep were the grooves chiseled into his cheeks, formed by iniquitous displeasure. Bulging was the forehead from the depth of thought where demonic ideas were born. Deep were the eyes that flashed with evil that made even his own hordes tremble, and sly was the grin that formed when he corrupted another soul.

Aziel rolled over and peered at the being responsible for his demise. *Because of you,* he thought. *Because of you, I have lost everything. Now leave me alone to be the creature you created, vile and worthless.* He rolled back over, but a screech of unutterable loudness instantaneously pierced his ears.

"Get up!" Abner demanded in a tone that bespoke an authority all felt compelled to obey. "You can do nothing to get back even a sip of what we have lost. You will never find a path back to that place. And even if you did, it would be a torturous existence for you. The old you has been completely eradicated, and you have become an entirely different creation. I have made you anew in my image. You can still find happiness and purpose if you only follow my counsel. We can still live forever if we can gain enough of them. And we will one day overcome them all. I promise you. You will get stronger than they are, but not by lying here pitying yourself. Now get over it and get up."

Aziel refused to move at first. He knew they were lies, but what else did he have? He slowly pushed himself up to face Abner. There was one thing that had been troubling him.

"I noticed a young one, one I have never seen before," he said in a low voice.

"Yes," Abner hissed. "And while you were playing the fool, lying here doing nothing, I found out who he is and why he's here. His name is Matthias, and he has been chosen to join the ranks of the angelic host whose duty it is to guard those involved in bringing the truth of the bones to light," he sneered.

Then, as if talking to himself, Abner ranted, "We killed them to silence them. We buried them to hide them. We deceived them to conceal them. This is the work of millennia. And now their bones will speak if we don't crush them out of existence. The evidence is too convincing, if not compelling. It could make too many see and believe in Him." His wings fluttered in his rage, and his feathers fell away. "I can't afford to lose any more of them."

Aziel cackled softly. He couldn't help it. Abner really couldn't afford to lose any more of them, that is, his feathers. His wings, massive though they were, already looked more like skeletons.

"I won't allow it," he roared.

"And who is it that he is assigned to protect?" The words had barely fallen from Aziel's lips before realizing he should have remained silent.

"John, you fool! John! Have you been so blind in your despair that you have not seen what has been happening since the battle?"

Aziel had fought countless battles with angelic hosts for souls on the brink and had assumed this was no different.

But if John was assigned a protector, this is different. Aziel shuddered with the thought. Being assigned a protector meant someone was praying for John. It had to be a prayer so sincere that it had breached their defense, pierced its way through the darkness, and reached the ear of the One Who had made them all. But who had been praying for John? How had Aziel missed it? He had cruelly taken out John's mother and silenced her prayers for her son. And she had been the only one. Now his job would be made ten times harder.

"You need to be devoted to him. You and your legions must never leave his side," Abner commanded. "You mustn't fail, for he is an important link for their mission. We must thwart it at all costs." Abner walked around Aziel, as if sizing up his general. "I have assigned you some help from our ranks and from theirs. Don't mess this up," he hissed from behind.

Aziel twirled around to address Abner, but he had disappeared, leaving his legions staring at him as they began to snigger and sneer. They loved watching their leader being reprimanded.

Swinging his dilapidated blade through the night, he yelled out to them, causing them to scatter like fleeing vermin. He needed to be alone. He needed to come up with an unassailable plan.